JADWIGA'S RING

A biographical fiction recounting the life of Jadwiga of Anjou,
king of Poland
1374–1399

DAWN IBRAHIM

ISBN 978-1-0980-0712-6 (paperback)
ISBN 978-1-0980-0713-3 (digital)

Christian Faith Publishing, Inc.
832 Park Avenue
Meadville, PA 16335
www.christianfaithpublishing.com

Cover art: *Dymitr of Goraj and Jadwiga of Poland*, Jan Matejko

Printed in the United States of America

With love to my family and to all those who lit my life with the light of their faith and love for God and neighbor, and for those who work for peace.

His Holiness St. Pope John Paul II

CONTENTS

Saint...7
Introduction..9
Prologue...11
    Provocation (AD 1373, Northern Poland)........................11
    Gathering a Storm of Revenge
    (Southern Prussia, Marienburg)...................................14
    Jadwiga's Birth (February AD 1373)............................20
    Sabotage..22
    War Is Hell..27
    Distractions and a New Horizon..................................29
    Truce...34
    Appeasing the Poles...39
    Home at Last...42

Chapter 1: The Sponsalia de praesenti in Hainburg
            (July AD 1377) 45
Chapter 2: The Apprenticeship of Young Jadwiga 63
Chapter 3: Tragedy and New Directions 74
Chapter 4: Home Again...77
Chapter 5: Growing Up in Buda (AD 1382)........................81
Chapter 6: Death and Commissioning.................................88
Chapter 7: Determining Destinies 94
Chapter 8: A Vacancy and Ambition...................................97
Chapter 9: Diversions 102
Chapter 10: Leaving Home for Good 107
Chapter 11: Travels to New Lands 111
Chapter 12: Poland Has a King..121

Chapter 13: Tested Resolutions..129

Chapter 14: Rethinking Past Resolutions 134

Chapter 15: Tempers on the Horizons 138

Chapter 16: Tempers and Recommitment on the
Western Front 142

Chapter 17: Duty and Destiny...148

Chapter 18: The Promise of a Wedding 161

Chapter 19: Day of Decision: The Feast of the Assumption.......175

Chapter 20: Resignation 188

Chapter 21: The King from the East..199

Chapter 22: Deception 211

Chapter 23: Regicide on the Eastern Front 219

Chapter 24: Baptisms, Wedding, and Coronation Days............227

Part 2: Jadwiga's Legacy 241

Chapter 25: Tears...243

Chapter 26: Tears of Change and Long-Suffering 251

Chapter 27: Alone 260

Chapter 28: Reunited 271

Chapter 29: Justice...281

Chapter 30: Perpetual Praises 291

Chapter 31: Glory 297

Chapter 32: Valley of Tears 310

Afterword...333

Bibliography/References 337

Photo and Illustration Acknowledgments 339

Saint

Standing on the shoulders
Of the saintly lives of others
Raised high to see the way

Docile to the Spirit
Humble and obedient
Guided gently along the way
Spirit of service and gladness

Tears and trials but prove
A trust beyond compare
Their vision seems so narrow
But spans the universe tomorrow

Understanding and wisdom embraced
Eyes fixed on the Ruler
All things are measured accordingly
And for a time may look left or right

But with the morning light
Are found along a straight and narrow path
With the Maker as their guide
And love for Him above all created things.
Light Great Light and lead great Leader
You know the Way
The Truth
And the Life
Love and sacrifice as the key to
The door that opens wide for others,
Not by might,
Nor by power,
But by my Spirit says the Lord.

INTRODUCTION

Dear reader,

In studying the life of Jadwiga, the presence of her father, Louis of Anjou, was so large it didn't seem right to ignore his significance. The focus on the larger context in which she is born in the prologue is to set the stage for a better understanding of the relationships and world of Eastern Europe in the Middle Ages. Many of these characters or circumstances played a major role in her life and ideals as well as the world as she inherited it.

 This story is biographical fiction; the intention is to keep the information as close to historical fact as possible and tell a great story, but as soon as one puts words into people's mouths, creates scenes, or focuses on the antagonistic aspects of characters, it becomes more fictional than historical. The facts aren't always correct or exact. Some chapters are completely fictional. *The Annals of Jan Dlugosz* is not necessarily based on complete facts. The romance of William and Jadwiga may have been exaggerated or maybe not. Rottenstein is a coalescence of three Teutonic leaders. The Teutonic Knights have been a charitable and valuable contributor in history despite the negative impact of a few leaders whose role is infamous in the life of Jadwiga. Slander of real people is a daunting endeavor, but the history books speak of these acts, and they are used to teach us important lessons. As a good older friend used to say, "It's okay to make mistakes as long as we learn from them, but it's even more important to learn from other's mistakes."

I do not speak Polish thus had to discount other possibly important Polish sources that might have informed the research. *The Annals of Jan Dlugosz* translated by Maurice Michael, Oscar Halecki's *Jadwiga of Anjou and the Rise of East Central Europe*, and Father Boleslaw Przbybszewski's *Saint Jadwiga Queen of Poland* 1374–1399, Postulate for the Canonization of Blessed Queen Jadwiga, were excellent sources.

Jadwiga's contributions were highly regarded by both the people of her time and by historians such as Oscar Halecki. She was canonized a saint by Saint John Paul II on June 8, 1997, testifying to her strong inner spiritual life. To strip this aspect from the story would be to do a great injustice to who she really was at her core as well as life for Christians of the Middle Ages who, because of plague and the times, were always close to death and feared judgment and hell. Her family was also deeply religious as was everyone around her. The church was a revered contributor to culture and society. Religious experience was a significant and acceptable experience informing and forming the souls of mankind as it does today. Gloria Patri, et Filio, et Spiritui Sancto!

PROLOGUE

Provocation
(AD 1373, Northern Poland)

As the autumn sun rose upon the northeastern plains of Poland on frostbitten crops, villagers trickled out to various tasks, carrying lunches and simple tools. The last rooster gave practice, and shepherds were sent off with provisions in further pastures. Peace infused the sky, the riverbank, the nearby forest, the fresh air, the gentle farm creatures, and the souls of men, women, and children.

Miles away, newly ordained brothers sang their morning lauds, appointed by the former Pope Gregory. It was chant like "Puer Natus in Bethlehem." The young men sang with sincerity and piety, row on row, facing each other across the platform of the altar, emptied of all desire and will, obedient to the voice of the superior who would send them to claim the minds and hearts of countless souls for truth. Their song could be heard from miles around, a song of peace and humble submission and abstinence from self-will and pride.

The villagers worked diligently as their families for generations. Their survival and minimal comfort depended on perseverance. No one except the elderly and the sick and the very young were permitted idle entertainment. More in the winter months, but not now when the beauty of Indian summer was matched by the urgency of fall. A young couple stole a quick and hidden kiss behind a cottage then went off to their duties. Mothers prepared and smoked meats, dried and stored onions, washed laundry, and slaughtered chicken for the evening meal. None perceived the impending destruction.

All would be made slaves, even the maiden given to a Lithuanian of stature at the hands of Witold.

Witold was a young bold man in his early twenties. His greatest flaw to his enemy was his greatest strength to his countrymen. He resorted to destruction and thievery for the sake of his kingdom and its prosperity. He found little comfort in relationships or communities or cultures not his own. He had slaughtered any Mongol he encountered from the East, and though the Poles to his west were never such a penetrating influence, he counted them as his enemy. Mostly he despised the Teutonic Knights. They were wealthy disrespectful men, all dressed as in a circus, unnatural to him because they had no women and lived in large castles. He had encountered them on countless occasions in Northern Lithuania, where they constantly tried to conquer his ancestors' lands, stealing wood and game.

Witold rushed upon his dark stallion through the thick forest paths with two hundred men on small ponies, a tactic inherited from the Mongols. Their purpose was simple: to pillage all that they could for the long winter ahead and to provide what had been taken in the same manner.

A donkey in the pasture closest to the forest began to bray. Geese began to honk loudly. A young girl gathering firewood near the forest edge was the first to notice the strange and frightening sound emerging from the forest as birds rose from the forest canopy. The child stood frozen and bewildered, for never in her peaceful life had the likes been known to her. Slowly, women began to take note of the animals. A middle-aged mother terrifyingly shouted for her young children to run to her and guided them quickly into the closest animal shelter, commanding them, "Hide!" and "Keep silent!" She rushed to her elderly father taking in sun, urging him quickly to come. By now, all the villagers knew the signs and sent their boys running to the fields to warn the men. Obediently, they ran, their hearts bursting with terror from the enemies they could now see emerging.

The little girl stood paralyzed but, upon hearing her mother's heartfelt plea to run and hide, ducked behind a pile of boulders cleared out by her forefathers. She was the first witness to the assault about to befall her people. Terror seized her heart as various-colored ponies blurred past and a large black monstrous stallion appeared snorting and breathless, which towered above the riders. The chilling rider came to a halt with two men at his side, pointing steadily in the direction of the village, giving a silent command. The men wore fur and rugged clothing, their faces and horses marked with strange symbols. It was a terrifying nightmare from which she would never awake. The men gave out screams of terror and whooping. She buried her head in her hands and sunk low to the ground—she was just old enough to understand the need to hide but not old enough to understand the need for hate.

The warriors brought with them carts and began to load goods (each executing their task in villainous fashion) farm creatures, clothing, food, furnishings, chairs, or tables. The villagers stood helpless. To not cooperate meant certain death, and they cried and mourned for the loss they knew was imminent.

Witold and some of his men rode to the edge of town where a simple church had been erected. They shoved out the elderly parish priest and his young assistant, both with breviaries in hand. Like lambs to the slaughter, they stood silent and submissive. They offered themselves to their Lord as martyrs, praying for the strength to love their enemies, praying they could live the words they understood.

Other of Witold's men exited the church, shamelessly loading candles, chalices or patens, linens, and furnishings. The elderly priest looked to the younger one with sincerity and love. "My son, our time has come. We lived as Christ, gave everything to Him—and now, we offer ourselves as a living sacrifice. Let us pray for the conversion of these men."

The young priest, who had been trembling and looking down at his feet as tears streamed down his cheeks, was the only one to understand him as it was spoken in Polish. Upon hearing the words of his loving, gentle, and meek mentor, he wiped his tears and nodded. A sudden peace and confidence inspired his being. He did not look up as his beloved elder took a blow to the head, then a second and a third. He did not look up for fear that his very last act may be one of judgment or worst yet hostility or hatred. Instead, he looked down as a sword blade, with one stroke, sliced his head to the ground.

By afternoon, the savage pillagers had all they had come for. As hastily as they had come, they left three by three, guarding their tied prisoners: weeping women, children, and some young men to be used as slaves. They began their journey to Vilno, Lithuania's capital. Witold, like a medieval cowboy, surveyed the burning village and surrounding area then rode off satisfied toward hundreds of miles of wilderness to the heart of his country.

Gathering a Storm of Revenge
(Southern Prussia, Marienburg)

It seemed like all of Europe was converging upon Marienburg, north of Poland. On the horizon was the great ominous castle headquarters of the Teutonic Knights. They had invited the kings of Europe and their best knights to protect the eastern border. The intention was to strike back at the Lithuanians for attacks on the civilians of Poland.

Thousands of European men settled on the meadows surrounding Marienburg. Peasants, soldiers, knights, and the like rallied east of Germany and north of Poland. To not react would indicate submission and invite the enemy to the table of their country. Men tended their horses, those who were wealthy or influential enough to attain them, while others tended meat on smoky fires or rough tent structures. An early February snow began to fall upon the evening's frigid surroundings.

In the distance, on the opposite horizon leading south, dramatically emerged a party of riders. Standard bearers carrying flags of Poland, Hungary, and Austria preceded the group. A sudden excitement and gossip filled the meadows. Here at last had arrived the legendary Louis of Anjou, king of Hungary and Poland, with his greatest ally and friend, Leopold of Austria. The two together had persistently taken up the gauntlet of the southeast for Europe. Their strong, heavy, and bold arms acted like a barrier to Constantinople, which had fallen now to the Mohammedans. They were living legends in a world of knights and kings and knew no distinction between their roles. They fought and bled risking all to be exemplary.

Louis was nephew of both the late great King Casimir of Poland and King Saint Louis of France, and his brotherhood with Western Europe was strong because of past marriages. To the Hungarians, he was known as Louis the Great. By the Poles, however, as the closest living male descendant of the late Casimir the Great, he was named Louis the Hungarian, so often did he spend his days in his beloved home nation at Buda.

Today, he was in Prussia, offering protection and offensive attack. All men paid reverence to the famous warrior team as they made their way to the castle with an impressive team of bodyguards and knights and a thousand more warriors following. Most were only able to see a quick, obstructed view of the legendary leaders.

In the basement foundations of Marienburg Castle was a large industry of ironworks, precious metals, and jewels. Men worked in ragged clothing, thin and worn with filthy garments, resembling creatures a little less than human. They labored at the foundry, fueling large ovens for the ironworks and each toiling at their crafts of weapons, chain mail, armor, and swords. All for immense profits of the knights who took every opportunity to acquire any lands to meet metal quotas. The air was thin and stinging.

In one corner, in the extreme heat and light of the brilliant fires, worked an elderly jeweler, crafting with rare metal of another type— gold. He wiped his brow from the droplets of sweat and frantically polished a beautiful, exquisite ring adorned with amber and a cat's-eye sapphire, examining it at eye level. He twitched nervously as he heard a door slam and the dreaded voice of the leader of the Teutonic Knights, Conrad Von Rottenstein.

Rottenstein made his way down the stairs toward the ragged jeweler, all the while consulting with his military leader in impatient and angry tones, "We must take Vilno now, with all of Europe's strength gathered. Now is the time to go straight to the heart of Lithuania and submit them to the rest of Europe! The end of paganism, think of it, Zolner! This will give us all the lands that Witold has been hoarding! Our new enemy will be the Mongols. Gone will be the pestilent Lithuanians." He reached the seasoned craftsman, whose talent very few in Europe possessed. "Well, old man, will we have to wait another century for you to finish?" The man offered the ring to him, shaking and bowing to avoid eye contact. "Good, but not excellent, and King Louis rides this way, arriving any moment! It will have to do, but you old donkey! What must I do to get the quality of work befitting a king?" He landed his fist on the cheek of the jeweler, who staggered backward, caught by a younger apprentice. Rottenstein, too much in a hurry to continue his aggressions, rushed back upstairs. His aid, Conrad Zolner, unapologetically snatched up a wooden chest, examined the contents, and, placing the ring inside, snapped it shut.

Rottenstein and Zolner arrived in the receiving room of the castle to find servants busily finishing setting up dinner tables. "Wenches and donkey's assess! All this time and you have not finished the preparation? The king is a stone's throw away, and yet you milk the cow and collect the hen's eggs! Hastily! Finish!" The servants scurried from the dining area as a hawk scatters hens from the hen yard. From down the corridor came the voices of men mingling in hearty welcome.

Louis was well loved by all who knew him. He was a large bearded man in his midforties. He was handsome, with gentle wise eyes, looking as if he wore his beard to advance the severity of his expression. He was grown to be king from his youth, and he loved and carried out his duty as if given by God Himself. It was his life's vocation. Nothing took him away from the seriousness of his duty or stopped him from doing whatever he felt obligated in either one of the countries for which he was named king. He was ready to assist whoever asked him.

As devoted to war as he felt he had to be for his time, his heart and mind were convinced that it wasn't war that was the answer to the crisis he encountered but rather education and a proper understanding and respect of Christianity, of living out Christianity. That was really the war that would win the world to peace. He felt bound to the methods of his day. With constant bombardment from enemy forces, how was a king to live a life of peace? He rarely issued offensive attacks. But having been asked by his fellow "brothers" and being the King of Poland, he had a duty to his subjects. He came obligingly, bound by a principle that was not his own but of his time. What he dreamed of was a civilized world with schools, universities and towns, of citizens who could form beautiful serene hamlets and live in peace. Above all duties, Louis loved his family, and nothing except perhaps his love and devotion to God and the church was greater.

Jan Matejko, Louis I Hungary

Rottenstein greeted Louis with a bow. "Finally! Great kings of the Eastern border! Finally, we set eyes on you! And blessed be God who has brought my brothers safe to Marienburg!"

"Thanks to you, Rottenstein, for your invitation, for which we are pleased to respond to assist you in your needs and the needs of Poland. Blessed be God! You have not yet met Leopold of Austria, my closest ally and best of friends."

Leopold was of a different nature than the more gentile Louis. He was large and robust, well fed and well fought. He was a warrior, skilled and excellent in the art of war. He enjoyed any reason to show his prowess and might. His voice was deep and commanding. When he spoke, all that was heard was his heart's desire. Most men cowered in his presence, but not Louis, who knew him as the very best friend to whom his growling had only the feel of a threatening but beloved pet who would always remain loyal. They were like brothers since Louis's brother Robert had been killed in Italy.

"Come, let us eat! Let us not delay as our table is set. You must be hungry and tired by your long journey all this way south of the Carpathian Mountains!" They were seated and, in unison led by the king, made the sign of the cross and began grace before meals piously and sincerely: *"Be blessed, O Heavenly Father, provider of all that is good and whose bounty is endless. Be blessed and ever praised! May your works be blessed for generations to come! Give strength and peace to your just ones and be extolled in all your creation. Amen!"*

Just prior to the servants bringing in platters of vegetables and roasted meats, Rottenstein signaled a servant to come forward, bearing the gifts. The servant came to King Louis, knelt, and held up the carved box, revealing many various rare and precious metals including amber, gold, and pearls. Rottenstein waved a finger to another nearby servant who entered the room with a very large hunting hawk tethered to his wrist. It was eager but well-mannered. peering about, waiting for a command. The whole company was visibly impressed.

"Rottenstein, the great symbol of Marienburg? Exquisite!" King Louis picked up the ring from the center of the box, appreciating its beauty and marveled at its craftsmanship. What could accepting these gifts mean? He was not fully allied with the Teutonic Knights because they had too often crossed the fine line between defensive and offensive war. They thought little of raiding Polish villages and did not respect anything except the Germanic cause. Louis was willing to ally himself with them only for the greater good of defeating a greater enemy. As he held the jewel in his hand he wondered if he should even accept the gift from this questionable ally who he knew to be conniving and self-serving. What would acceptance bring for his descendants and subjects, peace or warfare? Could someone like Rottenstein ever be satisfied? Would Rottenstein even allow his posterity and future generations to rule Poland, or would he devour whoever came in the way of his material progress? An order appointed by the Pope should conduct itself less like a kingdom concerned with material wealth and prosperity and occupy itself more with the things of heaven. He wondered if the knights had lost their way to serve another master. "The ring is of the greatest quality. I will send some craftsmen here to learn the art. The hawk will also be of use to us."

Rottenstein, looking pleased to have his gifts well received, raised a goblet of wine and declared, "Let us eat, for tomorrow, we wage war."

Jadwiga's Birth
(February AD 1373)

Louis waited eagerly for news of a son. For a king, his son would take his place, and he could die knowing that his kingdom would be bequeathed to a man of his own blood and mind. As yet, possibly due to the duties that took him away from home, Louis had not fathered a surviving son. He had two daughters, Maria and Catherine, from his Croatian wife, Elizabieta, whom he loved and cherished.

The winter winds howled through the Buda valley. Within the castle was a nervous and excited but hushed rushing to and fro. The Poor Clare sisters' prayers to the Holy Trinity for a safe and healthy delivery hummed like a gentle mantra to heaven.

Elizabieta was the third wife of Louis. She was an exquisite, graceful, fair-haired Croatian princess. Of his former deceased wives, she was the most beautiful. Her daughter, Jadwiga, was to take after her elegant, graceful poise and demeanor. Jadwiga, however, would be groomed for royal duty, unlike Elizabieta, who happily and lovingly played the role of mother and queen while being timid in regard to political and state matters.

"My lady, the baby is almost out, I see a head, push at the next pain, push!" A brave Elizabieta nodded. "Breathe now, breathe, stay calm," urged the angelic, white-haired midwife. "It's a girl, my lady, a beautiful healthy, lovely girl!"

"Oh," declared Elizabieta with exhausted delight. The sisters sighed with relief and now offered prayers of thanksgiving.

"A healthy, lively baby is always a gift from God. All decisions are in the hands of the Creator," the nurse reminded. No one dared complain or think that God had made a mistake. Still, there remained the unspoken understanding that Elizabieta was young enough and could bare the king a son in due time, and as she gazed lovingly at the beautiful girl in her arms; any sign of disappointment dissipated.

Briskly, in came Louis's mother, also named Elizabeth. Though similarly named, they were substantially different. The Queen Mother Elizabeth was a war-hardened woman who had lost her other son and had endured treason in Poland, which she attempted to rule as her right after the death of her Uncle Casimir. She was wise to the affairs of defense and politics and never hesitated to direct the household on Louis's behalf as well as most often take over duties to which the wife of the king should have privilege. She appeared insensitive and over-bearing, but the queen mother was given all due respect; and no one, not even Elizabieta, dared to question or hesitate to fulfill the least of her inclinations. Even the king himself respected her above all.

"Oh, why was I not called until now?" the queen mother queried. She rushed to the bedside and examined the new addition. "Oh, he is most beautiful Elizabieta, at last, you have done well, my love."

Elizabieta exchanged a brief glance with the maidservant, who gave a sympathetic smile to Elizabieta. "*She*, Mother, *she*! It is another princess for Louis, and she is beautiful!"

The elder Elizabeth froze. Would God Himself not hear her appeal for a son to inherit the throne? Where was the son they had urged heaven to send? A woman could never hold the Eastern border of Europe from God's enemies! This required a man. She gazed pensively, attempting to discern God's intention. The beautiful child was plump and healthy, and the moment captured her grandmotherly heart. As she touched the cheek of the beautiful baby, she quickly submitted her plans. She was wise enough to know that it was God who set rulers above men, not queen mothers.

"Her name is Jadwiga, like her ancestor before her who was so holy," offered Elizabieta.

The queen mother nodded with resignation. "Jadwiga. What a great name. We shall send word to her father at once that he has another daughter. She will do great things."

Suddenly, in ran two beautiful rosy-cheeked children, ages four years and two. "Catherine! Maria! Come see your beautiful new sister!" exclaimed the queen mother. The children delightedly gazed at the swaddled newborn infant, fascinated with the prospect.

"Mama, I thought we needed a boy," offered Catherine.

"Well, my love, you see, God sent us a girl, so we must have needed her more," replied Elizabieta with a gentle laugh.

"Papa said it would be a boy," pressed Maria with a tinge of disappointment and concern.

"A brother will come, just not at this time. Now, kiss the baby and thank God for such a healthy sister. She will be a blessing to us all." What they didn't know was the great role this baby girl would play in bringing peace and unity to Eastern Europe.

Sabotage

Thousands of European warriors were well into the forests of Lithuania, marching in linear fashion on a narrow well-worn path. Near the head of the troops rode Louis, discerning the situation of Western Europe with Enguerrand de Coucy, one of France's best-known knights and aids to the king of France, as well as the Duc de Bar of France and the Duke of Lancaster, England.

Because of his French heritage, Louis was able to converse well with the French nobles, but less with the English Lord. "How fares France and good King Charles, my great-granduncle? What news of the situation there?" Louis asked Coucy to bridge the long silence.

"Truthfully, the plague has ravaged our nation. Fields are left unplowed, homes abandoned, economy obliterated, priest, parent, child, departed for eternity. It is as though God has sent judgment on all of Europe, with no favoritism, except perhaps in the east here," he answered.

Louis replied, "We have taken measures to ensure our borders are secure of travelers from the west who might carry this scourge, as recommended by my physician Jon Radcliffe, and, as such, have kept in good health, thanks be to God… What of your wars?"

The Hundred Years' War of France and England was underway, and Coucy replied, "We are in truce with England," he nodded toward the English Duke of Lancaster, who only slightly acknowledged him with disdain. "And are eager to pursue more significant work for the glory of France and our good King Charles."

Louis's tone changed to subtle impatience and solemn, genuine paternal concern. "And what of your Pope elect? France has become like a world unto itself wherein dwells its own French Pope. A new Rome is Avignon!" He continued sternly, "Where has the good faith of our ancestors gone and the blood of countless Christian men spilled for the glory of God? Charlemagne, good King Louis, who died in Egypt for Rome's great cause! Would they not tear down the veil that lies between this place and eternity and barrage the borders of France and now turn his defeated crusade to the minds and hearts of the French to urge them to abandon such earthly and evil inspired folly? Within your own land lies duty enough in regard to the glory of God!"

Coucy answered the king respectfully, "Yes, my Lord, and there are many hearts united to yours in this regard. The church is torn apart by the simple and pervasive scourge of pride. By God's will, good men's prayers will be answered, the church will be one again, and there will be one pope in *Rome*."

By this time, the royal group had just crossed a bridge over a swift flowing river, and Louis and his immediate entourage dismounted to water their horses. As forty or so men made their way across the bridge, a loud snapping of wood was heard as the bridge gave out. Men scrambled on both edges of the riverbank to safety, climbing wooden beam structures or swimming to shore.

A young teenage man was caught up in the strong central current but, not knowing how to swim, was brought under, arms flailing wildly. With a great heart of pity, courage, and concern, Louis mounted his large stallion and urged him recklessly into the river.

The horse swam toward the young man who could be seen less and less.

The king grasped his arm the next time it came into view. Four bodyguards had scrambled to assist the king as hundreds of men looked on with awe and reverence that the king would risk his life for a common man. The woods were silent and time frozen as a bodyguard reached to hoist the young man to Louis's horse. Another few men had been pulled away from the bridge structure into the current, only to be aided by other guards.

Louis arrived to shore where other men assisted to lower the partially drowned man from the horse. They pounded his back as he sputtered and gasped for breath. The men surrounded him as the various guards also came out of the river, freezing and wet, but all accounted for. Most were breathless and speechless while army commanders and knights began mobilizing the startled men and troops, shouting and yelling orders to build fires and begin chopping down trees to rebuild the bridge. Others were ordered to investigate why the bridge had collapsed, whether it was accidental or intended. Everyone was on high alert.

The young man regained consciousness as the men said, "It was King Louis who saved you! You owe him your life."

He sat up shakily and touched the bottom of the cloak of the king. "Most gracious lord, my king, you risk your life for me. What am I to you? I owe you everything! I am your humble and true servant. You have given me my life back." Overwhelmed, he buried his head in the king's wet clothing and sobbed.

"Son, it was God who saved you and I both and gave us the courage to save you from your death. Thank Him, not His servants," Louis suggested kindly. The surrounding bodyguards pulled him away to a fire.

The enemy was not far off. From a hidden vantage under thick underbrush, a small group of Lithuanians led by the sons of King Olgierd of Lithuania observed.

"King Louis of Hungary?" Skiergiello asked.

Jagiello nodded, every bit as fascinated by the display of heroism than the result of their efforts to slow the European troops. "It should slow them down for a day or so. They are close, but it will give us time to get more men to the battlefront."

Jagiello was a remarkably large and handsome young man in his midtwenties. He was not like his cousin Witold. He did the bidding of his father loyally, but reluctantly when it involved bloodshed and war. He was as strong as any man, stronger than Witold even; and he loved the hunt, for he saw purpose in it. He had love and respect for all men and creatures. He was often thrust into the bidding of his father's ideas and silently obeyed his will, although he had the mind-set of his mother. He had all the makings of a statesman. His very presence and demeanor invoked love and respect. He was dark haired and handsome, which made one look upon once because of his princely position and secondly because one could not help but be impressed by his beauty. Only the beauty of his soul matched it, which was not filled with pride, ambition, or hatred but humility, patience, charity, and respect. He knew his heart was different than his father's and grandfather's. He was fascinated by Western Europe and cared little for the east beyond Lithuania. He did everything to educate himself about Western Europe.

His father knew his heart well and always gave over major war tasks to Witold, who was energetic and talented in that field over Jagiello. War had come too close to the capital of Vilno, and all were on the defensive, even Jagiello. "It will give us time," he repeated, as he was a man of few words. They left hastily toward Vilno to report this intelligence to his father, the king.

King Olgierd conferenced with Witold about battle strategy. Jagiello and Skirgiello entered late night into the wooden army quarters, surrounded by thousands of Lithuanian troops. They bowed to their father and nodded in Witold's direction. The Lithuanian king's sons had more of the luxury and pampered nature of power and an overbearing mother who claimed the rights of her sons' protection from war due to their Christian heritage.

Witold was to the king as precious as his own sons. Without the efforts of Witold, Lithuania would be but a western outpost for the Mongols and an eastern outpost for Europe, a barrier for the rest of

Europe against their assaults, who for generations had assailed them straight to the heart of their country.

"Father, our men are ready, well armed with many personal weapons from homes and farms. They are ready to fight and have willing hearts. The bridge was collapsed, but the Europeans are quickly rebuilding. It will give us an opportunity to acquire hundreds more in a matter of days."

"The German swine will advance little and turn back to home soon. Witold! Are we prepared?" the elderly gray-haired, battle-hardened king asked.

"As always, Uncle, we are," Witold replied.

"Where does their weakness lie?" inquired the king.

Jagiello replied, "We have learned that they have King Louis, his army, as well as thousands from France, England, and Germany. The Teutonic Knights gave us enough struggles, and now, they have the arms of Europe. We are strong, but they are sure to massacre thousands."

Witold grew suddenly impatient and angry. "They will reach Vilno before the Feast of Snakes, cut our Holy Oaks, and strip us of our heritage and honor. We must defend a quick and ferocious battle and rely on their 'Christ' to soften their hearts with a truce."

Olgierd conceded. "The truce must only come after a great show of force. They must know that we will stop them whatever the cost."

Jagiello, not interested in more war talk than necessary, bowed to his father before exiting. Olgierd could count on his son but respected his character enough to carry on battle strategies with Witold.

Jagiello could barely contain his anger as he confided to Skirgiello, frustrated and impatiently, "We stand to lose thousands of men and homes and risk the destruction of crops, why? Because Witold decides he must push the western border into Poland and cause havoc there. Jackass! He might as well have enraged the gods by that pathetic display of savagery to Poland. Poland was appeased, good neighbors until his viper's fangs had to sink in."

"One part jackass, one part snake, and a third part Mongol!"

Jagiello laughed at his brother's veritable insults, satisfied Witold was the one left with their father to fine-tune battle plans instead of them. Witold was too much a part of generations of old who clung to barbarism instead of diplomacy, which Jagiello was sensitive and prudent enough to know was the way of the future.

War Is Hell

The European troop had priests who provided mass for them daily and confession as death was always so close at hand. It was a young new Franciscan preacher who pressed the hearts of the kings as he preached to them one Sunday during mass, "Though there may be a time for every purpose under heaven, why must intelligent human beings express discord through the brutal evil of war? Humans, the most enlightened creatures of this earth who claim a spiritual dimension, yet feel the need to change things by use of force? By killing in the most brutal fashion? Do not deceive yourselves! Taking and giving of life belongs to God and God *alone*! It is never your right to take a life, this is God's right *only*! Throughout the ages, we have thought of the most brutal ways to destroy other humans for our own 'benefit,' and we have not understood Jesus until we have fully embraced his message of love and peace… For a moment in time, reality is suspended. What reality? That there is a Creator God who gave life, Giver of Life, Who in His work and very nature created us free but responsible and sees all humans as his children—the way parents see and know that the bond that join their own children is sacred and the worst possible evil would be for a brother or sister to kill his own. For a moment, the true, good, and beautiful is discarded and suspended, and we trade it for what is a lie. God is not in it! He has no part or takes no sides because to do so would be a contradiction in His nature. True progress of humans will be achieved when there is peace in the Truth, in what is true, good, and beautiful. That begins by the love that we have for this life, for our Creator and our fellow man. Love God, love your neighbor as yourself…and God's greatest challenge, love your *enemy*. When this is recognized in the world and in our hearts and in the hearts of the prideful, who have the most narrow view of reality possible, then war will be no more. Before we can achieve a world without war, we need to dream of it and do everything in our power to achieve it."

Each king and nobleman was challenged by the simplicity and humility of the Franciscan who with seeming disregard for their status or intentions preached his message.

Rottenstein stood up, huffed, and gestured toward the priest as though he was ignorant and walked out. The kings and leaders were all quite somber and reflective, now more cautious about their intentions and purposes.

⁓

But now, it was a time for war and the clashing of swords—that evil, brutal time when all creation cringes. Jagiello and Louis were kindred spirits underlying their collective duties and present-day realities. They had in their hearts a hatred of war and a strong desire for peace and the education of people as a means to achieve it. But both were now caught up in this present reality and so took up the loathsome duty of medieval war.

As leaders, it was their duty to fight in a way that was participatory but only as much as that meant they did not lose their life. They knew in their humble souls that their worth was not greater than the husband farmer or newly married young man expecting a son or the young man who would never experience such relations. They each detested the duties of this day with a deep existential loathing.

Jagiello was with his brother Skirgiello. His lighthearted and well-humored brother did not mind killing so much, his most important duty to protect his brother, for whom he would have given his life if necessary. They fought closely, for Skirgiello had promised his mother to help protect Jagiello from his own lack of will toward the murder of a fellow man.

Skirgiello rushed over to a reluctant Jagiello, who had stalled over a wounded peasant knowing he had received a deadly blow but was still alive. Jagiello could not bring himself to kill but instead fell to his knees and embraced the head of his young enemy and held him as he left the world.

"I didn't want to die here."

"I know," answered Jagiello. "God forgive us…" And he wept.

His brother quickly pierced the man through his heart to relieve an agonizing prolonged death. "God forgive us," Skirgiello repeated in disgust as if slaughtering a wounded animal.

Distractions and a New Horizon

It was to the benefit of the Lithuanians now with spring farming approaching to have the Europeans leave their territories. The same was true for the Europeans. Thousands had been killed or wounded. Both parties wanted it over.

One evening, as the darkness fell around the forest camps and fires blazed, the duke of Lancaster, England, expressed his views impatiently to the group of European leaders. "It has been a fortnight, and yet they continue full force defense on their land. This bitter cold April is winter battle. Our losses are a thousand. We cannot continue this for months, and yet our retreat will impress upon them a weak intention to subdue them."

His French opponent countered strongly, "We will fight this battle to its proper end, or why should we have begun it? If we misjudged them, so be it! We go home with less numbers, but victorious. We have gained miles heading toward Vilno. The closer we come, the more willing they will be for truce."

King Louis added, "They are stubborn men. So far, we have had no word. No talk of truce, but we will see them come to us for terms. Full force, another week."

"We should *take* Vilno now! Convert these pagans for all of Christendom and the glory of God," urged Rottenstein.

Leopold approached the group accompanied by his elder brother Albrect and Peter Suchenwrit, an Austrian court poet, philosopher, entertainer, and musician. Men in the company cheered and gathered round.

Peter was short, stout, with chubby rosy cheeks and a face that made men smile. Leopold was cheerful, happy to introduce a diversion and moral support to the battle-weary group. "Albrect, my brother, has joined us from Austria. Late and close to victory, but *here* nonetheless!" He announced as he patted Albrect on the back with affection.

"My brother, I was with you in spirit and prayer, and delayed by a nagging wife," his voice became high pitched, rolling his eyes and mimicking his wife. "'Another *crusade*? You're too old for this. Look, you're a grandfather. Stay home, or you will meet your death of cold and old age, which has made you slow and weak… You are sure to diiiiiiiiiiiiiiiiiiiee!'" Albrect's act brought about hearty laughter from the surrounding group. "But most important, I brought one of Vienna's greatest treasures, Peter Suchenwrit and company, court poet, to lift your weary spirits…" Peter took his cue and bowed energetically as the surrounding men cheered and were encouraged to come and enjoy the show.

Peter climbed onto a fallen limb as his stage. "That I will…and if you may, lift a pint of spirits"—he lifted a mug of ale—"so that I may lift your spirits higher and for your ear my music to cheer, it will sound better after beer! And if I may commence, my great King Louis…" He bowed to Louis, who nodded. Peter began strumming his medieval instrument with an accompanying musician and broke into a fun and entertaining song. By now, all were closing in to take advantage of his rock star appeal.

As Alexander the Great was known to be one of the most widespread heroes of the age, Peter began his humorous jingle:

> Let us go back further, before Roman rule or law
> Before Latin…
> Or matins…
> But after writing on cave walls
> Before Christ [respectfully, he made the sign of
> the cross; all men copied]
> The God in heaven come as man

Yet after Plato
Who first from head and next to mouth words ran
Whose devout pupil Aristotle from Greece was
sent to tutor
A young prince named part god by his devoted
mother
Beloved son of Philip, kingly father,
To the land of Macedonia at the shores of the
Aegean Sea
This Aristotle came
To teach Alexander, as he was called by name
Known to us as Alexander, "the great,"
Who lived not with love,
Nor hate,
But to fulfill his divinely appointed mission
To bring Greek culture and law to full fruition
Not just within his tiny realm
But all across this earth at the helm

And from the mouth of philosophers
His imagination filled,
Yet from his mother pride and ambition willed
To set out from such a tiny kingdom
With great armies

And his horse, Bucephalis, we cannot fail to tell
No greater horse no rider ever mounted
Energy and nerve of metal all accounted

Really what men saw
Was a man seated upon the throne
Even of great Persia
Where there his manly weakness caved in to desire
A woman, daughter of King Darius,
Led the world to know
Not a god, but mortal man, 'twas so…

And after conquering the East
He ventured to lands unheard
So even all his men, ill and wanting to go home
Did try to pull him from his endless roam

Yet eastward on he pressed
Believing that heaven would always hear his urg-
ing request
To conquer earth's darkest corners
But… He one day felt the wrath
Of that true God who turned His sacred head
from heaven's throne
To let Alexander know, that he was spirit, Yes!
But also flesh and bone
And in the heat of summer's day
Marched his army and Bucephalis into walls of gray!

Suddenly, the galloping of hooves could be heard loudly. Peter hurried his poetic song, unconsciously rising in volume as he was coming closer to his important conclusion:

A living grey wall of el-a-phants
For which Bucephalis became as horse to dog,
and dog to ant!
And at the hand of Prince, *Por-us* [motioning for
more ale]
Of great India

With sickness and mortal nature bearing down
Rode on, to be brought down
By elephants who with great *crash*!

Peter simultaneously was extremely startled by a horse that jumped through the forest brush and came to a halt near to the intrigued group of men. Peter fell sprawling from the log only to realize it was a young Teutonic messenger. He regained his composure and stage presence to finish…

Brought Alexander upon his *ash*!

The men laughed heartily. The bodyguards had drawn their swords, and now realizing the messenger was safe, put their swords away and retreated along with the men, leaving Louis privacy.

"Michael! Why the rush? You startle us! We *are* at war no doubt you have heard? You could have been killed!" Rottenstein snarled, trying to ward embarrassment.

Michael bowed. "Your graces, I have a message for the good king…," he stammered as he gestured toward Louis. Louis, concerned and anxious, stood.

Rottenstein snapped, "Well then, let's have it!!" He snatched a scroll from the young page's hand, who hesitated in disbelief that he was in the presence of the king and so many great legendary nobles and knights and making his way back to the horse, stumbled and tripped over a log. The nobles laughed as Rottenstein gave them a stern glance and nodded toward the king, settling the men into a solemn silence.

Louis seemed relieved but appeared to attempt to hide an underlying disappointment. "God be praised!" The group of men waited expectantly for the king to share his news. "My wife is well, God be praised, she, Elizabieta, has delivered five weeks ago, a healthy baby girl." Louis de-emphasized *girl*, claiming it mildly. The group of men, realizing that any king awaits anxiously news of a son and heir to such a vast kingdom, acknowledged the king's news with silence and pensiveness, calculating how this would affect them and their countries.

"God has granted me a healthy daughter and has kept safe my wife, thanks to the intercession of the Blessed Lady." The men offered their congratulations.

Duke Lancaster, trying to flatter the king, toasted. "Here's to Hungary's good fortune and to her great King Louis"—as he bowed toward Louis—"and the good fortune of all of Christendom. At his majesty's request, upon my return to England, I will recommend that from the house of England and England's great King Edward shall issue a potential spouse and future marriage to benefit all of the lands claimed for Christ and his church from west to east."

Louis did not respond. It was not in his interest, but he appreciated the flattery under the circumstances. Coucy of France, the Englishman's rival, rolled his eyes and shook his head. All were now led by Leopold, who began in his booming voice, "Hear, hear!" to which all present replied in unison as knights, *"God's will now and forever!"* A new day was dawning with the birth of Jadwiga.

Truce

Once sanity regained its place in the minds of men, after bloodshed and hate had run its course and won its purpose, men came to uneasy truces because they have learned that their greed or pride has already cost too much. They were left with the nauseating aroma of death and decay and suddenly began to yearn for peace and life. It was sad that they could not come to terms with the beauty of peace, before they cost so many so much. *"The way of war is the way of evil, not of God. Those who rejoice in war cannot be following the will of God."* These words ran through Louis's mind strongly in the last few days.

Less than a fortnight passed, and Louis and his men, one spring morning, gathered on the edge of a plain to recommence warfare after a brief fighting intermission. The knights and men were positioning to size up new landscape and discuss new battle strategies. Considering their significant industrial advantage, sheer determination, and brutality was taking its toll on the Europeans.

Coucy of France mused after breathing the spring air, "They will soon be needing to regain their land to begin planting their crops..."

His close confidant replied, wishing, "And we to a church for Easter tide."

Rottenstein intrusively replied, "Yes, but for now, we are in Lenten tide, which we know means that we bear the cross and the mark of suffering, for still a while." As the elder Teutonic Knight unwittingly reminded, they suddenly perceived him to be the root of the hell they had been thrust into. It was his leadership and greed into all the surrounding areas that had provoked the Lithuanian retaliations in the first place. They all realized that their alliance was extremely fragile. They knew they were not committed to the same degree as the Teutonic Knights and for the same reasons.

Louis replied, tired of it all, "Yes, today, we bear the cross."

A bodyguard excitedly interrupted; suddenly, hope was on the horizon, "And, Your Majesty, today the pagan bear the white flag!" A Lithuanian delegation approached with the white flag of truce while a large group of Lithuanian nobles rode forward.

The major nobles—King Louis, Rottenstein, Coucy, Lancaster, and Leopold—rode forward guardedly with their bodyguards toward the approaching nobility. A Lithuanian interpreter came forward.

"King Olgierd, I present Louis, king of Hungary and Poland...," the interpreter began. They were suddenly energized and impressed by each other's presence, at last each other's enemy face-to-face, all false images and prejudices stripped away. Olgierd appeared less than satisfied. He was a large but not a giant man, with long braided graying hair. He was rugged and scarred. Olgierd and Witold were stoic. Witold managed a hateful glare, spitting toward Rottenstein. He was really their worst enemy. The interpreter continued, "And to your Grace, I present King Olgierd, joint ruler of Lithuania, Witold his nephew, Jagiello, his son, Skirgiello, his son, and Korybut, another son."

Louis responded, "If you had advised us of your intention last evening, we would have dressed better for the occasion." Witold tightened the grip on his sword. Jagiello rode up ahead of the group.

Jagiello addressed them respectfully, bowing to King Louis. "I am Jagiello. Olgierd, my father, will hear your terms."

"Our terms..." Louis replied, glancing toward his fellow leaders and Rottenstein. They had not yet fully worked out details of the terms. "Our terms are that all Polish prisoners and prisoners of war be returned to us, and because of our approaching feast of Easter, our holiest day, we will return all prisoners to you." Jagiello watched for his father's response. His father nodded reluctantly.

"Agreed," Jagiello stated firmly.

Louis continued, "That you refrain from breaking the great trust forged from generations of friendship between Poland and Lithuania, and you swear not to cross the borders as established during the reign of my great uncle Casimir..." Witold looked beyond the delegation, his loathing evident.

Jagiello simply replied, "Agreed."

Rottenstein coughed nervously. "And great King Louis, furthermore...," he interjected rudely, but Louis cut him off from offending the fragile situation further.

"Yes, and our comrade Rottenstein wishes to inform you that if you do not convert soon to Christianity, you will feel his wrath once again. Understand it is in your best interest to gain heaven and avoid hell by your conversion to God incarnate, who lives within us all and by whose power we have our being and who has left his church for all men of good will."

Olgierd, who until now had been silently dignified, replied. "I am a free man, I am what I am. Why should I give up what is real to me, my heritage passed on from my father and his father before him? I will not bow to your wishes, and this will not be a term for this truce. On my land, in my country, me and my people will be free to live as our ancestors!" He ended his statement, angry and insulted with his fist raised.

Louis shifted in his saddle, knowing that the Teutonic Knights wanted to push to the capital and overtake the country. He personally felt that the retaliation he came to achieve on behalf of Poland was complete.

Rottenstein moved in close to him and quietly counseled. "We can end it now! These are not *my* terms! They have lied and put off conversion too long! We cannot accept these terms."

Jagiello knew the motives of Rottenstein but, wanting to ensure the end of the war, came forward, having understood his determination. "I will convert to Christianity within the next ten years, you have my word."

Rottenstein, realizing he was losing, shouted. "His word is water—one day solid, the next day liquid, and the third day, gone into the wind!"

Spytek of Northern Poland, also the victim of Teutonic aggressions, spoke with his usual snarl of sarcasm. "Jagiello has been known to me for many years now. I believe him to be a man of his word, and further…," addressing Rottenstein, "his mother is a devout Orthodox Christian most likely praying, like good St. Monica for her son, with tears and supplications to the Almighty!" Some chuckled at his attempt at sincerity.

Louis regained the negotiation process, expressing passionately "We are men of peace. I know that we have shown ourselves to be men of war, but you must know and understand that we are men of peace. Our Lord and God commands us to love our enemies, and in as much as we have harmed you, we have betrayed our God. It is a peculiar thing for you to have known us in battle and not to have known that in our hearts, there reigns a King of Peace who would rather have us injured then to invoke injury. Because of our human nature, we deny our Lord and God that which he commands of us that we be instruments of His peace and love. Our Lord wants all of us to live as brothers, in peace, and all His children—even those who may not yet know Him and serve Him—to be one, to be brothers. This is my heart, which I bear to you here in your country, to you so that you know that though we call truce, we are not the victors, nor do we glory in this bloody victory, but that we have suffered in order to attain peace for our country, and by God, we pray you will grant it to us."

Olgierd's face riled in contempt as he answered Louis as if he was less than manly, "I have heard of Him your God, usually from the lips of women and their subtle pleas, that *I* should join them in their prayers and beliefs. I will die before I turn my back on the beliefs of my forefathers and betray their sacred trust given to me to guard and uphold. But I will grant you your peace, and you have my word that in my power, Poland will not be disturbed by men of Lithuania. You have my word on this."

Louis nodded, dismounted, and came happily toward Olgierd, who also came to meet him. Much to the horror of Rottenstein, the king of Hungary and Poland stretched his arms to embrace Olgierd rather than the traditional shake of hands. Olgierd, taken aback, weakly embraced him also.

"So be it." Louis patted his back strongly. "We have our terms and fight no more but return us both to our hearth and families who await us."

"You have leave to return by the way you came. And subdue your men under the terms of this truce not to abuse, plunder, or disturb our peasants and villagers to the point of ruin," Olgierd replied.

Louis replied, "In the name of my sovereign Lord, Jesus Christ, we will do no such harm and will severely discipline anyone who is found to betray this term."

Each man bowed, and the two parties turned their backs on each other, commanding each army to turn and begin the long march home, with rearguards still vigilant. Jagiello was left, glancing toward his brother Skirgiello, incredulous at the proximity to friendship they had just witnessed blossom out of the painful context from which they had just emerged.

⚬

Later that night, Rottenstein, like a pot that had reached its boiling point, stormed into Louis's tent. "The mission was a failure!" he shouted accusingly. "You brought about the end of this too quickly."

"A quick end and another beginning!" Louis answered with his back still to Rottenstein, picking up his goblet of wine while overlooking maps for the way home. He tried not to let his impatience at Rottenstein's insolence get the best of him.

Trying to restrain himself, Rottenstein answered, "How will such a soft blow serve to better our cause and the cause of the *Holy Roman Empire*?" He slammed his fist to the table, alarming everyone present.

Louis replied unapologetically. "The cause of the empire is best served by mercy, not by merciless brutality and dominance. The Lithuanians will come in good time. Not by force, weapons, and warfare but with patient negotiations. You know, Rottenstein, there will be no solution until your German order ceases to take their lands as well as lands of Poland. When your greed ends, there will be the solution to warfare and an era of peace! Some persons are blinded by their ambitions and do not see that they hinder the kingdom of heaven because they will not exemplify our Lord in meekness and *humility*."

Rottenstein, humiliated by the king's patronizing admonished, "How easily our king turns military strategy into gospel love. It's not your duty to preach to us, our purpose given by the Holy Father. We, Teutonic Knights, defend Christendom against the gates of hell, with our very *lives*, and all we get is ingratitude and mockery from its kings and princes!" He turned and left, leaving Louis to smile satisfied, knowing that this would be the last time he would see Rottenstein for some time as he was headed home to his family.

Appeasing the Poles

Louis headed south toward Buda, Hungary, but had business to attend in the Polish capital. The nobles secretly complained about the mandatory meeting with Louis "the Hungarian" in Krakow. Being the most direct nephew and heir to Casimir the Great before him, he was liberal in granting the nobles and trusted counsel of Poland many rights and liberties, which reflected self-rule.

Ladislau of Opole, one of his most important and trustworthy statesmen and closest relative, was at the capital to greet him with joy. "I see you have taken my advice and brought with you the daughters of our late King Casimir. Of course, for their protection and education under your watchful eye in Hungary, your nieces are much better off with you as guardian."

"It is for their protection and the interests of my daughters. Each will aspire to great things and marry to the greatest dynasties of Europe. Each a crown! The girls make for good alliances."

The polish delegates arrived gradually. Nobility of Poland entered and bowed to Louis, presenting gifts and signs of homage including Spytek, who represented the interests of Northern Poland. Louis called the delegation to order. "Good men of Poland! I know you to be devoted subjects, and the difficulties are inherent in ruling such immense territories, stretching from south to the northern expanses. You have shown fidelity and support, even recently as I traveled the realm and, in hospitality and warfare, have been superb hosts. I called you together to bestow great and lasting benefits to reward your fidelity to the Piast Dynasty and the House of Anjou! Each of your territories is to be expanded, and taxes are to be diminished in accordance with the laws written and signed by me. May the sons of Poland rejoice and thrive in the reign of Louis and by the grace of God and his Holy Church…"

The nobility was at ease and rejoiced in the elaborate benefits bestowed freely and expressed by different comments and general astonishment. One eager noble shouted, "All hail King Louis!"

Louis continued. "These privileges and rights granted and written into law and deeds, freely bestowed, your good king is asking but one right—not for myself, but for my heritage, which at this point is endowed by the blessed daughters of Eve," he continued lighthearted and happily, "that you accept upon my death a daughter of mine to succeed me on the throne of Poland."

The nobility now shifted their mood as they realized the price was to compromise their views toward female rule and limit their choice to one of Louis's daughters.

"Unless by God's generous nature he grants a son to me to rule in my place, the kingdoms of Hungary and Poland as by his father! I salute all of my subjects and thank them for their trust that in Hungary, I will prepare for them the best of rulers in government, warfare, and scholarly endeavor: a son or daughter to benefit your— *our—great realm.* For the greater glory of God and the Church!"

Ladislau of Opole came forward with documentation. "Each noble of Poland, in receiving the great benefits bestowed by the king, is to sign in agreement." They could not oppose without endangering their status.

Louis continued, "Ladislau will oversee the consensus of every loyal subject. Poland made safe of late by the efforts of your good people together with their loving king from the threat of pagan Lithuania, not yet converted. I must turn my attention to the affairs of Hungary and leave your territories in your capable hands. If cause comes whereby you are in need of your king's presence, I will come to your aid and assistance. God Bless Poland and its many great representatives!"

The meeting at the great meeting hall was followed by a large dinner as a symbol of unity. Leopold, travelling southward with Louis, sitting close by to him, leaned in when the festivities were well underway.

"Louis, if I can speak to you on the matter regarding your daughter. I have a four-year-old son, William, who is in excellent health and sound mind who is promising to be an excellent young man. Having another daughter now, why don't we promise these to each other? She could come to Austria. The alliance and friendship we have forged can continue for generations."

Louis studied his best friend with sincerity, realizing that Austria was one of the jewels of Europe, and thought it fitting and an honor as there was nowhere he would rather see his young daughter than under the protection and care of Leopold. "Yes, Leopold, it would be an honor. This young newborn child will be a princess of Austria, and I consider it an honor that you would desire it so." They grasped each other in a long-armed grasp and, with the best of intentions, forged their children's destinies.

Home at Last

It was late summer by the time Louis had finished business in Poland and made his way through the Carpathian Mountains toward his beloved Buda. As he rounded the last bend toward his city, his home in the valley stood safe and secure, the church spires, and university buildings he had founded appeared in sight. Many delegates had raced ahead to give news of his arrival to his family. He strained to get a glimpse of those he cherished most in his world, his wife and children, knowing the one he had not laid eyes on would be there.

There was his beautiful Croatian young wife holding a beautiful healthy five-month-old baby, the sight of whom made his aggressions and hardness of heart melt away like a thousand snowflakes. He rushed from his horse to embrace his wife with a passionate kiss and kissed his children.

His mother, Elizabeth, allowing him this moment undisturbed, refrained from embracing him after knowing the dangers and travels he had endured for the sake of his duty. Finally, after she allowed his wife and children priority, she embraced him with tears of happiness. "We have much to discuss, son."

Later that night, everything faded from Louis's attention except his wife, whom he loved with all his heart. She was graceful, beautiful, submissive, soft spoken, and intelligent, but never interfering with his duties. They had nothing in the universe but each other.

"Elizabieta, I've been gone too long. I'm finished with long journeys away from all of you and home. Poland will take care of itself.

There are many good men there, and the Lithuanians are subdued. I am sorry the affairs of state have kept me so long."

"My lord! I would never ask any such thing of you! You know that."

"I have fought hard and long and am feeling my age. I have earned the right to be a king and govern my country and not stretch my affairs beyond what is possible for one man…" As Louis embraced and kissed her again, he added, "And to love my wife as a man should, and his children. What troubles you tonight when you should be happy I've returned?"

Elizabieta answered shyly, "I know you love us, and I know you love your daughters…"

"A great part of my mission was to secure their heritage rights."

Elizabieta continued, "But… I have failed to give you a son—a strong heir for your posterity."

Louis sat up, "Elizabieta, you're young and beautiful, and if I'm home, there will be plenty of time for a son in years to come."

"My maidens say some women are prone to sons. All I have ever born for you are daughters. Beautiful gifts of heaven, but not strong knightly kings who can save us from enemies from the east and keep unity and peace within the walls of our kingdom… I want… I think you may, my lord…find a woman…for the good of Hungary and your name—a woman who may bear your son for your namesake." Tears began to stream down her cheeks.

"Don't ever say such things. How could you? It is adultery, even for a king! I am not above the laws of God."

"Nor was Abraham, who bore a son through the maidservant, Hagar. Nor King David himself who from another woman bore Solomon, wisest king ever born to man, or Jacob, from whom the twelve tribes of Israel sprang from *two* women."

"Eliz, that was all before Christ, who showed us a better way to sanctity! How could you think of such things?"

"Your mother," she replied unaccusingly. "It was her idea, but she is right to say so!"

"Mother! You women! All emotion and you convince yourselves that you know for certain the way a man must take. No, Elizabieta, there is none but you, and that is God's will from the beginning." And they spoke no more that night.

The next morning was beautiful, lighting the interior of the stone castle with a warm pastoral light. The family was finally together around the table. Louis held the baby while finishing eating and was noticeably quiet and pensive, as well as Elizabieta.

Elizabeth, his mother, had ruled in Poland with her husband, but the Poles had rejected her rule after his death. "Louis, I am so happy you are home. There is such an empty space when you are gone... How are those *gentlemen* of Poland?" she asked sarcastically. They had not been kind to her or her sons during her reign there.

"They have agreed to accept one of my daughters to reign. It will be Maria."

"There will be much training of these five girls."

"We have our work cut out for us...," Louis replied.

CHAPTER 1

The Sponsalia de praesenti in Hainburg (July AD 1377)

"Jadwiga, Jadwiga! Get up, hurry!" The sun's first rays crept over the horizon and gently kissed her cheeks through the castle window as she rubbed her eyes. She loved the glorious chorus of the songbirds as she relied on them to lift her from her bed. Catherine and Maria, always the first up, relentlessly pushed and prodded her like Christmas morning. "Jadwiga, hurry…" Nannies entered upon hearing the Hungarian princesses had arisen, scurrying and dressing the girls. "We can't be late," urged Catherine. Now, the chorus from the castle cathedral brothers' choir could be heard, singing out a Gregorian chant of praise welcoming the morning, *Puer Natis in Bethlehem.*

The three sisters entered the chapel and joined Mama, Papa, Grandma Elizabeth, and a larger number of servants and bodyguards.

Now, the morning light streamed in, seeming to bless the day and its plans. Jadwiga noticed her parents and grandmother smiling in mixed emotions at her as she stared at them with her wide-eyed perceptive glance. Papa was tall and handsome and smiled a gentle loving smile at her but quickly returned to his prayers. Mama looked so beautiful this morning with her golden hair touched by the sun. She stared longer at her four-year-old beautiful daughter, and Jadwiga looked again to notice a tear, like a jewel sparkling in the corner of her eye. Mama, seeming to swallow her hardships and desires, gave Jadwiga an encouraging smile and returned to her prayers. Grandma, as usual, was completely involved in the mass, and Jadwiga followed her gaze to the front of the chapel, where the summer sun also now brightly lit a large crucifix.

All three sisters were well behaved, still waking up. They were relieved when the priest finally gave his final blessing, and they could run ahead to the dining room where a spread of freshly baked bread, butter, eggs, berries, and Hungarian sausage adorned the breakfast table. Everyone filed in to join the children, a much larger group than most mornings.

Jadwiga and her sisters ate quietly, as was always expected but competed giggling over who could make the biggest milk mustache, seemingly oblivious to the adult's conversation but always having one ear to the news for the day. Papa was talking to Misteke, the head of the guard, about the day's journey, and Jadwiga overheard they would stop at her distant cousin's home that evening to sleep. Hainburg was only a half-day's journey from there, and they would arrive some time tomorrow afternoon. Good! It wasn't going to be today.

She turned toward Mama and Grandma's conversation. Were the dresses ready and packed? Was Jadwiga's wedding dress ready and packed also? Mama assured Grandmother everything was ready. Grandmother looked over her shoulder at Jadwiga and gave her a wink. "The weather looks promising for travelling today," was the last thing Jadwiga heard her say as Catherine and Maria began to pull on her and motioned for her to follow them.

Catherine asked, "Papa?" and pulled gently on his sleeve.

"Yes, you may be excused, but we are leaving shortly, so stay near the front entrance, and whatever you wish to bring, get it quickly." Catherine nodded and led her two younger sisters by the hand. She seemed more concerned than normal, sad and almost fretting once she left the comfort of the dining room. Jadwiga felt worried as she could see eight-year-old Catherine's concern grow as she escorted her two younger sisters outside.

"Where are you taking us, Catherine? Papa said stay near the front," Maria asked. Catherine determinedly guided the girls outside away from the front, toward the castle stables. A watchful bodyguard signaled another guard to follow the children. Catherine led the girls down a gentle rolling hill, still on castle grounds, toward the barns and river. As they began to run, holding each other's hands tightly, Jadwiga tripped, only to be quickly helped up by her sisters.

"Hurry!" They sensed the urgency in Catherine's voice as they approached the barnyard. Catherine led them through the muddy barnyard, behind a haystack, with Jadwiga and Maria beginning to protest.

"No, no, Catherine, we will get dirty. Mama will be upset!"

"Mama does not want us to leave, now *be quiet and come*," Catherine commanded.

The two sisters allowed themselves to be led into the barns where Catherine checked until she found an empty stall filled with clean hay. "You two hide, and don't make a sound!" She commanded as she buried them in the fresh hay.

"Not even if someone comes, do not stir!"

They were quiet for what seemed like a long time, when suddenly, they could hear Mother calling from outside the barn. "Girls, girls! Are you in here?" She sounded distressed and frustrated.

"If you are here and hiding, you must come out. The carriages are packed, and Papa and the entourage are waiting. Are you in here?"

The girls remained still, with Catherine shaking her head back and forth, giving them both a warning finger to her mouth. "Shhhhhh…" The girls thought it a game they must play along with. Mama finally looked into the stall, and realizing they were found, Jadwiga jumped up out of the hay to frighten her mother, laughing.

Thinking from her voice that she would scold them, Jadwiga was surprised at their mother's reaction to the dirty girls whose hair were messed and filled with hay. Jadwiga knew that on a normal day, her mother would laugh and throw hay at them, but today was not a normal day. Instead of joining in the fun, Mama came to the girls, scolding Catherine, yet embraced all three. She knelt helplessly to the ground and suddenly began to weep, with their heads together in a huddle. Catherine also began to cry, leading to a chain reaction of tears.

Now they could hear Papa's deep commanding voice and knew there would be trouble, and the time for tears was over. They began to dry their eyes as Papa rounded the stall as well. Sympathy flooded and softened his heart as he observed his wife and trio of girls in a firm, sad embrace.

"Now, now, we must be brave and see that God has blessed this day with every grace and blessing. He is blessing us on our way, and our strength must come from Him, from above. It is a beautiful day." He stopped and hugged his family. He became pensive but continued strongly. "This is the day the Lord has made, let us rejoice and be glad in it, shall we?" He reminded them of the words they had just heard in the morning psalm.

Jadwiga and her sisters embraced him lovingly. He was firm and so well disciplined. They relied on him for their strength. Catherine signaled for Maria and Jadwiga to follow him. Jadwiga stayed in the lingering embrace of her mother, who didn't seem to want to let her go, and finally did so reluctantly.

Jadwiga found her pet lamb, which she had nurtured in the cold spring and was now becoming just old enough to fend for itself. She paused at its stall and knelt and embraced and buried her face in its fleece as Elizabieta looked on.

"Come now, Jadwiga, we must go," Mama ordered.

"I'll miss you," Jadwiga gave her pet a last kiss. "But I'll see you next year." She ran ahead of her mother and sisters, pulled on Papa's long shirt, and ran off once again in a different direction to delay the inevitable trip. Papa gave chase, caught her up in his arms, and carried her over his shoulder.

"Noooooo…" Jadwiga laughed. It was a game they often played. From up in Papa's arms, the world seemed smaller, more manageable, and more secure. Everything was fine, and that's what Papa's arms told her heart. Papa always protected his family, and where his arms led her, Jadwiga knew there was goodness, something to learn—and adventure, always adventure. He only set her down with the castle entrance a reasonable distance away. When Papa spoke, everyone listened, and there was no question.

"Go change quickly…the day is moving along, and we must depart for Austria… Run, hurry, girls. Jadwiga, your prince and husband awaits!" This time, there was no more time for games or interference. Papa had commanded them, and they went and came at his bidding.

Elizabeth, queen mother, huffed impatiently as everyone else was ready to leave. Louis joined her in the carriage, and she leaned in to be sure her opinion was well understood. "You know, sons don't do this kind of nonsense, just daughters!"

"Well, Mother, how would you know as you only had sons?"

"Exactly. You and Andrew never did these things. What do most women know about ruling anyway? You know I always thought a man was best for ruling. Look at the mistakes I made, with the best of intentions. Jadwiga is four now, and still no younger sibling, or *brother*, you know…"

"I know, Mother, it's the son with the strong hand that inherits his father's throne, the daughter her mother's loom."

"Something's got to be done…," Elizabeth mused.

"Well, something *is* being done. My sons will be by marriage, as God Himself has seemed to will it. With strong alliances with Austria and Europe, these young men will reign as equals with my daughters and take my place before long." His last words came out of his mouth, and he didn't know why.

"Nonsense! You are well and will live long as Uncle Casimir!"

The girls boarded the coach, Jadwiga's heart now filled with sadness as each step onto the coach lifted her from the land she knew and loved. Jadwiga could not take her eyes off her home until they turned a corner and it was finally out of sight, tears betraying her fear and uncertainty despite her efforts to be brave.

Great Uncle Ladislau from Poland joined them for the trip to the special event in Hainburg, Austria. Jadwiga liked his white mustache and air, and his rosy pudgy complexion. When Uncle Ladislau came, he brought treats and gifts and dolls she had never imagined existed; and today, his presence comforted her greatly.

"How are things in Poland, Ladislau?" Grandma asked. Jadwiga, as always, listened carefully.

"As you know best, they still enjoy self-government over rule of queen or king. They have kindly agreed to acknowledge a descendant of the house of Anjou to the throne. So, Louis, now, Jadwiga will be a princess of Austria, married to Leopold's William... And don't you fret, young lady. We adults like to make all these plans, but if it turns out you don't like this Austrian when you are twelve, you know you don't have to go through with all this anyway?" He pretended to snatch Jadwiga's nose, trying to cheer her up. She sat at his feet, leaning on his legs, listening solemnly to everything he said as she played with a cloth doll he had brought her. "What about the other girls, Louis? Catherine and Maria, who will you girls marry now that your baby sister is going to be the first one married and beat you all to it?" He teased them and tugged on Catherine's hair playfully.

"After great thought and patient negotiations, Mary will rule Poland someday with Sigismund, son of Holy Emperor Frederick."

Elizabeth enthusiastically and satisfied replied, "A *German*?" She was amused at the discomfort this would cause the Polish nobility.

"Louis, are you sure about that? I don't know how *that* news will be received in Poland," Ladislau commented nonchalantly.

Eight-year-old Catherine came to her father's side expectantly. "And me, Papa?" she asked.

Louis pinched her cheek affectionately. "You will marry the Duke of Orleans, Louis of Touraine, younger heir of Charles V of

France, and together, you will rule Hungary." She smiled, satisfied even though she knew nothing of the people or places, except for her Hungary.

"And with Jadwiga marrying William, there will be great queens in the Eastern Empire! And great princesses of Christ's church to guard its eastern borders!" Uncle Ladislau exclaimed energetically.

"Yes, unless a son is born," Grandmother replied hopefully.

Leopold and Louis's former promise was now about to come partially to fruition in the marriage of sponsalia.

⌁

Miles had led to miles, and Uncle was in a deep slumber despite the rattling and churning of the carriage. The pine-scented forests were interrupted from time to time by a series of farmsteads or the odd cabin that dotted the roadway. Jadwiga breathed deeply the fresh summer air, enjoying now the nature and birdcalls that pierced the silence, her sisters and her eyes glued to the thick forests for a glimpse of a wild deer or elk or even a bear. They saw farmers at work and encountered some travelers along the way.

The castle was far behind, and travel was becoming monotonous as Maria urged, "Papa, tell us a story, please…"

"Well. Hmmm. What about of my great uncle St. Louis of France, after whom I was named? He would feed beggars at his table and eat their scraps, tend to the sick, and build homes and shelters for women and children. He loved to say, 'Better to die than to commit a mortal sin.'"

Catherine finished, "And he died in Egypt, fighting the crusades…"

Louis continued, "Yes, while my grandfather, his brother, was given Naples by marriage. Naples is a glorious and beautiful land. One of the jewels of the whole earth…with walls of rock, oceans as warm and bluer than you've ever seen…"

"Except for Croatia," added Elizabieta.

"Except Croatia of course!" Louis's mind wandered.

Grandma Elizabeth, less able to restrain her anger, snapped, "And with evil women who kill their husbands…!"

"We do not speak of these things!" intervened Elizabieta, motioning toward the children.

Catherine pressed, "Papa?"

"Catherine, this will be a story for another day."

"Tell us about Poland, Papa," Maria pressed, knowing that she would live there. "Poland is beautiful, equal to everything you see. It is where I was raised, my first home, and I really love it. I feel quite at home there—many beautiful rivers, lakes, mountains, great farms, hunting, much like our Hungary. You will be happy there."

"Don't worry, Maria, I'll visit you all the time," Jadwiga assured her.

"And I will visit you in Austria," Maria reached over to hug Jadwiga.

"And you can both come home to Hungary often for tea," added Catherine. The adults smiled lovingly as the three sisters hugged as a sign of their promise.

The next morning, still a day's travel to Hainburg, shortly after dawn, the royal family departed from a delightful peasant cottage that belonged to a distant relative of Louis. The owners had happily taken shelter in the barn to allow the family use of their humble residence. Jadwiga noticed the happy family observing them departing their home and reboarding their carriages. The children were barefeet, some in worn tethered clothes but clean and healthy looking, and a rosy-cheeked blond-haired baby rested on the hip of a girl no older than Catherine. They didn't have nannies or servants or security guards, and the father and mother were also dressed in simple clothing, but she could see it: they had love. Some of the boys sat on the thatched roof of the barn or on the trees to get the best look, one holding a bucket to milk the cow, another his hoe to begin his work in the kitchen garden before the heat of the day. The animals made their way to the pasture.

Jadwiga waved happily to the children and neighbor friends who had come to witness the spectacle. The children excitedly waved back. Jadwiga could not move her gaze from them as the simplicity of their farm life appeared to her as poverty. She was moved by love and compassion for them even though as all children do, they did not see themselves to be lacking, but took everything for granted.

"Papa, can we come here again and stay a while?" Jadwiga asked.

"Maybe on the way home next year," Papa answered.

As the carriages began to pull away, the children emerged from the barn area, walking and then running after the royals waving, jumping, and smiling happily. The bodyguards did not stop their approach. Jadwiga's heart leapt for joy at their excitement, and she so wanted to help them and share everything she had. She dug into her father's pocket and brought out a handful of coins stamped with the image of her father. Managing the coins with both hands full, Jadwiga motioned toward the children.

"Papa?"

Louis nodded. "Yes, go."

Jadwiga leaned over the cart and tossed the coins toward the children while Maria grabbed her dress. The children squealed with excitement as they scrambled for the coins. Catherine and Maria, catching the spirit, uncovered a basket of honey biscuits and tossed them to the teens. The children shouted, "Blessings, blessings!" Their eyes shined with delight and thanks as they jumped, waving and shouting, "God bless King Louis!"

The trip was spent chattering happily and listening to stories and discussions from Grandma, Uncle, Papa, and Mama and observing the beautiful summer landscapes. Jadwiga reached into her father's pocket to find another coin and studied it carefully. Louis, by nature a teacher, asked, "What do you see there?"

Jadwiga answered, "The Blessed Virgin and a man kneeling to her."

Maria jumped up toward them and exclaimed confidently, "It's you, Papa!"

Grandmother replied, "Yes, it is your papa, kneeling before our Mother to show his subjects that all in his domain really belongs to God."

Papa added, "That all men may know that within these borders, she is held as the greatest counselor, intercessor, and aid, even to me. Everything here belongs to God. If we do not stand on faith, we do not stand at all." Papa motioned with his hand at the glorious natural surroundings near Austria. Jadwiga nodded in agreement.

The family finally arrived late afternoon to a decorated, beautifully scenic medieval town. Jadwiga noticed the river meandering gently through small mountains and pointed out the castle perched watchfully on the mount, overlooking the village. Carefully tended grapevines ran to the borders of the village. The smells of bread, cooking meats, and children running and laughing on the streets greeted Jadwiga.

Townspeople were thrilled and excited at the prospect of a royal wedding. They waved bits of silk clothes of variously dyed colors in welcome as they caught their first glimpse of Princess Jadwiga, the young bride-to-be.

They finally arrived at Hainburg Castle. Jadwiga saw Leopold's familiar smile. She knew him from his regular visits home with Papa. He always had treated her as his favorite as she was to be his daughter-in-law. Leopold's voice could be heard over the commotion as he eagerly came to help them from their carriages and greet them hospitably, his family standing reservedly behind him. "Welcome, welcome! I hope you had a good trip. Lady Jadwiga, you're here at last! Come and meet my family that you haven't met. Elizabieta, children, Mother, this is my beautiful wife, Viridia, who as you know doesn't like to travel." Viridia was of the important Italian Visconti family, and her dark hair and beautiful features were dignified, aristocratic, and friendly.

"Welcome, feel at home here, please," she struggled in broken Hungarian.

"And of course, my son, William, our young groom!" Leopold gently shoved William to the front of the group. "Shake hands and say hello, William."

"Hello," William obediently greeted everyone. He was thin with blond hair, friendly blue eyes, and a winning smile. Jadwiga shook hands with him as the parents looked on. He seemed nice, she thought as he gave her a hug. Everyone laughed, but Jadwiga felt timid as all eyes were on her, and she quickly moved back toward Papa.

Other priests, bishops, and family were present to greet the family. Jadwiga felt as though she had come to visit relatives on a summer holiday, as everyone was so friendly and welcoming. She was happy to be here; it already felt a little like home.

◦────∽◦∾────◦

The wedding day arrived, a sunny, warm summer day. Catherine and Maria were twirling and dancing, finished dressing and braiding their hair in the most admirable patterns, and all were dressed in the best of medieval finery. The women all now turned their attention to the child bride. Elizabieta stood in the background trying to hide her tears of joy and sadness from the child who could never possibly understand them.

Jadwiga's new Austrian nanny, Constance, was fussing and placing a wreath of freshly woven flowers and a veil upon her head. Jadwiga enjoyed Constance from the moment she had met her as she had a kind heart and smile like a big sister. Jadwiga felt how loving, patient, and kind she was in every touch and kind word. She was helpful, loving, and doting over Jadwiga, her new charge. Jadwiga loved her right away. She gave Jadwiga a reassuring hug.

"Do you like it, Mama and Grandma?" asked Jadwiga, lifting the veil from her face.

"Yes, sheer beauty!" Grandma replied.

Louis walked in to inspect the status of the women. He came at once to Jadwiga, kneeling in front of her on one knee, and lifted the veil from her face. "Radiant," he said lovingly, seeing a touch of sadness and hesitation in the face of his baby.

Jadwiga asked, "Papa, will you still be my father?"

"Forever," Louis replied, kissing and hugging her. "And your father found the best country in all of this world for you to live in. Now, be brave and remember, no matter what, God is always with you, right here," pointing to her heart. "So you have nothing to fear, ever. Understand?"

She nodded in agreement, wiping a stray tear. "Yes, Papa."

"You've seen William? He is a very nice boy, no?" She nodded but looked through her tears as she wiped her eyes to see Mama's quiet tears and Grandma even looking softly, and suddenly, Catherine and Maria joined in the tears. Papa, now surrounded by a flood of tears, comforted, "We aren't losing anyone, we are and will always be family, always together, and we are just adding many people to our family! Adding a brother. Girls, it is a cause for joy!" He hugged them all now reassuringly. "Jadwiga, you will stay here to learn the language. Will it not be good for you to learn the language of your subjects?" She nodded again, sniffling, as Constance stepped up to wipe her eyes and clean her nose. Mama came and hugged her tightly. Papa continued, "You must smile, a princess must always smile. No matter the hardships, she must bear them for the good of the people. No one wants to see a tearful princess, or queen…" And he looked up at his wife and winked. "This boy is the best I could find in the whole world for you, and he is the luckiest young man in the world." Jadwiga nodded as the family assembled in a solemn but joyful family embrace. "We must offer our sacrifices to God, like Jesus on the cross. He offered Himself, and in the mass today, you will offer yourself to God, for his purpose and will. Offer it up, offer it up to God!" The family nodded in agreement with Jadwiga. How often Papa had given her this advice whenever she had a headache or illness. Papa would say, "Give it to God." It always worked. Today, she tried again in her heart to offer a different kind of pain with Jesus to the Father, and as always, it was a sudden remedy. Her fear quickly dissipated into confidence and peace.

Jadwiga, young, beautiful, and innocent as any four-year-old child, stood at the back of the cathedral at Hainburg, the sun bursting brightly through the multicolored stained glass windows on this glorious summer day. The day was beautiful in this pastoral town, with the fragrance of many picked flowers, and where the fresh air from the farms and river brought a refreshing breeze into the cathedral and the singing of birds joined the singing of the local community of priests in the choir. It gave her mind peace and strength as she was led happily down the aisle of the great cathedral.

She observed the smiling, friendly faces of many local nobility and persons gathered for the great marriage. Jadwiga smiled at them, clutching her roses and daisies, all trace of the tears of fear behind them all, delighting every observer. Maria and Catherine led them, tossing rose petals gently on her path. Papa held her hand tightly as he led her to the front of the church and offered her to God and the kingdom of Austria, smiling reassuringly every step of the way. She was very familiar with the traditional *Introit* hymn; her confident smile reflected her love of its familiar sound.

She could see William at the front with Leopold, a boy of eight who she had known for under a week. His handsome, pleasant, friendly, winning charm and smile pleased her greatly. Papa gave her hand to William, who led her on to the altar, as he had been instructed. He was an obedient boy, old enough to know that they weren't really going to be married until they were older. He tried to be brave like his father and exude that bravery to his future wife. The children were made to sit next to each other and were very well behaved much to the satisfaction of the onlooking crowd.

After a sermon that was spoken with words mostly too large and foreign to Jadwiga, the priest finally stood over the two children, who were instructed to kneel for the matrimonial blessing. His large white mantle outstretched over them, creating a tent over the children, who smiled. William made a funny face at her, and Jadwiga had to cover her mouth to stop from giggling as the long prayer of blessing continued. Jadwiga felt sheltered and secure.

After the marriage blessing, the children were made to stand face-to-face and hold hands. Suddenly, the priest was asking Jadwiga and William to kiss. William understood, but Jadwiga did not. A nearby Hungarian priest gave the instruction to Jadwiga so she understood. William wasn't sure, but Jadwiga was obedient. They managed the command and innocently exchanged a kiss to the delight of the crowd, who clapped and cheered. The cathedral was now a house of delight and joy.

The festivities of the day were as elaborate as any medieval feast. There was roasted food, music, dancing, and sweets. The children at the wedding party were dancing and having fun, accompanied by hundreds of guests. All the difficulties of the earlier part of the day were dispersed by the strength and certainty the families had shared in their common faith at mass. Now, everyone seemed certain, happy, celebratory, and confident that the very best had been achieved for both families.

The night was growing old, and the children were sitting on thrones, fatigued by the feasting, playing, and dancing. They had resigned themselves to this grand game the adults had asked them to take part in: William acting his part as "husband," Jadwiga acting the part of "wife." Mama and Viridia came to tell them it was time to come to bed.

The children were led to their room, dressed separately, and kissed good night by their mothers. Jadwiga yawned and had to be guided to the bed. They both wore modest full-length white night-gowns and were placed by their mothers onto a large bed, with many hugs and kisses. The mothers left the room with their nannies within listening of the children in case they were needed. Jadwiga requested some candles remain lit. As the door closed, after a few moments, Jadwiga took a pillow and hit William with it as she had done with her sisters so many times and laughed delightedly. Sometime later, the nannies came in to check on their charges to find the two lying on a large sheepskin rug on the floor surrounded by pillows, nes-tled closely together for warmth. The nannies brought a wind-dried white sheet and, holding the corners, snapped it upward like a para-chute over the sleeping children.

The day before the family was to leave, Grandmama wanted to spend some time with Jadwiga and her sisters and took it upon herself to have a picnic lunch packed, and they rode out to the coun-try surrounding Hainburg to sit and talk before the long separation that was to come. Grandmama loved her granddaughters so much, and this situation they all found themselves in was leaving her heart feeling heavy. Four and a half years old—it seemed so young to leave such an innocent and vulnerable child behind. The older she became, the more she realized the risks even though the family was so good.

Catherine was climbing a nearby tree. Maria was feeding a colt some grass through a wooden fence, and Jadwiga was playing with some ants on the edge of the blanket, not wanting to leave Grandmama alone. The gentle gurgling and breeze from the cool stream and the shade of the tree made the summer heat just bearable.

"Jadwiga, we'll be leaving tomorrow. This place will be your new home for a time, and then next summer, we will come and get you and take you home again. You need to learn the language. Austrian, you know."

Jadwiga nodded and shrugged. "Yes, Grandmama."

Elizabeth observed her carefully for signs of fear or concern but saw that Jadwiga seemed happy and confident, or just naïve about how long a year was for a small child. "You know, I used to think that mostly men could rule better than women, and in many cases, this may be true. But, Jadwiga, God has chosen you and your sisters for very important jobs. You will never be like other girls, milking cows or spinning wool or a maidservant cooking food or cleaning all day long. I am not saying that you shouldn't learn those things or embroidery—I just mean you should pay close attention to the matters of the *court* and *listen* carefully to what is going on in the world of men. Jadwiga, come here and listen to me..."

Jadwiga obediently wiggled right next to Grandma, leaning on her leg. Despite the peaceful, relaxed surroundings, she wanted her undivided attention. Jadwiga focused only on Grandma. *This young one seems to understand so well for her age.* She seemed something like a prodigy.

Grandmama continued. "When I was young like you my father didn't think to educate me and teach me languages, reading, philosophy, history, and the mathematics as Papa has. I was taught the womanly things only. And when the time came for me, because your Grandpapa died and left me with Papa and Robert... I knew little, truly, of what it meant to rule. I felt so lost and alone and had to rely on others..." She checked Jadwiga's expression carefully to see if she was following her. Grandma looked down, feeling ashamed. "I know I come across brave, but the truth was...is... I made mistakes because I didn't know the world I came into, didn't really understand the way it really worked, and had only known the surface of it because no one ever educated me about it. I was sheltered really. But, Jadwiga, you are being given a tremendous opportunity from Papa and Lord Albrect to learn about everything around you: history and the philosophy and politics..."

"*Grandmama!*" Catherine interrupted from a large drooping tree limb. "Grandmama, please, I am stuck, and I can't get down, *please help!*" Catherine urged.

"Yes, Catherine, I'm coming, one moment! Please Jadwiga, *I beg you.*" Grandmama ignored Catherine's urgent plea, imparting the importance of what she had to say. "And the politics, you must not ignore or remain ignorant of the *politics*, being happy only to spin and weave. Leave that to the maids and servants and use your entire mind to understand everything you can about the world and what the council speaks of…about what is happening in the courts and in the church. Don't make the same mistake I did and be ignorant. A woman can know these things as well as a man, and *act* when action is needed. My greatest mistake was not acting on the difficult things when I needed to, and it made me weak and useless really…"

"Grandmama, *please help me!*" Catherine brought her to reality. Maria was jumping up and down under the limb but couldn't help.

She sighed. "Yes, Catherine, I'm *coming!*"

"Don't be sad or pout or miss us but use every opportunity to learn, and you will come home stronger, better, and more educated than before. Have you understood?" It was a lot to ask from a four-and-a-half-year-old.

She hugged Jadwiga and got up abruptly to assist Catherine. "Good then, when you think of me, think of these words and remember, do everything you do for the glory of God… Seek first the kingdom of God, and all these things will be given to you. Wisdom, courage, prudence, fortitude…"

"Grandmama!"

Jadwiga held Grandmother's hand tightly. "Yes, Grandmama, I will remember…" Jadwiga assured her as they walked to help Catherine.

A week passed with the spirit of the summer marriage festivities prevailing. It was time to return to their routines. The reality of the trading of children was beginning to set in, as now, the time had come to leave. Jadwiga felt loved as one of Austria and Leopold's family's own. The morning came for the families to part and for Jadwiga to see her family and William return to Buda without her.

Everyone was quiet and pensive after a collective family breakfast. "Well, the day has come, Jadwiga. Now you will stay with us." Leopold's loud voice seemed to echo in the great hall. "William, are you ready to visit beautiful Hungary? You will most certainly love Buda!" William nodded.

The family exited to the waiting entourage, each member of each family in turn hugging their beloved brother, sister, child, or grandchild. Emotions were suppressed to be strong for the four-year-old child they were leaving behind and the eight-year-old they were losing. Her sisters were sad and kissed her, only consoled by the presence of the new brother they never had.

One family member that Jadwiga had grown close to and fond of as a grandfather she didn't have before was Albrect, Leopold's elder brother. Papa gave her a last hug. "It will be all right," he reassured her. "We'll be together again soon." Jadwiga stood close to Albrect, who put his arms gently on her shoulders, as if to help make her strong and sure.

The priest came forward and gave a final blessing to both groups, then hugged Jadwiga with a welcoming hug. Jadwiga took great comfort in his attention and affection. Her new family crowded around her. Mama gave a final long embrace and smiled bravely. The carriage finally began to pull away. The families waved to each other as Maria, Catherine, and William fought to keep looking at her. Grandma waved and blew her nose. Uncle Ladislau waved furiously with both hands to make her laugh. Her sisters and Louis brightened the mood by excitedly and energetically waving and yelling out, "Bye, Jadwiga, Bye, see you sooooon..." She could see Papa smile at William, roughing his hair. They turned a bend, and they were no longer visible to Jadwiga. Albrect smiled down at her. "And now, your apprenticeship begins..."

CHAPTER 2

The Apprenticeship of Young Jadwiga

Jadwiga's new family loved her dearly and treasured her. She was a beautiful, intelligent, irresistible four-year-old who won over the hearts of every person she met as the new little princess of Austria.

Leopold, having to defend Austria, would have to bear himself to arms once again over one cause or another, or so he thought, and was often away. Viridia Visconti was an Italian princess and ran a meticulous household. She was preoccupied with the day-to-day functioning of the house and the servants under her charge. She was kind and attentive but not given to education, except of typical skills such as embroidery or knitting. She was hardworking, and Jadwiga learned many tasks by being near her.

The older patriarch of the family, more philosophical and gentle in nature, was Uncle Albrect, Leopold's brother. He was a philosopher, peacemaker, and pacifist at heart who despised war and took every opportunity to divert war by peaceful negotiations. He undertook her education and training as requested by Leopold but also, being of a grandfatherly age and occupation, took to heart as his personal duty to educate Jadwiga as a well-rounded princess, many faceted as her father had insisted. With Albrect, a deep love and connection flourished quickly with Jadwiga, whose mind was like a garden, ready to be nourished and tended to grow fruitful things.

One day, weeks after the marriage, Jadwiga wandered off to explore the living quarters of the palace. She overheard behind a screen in Albrect's study room Leopold and Albrect in a heated argument. Nearby stood Jonas, trusted servant of Albrect. Leopold's voice dominated and echoed throughout the room. He sounded angry, frustrated, and very determined as he often was.

"I *must* go, it is important for Austria…"

Albrect humbly replied, "Leopold, your family needs you. Your life is here."

"Your life here is good because of all my efforts," Leopold thundered angrily.

"But you strike offensively…they are not just wars and the matter of the Holy Father. Why do you support the Pope of Avignon, because of political gain? For shame, to ever think that a country or king could lay claim to the church of Christ…" Albrect was also determined in a calm, intelligent manner that was always characteristic of him.

"Albrect, go back to your books while I deal with reality. And don't you ever forget that it is from the efforts of men like me that Europe gains its peace!" Leopold stomped out of the room.

Albrect shook his head and dejectedly called out, "What about the pope in Rome? Did Christ appoint two heads? A body with two heads, what an atrocity!" Albrect shook his head.

Jadwiga walked quietly to Albrect's chair. There was something about Albrect that drew her to him. He was devout, committed to education; and there was something about the two of them like kindred spirits. And although she loved Leopold, she sided with Albrect. She was horrified that Leopold was off to battle, and she shuddered at the idea that he might never return. Albrect noticed Jadwiga and smiled sweetly. The storm gave way to a great strong ray of sunshine. "Hello, little princess! I hope Vienna is delighting you?" He patted her hand, which she had placed gently on his arm.

"There should be one," Jadwiga replied. "Holy Father…one… That is what Papa says," she continued.

Albrect was astonished by the capacity of the four-year-old-child in front of him. "He is right, my child. And you should not worry about us men. We speak as enemies, but we are always loving brothers. Jonas…" Jonas came quickly to Albrect's side. "Jadwiga is here. Do you think Father Thomas is nearby to meet our young prodigy? Let us go see." He slowly lifted himself from his chair, motioning for Jadwiga to come and pull him up. Together, they exited the library toward a study room.

Here, they found a group of children sitting attentively, listening to a young Franciscan friar with a brown habit with a rope around his waist, reciting Latin with the children. "Amo, amas, amat, amamus, amatis, amant…" The group was chanting. Jadwiga was drawn toward some shelves of books and slowly ran her hand across them as she walked with Albrect. She was too young to read but old enough to know the wonders of them.

The friar stopped his lesson and came to Albrect and Jadwiga. The children squirmed in their spots and couldn't help but listen curiously. Father Thomas affectionately embraced Albrect. "Lord Albrect! Now this cannot be Princess Jadwiga? She is so big!" Taking her hand in his, he kissed it. He was young and very friendly. He had an awkward gap in his front teeth and a boyish grin that gave him a look like he would never grow old. His brown robe had only a ceinture and rosary, and he wore simple sandals; his hair was shaved in traditional Franciscan style. She liked him at once.

"Yes, here she is. Jadwiga, Father Thomas will be your teacher. He will teach you Latin, more Austrian, German, and answer any questions you may have about God, the powers that rule, temporal and spiritual, about philosophy, how to speak well, how to think well, anything, everything…"

Jadwiga replied excitedly, "My own teacher? Will you read to me?" They laughed at the level of her delight, as if there was no greater gift they could give her.

"With great pleasure," answered Father Thomas.

Albrect spoke to Father Thomas, "In her free time, she will be with me, observing the affairs of state, or with Lady Viridia learning needlepoint…" As the two continued, Jadwiga observed the group of kids to see two boys surprisingly lunge for each other and begin punching and wrestling each other to the floor and pulling hair. Father Thomas rushed back to the two boys. "Luke! Nichola! Please stop this at once," he cried out while separating them. "Why must this go on? Jadwiga, I am sorry, Albrect…you boys apologize," he urged as he gently pushed their heads toward Albrect.

"If you are to come to class at the castle, then this must end," Albrect admonished gently. "Now please apologize to each other. Your parents do not want to hear of such behavior!"

"Sorry, we will not fight," the boys agreed, red in the face and ashamed, and apologized to each other.

"Now sit and back to work then," Albrect advised.

Father Thomas continued his lesson. "Yesterday, we talked about 'why does God permit sin?'"

Nicholas eagerly blurted, "Because man has free will…"

Father Thomas replied, "In part, yes. What will we ask today?" Everyone was quiet and somewhat shy with the new student present. Jadwiga stood. "Jadwiga?"

"Why must there be war? Why can't there be peace?"

Nicholas replied eagerly, "Sometimes, the Huns attack, and we have to stop them."

"Good, good, John?"

"They want to take something that isn't theirs."

Father Thomas again agreed. "Yes, sometimes," and, noticing Lord Albrect, motioned with his hand, "Lord Albrect?"

"Sometimes, war is just a way of living, an industry. Your father, Luke, what does he do?"

Luke answered, "He makes swords and chainmail."

"Yes, and what would he and all his men do if not that? They make money from it. It is a way of life for many people," Albrect questioned.

Father Thomas addressed Jadwiga finally, to answer her mature question. "Sometimes, we go to war to attain a greater peace. Just war is war served in order to achieve a greater good for society, to preserve a society against harm, or preserve one group's rights."

"The Crusades!" Nicholas shouted.

"Indeed, the Crusades are meant to enforce rights of Christians to the Holy Land and in defense of those attempting to conquer the Eastern Empire, built and ruled by Christian men. The church calls this 'just war.' Christians are not permitted to wage war without just cause—for example, to take what belongs to another…"

"Jesus was not a warrior. He wants peace," Jadwiga said convincingly.

Father Thomas, impressed by her truthful simplicity, addressed the group. "Bella in cordibus hominum incipient." And he motioned for the children to repeat, "Bella in cordibus hominum incipient." They repeated. "Translation: *Wars start in men's hearts*," and he replied again, cautioning each child, more slowly to make sure they soaked in the full meaning, pointing to Nicholas's heart. "Wars…start… in men's…hearts. Never forget that as men, God has given to us the tremendous gift of free will so what we will, will happen."

Albrect completed the thought in agreement, "Will peace and act thus. Through God's grace, the good will of men, peace will come…"

Father Thomas finished, "Very good! Let us recite the prayer of St. Francis of Assisi."

The children were familiar with the prayer, so all prayed in unison, "Lord, make me an instrument of thy peace… Where there is hatred, let me bring your love; where there is injury, your pardon; where there is doubt, true faith; and where there's sadness, joy. Oh, Master, grant that I may never seek to be consoled, as to console another, to be understood as to understand another, to be loved as to love the other…"

Winter came, and with it the great feast of Christmas. A large celebration was underway, extravagant by medieval standards, bordering on excessive. Food was laid out—meats, vegetables, and sweets and pastries reserved for Christmas after a month of the Advent fasting. Viridia, with a small group of women, was sitting talking, laughing, enjoying the music and dancing. Jadwiga was playing with her new cousins and friends of the family who were her schoolmates as well.

Albrect entered, clapping and gaining the attention of everyone; Peter Suchenwrit was at his side with his musicians. The children and Jadwiga shouted gleefully and gathered around. Albrect motioned for quiet and to sit down. "Attention, attention, quiet... May I introduce Peter Suchenwrit!"

A loud cheer went up from the children and men. A medieval melody began, and Peter wasted no time. "Let's see, what shall I sing of tonight? Of knights?"

"Yes, yes," shouted the children.

"Of glorious knights? Or *days*?" Peter teased.

"No, not days!" the children whined and shouted.

"*Days* when men of valor..."

"Yes, yes!" shouted the children.

Searched the world for honor
For a deed that will be written
Long after they are smitten
But now, let me tell you about Lords Albrect and Leopold
Who with the father of Princess Jadwiga, King Louis
Made war with the great Knights of Teutonia
Against the last great settlement of pagans in Lithuania
Who worst than hairy beasts of wild
Took captive father, wife and child
And burned them to their evil god
At stakes of wood, flames higher and higher stood...

The children sat enthralled, their imaginations, including Jadwiga's young impressionable mind, enraptured with the gruesome tale…

> They worshipped snakes, ohhhhhh,
> What soulless beasts were they to battle
> Your beloved knights and sturdy horses
> With sword and bloodshed alone
> Could put an end to hearts of stone
> Beasts, not men, how can Christ himself redeem?
> Animals and criminals t'would seem
> Yet for us all He came this holy night
> To put all pagan gods to flight
> And conquer men with words of love
> First came as baby, then died as lamb above
> No sword shall slay this holy night
> Only death in every manner put to flight!
> Hosanna, let you children sing
> Hosanna! To the newborn King!

Peter ended the ballad with wild-eyed excitement and energy to the gratitude of men and children. Everyone clapped and cheered and carried on with their feasting and drinking. The music continued, many dancing again after the brief interlude.

Jadwiga sat quietly amidst the festivities apart from her friends and chaos, looking out a window, pensive, almost melancholic. She noticed the full moon outside, intrigued still by the lyric, *"Who worst than hairy beasts of wild…"* As she tried to imagine any of God's men who would resemble beasts, images conjured in her mind made her shiver, and she began to fret. She decided that this would be a question later for Albrect or Father Thomas. Her father had to slay hairy beasts of wild? She looked down out of the castle window and noticed the snow shining like diamonds, and some peasants bundled in wool and fur on this freezing night. This was a story father had never told. Her concern began to fill her with anxiety until a gentle sweet voice broke upon her imaginings…it was Viridia.

"What are you thinking of, child? Do you miss home? Come to me."

Jadwiga nodded. She had been thinking of Mama and Papa, her sisters, and Grandma. She left the group of children behind, some playing and laughing with dolls, boys with wooden swords, and she came to her mother-in-law, who put down her embroidery work, fussing over her clothing and hair. She hugged and kissed her gently.

"My, this child is a beauty," she mused to the other women. "My William is lucky to have you as his little wife. You have learned Austrian so quickly, more quickly than I did." Jadwiga smiled and nodded, comforted. Jadwiga noticed a line of servants bringing in yet more food and drink after everyone was so full already.

"When can I give the extra food to the poor? May I go now, my lady? They must be cold and hungry."

Jadwiga had grown fond of the castle duty of giving to the poor and asked sweetly and with such great love and pity in her eyes that Viridia and the women could not help but be touched deeply. "Well, I suppose you may go now." Viridia called out to a servant about bringing out the Christmas gifts for the locals.

Jadwiga nodded and quietly slipped through the crowd of partygoers, observed by Albrect. She took a basket, filling it with much leftover foods of all kind, and headed to the exit of the room with the servants, followed by Albrect, her ever-watchful guardian.

The wind blew snow softly this moonlit night, but it was freezing outside the great castle hall. Outside, unbelievably, were huddled a group of mostly poor fathers who, despite the cold, knew that many Christmas leftovers would make the wait worthwhile. A guard opened a large wooden service entrance. Jadwiga emerged from the castle dressed in winter attire, wool and fur. She distributed the food to those waiting with some servants. The guard emerged with bushels of breads and cakes for their Christmas-morning breakfasts. The beggars were grateful and took a share of the goods, thanking Jadwiga. Jadwiga noticed within the crowd, so late on this icy night, a mother with a girl her age, who did not have proper clothing. She suddenly felt a deep sympathy for the girl. Why was she out so late and didn't she have a father to come and collect the food? Knowing she could have another made or purchased easily, she took her winter fur coat and wrapped it around the little girl. "Here...you take it..."

The mother of the child happily exclaimed, "God bless you, Princess Jadwiga..." The child responded, "Blessed Christmas." Jadwiga looked on as they turned to walk home. The girl looked back at Jadwiga and waved. Jadwiga was filled with great empathy, wishing she could do more as she waved back.

She suddenly felt the cold and heard the guard protectively and gently call to her, "Princess...come..." He gestured, at which she turned and preceded the guard into the castle. Down the dark hallway, lit only by the occasional torch, she saw Albrect walking away. Knowing that he had likely come to be sure she was safe and happy, Jadwiga ran toward him and gave him a hug around the legs. He put his outer cloak around her to warm her.

Albrect spoke soft and admiringly. "Feeding the hungry? Clothing the naked? So late at night?"

Jadwiga questioned, "Where are you going Uncle Albrect?"

Albrect replied, "Follow me and see."

As they walked down the great halls, Jadwiga asked, "Uncle Albrect, what was Peter singing about in his song? He talked about Papa and the beasts you had to fight. What were they like? Did you really have to fight beast humans?"

Albrect laughed, surprised that the lyrics had taken such a hold of Jadwiga's imagination. He paused, looking amused at the child's literal mind. "Jadwiga, the truth is that Peter likes to exaggerate and make stories for us, but the Lithuanians we fought were frighteningly similar to ourselves—not beasts, but men, fighting for causes that were dear to them, fighting for their property. Now they were pagan, but soon going to convert to Christianity. They are this close," as he held his fingers together with about an inch of space. "They were not beasts, Jadwiga, but men of flesh and blood much like ourselves."

"So they were not beasts?"

Albrect laughed. "Never mind Peter, he's an entertainer... No, they are not *beasts*! The problem came when the Teutonic Knights fought in *their* lands, not defending Christendom but robbing their lands for industry and greed. *They* were attacked first by supposed servants of the church. In the world, my dear, things may not be as you would think, and evil and darkness can be found in many places where light and goodness should be.

Often who seems evil, or to be your enemy, is your brother and an opportunity to love. Do you understand?" Jadwiga nodded, relieved. "Our Lord did tell us to be aware of wolves in sheep's clothing, and the knights are like that now that their leader, Conrad Von Rottenstein, cares little for the peace. Rottenstein is a wolf in sheep's clothing. These people are to be feared the most because they refuse to bring peace to the lives of others and, even yet, use God as a shield for their defiance of Him. These are the people who we need to fear in life. They're the ones who will not allow peace and harmony to prevail in the world. Have you understood?"

"Yes." Jadwiga took all he said to heart and tried her best to understand.

Albrect turned into a small lower-level chapel lit only by candlelight, occupied by a brother, a priest, sisters, and servants who had finished their long day of work. They prayed in front of the Blessed Sacrament, held and adorned by a golden monstrance on the altar. Albrect genuflected reverently, as did Jadwiga, a gesture she was familiar with observing her own father. All was silent. In the distance, the music of the festivities could still be heard. Below the altar was a nativity scene carved of wood, with the intriguing figures of Mary, Joseph, the wise men, and animals, which pictured the special night when God himself came upon the earth in the person of Jesus, so humbly in a manger. Albrect knelt down, totally absorbed in contemplation and adoration, as though transformed to another world. Jadwiga observed him closely and copied. She felt awakened from the cold and spoke in her heart to the God she could not see, except in this little child, *"You must love the barn as I do, Lord, for you made it your first house. I know how sweet and beautiful the hay can smell, and the gentle noises and peaceful animals—they were your creatures and the shepherds beholding their Creator that night, but I know why you came there… It was because you came to share in our life…you are like me, you love the barn."* She knew it was typical for her not to hear back from the large silent God she knew and felt in her soul. A sister began to sing "Adoro te Devote" (St. Thomas Aquinas) with love and devotion. Jadwiga exchanged a joyful, peaceful smile with Albrect and felt all is well in the universe, for God has come to us. It was Christmas night, and the light was forever going to be brighter than the darkness.

CHAPTER 3

Tragedy and New Directions

Winter receded, and the children delighted in the glory of spring-time. The castle filled with summer breezes, fresh from spring-cleaning. The farms and woods came back to life, and the berries, fresh milk, cheese, and greens were back on the table. Lambs, calves, and colts appeared in the fields with their mothers. Father Thomas took his eager students outside every day they could. They went on hikes in the woods, fields, and nearby farms. They left the clutter of town and the shadows of the castle that sheltered them through the long winter, always accompanied by the watchful eye of guards. Father Thomas was particularly fond of the outdoors and the tremendous power and effect it had. All that humans built loomed small under the grandeur of the cosmos. Nature trivialized the workings of men, and he knew how important it was to balance these privileged children by bringing them closer to nature.

Father Thomas taught them botany, both useful and danger-ous plants, and helped them collect the plants of early spring. They observed the work of many nearby farms and communities as it was their duty to be educated in the workings of the subjects of the kingdom. They were taken to industries to observe the workings of every-day people: blacksmith, weaver, clay worker, and even the glassworks shop.

It was a sunny, warm spring day that the group, returning from their excursions, decided to play and swim in a nearby stream. The bodyguards on horseback stood nearby—an ever-watchful presence, relaxed and relatively unconcerned of danger. Jadwiga was splashing happily with the children to cool down. She liked collecting shiny rocks and pebbles from the stream, and they were busy finding the best ones.

Suddenly from the town limits, a woman was running to them through the pastures, hurriedly, raising her skirts to speed her and waving to draw attention to herself. It was Constance, Jadwiga's nanny, and she continued to wave, calling as she came closer for Jadwiga.

A bodyguard rode closer to the stream toward the children who, with loud squeals of delight, did not perceive the distressed nanny. "Princess Jadwiga..." His deep commanding voice over the rabble caught everyone's attention. He motioned toward the approaching nanny. "She calls for you..." Fr. Thomas stood upright and strained to see Constance, who seemed upset and red from the hot sun.

"Jadwiga must come at once!" she urged. Everyone including Jadwiga suddenly joined in the serious mood, concerned and surprised, for Constance was in tears. Jadwiga wasn't sure what was wrong, but she dropped her stones and quickly went to Constance, who she had never seen cry. She cupped her hands on Constance's cheeks, trying to comfort her. "What is it, Constance?"

Jadwiga was brought quickly back to the castle on horseback. It was not Constance's place to address why she had brought her hastily to the family. She kept her lips pressed tight together and hugged Jadwiga and repeated, "It will be all right, dear." Jadwiga, now five and a half, was concerned but didn't know why.

When they came to Leopold's study, Viridia, Leopold, Albrect, and William were all present. Everyone was serious, concerned, on edge, and Viridia and William were crying. Jadwiga observed everyone carefully and seriously. She could not even be sure that the boy she saw was William, for it had been nine months, and he was like a stranger to her again. Viridia gently pushed him forward to Jadwiga to hug her. "Say hello to Jadwiga, William." William reluctantly obeyed. Viridia, in tears, came to Jadwiga and embraced her, "My dove." Leopold stepped forward and knelt eye level with her with a furrowed brow.

She did not fear this kind, loving man but admired his large-ness and strength. "Jadwiga, we have news from home. It's not good. Your eldest sister, Catherine…heaven help us! She is gone to heaven child…she has died." Jadwiga was disturbed by the grief of everyone, but she did not understand the reality or implications of what she had been told. It had been nine months since she had seen her sister. Leopold continued, "William has come home for summer. You are to return home immediately. William will return to you in autumn."

Jadwiga rushed to Albrect. He put his hand on her shoulder. She looked up at him. "Home? To Buda?"

She had been excited by the fact that it would be soon time to return to Buda, but now that she could go home, her excitement was overshadowed by the news of her sister's death, which had not fully sunk in. She wasn't sure how to react. He smiled down at her. "Your parents need you home now," he managed to say, wiping a tear. Jadwiga was in shock, not knowing what to say or do; but the sorrow of everyone made her cry as she struggled to remember her beloved Catherine—her soft long brown curls, kind protective ways, and her smile.

Constance comforted her. "I will pack her belongings. I will go with you, Jadwiga."

"Of course, yes," Leopold answered, not his self.

CHAPTER 4

Home Again

Jadwiga was sent speedily home to Buda, accompanied by Leopold. Her family eagerly awaited her arrival after almost ten months, and after the family's sad loss, her return was extremely important to them all. Catherine's funeral had already taken place. The whole heart of Buda was broken.

As Jadwiga neared Buda and the beautiful river and castle walls, she squinted toward home to see her family gathered at the front entrance of the castle. They were eager to lay eyes on the sister and daughter they still possessed. Louis greeted Leopold with a warm embrace and then anxiously came to Jadwiga and picked her up lovingly from the carriage, hugging her tightly. Jadwiga wanted to say something to Papa, but the only thing that came were tears and sobbing, and she didn't know why. He could not put her down for some time. Papa carried her into the castle, only stopping for Mama and Maria to hug her. It was difficult to see her father and protector cry. All the emotions tied in being away for so long and trying to be strong melted away. Even Leopold and Grandmama were reduced to tears. Elizabieta took Jadwiga and kissed her over and over and hugged her tightly.

"Thank you, Constance, thank you for all your care. We have heard you have been so good to Jadwiga in our absence," Mama gently thanked Jadwiga's favorite nanny.

"You must be hungry after such a long journey," Papa said. After some time, the women walked to the kitchen to get some food for Jadwiga and some tea.

Louis watched pensively, absorbed with Jadwiga. She had grown so much and gotten so much taller. Louis placed his arm on Leopold's shoulder, leading him to a room with a desk and documents spread out. A warm fire lit the room with a peaceful glow. Both men sat and stared silently into the fire, watching its transforming energy dance and crackle, both caught up in their own train of thought. Louis was still in shock from Catherine's sudden death, and he tried to think clearly how to rearrange the politics, but it was really muddled in his mind. It was too soon. He couldn't help but think that he and Leopold were two of the most powerful men in Europe, but how powerless and really small they were in the great mechanism that was creation and nature.

Leopold was the first to break the silence in a businesslike way. "Louis, I have to return today. I won't stay, but in regard to the marriage, and I don't feel comfortable discussing this in haste, but will the marriage arrangements still be upheld as agreed upon? Your situation has changed." The death of Catherine meant a shift in plans and loyalties, and no one was certain how it would affect the arrangements that had been determined at Hainburg. Despite their great friendship, the relationships that had been so lovingly and carefully crafted were now in question.

Louis answered in a disheartened tone, more distantly concerned than normal. "Yes, yes, they will, Leopold, no need for worry. I will have my scribes script an agreement reverifying our plans. Elizabieta and I, with the clergy, will sign our consent. Now, William will be presented as my legal successor in Hungary, together with Jadwiga."

"For my part, I will move the date for the dowry, 250,000 florins, one year sooner, and we will ensure that the marriage is consummated as soon, or near to soon as Jadwiga is twelve. Louis, also…the nanny… Constance. I spoke to her, and she is willing to stay. She loves Jadwiga. They have a strong bond. They get along so well. For now, Constance is willing to stay. She comes from one of the best families in Vienna."

"Yes, of course, thank you for arranging that. She will be free to return to Vienna when she wishes." Louis was happy to have the stability for Jadwiga.

"She has expressed a strong desire to stay with the child, to help her through these difficult times." Leopold reassured. They shook hands. Leopold, shaking his head still at the sad turn of events, with empathy and sorrow, continued, "This should be a glorious day for our family, and for me, but it is a privilege granted through unfortunate circumstances. It may not be until the two are officially wed that we will recapture the joy and glory of this benefit. I will send William in the autumn." Once again, the two men embraced with empathy and sorrow in their hearts.

Louis patted Leopold firmly on the back. "The Almighty Father oversees all by His providence. Come and have something to eat."

Sometime after the death of Catherine, Jadwiga began to have trouble going to sleep at night. For a time, she would come and find Mama and Papa at night, when she was to go to sleep. She couldn't breathe. She imagined Catherine buried underground and herself being buried also. These thoughts terrorized her, but she didn't speak of them. Only sitting on Papa's lap, with him holding her tight and humming songs to her, would settle her to sleep, and he would have to carry her to bed. This went on for some time. One day, Jadwiga asked Papa, "What happens when we die?"

Papa answered, "Well, our body dies, but our soul lives and goes to a new place, heaven."

"Where's my soul, Papa?"

"Well, it's right here," Papa suggested as he drew a line right next to her spine. "And it's bright and shining." She imagined her soul, long and tall and glowing white.

"Where's heaven, Papa?"

"Not too far away. Maybe souls in heaven can see us. Jesus told us he is going to prepare a place for us, so you can guess that it's like here—only better, because there's no evil there, only good. And colors, lots of different colors and beautiful things you've never even seen before."

"Is Catherine happy there?"

"Happier than the happiest feeling here. But we are sad because we miss her."

"Will we see her again?"

"Yes, we will all see each other in heaven after."

"But I don't want to die, Papa."

"The strange thing about dying is that when it comes to you, somehow, you are just ready. It's your time, and it's okay. We have the sacrament of the dying to give us strength for it. We offer this final suffering to God, to make up for the sins of our life. Death, you see, is a punishment for our sins. If we accept that and repent for our sins, it is redemptive suffering, and we can go to heaven soon."

"But Jesus didn't sin, and He died."

"Ah, and that is the glory of Jesus, that he chose death to make up for our sins and the sins of all mankind. He was the perfect offering for the sins of mankind. He underwent death to make up for all *our* sins, and his life was that valuable because it was perfect, perfect in love of God and neighbor. He died so we could inherit eternal life. He paid the price for us. And death wasn't the end of the story... remember why?"

"He rose!" answered Jadwiga happily.

"To show us it is true, life after is real and true, and to show that death has no power over God. It's just something we will understand better after."

Jadwiga sighed deeply, nodded, and put her head comfortably on his chest, resigning herself to the great designs of God, putting all her trust in her father's words and the great God who created them all.

CHAPTER 5

Growing Up in Buda (AD 1382)

Years passed, and the family settled together in Buda, with Louis going away on occasion to Poland for business or campaigns but being home as often as he could with his family. He and Elizabieta had no more children, and the sons of the household were the future sons who would marry their daughters. They came for long extended stays in Buda, mostly during summer months, to learn of the heritage and languages of the lands they would someday possess and rule together with their wives. This included William and Mary's future husband, Sigismund (Margrave of Brandenburg), who was the eldest of the four children. Sigismund Luxemburg was the son of the reigning emperor, Charles IV.

They were often at court, watching court proceedings and government meetings, or sent for instruction to priests for learning. Louis had always been a tremendous advocate for schooling and higher education and saw it befitting for his daughters and his future sons-in-law both to receive education. Four years after her sad return to Buda, Jadwiga was now eight years old; William, twelve; Mary, ten; and Sigismund, sixteen. The group was frequently seen together. Of the group, Sigismund, perhaps because he was the oldest, had a more serious and intense disposition. He did not have a free spirit but seemed more dutiful and understood the responsibilities of governing better than the other children.

The three younger ones seemed often a nuisance to him, a young man, while they were still so young. They often played pranks and tricks on him to see his temper flare at them. For William, it was a great sport. Jadwiga would often smile and laugh to think of the times at court when Sigismund would doze off only to be awakened by William poking his nostrils with a small twig.

There was the time that William had gotten Sigismund drunk by "mistakenly" serving him fruit Cassis liqueur, insisting that it was fruit juice. Sigismund entertained them for the first time, and they found he in fact did have a sense of humor, until he got sick and swore revenge on William.

There was that summer twilight sunset when an unusual blazing orange, pink, and purple-red sky that looked like a giant fire stretched unusually across half the sky. The group was still playing by the river after late-afternoon fishing. Jadwiga was wading at the shore, catching tadpoles, the blazing colors reflecting on the river. Sigismund ran up the grassy bank, outstretched his arms with a stick posing as his staff, and yelled out frantically at the top of his lungs, *"It is the end of the world!* Look at the *sky,* it's the end of the *world!"* and proceeded to sing out loudly, chanting part of the mass, his shadowy figure and deepening dramatic song echoing on the city and castle walls. *"Per ipsum, et cum ipso, et in ipso, est tibi Deo Patri omnipoténti, in unitáte Spíritus Sancti, omnis honor et glória per ómnia, sæcula sæculorum et glória per ómnia, sæcula sæculorum! et glória per ómnia, sæcula sæculorum..."* The chanting made the whole scene strike a certain terror of near death and judgement in her heart. In the strange surreal surroundings, Jadwiga suddenly imagined it was truly the end, and her heart began to beat twice as fast. Jadwiga screeched and dropped her tadpoles, running with all her might, following William and Maria, who also screeched and ran toward the town trying to escape the end. Only Sigmund's jeers and laughing corrected their fears as they ran toward home.

On another occasion, the group was being given a tour of the royal prisons, looking at the various prisoners and their state, some calling loudly out to the young rulers, some bowing, some staring silently, and some very old or nearing death. It was Jadwiga's first time there, and the darkness and dreariness felt like it could be hell. She wondered what exactly these poor souls, mere shadows, could have done to deserve this torment. She recalled all the trials and court cases she had heard in the courtroom, but until now, she did not understand what a punishment imprisonment was. The men were thin, ragged, and dirty. The sights and sounds were repulsive, but this morning when Sigismund and William had recommended the girls not join them for the tour, Jadwiga had insisted on coming, always with Grandmama's encouragement in mind that she should know everything the men knew. So she went with them.

They came upon a younger man with a dark beard and skin, dressed very differently. When they walked by, they found him kneeling on a mat, forehead bowed down, touching the floor, facing the prison wall, which only held a very small and narrow window. He stood and prayed with his back to them. He knelt again, bowing his forehead to the ground again. The young royalty watched in quiet fascination. The guard, upon noticing his lack of attention to the royals, unlocked the cell, walked toward him hastily, grabbed the man from his kneeling position, and made him pay attention to the young royals.

William called out, "What were you doing?" The prisoner did not understand.

Sigismund answered, "He was praying."

The guard answered, "He is of Mohammad. He must face southeast when he prays, towards Mecca, and he must pray five times each day. He was imprisoned because they think he is a spy, but he can't speak Hungarian."

Jadwiga and her sister seemed surprised. "Face Mecca, why?" Jadwiga asked, "Is God not everywhere? Do not distract him from his prayers." She made a personal commitment to follow his example and pray at least five times a day. "We should learn from this man that we must pray often. What if he is not a spy?" She bowed slightly to him and smiled, finding him different from the other prisoners. She reached deep into her pocket and produced a rosary, handing it to him through the bars. He touched her hand and smiled thankfully.

They routinely entered the city cathedral where an old teacher, commonly referred to as Scribe John, tutored the royals. Jadwiga and Maria chanted as they entered the great church, making the sign of the cross, "Holy water, wash away my sins. Precious blood of Jesus, take away my sins." The four wove their way through the cathedral and back to a hallway leading to a room that was office of Scribe John.

He was sitting at his desk, with his back to the group, engulfed in his work, his desk being right up to the only window so he could catch as much sunlight as possible for his reading and writing. He was muttering, "Uh-huh, uh-huh." He began to write furiously. The bodyguard coughed loudly to gain his attention. Scribe John stood and turned, bowing slightly, "Oh yes, yes, my children…come… come…" He motioned for the group to be seated.

"How shall we begin today?" Scribe John asked.

"Tell us a story," responded Maria.

"Well, you know about Rome, Greece, Hungary, and Poland," he listed… None of those seemed to appeal to him. "When we write or speak or act, men who have lived and died, we all shall die, what moves men to do what they do?"

William answered, "Sometimes good, sometimes evil."

Scribe John answered, "Yes, when we're moved by good, we are responding to the Holy Spirit. We hear God's voice and do His will." He took the Bible from his desk and flipped through. "Yes, here it is, Psalm 95:8: 'If today you hear God's voice, harden not your hearts.'"

Jadwiga thought for a moment, "But how can we know God's will? How can we hear his voice?"

Maria answered, "I do not hear him speak to me as I hear you."

Sigismund, normally skeptical about the value of even spending time here at all, asked, "How does God speak to us?"

Scribe John paused then answered, "Sometimes through others, most times through others, but even the baptized child hears God within themselves."

William honestly responded, "But I've *never* heard him."

Scribe John replied, "When you hear the Bible, the Word of God, read or explained at mass, does it move your heart, stir within you, build your spirit?"

"Well, yes," William replied.

"Then you have heard His voice. Have you ever wanted to do bad, or not just bad but you really had a passion to do something… but something tells you no, no *this* is the way, walk in it?" The children reflected for a moment, and Sigismund nodded.

"God speaks to us in urges within the core of our true selves, our soul. It is not exactly like our voices, but subtle to our intellect. It is the language of our soul and God's soul. Abraham and the prophets all fine-tuned this sense by silence and prayer. Prayer…that is openness to listening in the best way we know how. The Word of God is the school and language for this purpose. Now, we sometimes hear about hardening of hearts in God's Word." The children nodded. "The prophets and Moses complained about this, even Jesus. When people will not listen to God's voice within them. Be on guard, alert, not to harden your heart. Stay with it no matter what. Never close your mind and heart to God in all these ways, and He will guide you." Jadwiga was pensive and reflective, taking every word in of her beloved teacher.

"Now, back to Latin…," Scribe John urged.

Grandmama was nearing death and visibly ailing, so she summoned Jadwiga and Maria to her. It was spring, and the children came to the orchard where Uncle Ladislau of Opole, grandmother's cousin, had brought them. She was lying sitting up on a wooden chair, with a thin woolen blanket to keep her warm. The cherry and fruit trees were in full bloom; cherry blossoms fell gently like snow on the ground, surrounding the girls and their grandmother with the sweet smell of spring.

"I had you come… I want you to know that I love you both. I am leaving you each a crown: Mary of Poland and Jadwiga for Hungary." The girls nodded, beginning to feel somewhat serious and realizing this may be one of their last visits. She had changed greatly, for weakness never had been a part of Grandmama's constitution.

"When you were young, you used to ask me so often, 'What happened to your hand?' I could not answer you." Elizabeth raised her mutilated hand that had three fingers cut off. The girls were just big enough and used to it enough that they nodded sympathetically, only slightly repulsed. "You were so young, I could not answer you… I had *two* sons, you know." Both sisters nodded. "And those Polish, well, sometimes, they can be stubborn…rebels some, breeched the castle, and almost assassinated Papa and his dear brother Robert when they were little, like you…" She reached out and touched Jadwiga's face, knowing her grandchildren were her greatest possession. Smiling, she continued, "Thanks be to God, all they got were my fingers…"

Elizabeth summoned Ladislau. He came holding two beautifully decorated crowns. She weakened, "Ladislau, you tell them about Robert… Please…"

"What you have not been told is that your Uncle Robert, your father's brother, as a young man, was married off to his second cousin Joan of Naples and not a year later was killed by her, *by her own hands!*" The girls were appalled. They were old enough to understand the horror and the implications of an arranged marriage gone badly. Ladislau shook his head. "A woman evil of heart and deed, known even to the Holy Father as such."

"Grandmama, his wife killed him?" Jadwiga clarified.

"Papa's brother?" Maria asked. Details about this brother had never been revealed to them. Jadwiga could not believe it. Her heart ached for Papa and Grandmama.

"I do not tell you these things to frighten you but so that you know the evil one is always at work... And if I could undo history..." The old, battle-hardened grandmother began to weep, too weak to speak, and Mary and Jadwiga finally saw the sorrow she had been carrying all these years. Elizabeth continued, "They took my son... took his life..." They all began to cry. The children embraced her. "How different things would have been and would be if he had ruled with your father..."

Suddenly, Grandmama regained her strength, breathed strongly, and smacked them each on the cheek, surprisingly hard. Maria was stunned at the strength of it and hurt that she would do such an undignified thing. With her hand to her cheek and her jaw dropped, she whined, "Grandma, why did you *do* that?" Jadwiga wondered if she was losing her senses and waited, wide-eyed, for an explanation.

"That is so you don't forget me..." She insisted, wagging her pointing finger at them, all still in tears. "And Catherine, we miss her so..."

Maria spoke softly, "Grandmama, rest...shhhhhh...shhhh... rest now..." and kissed her on the forehead. "We won't ever forget you, Grandmama."

Jadwiga assured her, "The Lord observes all things, Grandma. Robert and Catherine are in his care." And she kissed and hugged Grandmama, wondering just how much time they had left together.

Elizabeth put a hand on Jadwiga's face, "I will join them soon...," she said, resigned, drifting off to sleep. "Choose your paths wisely with God's light..." Ladislau put his hands on the girls' shoulders and led them away. Elizabeth died that winter, on December 29, 1381.

CHAPTER 6

Death and Commissioning

When Jadwiga was eight years old, another tragedy struck the family. Louis had been gone on business for some time, and there arrived a bodyguard to Buda castle with tragic news. Elizabieta looked fearfully at the approaching men, one who would have always been at Louis's side but now was here without him, and terror struck through her heart. She thought Louis must be dead. Was he killed? Was it accidental? Although his health had deteriorated since the death of Catherine and then his mother, Louis was only in his fifties, far too young to have died. The castle chaplain accompanied him. "Majesty, we have pressing matters concerning the king...my lady, our king, your husband, requests your presence immediately!"

Elizabieta sobbed. Jadwiga and Mary entered the room. Jadwiga heard the chaplain say, "He is very ill and has received the last rite... You must all come to him now. He wishes for you and the princesses to come. On his return journey to Buda, his illness took a turn for the worst. He is at a peasant's home at Trnava and has not been able to leave but has been given every comfort possible."

Mama commanded, "Girls, we must go..."

They had not informed the family of his condition until they realized how serious it was. William was with them, but not Sigismund as he was in Poland trying to gain support for his upcoming rule.

As they rode toward Trnava, everyone was quiet and pensive.

"What state of mind is he in?" Mama asked.

The bishop answered, "He has full presence of mind and yet suffers a fever. He is strong. So he lived, so he dies… One grace at this hour is that he sheds tears for the death and suffering at his hand through war and revokes any evildoing by use of force or brutality."

Elizabieta pondered, incredulous, "By grace, he sheds tears…" They found it hard to imagine because Louis had always been such a pillar of strength.

Finally, they arrived at the cottage. Elizabieta referred to an assistant, "See to it that the family is well compensated." Elizabieta and the girls rushed to Louis's side, overcome with love, devotion, and tears. Jadwiga thought the cottage was rather comfortable and Papa was well accommodated. It was not possible that he would die, perhaps just be too sick to travel home.

The great king was lying on a simple bed by a fire attended by the peasant family, the bishop, and his chief advisors. Papa saw them come in and struggled to say their names, "Elizabieta… Mary, Jadya…"

Grasping Louis's hand, Mama pressed his hand to her lips then kissed his forehead and lips, kneeling devotedly beside him in tears. The girls and William stood on the opposite side of the bed in disbelief. Louis offered them his hand, and they grasped it. The girls knelt also beside his bed, their hearts and eyes filled with great love and devotion. William looked quietly on. It was worse than any of them had imagined—Papa feverish and extremely weak, his eyes bloodshot. Jadwiga looked at William, who shook his head sadly at her as if to say, "This doesn't look good," and he looked so sorry, for he also had gained so much love and respect for Louis, who had treated him like a son.

Louis gained enough strength to bequeath his last testament. "Here we are on the threshold of tomorrow…" He had difficulty breathing and speaking. Jadwiga stoically and composedly took in every one of her father's precious last words. Papa managed a loving smile to them. "But tomorrow you face alone… Let Jesus be your guide, your strength and joy…the future of Poland, Mary… And Hungary, William and Jad…is yours and your espoused." Tears began to stream down his cheeks, "I begged God in heaven for a son… And He who is capable of all things saw to grant me daughters…" He stated this with love and acceptance. The girls shared in his regret that they never had a brother.

They all wiped away their tears now, trying to be strong, but feeling very small and helpless. Louis lifted up Jadwiga's chin lovingly, looking deeply into her eyes. "His will is perfect…it is the will of the Prince of Peace to grant a time of peace. Wherever possible, bring peace here and now, for here lies the dignity of a Christian. Not that he has fought well and strong and killed in the name of God, but that he has built the road that leads to peace. There lies strength stronger than power and might… The kingdom has been entrusted to the hearts of women and men who will love well, love peace well, for God's sake… He lives. He most surely lived…" The family, helpless in light of the inevitable, stood silently by, attending to his needs until he breathed his last on September 13, 1382.

Ludwik Węgierski (Louis of Hungary and
Poland) Marcello Bacciarelli, 1768–1771

Elizabeth and Mary mourning at the tomb of
Louis I, by Sándor Liezen-Mayer, 1864.

The funeral of Louis in Buda was large and well attended as the entire country was in mourning for this beloved and treasured king, who had died far too young as far as all were concerned. Scholars from the university he founded, priests, bishops, peasants, nobles, representatives from Poland all mourning at the loss of so great a king. The coffin of Louis was processioned throughout his city, and he was buried in the nearby Catholic cemetery.

Peasants lined the streets as far and deep as they could to show their respect and love for the king and his family. As the church bells pealed, the love and fidelity of his countrymen was strong and true.

Elizabieta sighed, wiping away another of the endless stream of tears. Not even all this love and respect was enough to comfort her heart or her daughters' left behind to govern. They could not reduce the number of tears they cried, even after so many days, nor could they understand the helpless and defenseless position they found themselves in now that their protector had been taken away from them. In a man's world, with man's games, how could they play, how could they replace this king? Jadwiga knew the truth in her heart. Louis was irreplaceable, and the future of both Hungary and Poland was now left in the hands of a mother, two daughters, and two very young teenage sons-in-law-to-be. She felt the future at this moment weighted down by doubt and helplessness. What would they do now?

CHAPTER 7

Determining Destinies

Elizabieta always dressed in black now. Days after the funeral, she could not drag her heart from the deep pit into which it had sunk. Even with her daughters around her, she felt terribly small and weak, knowing that shortly, Maria would have to be separated from her for Poland.

Wedding arrangements for Maria and Sigismund would have to begin, and yet Maria had confided to Elizabieta that she did not love or even like Sigismund at all, especially as a future husband. She had tried to bring this up to Louis but thought there would be time to discuss it. Elizabieta tried hard to focus on the issue she knew they would soon be bothering her to address. She too had grown to despise Sigismund's selfish and arrogant manners and the way he often would be looking at other young women of the court. His heart did not seem loyal to Maria.

The marriage plans negotiated by Louis, to her, suddenly seemed impossible to fulfill. How would her remaking of the arrangements made by Louis look to everyone in her court and the kingdom?

Ladislau knocked and came in, breaking her train of thought. He had been a trusted Polish advisor to Louis and aid to his mother Elizabeth throughout Jadwiga's life, and now here with the family as a family member, he was the one person she felt she could completely trust and confide in. She knew he genuinely cared for the girls' best interest. She held out her hand to him. "Ladislau, I am so grateful for your presence. I don't know what I would do without you here."

"I'm pleased to be here Elizabieta, there is no where I'd rather be." He shook his head sadly and seriously. They sat quietly for moments. "Madame, there is a matter for which I must bother you even though it is so soon after Louis's death. The Hungarian nobles have already met and are insisting that under the circumstances, *Maria* should be crowned queen immediately, *in Hungary*, as she is the eldest. They do not want the throne vacant."

She couldn't believe it. She had been so concerned about how changing Louis's plans for the girls would look to everyone, and here, the nobles and court were busy meeting and changing all his plans anyway! "They are like wolves circling the prey! Why can't they honor him through his wishes? It was for Jadwiga to have Hungary, and William!"

Ladislau answered sympathetically, "My lady, you are correct to feel this way, but a kingdom without a king is in itself subject to the wolves. Jadwiga is almost ten, too much a child. They want Maria crowned immediately, understandably for security of the kingdom. Charles D'Urazzo also may attempt to take the crown if we do not act quickly."

Charles D'Urazzo, the Italian cousin of Louis? Louis never trusted him and would turn in his grave to know it. He would dare come now? She grasped her head, which began to pound, and began to feel nauseated. She went over to the window to get some air and breathed deeply, the warm sun streaming on her face. Suddenly, a peace came over her. Keeping Maria here and crowning her queen would leave plenty of time to rethink who her husband could be besides Sigismund. It would keep her close.

"I am tired, Ladislau, what else can we do, is this clear thinking? When a person is young, you seldom realize the consequences of simple paths, how they can form a destiny…"

"My lady, the other option is to crown Jadwiga, but she is only eight. The Poles in Poland are rejecting Sigismund. If you follow through with what Louis desired, there will be rebellion and unrest, perhaps civil war, in Poland. Mary and Sigismund would be in danger, and their reign would be marked with strife. Louis did not foresee this. Sigismund will have to launch campaigns to take Poland by force and now is hated in most of Poland."

Elizabieta weakly consented, "So be it. Let them crown Mary. Between you and I, Ladislau, my heart is not with Sigismund either… He is cold, detached…unaffectionate, and has eyes for women. He is the last man I would have Maria married to. I cannot blame the Poles for the way they feel."

"It's politics really. For now, it will be Mary as queen then. We are here to assist."

"So be it…" Elizabieta sighed, scarcely having enough time to think through what she had consented to. It was with such unintentional circumstantial discussions that the destinies of the young princesses were formed.

Five days after her father's death, Cardinal Demetrius Kapolyai crowned Maria "King of Hungary." She smiled confidently but timidly to Jadwiga and Mama, and nodded at them. She wanted to be strong for them even though her stomach was in knots and her heart filled with dread. She tried to mask it with a smile. Mama gave her best game face and looked at Jadwiga with confidence. *I'm only twelve.* Jadwiga and William looked on, trying to smile back.

Hungary had asked for a queen and, in receiving Maria, had crowned her "king," leaving little room for doubt that they intended her to be the primary ruler along with the nobles and councilmen.

CHAPTER 8

A Vacancy and Ambition

Six months passed as everyone adjusted to the new situation. Elizabieta left most of the running of the country to her trusted advisors, men who had been devoted and faithful to Louis. Ladislau was always her trusted representative at court, assisting her with council and decisions. Now, Ladislau was being pressed by the Polish council to take action.

"Ladislau, she is only nine, and I fear for her safety most of all. I am not ready to send Jadwiga to Poland, she is not ready, just a child…"

"Jadwiga will be secure on the throne of Poland, I will personally see to it. There are many good men who will operate as her advisors. You must send her soon. An interregnum will be devastating to Poland as civil war is beginning. My lady, for peace's sake, we must send her. It is already six months with a vacant throne."

"Not so, Mary is upon the throne," Elizabieta replied, frustrated.

"The Poles never wanted a vacant monarch, of this they are certain," Ladislau informed her.

Jadwiga came running by, playing with some local friends, and hugged her mother. "Uncle Ladislau!" She hugged him also and ran off chasing the children with their dogs and a small pony.

Elizabieta looked on after her, realizing she did have some authority in the matter.

"Fine Ladislau. I will appoint you as viceroy. I will allow her to be crowned, but due to her young age, she must be returned to Buda and live with us for three years, at which time she will be marriage age, thus we will have a hand in determining the future."

In a typically obedient and respectful manner, Ladislau replied simply, "Yes, my lady, as you desire." It was a good-enough compromise for now.

◦◦◦

The nobles of Poland were indeed becoming restless. Who could blame the Poles who already had compromised greatly by allowing Louis alone to determine the future of their country? Mary was supposed to have been their queen, but now, Mary was the queen of Hungary, and the Poles despised Sigismund.

A void existed, and Ladislau arrived in Krakow to find the arguments for succession were loud, boisterous, and inconclusive. One such occasion, the nobles were in a heated debate, roughly sanctioned into four groups, simultaneously trying to make their voices heard. Ladislau was sitting quietly by, feeling defeated. After so much time away, he knew he had to ease back into government despite being a direct relative of Louis. The archbishop was also present, looking worn and fed up with maintaining peace.

Ziemowit of Mazovia, on a slightly raised platform, attempted to gain the attention of the group. A large, fat Polish magnate gained their attention, elevating Ziemowit to a position where he could speak near the archbishop. Ziemowit was a very young, distant relative of Louis, and had led uprisings against Sigismund, but the nobles and church were not fully behind him for various reasons. The crowd finally, by the signal of the old, revered archbishop, settled to listen.

"There is no better choice for king than *me* in all of Poland. It was *I* who led uprisings against Sigismund when no one else dared. It was *I* who have led missions to conquer lands in Ruthenia. The time for Poland to have a man of nerve and action is now! And no one will make a better husband for the Princess Jadwiga then *me*."

The archbishop replied, "Perhaps Ziemowit has a case. He has proven himself battle-worthy, he is of native blood…maybe he is right to be crowned king, and when the good Queen Elizabieta decides to send Princess Jadwiga, she will be a fitting bride and queen, thus the solution to all this strife." His speech was slow and calculated, coming from a well-thought position.

The majority of the group seemed to calm and began to nod in agreement. It seemed like this may be the only solution to a long inconclusive debate. Ladislau despised Ziemowit. He was an uneducated, unrefined young man; and knowing his dear Jadwiga, there was no way he ever wanted her to be married to him. The crowd was quiet and pensive and little by little nodded in agreement and began to give consent to Ziemowit. Ladislau's stomach churned.

Some of the nobles declared their agreement. It looked like they would reach this conclusion out of exasperation alone when a very well-known older gentleman, John (Jasko) of Teczyn stood up near the archbishop, motioning for them to sit. "Good and benevolent Father, Ziemowit, men of Poland. It is with all due respect and with the permission of the court, that I ask a moment of listening."

Someone in the crowd shouted out "Jasko!" in a supporting voice, and the room erupted in laughter. He was well admired for his piety, humility, and integrity. Jasko proceeded, humbly and respectfully, "With all due respect, Ziemowit, the promise of succession *was in fact,* given to Louis at one such meeting. His daughter was to be given reign a priori. That was what we swore to…and how King Louis fattened our purses and bellies, do we not recall? Were we not all here present? It was our oath!"

Ziemowit yelled out defiantly, "Louis the Hungarian is *dead*," and some nodded in agreement.

"Yes, but we live, and so does our oath! As you live, so lives your oath! Let the princess come and be crowned and let her decide who she will marry." Again, Jasko spoke in his wise, calculated way.

"Not an Austrian!" Ziemowit yelled, cautioning. And in the crowd, many repeated, "Never an Austrian!"

Jasko motioned for the group to settle down and not get carried away again. "We have time, we have time. Ziemowit may be crowned our king in due time, but, brothers, in the manner we swore to our good King Louis."

At Jasko's last words, the crowd seemed to settle and quietly agree with this wise man's counsel. Ziemowit observed the sudden shift in loyalty and was visibly perturbed that Jasko had changed the general consensus again. Looking around frustrated, he exited through the crowd, quickly and angrily, while the men parted to let him out, slamming the door behind him.

The men shouted "Oooooohs," and "Aws," mocking the young man for his abruptness, and the assembly began to rise, laughing and discussing the failed ambitions of the young arrogant Ziemowit. Ladislau breathed a sigh of relief.

Jasko and the archbishop walked away together and began a private conversation of their own. "He is young and impulsive, I am not so sure he is best for king," Jasko began confidentially to the archbishop.

"I agree, Jasko. His heart is not with the church or Christ. He may, in the end, bring strife to Poland. Maybe it was by the grace of God you spoke and changed the consensus. Fiat. I am told Jadwiga of Anjou is a remarkable young girl, showing great intelligence and spirituality for her age. She will be a great queen, who Ziemowit would tarnish."

Jasko concurred, "King Louis in all was a king of charity, whose love for God and neighbor were evident. No doubt this heritage will continue in Jadwiga, who is due to arrive at Easter." Jasko now paused, hesitating to bring up the real underlying issue that kept nagging at his heart. Finally, he got the nerve to bring it up.

"There is, however, a matter of a Duke of Lithuania, Jagiello, whose brother Skirgiello has on three occasions approached me with marriage proposals from Jagiello."

The archbishop replied incredulously, "Jasko! A Lithuanian!? What ails your mind, brother, fever?" Both men suddenly stopped walking.

Jasko clarified, "Now, now, listen, my dear Francis, listen. He has proposed fascinating terms: his personal conversion to Catholicism as well the entire conversion of Lithuania. How would that do for national security?"

The archbishop was silent. He could not believe the proposal. What seemed a simple solution to a long-term, chronic problem for Poland. "Jasko! Are you serious? It must be a trick!"

"I thought so too at first, but now, after the third time, it would appear to be an honest proposal. Even his brothers are promising their baptism to Catholicism."

The archbishop skeptically questioned, "You believe them?"

Jasko pressed on, "Apparently, their mother is Orthodox Christian and has attempted to marry Jagiello to a cousin of Rus, but he would have to convert to Orthodox, and Jagiello seems to be more interested in choosing his own destiny, with an eye to Western Europe. Conversion is imminent for him."

The archbishop, tired and frustrated but understanding and believing the sincerity and possibility of it all, answered simply, "I will meet with him."

CHAPTER 9

Diversions

Early spring arrived, and Elizabieta could no longer put off sending Jadwiga to Poland, or the Poles would choose another successor. The day came when it was time to bring Jadwiga on another trip—this time to Poland, to a new destiny. Her mother, maids, Constance (who had stayed with Jadwiga since Austria together with her bodyguard) were travelling the journey through the forests and farms toward Poland. Everyone was quiet and nervous.

Mama broke the silence. "You know, Jadwiga, it was not what I wanted. You are too young to leave home now."

Jadwiga answered bravely, "I know, Mama, but with God's help and the help of good men, I can do this. I will do it, Mama. I will make Papa proud."

"I wanted you home a little while longer. They will try to control your life and your destiny. They may even resist William."

Jadwiga had grown extremely fond of William and he of her. There was great friendship and kinship between the two growing up knowing someday, they would be husband and wife. William had been through so much with her. "What do you mean they may resist William, Mama?"

"William is Austrian, and although Austria and Poland are not enemies, the Polish do not need ties with Austria, nor do they have any purpose in having an Austrian rule their kingdom."

"Well, I will be queen, Mama, so they will do as I wish."

Mama smiled., "You have your grandmother's blood and confidence! You will be fine."

Suddenly, their travel was interrupted by a few men on horseback who had stopped the party and were in heated argument with the head guard of their group. Elizabieta stood up. A bodyguard tried to stop her from going to see what was going on, but she persisted.

The bodyguard insisted, "My lady, it is a matter for the guard."

Jadwiga thought how Mama had changed since Papa's death and was less likely to be ordered when she was determined. "My good man, thank you, but I would like to see the matter." She exited the carriage and approached the men. Jadwiga followed curiously.

Jadwiga noticed a young man, with three others, about twenty-four years old and handsome trying to speak to Elizabieta. "My lady!" He dismounted and bowed low to Elizabieta and Jadwiga, sensing that they were important nobles.

Elizabieta asked, "What is the matter?"

Their bodyguard explained, "These men say there is a group of five hundred men on the Polish side of the Poprad River who are waiting to kidnap Princess Jadwiga of Hungary! There is a rumor that it is the men of Ziemowit of Mazovia. He wishes to take the princess and marry her by force so he may be king of Poland." Jadwiga's heart sank. She hugged Mama tight.

The young man seeming honest and genuinely concerned pressed, "My lady, do you know if the princess is coming this way anytime soon? We must warn them immediately! Such an armed group of men show the duke sincere in his intent."

Elizabieta responded, "And my good man, how do we know you to be sincere? Who are you and what is your occupation? Where are you from? You are Polish, are you not?"

The young man attempted to take something from under his cloak. The guards at once drew their swords, and two bodyguards stood in front of Jadwiga and her mother. All stood motionless, waiting for the next action. "Madame, I only wish to give proof of who we are. May your men allow me please?"

Elizabieta nodded. "Let him."

The young man removed from his cloak a medallion of Hungary, proof that they were border guards for Hungary. "We are guards! Now, my good lady, any word of Princess Jadwiga?"

Elizabieta looked to her guard, who nodded, believing him now to be who he said.

"I am Queen Elizabieta of Hungary, and my daughter Princess Jadwiga."

The young man, Henre, became wide-eyed in disbelief. He grabbed his hair and head in extreme happiness. "Oh, merciful glorious day, when I can repay such a debt!"

Elizabieta, suddenly seemed entertained and almost amused by the enthusiasm of the young man. "Yes, speak man."

"My name is Henre. I am a loyal servant of your husband, King Louis the Great. He saved my life years ago in the Lithuanian war. He saved my life! I almost drowned, but he came and saved me, a young, useless soldier. Risked his life to save me! I swore service to him. I owe him everything, and I owe everything to his family."

Jadwiga came forward cautiously. "You knew my father?"

"Only for a brief moment, when a bridge collapsed, and he saved me from drowning…" Jadwiga smiled and suddenly felt a deep connection with Henre.

"Well, good man," Elizabieta answered, "what is this you say about a small army?"

Henre was suddenly drawn back to the reality of the present danger. "Please…please turn back immediately—you must! There are not enough of us to defend against them. Ziemowit will take the princess. He may even chase, but we will stop them if you turn back. We will cut out the bridge at the Poprad crossing, and they will not be able to pursue you! My lady, please believe us, for King Louis's sake, and the princess!"

Jadwiga could sense that Mama was quite pleased at the sudden turn of events because it was just the excuse she needed to delay sending Jadwiga. "By all means, my good man. And God bless your work."

Henre nodded. "Long live the house of Louis of Anjou in Poland and Hungary!"

The entourage began to embark and turn back while Henre and his guard raced off in the direction they came from to destroy the bridge.

When the men at Wawel Castle, who had been eagerly awaiting and preparing for the arrival of Princess Jadwiga, heard of Ziemowit's sabotage and that the princess was turned away because of his planned kidnapping, they were infuriated. They had waited long enough for this day and now got news from Henre that Elizabieta had taken her daughter back home to Buda.

Here again convened the frustrated group of noblemen with Ladislau of Opole, who was to aid Jadwiga upon her arrival and Jasko. "Damn that weasel Ziemowit! We will teach him that he will not take the future matters of Poland into his own hands! This will be the last of him! He will no longer sit on council!" he spat in conclusion, both in disgust and as a sign that his word would be done.

Jasko, normally kind and patient, added, "Now Poland remains in danger of being without sovereign. Our security remains uncertain."

"The queen has put off sending the princess twice already! We will not be put off again," another nobleman scowled.

Jasko, in defense, answered, "This time it's excusable. They could not risk the security of the princess."

The persistent oppositional nobleman continued, "They have put us off, and the Queen Elizabieta only wants her way! They must send her immediately, or we will choose our own monarch! Tell the queen that if she does not send Jadwiga by summer's end, we will select our own monarch. Enough!"

Ladislau knew he was expressing the general consensus of the majority in Poland, who were losing patience in regard to the coming of the princess to fill a vacant throne.

CHAPTER 10

Leaving Home for Good

Late summer had come, and the family had managed one more sweet spring and summer together. Jadwiga was now nine and a half years, and Uncle Ladislau had returned from Poland.

"You are quite different now than you were a year ago, Jadwiga," he commented to her as they walked together in the flower garden.

"I feel different now, Uncle. I know you have come to take me to Poland."

"How are you feeling about leaving now? You understand Ziemowit has been banished from council? He will no longer be a threat, and the Poles are very concerned about the kingdom's security. Your presence is needed now in Poland."

Mama joined them in the garden just as Ladislau was finishing speaking. "Ladislau, you normally consult with me in these matters," Mama seemed to correct him.

"Uncle was just explaining that the situation with Ziemowit has been resolved and that perhaps it is time for me to go back to Poland," Jadwiga explained. "To stay."

A look of fear and concern came across Mama's face. Jadwiga thought she was stronger than this now, but Mama's timid nature always seemed to control her choices. Jadwiga often thought about Grandmama and Papa and how they never made choices out of fear. On many occasions, Papa had spoken to her about making decisions from prudent considerations, guided by the wisdom of others. Somehow in her heart, she knew it was time for her to go. She looked reassuringly at Mama. "I packed for the journey."

Somehow, the young child they all had seen grow up was to be taken at her word. In a mysterious way, they saw now that she had a commanding presence, a beautiful, wise presence, far above her age—this character carefully crafted by her father. The effects of the education and grooming he had tried to provide seemed to take effect and instill confidence in them all.

Surprisingly, Mama held out her arms to Jadwiga, and they all sat down on garden benches. Elizabieta held her tight. She knew also it was time. "Please don't worry, Mama. Uncle, what about William and my marriage? Will this be honored in Poland?" She wasn't sure how to read Uncle's face.

"You are not of marriage age for two years. William could join you at that time. For now, you are to be crowned as the sole ruler in your own right."

Jadwiga wasn't completely reassured by his answer.

This time, there was to be no interference. A small century of men had come from Poland, as well as a small army on the Polish roads was secured to ensure of the princess's uninhibited arrival safely to her new home in Krakow, Wawel Castle. Jadwiga was excited and more ready than ever to embark on this journey again—this time for real. Something within her gave her confidence that each step she would take now would be guided from above.

Elizabieta and Maria embraced and kissed Jadwiga. She climbed into the carriage accompanied by Constance and many other young ladies-in-waiting who, over the years, had become trusted companions. Mama was crying because she knew this was for real now. She would not accompany Jadwiga this time because of the demands of governing with Maria in Buda and fears about her safety.

"You know, I am ready for this now. The Lord will be with you and me. Everything will be all right. We will visit and soon enough William will come. We are not alone because God is with us." She wiped away a tear on Mama's cheek. "I'm ready. Maria, you will always be in my heart and in my prayers."

"You also Viga," Maria lovingly replied with a strong embrace. Jadwiga found she had to also wipe some tears from Maria's cheeks.

"Let's be strong, like Papa would have wanted," Jadwiga assured her.

William was there to see her depart and approached her to say good-bye. "So this is it, for real now. I'm heading back home soon too."

Jadwiga answered lovingly, "You'll come soon, William. I'll be alright till then." He hugged her tight. He was now fourteen years old, trained and tutored to have dealings with men for many years and had wisdom and maturity beyond his years.

Privately, in a low voice, William confided to Jadwiga as he noticed Ladislau and the family was distracted for a moment, "You will be the queen. Don't let them tell you what to do. I will come to you, and we will be married. We are married, but we will fulfill our marriage and always be together. I love you. Wait for me, and I will wait for you…" He affectionately had his hand on her cheek, and they embraced one more time and kissed each other as a brother and a sister, but on the lips. Jadwiga felt awkward and laughed lightly. He grasped her hands to his chest and kissed her hands. Jadwiga pulled away to leave. He still held one of her hands, kissed it gallantly, staring in her eyes. She tried to read his expression. He seemed sad and lost as he tried his best to smile reassuringly to her. He was definitely more serious at that moment than she had ever seen him. With so much on her mind and in front of her, it felt intimidating. She had to press forward.

Jadwiga looked at all she held most dear and spoke strongly to reassure them all.

"You know I am ready for this now. The Lord will be with you and me. Everything will be all right. We will visit and soon enough. William will come. We are not alone because God is with us." She wiped away a tear. "I'm ready." *I am ready. Thank you, Lord. Please give them peace and joy.*

The entourage pulled away. The two parties waved and blew kisses until they could no longer see each other.

CHAPTER 11

Travels to New Lands

Despite the sadness of leaving home, there is always something thrilling about taking a journey on new roads. As the carriage churned on down bumpy paths, Jadwiga thought about Mama, who also had to leave home at a young age to marry a powerful king of Europe, although not quite so young as Jadwiga was now. Mama had discussed with Jadwiga at great length prudent ways to think about her situation.

"Make the best of every moment," she had told Jadwiga. "Know that God is always with you. No matter what circumstances you may find yourself in, you are never alone. Take comfort in the fact that we will all be reunited in heaven someday. When you find yourself slipping into sadness or melancholy, realize that life is too short to be sad. Find beauty and joy in every moment. Create joy if there is none there. Take comfort in the church and in your husband and family, they are God's greatest gifts." All her mother's repeated sayings and attitudes flooded her heart as she left Buda.

Even though Jadwiga recalled often the difficulties her grand-mother had encountered there, Ladislau had reassured her these were no longer the circumstances and there was nothing to fear in her coming to Poland. Constance had been at her side for six years now and was like an aunt to her who would always remain so throughout her life. She smiled now at Jadwiga. And looking at Constance, all homesickness dispersed.

From the moment she left home, her heart was now set on the kingdom that was to be hers and someday William's also. Jadwiga's sadness now began to turn to delight and excitement. Somewhere in the course of her last few years, there had developed frequent thoughts that questioned and seemed to form her heart, and these came back to her today as each traveler became absorbed in their own thoughts. *"If you had a kingdom, all my own... how would you rule? If I had a kingdom all my own, what would you do? If I had a kingdom all your own, how would you rule?"* She pondered these things often, and now. the imaginary kingdom was at the end of her journey. She thought of Papa now, and a sharp sadness mixed with his greatest ideals for the countries he governed. As devoted to war as he felt he had to be for his time, she knew in his heart and mind that it wasn't war that was the answer but rather education and a proper understanding and respect of Christianity—of living out Christianity. That was really the war that would win the world to peace. What Papa dreamed of was a civilized world with schools, universities, and towns of citizens who could form beautiful serene hamlets and live in peace. And education! All its citizens educated! This he only began to achieve... Jadwiga pledged she would continue what Papa had himself continued after Great-Uncle Casimir's reign.

What would her kingdom look like? She envisioned the whole thing in her mind. It was beautiful, it was golden, it was sweet like honey, and she couldn't wait to get there.

～～～

The group finally arrived to an area where there was a checkpoint marking the Polish-Hungarian border. Here, Jadwiga noticed she had reached just beyond where she had travelled last time and as close to Poland as she had once come. She felt the presence of her father, as she knew so often he had travelled this way also. At the checkpoint, the group stopped to speak to the guards. Jadwiga noticed Henre, who her father had saved and who saved her last time from what may have been an unfortunate destiny with Ziemowit.

"Henre!" Jadwiga called as she waved and exited the carriage excitedly to greet him. He saw her also, came, and bowed to her and kissed her hand. "Still at your service my queen," he said with a happy smile.

"I cannot thank you enough for your assistance to us that day. I was not able to properly thank you. I am going to be the queen of Poland, Henre, and maybe you can come and work for me there..."

"Whatever you wish, my queen, my life is at your service. You should reach Krakow within days. Best wishes and God bless you." Jadwiga re-embarked on her journey and waved a last time to the young man her father had saved in Lithuania.

As they journeyed to Krakow castle, Ladislau often told her stories about what the city and surrounding areas and all of Poland was like. He loved his country of origin, and he enriched Jadwiga's heart with the same love before she even laid eyes on it. They entered the Carpathian Mountain region. Jadwiga had seen mountains at a distance, but now, they engulfed them as they made their way through the beautiful valley regions. Fresh gurgling streams filled with trout, forests, and the occasional small farm settlement dotted the valleys. The mountains made her feel small, but secure and sheltered. Here, she felt God's grandeur and majesty in a way she never had.

Ladislau arranged for the group to visit the Carpathian Mountains Wieliczka salt mine, which belonged to Poland. It was an important part of the Polish economy and was well known for its artistic carvings. Jadwiga, now a Polish official, visited the mine with the group and was impressed greatly by its magnitude as well as the artistry of the carvings. The talent and imaginative artistry were breathtaking. Before her eyes, etched in salt rock, were carvings of a humble workman, presenting Queen Kinga with her ring, her country people now better off. Many religious carvings and a beautiful chapel were found in the depths of the mines as well. *Lord, please help me inspire my people.*

An enthusiastic Ladislau was their guide, for his relatives worked and managed the mine. He explained the true legend of Queen Kinga, who had her men dig for salt when the economy was poor. "And then good Queen Kinga, needing a dowry and her country starving, dropped her ring into the narrow shaft and commanded her countrymen to dig for it. At her command, they began to dig, and that was the beginning of our great mine, as legend would have it." Jadwiga nodded in fascination, wide-eyed as she thought about the possibilities a leader could bring her people to with her encouragement.

Their travels continued through the mountains, with the group stopping to sleep and camp in tents on the journey. During these camp sessions, which the young princess and her ladies loved, they all shared lively discussions and stories. It was around a campfire that Ladislau entertained the group by telling them stories of Polish legends.

Ladislau began, "You know, Princess Jadwiga, it was a queen, a very beautiful woman, responsible for Poland's amber trade as well."

Jadwiga smiled, excited, as she sensed another story. "Truly? Tell us about it please, Ladislau!"

"Yes, she lived in an enormous amber castle. Do we have some amber here? Yes, your necklace. Well, she lived in a beautiful castle of amber. She took care of all the sea creatures. Did I mention it was under the ocean? The god of thunder and lightning loved her and protected her from storms. She heard one day of a handsome fisherman…" The girls giggled now at the prospect of young love. "A handsome young fisherman who was setting traps. When the sea creatures complained to her, she went to him to chastise him, but instead at once, they fell in love. The thunder god was jealous, so he stirred up a great storm, which destroyed her amber castle into millions of pieces."

Now the young girls were wide-eyed in disbelief and curiosity. "And the couple?"

"The young couple in love was killed by the hate of the jealous god. Fishermen still say they hear the moans of the young fisherman. Amber is always washing up on the shores."

The young, impressionable ladies were wooed by the tale of romance. "Please, sir, tell another one…"

"No, no, it's now time for bed, young ladies," Ladislau commanded.

"Uhhhh," the young ladies moaned together in sincere regret.

"There will be more time for stories later!" Ladislau yelled out as they began to stretch and walk toward their tents. "The day after tomorrow, we will be in Krakow. We have an early start tomorrow."

The ladies dispersed, and Constance called to Jadwiga, "Come, child."

"Go, Constance, I am coming," replied Jadwiga. "I just wanted to speak to Ladislau."

"Ladislau," she ventured as everyone had left. "I need to talk to you."

"Anything you need, Princess."

"Well, we are coming so close to the kingdom, and I am happy, but I cannot help but be concerned about my enemies."

"Your enemies?!" Ladislau replied.

"Yes, my enemies. Every kingdom has its enemies, and the story of Grandma Elizabeth, and they cut her fingers off—"

Ladislau interrupted, "My child, I have already told you that those men were just bandits and villains and were brought to justice and are long gone. You are not to worry about the likes of these, we have excellent security."

"But, Ladislau, my father was often to Poland fighting wars, who was he fighting? Are they still there? Was it the Lithuanians?"

"Hmm, well we did have to fight them, but, Jadwiga, we don't normally have problems with the Lithuanians since your Great Uncle Casimir made a peace with them last generation."

"Then why was Papa fighting them?" she asked.

"The truth about Poland is there are sometimes men who want to lay claim to its land and who want to take the lands of those who are already established, but it isn't usually the Lithuanians. In fact, the Teutonic Knights are really the worst enemies of Poland because they take what they like, when they like. It wasn't always so. It is more this leader of theirs today who has lost his way and his raison d'être…if you will." Jadwiga pondered this for a moment but needed to understand the best she could.

"Well, who are the Teutonic Knights? Are they Polish?"

"They actually were German and were an order of Knights that served to protect people who went to the Holy Land during the crusades, but since then, they have gained lands north of Poland, in Prussia, and have built great towns for themselves."

"Why are they in the north?"

"They are in the north to protect the onslaught of pagan nations into Europe, as a barrier, if you will, for Germany and even Poland against forces from the east."

"So they do help Europe," Jadwiga thoughtfully replied.

"Yes, they do—they did, but recently, they have been troublesome even for Christians to the Poles of the north and the Lithuanians, who probably feel that they took many lands in their north as well. Conrad Zolner Von Rottenstein, he is the troublemaker. I met him face-to-face, and he is one who is not to be trusted. He carries the flag with a cross, but it is a veil, he is a wolf. I would say as it stands, he is really Poland's greatest enemy."

"Then what of the Lithuanians to the east?" Jadwiga needed to resolve this question."

They are enemies with him but usually leave us in peace. They came to a truce with us at the time you were born."

"So what you are saying then is that who you would expect to be the greatest enemy of Poland, the pagans to the east, are not as great an enemy as the Teutonic Order to the north?" Ladislau nodded, to which Jadwiga simply replied, concluding the late-night conversation, "Then I should like to meet them myself."

Finally, the day arrived for Jadwiga to set eyes on her long-awaited kingdom. Everywhere she looked, she saw beauty in one form or another. A stream, a forest, mountains, and now farmer's fields with farms and livestock managed diligently and responsibly. Cozy cottages with villagers busy at work and children playing nearby. Wildflowers lined the roadways, and the tree-lined edges of fields were the backdrop to the rolling landscape. There were occasional wooded patches where she caught glimpses of foxes or deer. She dozed off in the afternoon sun to the rocking of the carriage, filled with so much peace and excitement at the near arrival to her new home.

Ladislau awakened her and pointed out on the distant horizon the Castle of Krakow, looming large above the town near the Vistula River. "Princess, your kingdom!" he called to her excitedly as he raised his arm and swept it over the whole region. "Can you see St. Mary's Basilica, with the copper roof, can you see it? And the castle wall lining the riverbank there, do you see?" Uncle was practically tripping himself with an excitement that was contagious. She could see the roof of the beautiful large basilica, a large bridge that led to the walled town and her new castle home, a combination of bright white and red brick, all built by Great-Uncle Casimir. Many people could be seen around the edge of town coming in and out. Boats floated peacefully by.

She nodded as they drove through a lake of golden august fields. She stood, surveying it with honor, joy, and excitement, a large smile on her face. The rolling landscape continued to the wide meandering river. Mirrored in the river was her new home above the riverbank. It had been Grandmama's home, and Papa's. Constance was even excited and smiled brilliantly at Jadwiga. Strangely, it seemed like they were coming home.

When she had lived in Buda, she had thought never would she find a home so beautiful as hers, but she couldn't help but think this new city was like its twin, filled with beauty and a people she would come to love.

Queen Jadwiga's Oath by Jozef Simmler, 1867

CHAPTER 12

Poland Has a King

Jadwiga did not fully understand the effect civil war had on the people of Poland and how a vacant throne had left most at unrest for two years. Ziemowit of Mazovia's claims to the throne, Sigismund fighting to maintain authority, and the general unrest that comes without a leader had left the whole country on guard. What the Polish people did not expect is how all of a sudden, amazingly, their bickering and fears would cease after the arrival of their queen.

Her presence brought about the same peace that had presided from the time of Casimir the Great before her father. The day of Jadwiga's arrival, excited townspeople lined the road to Krakow, having heard stories of the beauty, grace, intellect, and devotion of this new princess. Every person, child, and farmer gathered to the streets to catch a glimpse of her, waving the best cloth they had—banners of purple, green, blue, and yellow. Children and young ladies were throwing petals and flowers in the path of the procession. There was general excitement as Jadwiga waved to all. They were thrilled to finally have a leader of their own again because even though Louis had been loved, "Louis the Hungarian" had been most often away from the capital. Individuals strained to look beyond the body-guards on horseback. Those who caught a glimpse of her were visibly touched by her presence. People could be heard saying, "Oh, she is beautiful," cheering and clapping as the entourage continued. The entourage moved quickly through the crowd for security, but even guards strained to get a glimpse of the new child-ruler. Jadwiga could scarcely take in all that was happening. She was used to the attention that the people of the kingdom gave her in Buda, but the attention was usually toward her father or Mary. But today, she was the rising monarch of this kingdom of beautiful faces filled with hope, love, and devotion. The attention suddenly made her feel shy and blush. The last time she felt such admiration was at her Hainburg marriage.

The people captivated her, as did her new home from the moment she saw the Castle of Krakow on the horizon and the beautiful Vistula River. Now, she was so close to the castle; it loomed large, and the cathedral as well, which could scarcely be distinguished from the castle. It was even grander than her home at Buda, and she was filled with great peace and joy.

Even more comforting was a group of Franciscan friars who stood anxiously with bishops and a cardinal at the palace gates to receive her. They clasped their hands together with joy, as if she was the answer to their prayers; and the priests and cardinals blessed her, each welcoming her with delight. The day was joyful, almost to the point of bliss, and this joy would spread through the lands of Poland.

What would William think about this place? *Someday, he will come here and love this kingdom too.*

Jadwiga settled in her new home easily now that she had experienced such a warm and loving reception from her subjects. Everyone worked hospitably to make her feel happy and welcomed, and she did feel so much love that every evil imagining she had in regard to Poland dissipated. The language of Poland was even familiar to her, as it had been her Grandmama's and Papa's, and Papa had seen to it that the girls had been educated in the Polish language. She quickly picked up fluency in speaking and understanding. She spoke five languages—Hungarian, Croatian, Austrian, Polish and some German—all which would serve her kingship well. She understood now why Papa had emphasized languages.

The date for Jadwiga's coronation had been set to give enough time for the most important nobles and wealthiest of the Polish men to travel to Krakow. Jadwiga made sure to have a personal invitation sent to the Teutonic Knight's leader, Conrad Zolner Von Rottenstein. She also had a personal invitation for a meeting with him to be set just prior to her coronation, upon his arrival. Word of this young princess had reached through the kingdom and into Europe, so Rottenstein decided to come, given the personal nature of her request.

When Jadwiga received word of the arrival of the Teutonic Knights and Rottenstein, she began to doubt herself and her ability to speak to him. She had been taught from a young age to love her enemies and had consulted many in her council about the issues surrounding the Teutonic Knights. Her German was not strong, and she was told his Polish was not very good. She felt that although Ladislau had told her that he was their greatest enemy, she would hold no person as her enemy. She knew her grasp of things was simple, as she was still only a child, and prayed for wisdom from a deeper source. She had already received the sacrament of confirmation, anointed "Militis Christi natalitius," in preparation for her coronation. She would rely on the graces bestowed on her now that she was a soldier of Christ.

Days before her coronation, she finally came face-to-face with the Teutonic leader she had heard stories of since her childhood. He had claimed lands in Northern Poland for his order, he had disturbed the peace; and if there was anything Jadwiga wanted in her kingdom, it was peace. When the great meeting hall door opened, the room so large that she could scarcely see the man, she fidgeted nervously as the small entourage entered. Suddenly, a cold autumn wind blew through the room and somehow chilled her heart, making her timid. For the first time in her kingdom, she couldn't speak, and it was as if the cold breeze had frozen her tongue and tied her heart into a knot. For a moment, she forgot who else she was besides a nine-year-old girl. Panic suddenly set in, so she stood to accommodate her fears and anxiety.

As Rottenstein walked steadily up the aisle of the great meeting room toward the girl, she looked expectantly at him, hoping to see in front of her a Christian man. That, she had told herself, was their common ground, what made them one family under God.

Rottenstein had gotten much older from the time of her father—old in his thinking, old in his bitterness, greed, hate, and mercilessness. It seemed to have marked his countenance, and he seemed the picture of these things. He appeared serious, worn, battered, and lacking joy.

Suddenly, all her inhibitions gave way to pity. She saw past his physical appearance to the black-and-white Christian flags, which were born around him, and she saw deep within the person who had started out on a noble quest, a lover of God, who sin after sin had lost his way and was now so far on a lost road he could not find his way back.

As Rottenstein neared the throne, in his mind was the idea of obligation and what nonsense that a child was made the ruler of any country. Although he did not care much for Louis the Hungarian, for a moment, the beauty and innocence of this child did touch his heart, as she seemed to gaze at him with something that looked like a deep love. This quickly gave way to his more practical and less emotional nature, which was like a starving plant that had withered so long from lack of attention or watering and would soon die if it did not receive a storm of rain to bring it back to life.

"My Lord, thank you for coming!" Jadwiga spoke first and offered her hand and bowed slightly, as she was not yet anointed. He took her hand, upon which he now saw the ring that he had given to Louis just nine years ago.

Somehow, that she was wearing the ring impacted him in a way he could not explain. "My princess, I would do nothing other than come if you bid it. I see you are wearing the ring that I gave as a gift to your father just before your birth. I hope it will please you to know that we fought together side by side. I am happy that you wear it, and I am sorry for the loss of your father. He was a friend." This comment softened Jadwiga's heart, and she nodded in regret as she touched the ring on her finger.

"Yes, it was a tremendous loss to our family. Mama said he was too young. This was a gift from you?" she replied. Mama had given her the ring before leaving but had never made clear from where the ring had originated. He nodded. She decided it would be a sign for her that she would refuse to make this man her enemy and pray for him until he became a man of peace.

"You summoned me," he now remarked curtly, getting down to business. They were having a quiet, private discussion far away enough from the others, speaking low enough to keep the conversation private.

"I am to be crowned, 'king of Poland,'" she smiled and informed him childishly, knowing between, them the title was much larger than her. She understood well the irony.

"King?" Rottenstein replied with patronizing superiority, raising his eyebrows and looking doubtful, as if the Poles were just stupid.

"Yes, king, and as king of Poland, I am asking you a special favor."

Now Rottenstein decided to amuse himself for a brief moment. "Yes, anything you ask on the eve of your coronation, dear 'king.'" He leaned in closer.

"I have heard that you are taking lands in the north from my people," Jadwiga questioned simply.

"Yes…but this land has been in question for generations…"

Jadwiga pressed on, "My lord, I hear that you wage war on innocent farmers and villages, not only in Poland, but in Lithuania as well."

Rottenstein could no longer play the game of diplomatic, well-mannered visitor. He could no longer hide his impatience and wounded pride at now being chastised by a child, "king" or not. This was far too insulting, and if she had been any child, he would have smacked her to the ground and kicked her. "You know nothing, you are a child."

"You are partly correct, sir, I know little. But I know that the way to peace, especially by those who claim to love God so much, is never by hurting others and taking what belongs to others—that is *coveting other's goods, stealing* and *killing* your grace. You cannot ever possibly be doing God's work if you are doing these things." Jadwiga whispered loudly the last words to make sure no one heard her chastising her elder, and it was not her intention to shame him in front of those around them.

She wanted to speak to him heart-to-heart, and the truth of her words pierced him like a sword, shattering any pretense or words he intended to present. He was like a wounded lion becoming angered and caught somewhere between submission to the wound and killing the one who had inflicted it. Her words caused a gut-wrenching strength that tied his words into a knot because his pride and ego were never challenged without remorse on the other's part. He nodded silently and gave pretense of remorse but could not answer.

Jadwiga did not read his falseness properly and continued unafraid, again speaking softly. "I am requesting that as a gift to me, you will no longer invade Northern Poland or Lithuania, as my Great-Uncle Casimir had made peace with them. I want that to continue in my reign."

"You don't know what you are asking. You don't understand the workings of the adult world you are in. I cannot be sure to grant this." He replied, trying with all his might to control himself from a typical outburst.

"I will wear this ring that you have given my father and has come to me as a sign that we are kindred souls with a mission of peace," Jadwiga simply replied, noticing that the ring had large amber pieces embedded on it. Remembering Uncle Ladislau's story, it made her think that Rottenstein's greatest talent was economy, and he reminded her of the god in the story who could become jealous and kill the princess and her love. William! Was Rottenstein one of the men who she had been warned might not take kindly to his rule? Rottenstein stood silently, like a wolf, with his head bent low, watching what his prey would do next. Jadwiga questioned him one last time, "And William of Austria…what is your opinion about my future spouse?" She felt that while she had his undivided attention, she would be sure that his loyalty would be to William.

"Austria is Germany's closest ally. It would please us to have him on the throne by your side," he replied simply and truthfully. He had no malice whatsoever to William, so Jadwiga, ignoring all other reactions, believed him to be sincere in this matter.

She could say no more but "Thank you for this talk."

He simply replied, "Thank you as well," and turned to join his entourage, bearing flags of the Teutonic Order, a simple white flag with what Jadwiga thought appropriate and frightening as she watched them flutter as the group left the great hall, a black cross.

Something about Rottenstein and that flag scared her young heart as she reflected on the good choice someone had made to pick the color black against the background of white, which showed purity of intention with the irony of self-deception, evil, and sin.

Finally, coronation day arrived, and Jadwiga was happy and confident. It was a glorious autumn day. Jadwiga had already come, in the short time she had been in Krakow, to make these men, advisors, the religious, and workers within the palace like a family to her. They had shown her great love, fidelity, and hospitality since her arrival, and they loved her.

Constance was also present, always close by, attending to all of Jadwiga's needs. Jadwiga felt that this was her new home and God had sent her here. She was at peace. The coronation took place with great attendance inside and outside of the great cathedral at Krakow, and a feeling of a new day for Poland infused the celebrations. With great joy, she processioned up the aisle, with Gregorian chant filling the great cathedral, flowing gently upon the medieval city of Krakow.

Jadwiga knelt before the archbishop, who gave an anointing saved especially for rulers, and crowned Jadwiga "REX POLONIA" or "king of Poland." She received the title with all solemnity, dignity, and peace, as though she was born for it. She turned and faced everyone in the church, with the archbishop gesturing with open hands and arms, "Here, behold your sovereign." As she looked eagerly to the crowd, smiling with love and excitement, everyone applauded.

As she processioned out of the church, Jasko, Ladislau, Constance, ladies-in-waiting, various religious orders were all delighted. Poland finally had a live in monarch after a long vacancy. Crowned "king" meant that Jadwiga would always be the primary ruler of Poland as long as she lived, no matter who married her.

The great festivities and celebration carried on from within the castle throughout Krakow. There was plenty to eat, drink, and dessert on, as so many had contributed goods for the celebration. The whole region and people from varying regions gathered. There was dancing and instruments throughout the streets of Poland as well as within the great castle hall. For safety reasons, Jadwiga and her entourage were confined to celebrations within the castle.

In the castle celebration, Jadwiga was becoming tired by the day's events and was sitting quietly on her chair, resting her cheek in her hand, watching the events, trying to pray her rosary before she got too sleepy.

Jasko observed her intently. He had saved her from what may have been a difficult marriage to Ziemowit. The archbishop, observing her from a distance, commented to Jasko, "She learned that from her grandmother—loved festivities but prayer and God first, no matter what! God has blessed us with a great queen."

Jasko nodded in agreement. "She has requested the release of most prisoners from the Krakow jail in honor of her crowning. She is perhaps simply too merciful." Toasting their glasses, Jasko continued, "To our holy and merciful queen. She will certainly always want to do the right thing for God and Poland."

The archbishop, with genuine patronizing love, replied, "We will not frighten her with all responsibility just yet, Jasko, give it time. We will win her heart and her trust. She is sure to come to see things our way."

They toasted her privately, looking at her with love and admiration.

CHAPTER 13

Tested Resolutions

Jadwiga's new life, although she was so young, brought her great responsibilities that she was not sheltered from. She had an observatory role and was included and respected as the ruler of the country. She listened to the counselors she trusted since she had arrived and who had ruled the country without much interference for years. The respect was mutual. She could often be seen observing the goings on with her translators, still mastering the Polish language. She was always respected and included in the entire goings-on. So many people were surprised and pleased by the graciousness and wisdom she possessed as a young girl. Ladislau was always nearby to clarify or correct anything, and they often had discussions. He taught her about government and advised her the most. It was only Constance who really knew the difficulties and those moments when the pressures and reality of her life away from her family overwhelmed her. The loneliness and sacrifices she had made to fulfill her duties surfaced on occasion.

One such evening, winter still lingering, Constance entered her freezing bedroom and found Jadwiga sitting on a windowsill with the shutters open. The full moon gave a gentle ambiance as Constance entered the cold room, although a warm fire was burning in the fireplace. She rushed to close the shutters, tightly blocking out the moonlight that Jadwiga seemed to be basking in. "Child, you cannot sit here in the freezing cold. You will catch sick." She lifted her chin, turning her face and saw her eyes and cheeks filled with tears. "My dove, what is it? Shall I call the physician? The guard? Has someone hurt you?" Constance hugged her while Jadwiga sobbed quietly.

"No, no, Constance."

"What is it then?" Constance pressed.

"I just miss home and William. I see the moon, and I think, maybe Mama and Maria see it too, and William. Do you think they see it too, Constance?"

Constance's heart filled with motherly love. "Yes, of course my love, they see it too." She tucked her in bed and, wiping away Jadwiga's tears, gave her another hug and kiss. "Don't forget who you are. The *king* of Poland."

They laughed as Jadwiga wiped her tears, encouraged and strengthened by Constance's strength and determination. "I'm sorry, Constance. I'm all right."

"It's all right child, rest." she said as she took some warm water and a cloth, wiping Jadwiga's face. "You'll feel good in the morning. You are just homesick. But this is your home now. And you know soon, William will come, and you will be married." Jadwiga relaxed and began drifting off to sleep to Constance humming her favorite hymn, *Agnus Dei,* to comfort her. Both the song and the idea that William would come suddenly brought her so much peace.

Many weeks later, Jasko and the archbishop summoned Jadwiga to a meeting room after breakfast. As Jadwiga walked in with her ladies-in-waiting, the men stood and came to greet her with grandfatherly embraces. Jasko thanked her for coming and, looking toward her entourage, asked Jadwiga, "We were wondering if we could see you *alone*?"

Jadwiga motioned to the ladies. "Yes, of course."

Turning to her senior and trusted advisors, she became concerned; perceiving their serious countenances, she wondered what the problem might be. The archbishop, sensing her concern, advised, "My dear, please be at ease that this is serious, but state matters." Jadwiga nodded attentively, waiting for him to continue. "We have called you here to discuss a matter which no doubt is close to your heart but will be close to the heart of all of Poland as well. We understand that you have a marriage of consent to William of Austria, which only remains to be consummated. Are you aware of the hostility of many Poles toward Austrian rule?"

"Well, yes, but why?" Jadwiga asked.

Jasko now spoke, "My lady, we never brought these matters to you seriously because you were so young when you came, and we wanted you to come and feel at home here, and now, this question must be faced. The Poles have great and unquestionable devotion to you, but it is your espoused, William, who is of concern for your loyal subjects. They hated Sigismund, as he was German. They will not accept William…"

The subject of the conversation suddenly dawned on her, "Because he is Austrian… But, my good men, I am the king, they will listen to me and abide by my wishes…" Jadwiga said hopefully.

The archbishop continued the difficult and sensitive discussion. "Your grandmother must have taught you how fickle and stubborn the Poles are in regard to rulers. We have been blessed with their united devotion to you. You have brought peace, unity, joy, and hope, but William will be in real danger here, and it will bring conflict if you force your marriage vows. It will divide the nation."

Jadwiga, not believing what she was hearing, replied incredulously, "But… I never even would have thought about it! It was what my parents wanted, my father, Papa, always wanted. What are you saying? That I should *not* marry William?"

Jasko gently replied, "Well, you *are* the king, and the decision is yours, but by marrying William, you are putting his life in danger. There are too many who would see to it that no Austrian will rule. He could be assassinated."

Jadwiga sat down and looked out the castle window. In truth, this was a difficult thing the advisors were asking. They did not understand how dear William was to her, how all the long, lonely nights and moments of her longing heart, the thought that comforted her most, was that William would soon come and be her husband. This brought her solace and strength in all her difficult moments. They could not possibly realize the sword they were now bringing close to her heart. It was always the very thing she believed without doubt would happen, the very thing her dear father had worked so hard to ensure for her before his death. Fighting tears, she struggled to be strong and continued the discussion unemotionally for their sake.

The archbishop, not insensitive to her heart, continued, "My dearest one, what we have told you is difficult, but there is an alternative solution, one that would work for peace…" Jadwiga faced him, puzzled and hopeful, waiting silently for him to explain.

"A certain duke of Lithuania, Jagiello of Olgierd. He has come to us, and we have met on various occasions." Jadwiga could not help but think, what could this possibly do with her or William? "He is a fine, handsome man of honor and dignity, and although a pagan, he has his eye to the church and the West. He in fact, has offered a proposal of marriage…"

Suddenly, Jadwiga realized what the men were getting at. "For me, good men? But no…not for me…and William, I love William…!" *No way, it has to be William.*

"My child, he is a brother to you. You love him as a brother. Hear us out. Jagiello of Lithuania has offered a proposal a number of times, one so pervasive and unbelievable that I had to meet with him to discuss his terms, which I am sure you will find incredulous."

Jadwiga tried very hard to remain gracious and respectful. "A pagan Lithuanian? How could you even think of it?"

Jasko responded, "These are his terms. If you marry him, he will convert to Catholicism along with his brothers. Then he will convert all of Lithuania and destroy all its pagan temples. We have found him to be a man of great dignity and sincerity. His own mother is an Orthodox Christian, so he has been taught from her but has never been baptized because of his father. His proposal is incredulous! Think, dear one, of the good for all of Poland."

She sat down and tried to take it all in. *Conversion and the destruction of paganism?* This was huge. She answered, still surprised by their proposal. "But are such barbarous men capable of giving their word?" The two men smiled then laughed gently; rumors and common folktale and prejudice were always rampant.

The archbishop replied, "Yes, yes, child, be assured they are normal people, with souls. And just think, what better way to lose your enemies than to make them your family? The enemies to the east will no longer be enemies but family! And you will be queen of their realm as well."

Queen of Lithuania? Jadwiga understood that they were quite serious, and resorting suddenly to the idea that Mama would never consent to such a plan, she decided to shift the responsibility to her mother, who she felt would be sure to continue to support the will of Louis of Anjou. "We will have to send word to Mother. She would have to give her consent. She is also the one who betrothed me to William. She will have to make this decision."

"Well, if it is your wish, we will send for her consent on the matter."

Jadwiga, suddenly feeling the weight of the issue, answered meekly, "Please, do."

"One more thing, my lady, they—that is, a delegation with Jagiello's brother—are arriving tomorrow, and you are to meet with them."

Jadwiga, even more incredulous and feeling doubt about her power as "king," overwhelmed by her obligations and confusion, sat down. This was happening too quickly. Her heart sank. *Tomorrow?*

CHAPTER 14

Rethinking Past Resolutions

Elizabieta had fled home to beautiful coastal Croatia with Maria. She was attempting to arrange a new marriage for Maria, as all had become disenchanted with the idea of her marriage to Sigismund. He was unpopular in all political circles because of his cold and abrasive disposition. Elizabieta was attempting to control the situation by negotiating a new marriage for Maria to Louis of Orleans of France and had just met with a French delegation regarding her change in plans for Maria. Another delegation from the east arrived at the Croatian castle escorted by some delegates from both the court of Poland and Buda. This came as much as a surprise to Elizabieta as it had to Jadwiga.

This delegation was not led by Jagiello, but by his loyal brother Boris, also a prince of Lithuania. They were not a group of savage-looking brutes but handsome, well-groomed, well-educated young men and their fiercer-looking guards, who represented both the old and newer generations in an interesting mixture of personalities. They had found that their quest for permission for their brother

Jagiello's hand in marriage to Jadwiga, being a long trip to Buda, would now involve an even longer trip to the coast of the Adriatic, with Italy beyond on its other coast, almost in sight of it. So they had set out for the west.

They were met by Nicholas Gara, a fair-haired handsome and intelligent fifty-something who was now her trusted advisor, who seemed to have more than a dutiful love and devotion for his queen. Elizabieta trusted and loved him more than anyone in her charge. He assisted her with all her national and international business concerns and was almost second in command. She now turned to him for guidance, and they worked together closely.

As the entourage entered, Elizabieta anxiously watched their approach to the throne, anxious to hear news of her beloved Jadwiga. She knew the news was not bad, for no black flag warning of grim tidings was flown. She leaned forward with eagerness to hear why they had travelled so far from the east.

"My lady. We traveled to Hungary. Then realizing you were here in Croatia, we traveled here. My name is Nicholas Bogoria, chamberlain of Krakow. Our Polish delegation as well as Boris, a member of the family of Jagiello, grand duke of Lithuania, has come to seek your approval on an important matter regarding Queen Jadwiga."

"How is she?" Elizabieta asked passionately. *It's been a year since I've seen my baby.*

"She is fine, very well, I assure you, and adjusting excellently to her new life. She is well loved by everyone in Poland, and Poland thanks you again for the gift to us of your beautiful daughter, whose face has shown to be a blessing of peace for us, and now for neighboring countries also."

"Thanks be to God," Elizabieta replied quietly.

Boris, Jagiello's brother, now came forward and knelt humbly before the queen. She was struck by his handsome countenance and manners in light of past prejudices against the Lithuanians. Elizabieta, trying to hide that she was deeply impressed by his physical beauty and good disposition, answered anxiously, "Well, what is it?"

Nicholas Bogoria continued, "The matter is regarding Boris's brother, Jagiello, grand duke of Lithuania, who is known throughout

Poland and Lithuania as a dignified, intelligent leader and with whom the kings of Rus have desired to marry their daughters. It is thus a great honor that Jagiello has approached the Polish administrators, as well as Queen Jadwiga, asking for her hand in marriage. The honor has now fallen to you to become his mother, and to us to request that you would agree to give Jadwiga to him in Holy Matrimony."

Elizabieta was taken completely by surprise and, in virtual disbelief and unguarded, answered, "But…how would the clergy, and why would you want her to ever marry a pagan?"

Nicholas, anticipating her concerns, smiled widely. "My great queen, the best is yet to be heard. This great Jagiello, with a heart we believe to be sincere and true, has promised together with many relatives"—and with this he motioned to Boris who had remained kneeling humbly before her—"to be baptized into our great Catholic Church, to become one family under God." Elizabieta was astonished at this new revelation. It was almost unbelievable and suspicious. These were the same people her husband had been fighting against for peace just twelve years ago. She struggled to recall Louis and put him in her position. What would Louis think of this?

Nicholas continued, now excitedly realizing that here and now, he was an instrument of change, of history in the making, for which he had journeyed so far, "And there is more still, if you will agree, he will convert all of Lithuania to the Roman Catholic rite, and paganism and strife between Poland and Lithuania will be no more. The distinction of the privilege and magnitude of the apostolic endeavor has fallen into the hands of Jadwiga and the Angevin dynasty." His tone and excitement crescendoed to a delighted, irresistibly joyful, and inevitable proposition. "All that wars, missionaries, popes, and countless delegations has failed to accomplish now falls, by the consent of the house of Anjou, to be accomplished by *your* simple *fiat*."

Elizabieta sat back on her throne, quickly coming to understanding of the greatness of the matter, felt the choice—if in agreement with Poland was in tremendous favor of the church, culture—and peace, so how could she refuse? Wouldn't Louis agree?

"And of course, Jadwiga would be the new queen of Lithuania…" Nicholas added.

After a moment of intense silence, she replied, "But what about Leopold of Austria, and William? The Habsburgs…"

At the mention of this name, Boris sprang into action. He motioned toward an aid, who brought forth a treasury full of gold florins, addressing the queen briefly in his own language. Nicholas Bogoria explained, "Jagiello offers a vadium of 200,000 florins, which had been agreed upon by the former king of Hungary and duke of Austria. The payment has most certainly not been made by Leopold?"

Elizabieta turned to Nicholas Gara, who affirmed what she knew, that Leopold had not been heard from regarding this promise at all. Elizabieta shook her head no and looked to him to continue.

"And finally, all Polish prisoners are to be released of course, and all Polish lands to be returned to Poland. There is nothing but gain for Poland and good Queen Jadwiga."

Elizabieta, impressed and astonished, glanced to Nicholas of Gara, who nodded and gave a look of approval, as though saying to her "go ahead, there is nothing to lose." After a pause of silence, Elizabieta stood, answering formally, "I am glad to consent to anything that will be a worthy acquisition for the faith and kingdom of Poland, as would most certainly her father, Louis the Great—God rest his soul—would have agreed. I thereby give formal consent that the Polish prelates and lords, together with the consent of Jadwiga, do what they find to be in the best interest of Christendom and their kingdom." In fact, Elizabieta, true to her timid nature, had returned responsibility for the decision to Poland and Jadwiga.

A cheer went out from the delegates who had already, in their travels, become close allies. Nicholas Bogoria bowed to the queen, acknowledging her consent and, with a relieved and grateful expression, bowed again. A scribe came to the queen, handing her a quill, parchment, and seal. In the presence of all, she signed and sealed with her wax signet, the official document that in the hands of Nicholas of Bogoria became the fate of Jadwiga and Eastern Europe.

CHAPTER 15

Tempers on the Horizons

The negotiations had concluded, and far from Croatia, north of Poland, Marienburg Castle loomed as an ever-continuing industrious center of progress and toil. Within its walls, Rottenstein had gotten word of the new arrangements in Poland. Throwing a gauntlet across the room, missing hitting several servants, his weapon circled and circled until it found its place in a large wooden beam. "Damn! Cursed Lithuanians! How can this be? What black magic spell have they cast on the damn Poles and their prissy little king? What? What? What? How can this be? Have the Poles gone mad?" he raged hysterically, almost foaming at the mouth. This was something he never anticipated.

It was and has always been easier to exploit an enemy than an ally, and now, all he had spent so many years fighting for was at stake. His mind-set was fixed. "This is madness. *Madness!*" Everyone around him sat motionless. No one dared to provoke. He was so angry he was biting on the flesh that formed a fist. His crazed expression became pensive, conspiring any way conceivable to stop this new possibility from becoming reality. "We will have to stop them!" Turning to his advisor, he demanded, "Leopold of Austria! Where is he in all this? His son William was supposed to marry Queen Jadwiga! Has he been informed? Zolner!"

Zolner stood immediately, ready to obey every whim of the dictatorial leader. "Send a delegation—one large enough to fight if necessary—to Leopold. Tell him we are ready to fight the Poles with him for this. I will *die* before I allow a Lithuanian rule Poland. And may God curse them and smite every last Lithuanian." And with that, he sealed his word with a gross spit on the floor, Zolner scurrying to conform to his rage.

Months passed since Jadwiga had first received the news of the great changes in the circumstances that would determine her future. Jadwiga waited eagerly, some days feeling melancholic, and some sad. She understood the greater ramifications for peace and the world by marrying Jagiello instead of her William. She often imagined what he was doing and what he looked like as he was growing into manhood. She assured herself that Mama would side with William.

She had waited anxiously for news from Boris and Nicholas Bogoria regarding her mother's decision and had prayed fervently for God to give her the answer through her mother's decision. As much as she loved and took comfort in William, she was willing to do God's will because she knew in her heart that God's will was best. As it took months to hear back from this delegation, Jadwiga prepared herself to accept whichever decision her mother made to come from God himself. If God wanted this, then it would be declared in her mother's consent. So the weight of the decision fell back upon her shoulders when the delegation returned without the definite answer from Elizabieta—only that Jadwiga and the Polish government could do what they felt was "in the best interest of Christendom and their kingdom."

Mama had given her full respect and freedom to make the decision, but didn't Mama understand that she needed her to take the lead this time? She needed clarity, and Mama was not going to be the one to provide it. She felt the weight of the choice, as though God Himself was giving her rights of exercising free will. The power and responsibility of free will—she tried to cherish it rather than feel its burden.

The Polish clergy and governors, in the same spirit, left her some time to ponder the decision and did not force her but encouraged her to favor Jagiello. She often went for long walks to get away from the castle and clear her head. She preferred the idea of marrying William. She weighed out objectively what she should do now that God had given the great privilege and cross of power and authority. With this came tremendous responsibility and self-sacrifice. Papa had always instilled this in her from her earliest days. When she would complain to him as he would be leaving again on lengthy campaigns, leaving the family in fear that this would be the last time they might ever see him, praying always for his safe return, he would hold her close to his heart and whisper in her ear, "Duty before honor…," and his powerful words echoed in her mind and heart as she pondered her choice.

Finally, the day came that Jadwiga, all things considered, decided she must put aside her emotions and secret dreams of William—her fair-haired, rosy-cheeked, beautiful friendly soul mate of her youth; her prince and the knight in shining armor she had dreamed of and thought always of their last words, a kiss and a promise: "Wait for me, and I will wait for you…" These images she decided as they faded farther and farther from her new reality became something she set at the foot of the cross of Jesus, sacrificed and discounted as dreams of her youth as she made the final decision to marry Jagiello of Lithuania instead.

Jagiello, an unknown man three times her age. Her decision was not based on her lack of love for William but on her complete and total love for him. The idea that the Poles did not want an Austrian king echoed in the recesses of her heart, that her selfishness to make her childhood dreams come true could put him in danger. Because of her great love for him, she would never put him in harm's way.

For this and the higher good of achieving peace for Poland and Lithuania, she would give her consent to what she even would have thought unthinkable only six months before.

⌒⌒

Jadwiga, on this winter day, was seated on the throne, receiving the Lithuanian delegation including Skirgiello, Jagiello's dearest brother, who came offering beautiful gifts of gold, furs, and coats in a long procession. Jadwiga was mildly impressed by these as material things were secondary to her. Finally, as though in real understanding and empathy to what she treasured most, she was offered a golden crucifix on a golden chain. Somehow, these people from the East understood her heart by saving the best gift for last. How did Jagiello know?

Skirgiello finally spoke. He was as handsome as his brothers and strong and, to Jadwiga, seemed very old. "My brother offers all these gifts in honor of his potential espoused and wishes a final response from her majesty, the king, whether she will have him as husband and king of Poland and thus become the queen of Lithuania."

Jadwiga held the beautiful golden crucifix in her hands and kissed it. She saw also that the delegation up close were of men who resembled any fine man she had ever met. Gazing one last time on the cross and then at her advisors who smiled and nodded, she was assured and confident. She stood and reached her hands out to Skirgiello and, holding his hands replied, "Please brother, tell your brother that the king of Poland accepts his proposal and will pray and wait patiently for the time of the fulfillment of the marriage."

A spontaneous cheer went out from all present, both Poles and Lithuanians. They realized that years of strife and hardship was now given the kiss of peace and the breeze of reconciliation. Darkness and dread were giving way to a springtime of hope.

Skirgiello was touched and emotional. They had been trying to make this happen for years, and he knew in his heart that this was both Jagiello's dream and his destiny. He bowed joyfully, kissing Jadwiga's cheeks in a departing and welcoming greeting.

CHAPTER 16

Tempers and Recommitment on the Western Front

It was less than a month before another set of visitors graced the castle of Croatia, which Elizabieta was still calling home. This time, it was not a kind visit in the spirit of humility but Leopold, the largest and tallest man in the castle, a growling and angered lion letting everyone hear his discontent upon hearing the new turn of events from the northeast. He stormed Elizabieta's place of refuge like lightning moving across great distances. William, now a young man of sixteen, handsome, most especially to any young lady, followed behind his father. Though of a calmer disposition, he was tall like his father but slender, his height allowed him to keep up with his father. They approached together with their delegation from Austria.

Nicolas Gara, trying to soothe Leopold's temper, had to double his gait to keep up with him as he stormed through the palace toward the meeting room with Elizabieta. "Leopold, I realize you are upset, but please, she has just lost Maria to Sigismund with whom we have just averted battle. You must exercise patience, she is tired…"

Leopold shoved Nicholas from his path as he lunged to enter the meeting room doors. "Enough from you, Gara!" He burst through the doors, not waiting for the proper escort, sending guards flying in opposite directions as they were not prepared for a rude entry.

Elizabieta sat up, startled at his abrupt entry and the look of anger and almost rage on his face was new, as she had only met him with her husband under quite civil circumstances. Nicholas followed closely at his heels, out of control of this giant of a man. She was quite alarmed, but once she saw William close behind, she decided to handle Leopold by ignoring his bad manners and descended to embrace his golden-haired son, who grinned lovingly in recognition of a woman who in his childhood had been good and dear to him. She embraced him as a long-lost son and kissed his cheeks. He reminded her of the time when her life was peaceful, beautiful, and simple and her children were in her charge day after day but were lost to her now. William returned a greeting of love and respect to her as a mother who had been such an important part of his upbringing. It had been years since she had seen him, and in this short time, he had grown from a boy to a man. It suddenly dawned on her that she had done a great injustice to him and Leopold, and perhaps, her late husband. Suddenly, she did not know if she had made the right decision, and she didn't in fact know what decision had been reached in Poland by Jadwiga as news travelled very slowly in this time. So for a moment, she wasn't sure why they had come to her.

Leopold quickly cleared up the matter, slightly softening his tone. "Elizabieta, how could you? *How could you forget the Buda pact, 1375!* Hainburg and Zwolin, 1380? *Were you not there?* What about Louis and what he wanted? What has come over you?"

Elizabieta, now on her throne again, gathered herself quickly from the attack and attempted to converse in a clear and sovereign tone with the looming prince. "Leopold… Charles of Durazzo is trying to take the throne from Mary. Sigismund is coming for Mary, to take her by force…a woman is weak—she is the plaything of all the men in her world, not a force… I had not heard from you. *You* did not fulfill the terms of the dowry…not hearing from you, I thought maybe you had changed your mind. After all, you had lost the Hungarian throne, and *that* was what you and Louis had agreed to… I thought you had changed your mind…"

Scarcely had she finished that Leopold burst in, "Woman! Changed my mind? Ah, what do you know of ruling a kingdom? I don't have time to change my clothes let alone change my mind. You, you have no idea… Oh what I would give for Louis to be here now."

Elizabieta, now insulted by his rude manners, became less patient of his impatience. "Yes, talk, talk on, Leopold, and curse, that is what you do best, yet you never fulfilled the terms of the dowry and the 200,000 florins that you owed to Hungary was paid by a man of action, the grand duke of Lithuania." At this, Leopold's eyebrows narrowed, and his face grew disgruntled, as the seed of resentment that had been planted by the Teutonic Knights in his heart also sprouted into rage, he began to shake to control his temper. Elizabieta continued calmly, "We had not received payment from you, and actions are louder than words."

Leopold lunged for Cardinal Demetrius who was standing innocently by observing with concern the unfolding drama, grabbed him by his clerics, and pulled him to himself thundering, "Jadwiga's time is coming in six months! Something has to be done to stop this! The *Lithuanians*?" He shouted disgustedly, "Louis is turning in his grave at the sound of it! They are our *enemies*! You weren't there! We fought them, Louis and I—bloody, evil bloody war—Louis and *I*…we fought the barbarians face-to-face! They are swine! Evil, dirty, pagan swine who lie, pillage, and rape. They are *liars*!"

Letting go finally of the poor cardinal, who attempted to regain his composure, Leopold pointed to Nicolas, Elizabieta, and Maria, shouting and spitting, "And you, you have been deceived by the soulless devils!"

He now had swayed his audience and made each and every one lose any resolve they might have initially had. Elizabieta began to think they had made a grave mistake by allowing this possibility. Her stomach felt in knots. She stared at him silently as he caught his breath, not knowing what to say, afraid that perhaps Leopold was justified. It dawned on her that just maybe he was right, and an awkward silence permeated the group for what seemed like many moments. Who had she signed Jadwiga's life to? Had she been deceived? Her sudden panic made it difficult to breathe.

William silently and patiently observed with sympathy Elizabieta and Maria in front of him. He finally stepped up quietly to soften the blow struck by his father. He spoke with respect and yet determination and simply asked, "Is there something that can be done?"

Nicholas answered, concerned now, "If most of the Polish court has been swayed to this, there will certainly be a battle if you go to Poland, Leopold. As of now, they have no doubts and have put confidence in the duke's words. You cannot fight all of Poland over a marriage." He then turned to William, "William, they will not accept you. Your life may be in danger, as they did not accept Sigismund before you. I am sure that is why Jadwiga gave up your marriage, because of the harm that might have come to you. The Poles are obstinate in their choices."

William turned to the bishop, passionate and truthful in his innocent youth, "But we are betrothed, she is to be *my* wife. Something has to be done. She is my wife already!" Elizabieta could see that he was mature, genuine in love, and resolute to fulfill his destiny with Jadwiga as planned. He turned to her, "I think about her all the time, of our last meeting when she left for Poland. The last thing I said to her was, 'Wait for me, and I will wait for you.'"

She could see his love for Jadwiga was pure, and he was willing to take chances, even on his life for her sake; her heart sank as she realized she had wronged him greatly. Everyone stood pensive and sympathetic.

The cardinal finally broke the silence, trying to make amends, "Well, there is one thing…" Everyone looked expectantly at the older, wiser holy priest. "In rare cases, where the church deems, we can move up the consummation age. With my consent, William can go to Jadwiga and, with her consent, fulfill the marriage of sponsalia."

Without hesitating, Leopold alarmingly shouted above everyone, *"Scribe!"* A scribe came hurriedly and shaken with the quick turn of events. He set himself to work with his quill and parchment.

Leopold commenced in a dictatorial voice, commanding the situation, "Write *this*:"

> It is with careful prayer and discernment, I, Cardinal Demetrius have removed the prior conditions of the age of consent of Jadwiga of Anjou, due to her maturity of mind and intelligence…on the feast of the Assumption of the Blessed Virgin, or anytime thereafter is declared eligible for marriage… As witness to the consent of Queen Elizabieta, all here in the present company will sign."

Leopold continued,

> I, Elizabieta of Anjou, in the company of said witnesses, give consent to the fulfillment of the marriage vows of Queen Jadwiga of Poland to William of Austria, as agreed to in Hainburg Austria, 1378, who having reached the age of consent, as indicated by Cardinal Demetrius, on the feast of the Assumption of Mary, August 15, 1385, are to be finally and officially married. With Ladislau of Opole to act as plenipotentiary to oversee these commitments fulfilled.

Turning now to William, he commissioned his son, breathing into him the heart of boldness and courage he possessed. "Son, you must go. You have only three weeks' travel time. That leaves no time for delay! I cannot go with you. Bring the consent. Go to your beloved and, together, fulfill your destiny!"

Leopold accompanied William, his men-at-arms, and his trusted attendant Paco to their horses out into the hot July sun. Everyone present understood the strategy. There was no time to discuss details. Leopold's presence was not needed and might cause more problems than good. If this vow was to be fulfilled, it would have to be fulfilled in a quiet, subtle way so as not to arouse suspicions from the Poles and, as Nicholas had pointed out, without raising the prospects of war. William's heart raced with the thrill of the journey, of finally getting Jadwiga, of a resolution on the horizon. *Thank God Father is so strong.* He appreciated his father's bold, rash ways like never before.

Leopold shouted to encourage them, "You don't have a moment to lose! Ride like your life depends on it. Your life and your love do depend on it! Son, your destiny is in your hands now. Paco, you are his guardian in my place. Be me for him. Let nothing get in the way of him. Ride!" He smacked the horse's rump as the group took off at top speed, shouting, "Godspeed!" His hulking presence grew smaller and smaller as the group thundered off out of sight to the northeast toward Poland.

CHAPTER 17

Duty and Destiny

Wawel Castle gardens were joined in the back to the Franciscan property whose monastery was at the opposite end of the vast walled yard where four or more acres of land generously housed a few grazing sheep, chickens, and ponies, cows, orchards and vegetable, herb, and flower gardens. In the spring and summer months, for Jadwiga, it was a place of beauty, safety, and refuge. Here, she spent much time with the orphan children in the charge of the Franciscans, the visiting children of the castle workers, and her ladies-in-waiting. In this tiny paradise, all the problems in her larger world disappeared.

This day was a particularly warm and beautiful summer day. Jadwiga's ladies were sitting peacefully doing their embroidery. Jadwiga was entertaining the children. In the distance, a trumpet could be heard, the routine "Hejnal" from the Mariacki tower of the Church of St. Mary in the center of the city square, not a kilometer from where they stood.

Jadwiga, known for entertaining the children with stories accompanied with scenes played out dramatically, was being summoned by the children to perform. She liked to educate the children about history through stories. "Queen Jadwiga, *please* tell us about the trumpeter of Krakow!"

Jadwiga answered, "Again? But I told you that story just yesterday!"

"Oh, please tell us. Pleeeaase!" They gathered around her, pulling on her gown and sleeves from all sides, not allowing her freedom to walk or move.

"All right then, he who persists wins the war. Sit down. Not long ago, there were dark, dark days for Poland when good King Henry the bearded ruled. The Tartars of Asia, brutal men, sons of the great Ghengis Khan, merciless warriors who rode small horses, came as far as Kiev. They took Kiev, a beautiful city, and took all its rulers and magnates as slaves. They ruled it, only seven days' journey from where we now sit. What a terrible horde they were from the East, east even of Lithuania."

At the mention of Lithuania, she paused and thought briefly of her future husband, who she was to marry, thereby bringing safety to her kingdom. She tried to imagine what he looked like. She grasped the crucifix given to her by Jagiello. "They had only destruction in mind, *burning* and *killing* mercilessly." The children listened attentively while Jadwiga now began to make dramatic actions to mime a death as she spoke. Her face was solemn and dramatic. The ladies-in-waiting laughed at her drama and her enchanting effect on the children and called out, "Jad-wiga!" as if to say, "She's at it again! Bravo!" She continued with suspense and urgency in her voice.

"The Mongols burned *everything*, every village on their journey towards Krakow. The people of Krakow were celebrating, as they are often known to do, some feast or other when the dear trumpeter, whose job it was to warn of danger, keenly attending to his duties, noticed some Mongols entering the city, trying to take advantage of the good citizens who were in the midst of festivities. The good watchmen saw them, and blowing his trumpet..."

Jadwiga dramatized the last horrific but heroic moments of the trumpeter's life even mimicking his "Hejnel" tune, who, being shot in the throat cannot continue his song but has alarmed the people to the danger, continued the narration: "Dropped to the ground, shot with a Mongol arrow in his throat, has died a hero, to the end of Polish time. And that, my dear children, is why the song ends on a strange note, before it has its proper end, for he was shot in the middle of his warning tune. We are reminded of the bravery of that true Pole and reminded that we must each do our duty with honor and devotion. He saved the town that night." She bowed to indicate the end. The children clapped and cheered and began to copy Jadwiga's dramatic mimes of being shot in the throat and collapsing to the ground; some were the Mongol shooters with arrows and some trumpeting. One little girl made her way to Jadwiga and pulled on her dress. Jadwiga looked down, "Yes, child?"

The little girl, visibly afraid and disturbed by the story, asked timidly, "Will they come again?"

Jadwiga picked her up, swung her around, hugging her tightly, stroking her hair, held the orphaned child close to her heart as her own parents had done for her. Other of the more timid children came close as well for comfort. She came back to reality and with optimism answered, "No, never! They are gone now. Soon, Poland will have a great king, and we'll be able to feast without fear! The great *King Jagiello*." She finished her last sentence quietly and with resignation. The children smiled and went away, satisfied. The ladies-in-waiting smiled and continued their work. Jadwiga was reflective. Lithuania was a barrier zone between them and the Mongols.

◦⌒◦

Meanwhile, William's small, undetected delegation was quickly making its way to Krakow. William, together with his guardian Paco, Ladislau of Opole, some bodyguards, and ambassadors had stopped by a river, close to Krakow now. Their horses drank as they bathed, for their time of meeting was approaching quickly.

"I feel like I'm getting closer to her now. She's been in my dreams for a year now. I can't wait to see her. She's the one love of my life."

Paco, a handsome, cowboyish persona, acknowledged his state of mind with tolerant patience. "Careful now, young Tristan, you've lost your mind already before you even have her. Right now, you still have a lot of obstacles to face before your dreams become reality," he cautioned.

William passionately answered, "If I had only known the Poles were planning these things, I would have *never* waited, Paco! I would have come sooner and taken her to Austria. There is something between us, I can't explain—a love that is meant to be from eternity. I *love* her. And we have not seen her of late, but she is beautiful. There is no other as beautiful as her. No one gives me reason to dream of them. Her soul is pure, holy, and her physical beauty matches her soul."

Paco listened, rolling his eyeballs and shaking his head at young love—more realistic about the difficulties they were about to face in light of the optimism of the young prince. He chose to be silent and leave the prince to his innocent dreams and intentions; after all, who knew? Maybe everything would work out in Krakow.

"I will achieve my dreams by showing everyone in Krakow that nothing will stop me. I will have her despite all who would dare stand in my way." He finally came back to reality. "Tristan? *Tristan?* Pathetic!" as he splashed and shoved Paco.

Paco shook his head and laughed, replying with mocking pity. "Yes, and you are a knight, a princely knight without a castle, lady, or kingdom."

The older and seasoned Ladislau, who had been nearby quietly listening, took William more seriously. He had been with Jadwiga's family from the beginning, had been at the wedding of sponsalia and, knowing King Louis's intentions from the beginning, offered his own view. "Soon enough, he will have all three. I will see to it," he replied, serious and determined.

Paco responded with skeptical silence, again, his heart filled with doubt because of the overwhelming odds that such a small group would encounter trying to change the mind of all of Poland.

⚬⚬⚬

It was a dark, warm summer night, soon to give way to the break of a new dawn. In the stillness, a clear moon shone above the countryside. Besides the gentle plodding of cart horses' hooves and the churning of carriage wheels, crickets and night owl sounds were all that were heard. Because of the silence, even a nearby brook could be heard, gently running on its way alongside the country route. An open cart rumbled along this country road with Jadwiga as its passenger. Just ahead rode four Polish delegates: Jasko, the archbishop, Dymitr (the queen's knight), and a bodyguard riding on horses.

Jadwiga breathed deeply, surveying the predawn beauty of the nature around her. The sky was now glowing with pink and orange embers, giving a look of perfection to all of nature. In her hands, partially wrapped in a cloth, she cradled a precious glass vessel. Within the globe could be seen a luminescence radiating of multiple colors of gold and light, as if encapsulating the dawn. She was now preoccupied with holding it close to her and keeping it safe because she realized how fragile it was and did not want to damage it. It was her sole concern within the rambling cart to maintain it without damage. The light of dawn began to break through the darkness, revealing the beauty of the surrounding fields and farmers' fences marking boundaries. One of the men on the horses ahead of her turned to her and, motioning with his arm, respectful and with affection but authority, urged her, "My queen, let it go, leave it..."

The cart suddenly came to a halt. She descended, walking gracefully to the large brook, holding on to the radiant globe as if precious to her. She decisively bent and gently placed it into the strong moving stream and watched as it floated away from her, her heart weighing down as it moved farther and farther away. She sighed deeply and then followed the men on foot, who also now mysteriously were on foot.

They came to a barn and a sharp ninety-degree turn in the road. They turned and headed down this new direction. Suddenly, the men were ways ahead of Jadwiga, almost on the horizon. Jadwiga, more alone now and farther from the men, suddenly heard hoofbeats running and pounding from behind her with urgency. She stopped, trying to discern who might be approaching so urgently. Two horses approached Jadwiga.

Uncle Ladislau's voice could be heard, gently calling her, "Jadwiga…"

She turned to see William clearly only ten feet from her. They were surrounded by fog. They looked at each other with true and pure love. He was walking now toward her. Everything else was a blur to her; only his presence was clear.

He was holding something precious, carefully guarding it, and held it out to her now. It was the glass vessel she had given up. It was even more beautiful and radiant than before, its light shining comfortably between them. She gasped, looked up at him with love and understanding. All the love and admiration she had ever had for him came back to her—his charm, beauty, intellect and extroverted friendliness, his pure smile and the way he would greet her each day with love. She gazed at the globe he now offered her with disbelief. He had come to restore their love, and they looked at each other with pure, uninhibited love. He smiled as he stretched out his hand to give her back the globe, but as she tried to reach for it, it escaped her grasp and fell to the ground, shattered.

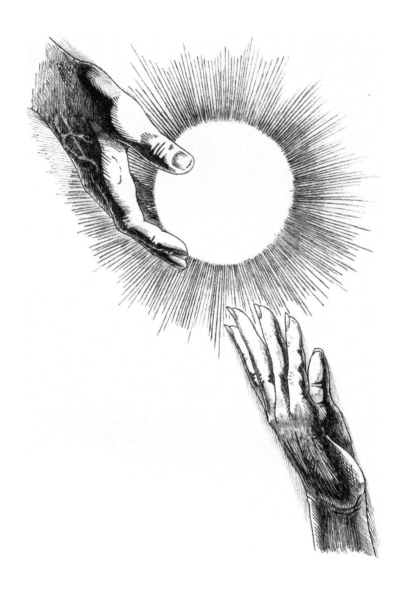

Her heart jumped, and she gasped from the pain she felt in her heart. She suddenly heard shutters opening and felt bright sun on her cheeks, squinting from the brightness, and a fresh August breeze danced in. Sitting up, her eyes welled with tears as she awoke from her dream. Constance rushed to her side, worrying about her tears and her gasping for breath, so distressed.

"I… I… I can't breathe…"

Constance attempted to calm her, hugging and soothing her. "Child, it was a dream, you're all right…shh…shh… What is it?"

Fully awake, she suddenly realized that she had betrayed all her true feelings about William and had succumbed to the pressure that her elders had put on her and denied her own will. She had in fact betrayed William.

～～◦～～

August 7, 1385, in Krakow, no one, including Jadwiga, knew that William and his delegation were approaching the walled city. Suddenly, on the horizon, the small royal delegation bearing the Austrian flag was seen approaching the city gate. William led the way as he could not contain his excitement and youthful optimism. He was dressed pristine and clean, a prince and almost a bridegroom. William had never seen Krakow, and as he approached, he noted the large walled castle grounds and cathedral that housed his true love. This would be his home, and he loved it.

They crossed the Vistula bridge, not unnoticed by many citizens surrounding the city gates and river. They were permitted entry by the guards who, accompanied by Ladislau, saw no threat in the small party. William smiled at the guards. Many citizens followed, curious to see what this entourage was and what business they might have in Krakow. Townspeople stopped and stared, mainly stunned by William's attractiveness. They quickly pieced the flag of Austria with this obviously princely delegation. This had to be the prince that they had heard of, that Jadwiga was supposed to have married, William of Austria. People whispered in hushed voices, but still could be heard as they rode by, "It's him, it's *William of Austria.*"

William, trying to win the crowd, politely smiled, nodded, and waved, hoping that soon, these would be his subjects. He saw in them friendly citizens, as in Austria or Hungary, which made him feel at home; they would be his people. And for the first time, they took notice of him in a new way he was not used to. He was ready for this now. It was his time. He and Jadwiga would do amazing things.

The people appeared both amazed and astonished, because the word announced throughout the kingdom was that Jadwiga was to marry Jagiello. In fact, most of the important Polish ambassadors and statesmen were currently meeting in Krewo to seal the deal with the Lithuanians as Jadwiga's age of maturity approached, completely unaware that William would dare to come to Krakow. They could see that this young prince seemed the perfect match for their queen.

A young boy ran through the crowd excitedly, the only herald of the group, making his way to the castle gate to inform the castle guard, "Prince William, of *Austria,* he's come, he's come *for the queen!*" He cried urgently to the guards, pointing excitedly to the delegation making its way through the crowd. A guard, suddenly noticing what all the fuss was about and trying to get a glance of the approaching delegation, sent one from his post to summon the castellan. Castellan Dobeslaus of Kurozweki immerged quickly to the gate from the castle.

Quickly surmising the events taking place, he shouted in a loud booming voice, which was heard echoing through the town. "Shut the castle gate! Shut the gate *immediately!*" William's peace was shattered by the sudden orders. He knew that tone, like Father's, unwavering, stubborn resolve. The guards were startled at his abrupt and decisive behavior, not understanding his logic, thinking the approaching delegation friendly and inoffensive, but quickly obeyed.

The delegation arrived to the gate, Ladislau of Opole now in the lead. As the polish representative for Queen Elizabieta and Jadwiga, William could see he was greatly disturbed by this rude reception. Now enraged, he shouted in an equally thunderous voice, feeling nothing but disdain for his fellow countryman, "Dobeslaus! Dobeslaus!"

William saw how cocky the castellan was behaving, that he had the upper hand. Dobeslaus reappeared unrepentant and unperturbed, "Yes, Ladislau? You do realize I am the castle governor, and this is a position kept by my family for *generations*."

"And I am the viceroy! This delegation requests the honor of an audience with the queen, and I am representative of her own mother—the queen mother, Elizabieta! Open these gates! Immediately, Dobeslaus! I have the queen's permission and a letter for her daughter! You follow *my* orders!"

Now he finally caught Dobeslaus's attention and concern. "What is it you have there? A letter?" he asked with a continuing attitude of disrespect. "Let me see it then."

"When hell freezes over! It is for the queen!" replied Ladislau.

"And the queen will only see who her castellan allows," replied Dobeslaus as he motioned for Ladislau again to hand over the document. "Now, Ladislau, we are countrymen you and I, who both love the queen and our country, only you have removed yourself from Poland for twenty years, and I, I have been loyal, so I know who is loyal and who is not. It's my job to know it. Now give me the document, or should I have you and your group held in the town prisons for treasonous attitudes?" He motioned once more with a threatening look, gesturing to give it to him. William observed the battle of wills silently.

Ladislau, hoping it would be their ticket for entry and knowing that it was not beyond Dobeslaus to imprison them, handed it to him begrudgingly, "Here then, but give it back and the queen will hear of this privacy breech. Give it back immediately!"

William wondered, was Jadwiga now a prisoner in her own castle? He would make this fool pay for his disrespect; it was only a matter of time. Dobeslaus examined the seal and seeing that it appeared authentic, asked, "May I?" intending to break the seal, "You know I am in charge here, all else have gone to Krewo." *You will pay for this, fool.*

Ladislau shook his head, becoming angered that he would even dare to open a letter designated for the queen. "Do *not*!" he ordered. *Don't you* dare, William thought.

Dobeslaus broke the seal, alarming everyone present that he would dare to do so, continued in a taunting, bullying voice after briefly scanning the contents of the letter. "And the irony here my friend is that good Queen Elizabieta has written and sealed the very same in favor, however, of Jagiello of Lithuania, and that document has accompanied our noble countrymen to Krewo and the delegates of Jagiello of Lithuania, who *as we speak*, are arranging his marriage to the most fair Queen Jadwiga. This then must be a forgery!" he exclaimed as he threw the document through the iron gate to the feet of Ladislau. *You will pay.*

William acted unperturbed and undaunted by his rudeness and inhospitable, stubborn attitude. Thinking that his youthful charm and grace may win him, he bent to pick up the document. "My good man, I only wish to see my long-lost sister, good Queen Jadwiga, that I may wish her well, and bring her these gifts of *friendship*, in light of her new engagement."

Dobeslaus, unmoved and even more resolved and distrusting, shouted, "William of *Austria*! That is not what the letter read! You will not be admitted to this castle, except over my dead body!"

Jadwiga was sheltered in her walled paradise with the women and children, sitting under the shade trees to protect from the summer heat. A maid came running urgently from the castle toward them, lifting her skirts to hurry, almost wild with excitement. Obviously delighted and incredulous, she breathlessly yelled her good tidings, "Queen Jadwiga, my queen, a *delegation!*" They were amused by her wild abandon as she rushed toward the group, unrefined and waving.

Jadwiga, amused and curious exclaimed, "A delegation?"

The serious maid came and fell to her knees, breathless in front of Jadwiga.

"Austria! *William!*" was all she managed.

It could only mean one thing. Shocked and reserved, Jadwiga replied seriously, "You mean, my girl, he is *here?* In Krakow? Now?" Her face turned red.

"At the front of the castle, right *now,*" the maid replied, gasping.

The ladies-in-waiting suddenly jumped up, excitedly exclaiming, "Oh, *he's come!* It *cannot be!* It's *not possible!*"

Every young lady in the kingdom knew the story of the prince of Austria, that he was a handsome and an honorable young man, and how Jadwiga was forsaking his love for the grand duke of Lithuania. Every young lady knew the possible implications of this visit. They suddenly all abandoned their daily work and walked quickly then ran toward the castle, putting away all reservations. Their curiosity made them completely forget themselves. Jadwiga also ran along, making a race out of it, intending to beat them all. Constance could only yell out a cautionary, "My lady, ladies, wait…," but was mostly ignored.

Once inside the castle, the girls stopped briefly to catch their breath, straighten each other's dresses, and fix their hair. Jadwiga was so excited. Was it a mistake? Was he here? Either way, she was as happy to see him, as she would have been her brother. The impressions of her dream suddenly filled her heart for a slight moment, and her heart dropped. Either way, she was overjoyed at the possibility of seeing him again.

As they composed themselves, Constance entered red and out of breath. "Prudence, my ladies—my lady, a queen *never* runs!"

Jadwiga, demonstrating an uncharacteristic unreserved joy and excitement that few saw in her, cupped Constance's face in her hands. "It's *William!* He's come! I am the king," Jadwiga jokingly reminded Constance. "I will run only when required!" The girls laughed and continued excitedly down the corridor, toward the front entrance of the castle to a window that would give a clear view of the arriving delegation; straightening their hair one last time, they immerged onto a front balcony.

Thinking William was entering the castle, Jadwiga and the girls were visibly confused and disappointed to see the Austrian flag and delegation moving away from the castle back into the city. Jadwiga, completely uninhibited, cried loudly to be heard throughout the town, sweetly with a heartfelt, soulful cry of both an innocent child and young woman, "William!" She waved frantically at her dearest love, her cry echoing on the surrounding buildings.

The Austrian delegation, with its back now to Krakow Castle seemed more serious and pensive as they withdrew. William, suddenly hearing his name called sweetly, knowing it had to be her, lightened up immediately and stopped his horse. Almost afraid to see his young love that he had dreamed of for a year or so, he paused, thinking briefly, as the pain on his face demonstrated, that he might not attain her after all in her guarded kingdom. He turned and looked toward the direction of her voice and beheld her, waving and smiling. He was not disappointed.

He smiled a winning smile, barely visible to Jadwiga from the distance between them, and put a finger to his lips as if to say "Shhh," pointed with his thumb to his heart, then his eye, and then to her as if to say, *I will see you soon.* Jadwiga could just barely make out the signs from where she stood. She could see Uncle with him. *Why was he leaving?* There must have been a mistake.

Simultaneously, Constance came on the balcony, pushing through the excited group of young ladies as William turned and continued riding away with his delegation. Constance's voice echoed in her brain like a dream, "My queen, Dobeslaus will not admit him."

It dawned on Jadwiga what was happening, and her mood quickly changed from passionate excitement to puzzlement and disappointment, even disbelief. She noticed Dobeslaus across the courtyard. *How could he? Why didn't he admit them?* Jadwiga scolded him loudly and passionately across the yard, so all could hear, "Dobeslaus, how could you turn them away?"

CHAPTER 18

The Promise of a Wedding

Another beautiful and peaceful moonlit summer night, with just a hint of a cooling breeze rustling the leaves, came upon the city of Krakow. In the shadows of the Wawel hill, pasture could be seen three figures jogging swiftly toward the Franciscan monastery. It was Jadwiga with Constance and Clara. They made their way through the orchards, vegetable, herb and flower gardens, finally arriving to a wooden back door of the simple monastery. They knocked softly and were quickly admitted.

Many candles lit up the length of the room, which had a fireplace with glowing embers and long tables and benches. Most Franciscan friars were in their cells by now. A few friars were present, one cleaning the hearth as the ladies entered the dining room. Friar John admitted them with a large hug. A hooded friar walked toward them. He was surprisingly young.

"This way, my lady, my queen," he urged as he took Jadwiga's hand to lead her. He came to a spot where the candlelight was greatest and paused, turned to Jadwiga, and removed his hood.

Jadwiga, delighted, exclaimed, "William, finally! I couldn't wait another moment to see you. Oh! You've come!" They hugged each other happily, and she felt timid, as William looked her over carefully from his taller perspective.

"I thought about you all the time." He paused and looked over to Clara, Constance, and the friar who unintentionally stared at the young couple with tenderness and sympathy. They suddenly realized their need for privacy, left the room and the two to their own discussion.

William joyfully continued, intrigued with the beautiful young woman he wanted to be his wife. "Jadwiga, I'm sorry I didn't come sooner...we thought our Hainburg vows were being honored. We were waiting until now to make the arrangements for next February when you would turn twelve. We didn't know the Poles were serious about this new arrangement. They wouldn't admit us to the castle earlier."

In the background, a Friar John was setting the table with some bread, cheese, and wine, and he motioned for the two to come and sit down. He lit some candles on the table. They sat across from each other. Both had butterflies in their stomachs because it had been over a year since they had left each other. Preoccupied only with each other, they could only nod appreciatively to the friar and continue their intense discussion, not able to eat or drink.

Jadwiga replied hesitatingly, feeling nervous in front of this young man she had not seen in what felt like years, "I..." She glanced downward shyly and then back to her childhood friend. "You mean you didn't know there had been a change in plans? Were you not informed?"

"We found out just over a month ago. Your mother sent this," he replied, as he took the signed document, unrolled it, and handed it to Jadwiga. "The seal was broken by Dobeslaus. He breeched your privacy, even with Ladislau there!" he apologized.

She began to read the letter that Leopold had hastily scribed on behalf of the Cardinal and Mama. She couldn't believe what she was now reading. It mentioned that she could now be married to William on the Feast of the Assumption, and plainly stated that the marriage was to be consummated within this week. She dropped the letter.

Suddenly everything became confusing—marriage to William *this week*? Her face turned redder as she tried to keep calm and assess the situation. She had thought the age of consent was twelve, which would be February. She thought William had come to visit, and that would have been enough to delight her heart. She had not come to this late-night visit expecting to encounter this complicated situation.

"But… Mother sent the letter of consent for my marriage to Jagiello of Lithuania, and I was afraid for your safety, so we consented to that now. My advisors are meeting in Krewo to arrange my marriage to him in February. What is this? Was that a forgery, William, or is this a forgery?" She looked to her good friend to help her discern the truth.

He explained passionately, infatuated by the beautiful young lady in front of him. "No, Jadwiga, when Papa found out from Ladislau and the Teutonic Knights that your mother had signed consent to a Lithuanian union, we had no idea that the Poles would do it. We were just waiting to make arrangements now, before your age of consent. We heard nothing from you or your mother. We thought all was well. Your mother was persuaded to allow your marriage to Jagiello, who had true consent, but we went to her in Croatia, demanding the terms and our wedding be honored. It was Father that made her keep the agreements made with your father. And the cardinal, he, under the circumstances, has said that your age of maturity is now. We can be married by August 15, the feast of the Assumption."

He came to Jadwiga's side of the table. Jadwiga pivoted around. The look on his face was happy, but serious as he came to her. He got down on one knee in front of her and produced a beautiful ring—more beautiful than any she had ever seen. It was a simple flower like a water lily, small cut multiple-colored jewels made up multiple layers of petals. The candlelight made it sparkle in a way that reminded her of the luminescent globe in her dreams. Uncertainty filled her heart. Startled by the sudden turn of events, she shook her head in disbelief of what was transpiring before her eyes. *Is he proposing marriage?* Her heart raced.

Lovingly and with the highest respect and devotion his heart could express, William continued, "So, my queen, true love and desire of my heart, my little wife," he offered the last point with a smile, reminding them both of their youth and their marriage of sponsalia. "I do not have much to offer you. I am in fact without a kingdom, palace, or fruitful employment. But I have a true heart filled with love and devotion and promise you a life of love and joy, seeing that your every wish and desire is fulfilled. My promise is to make a family of our own in the service of God, this country, and its people. Will you marry me *again?* Forever this time?"

Jadwiga, overcome with love and devotion, suddenly felt that her betrayal of him had been a grave mistake. All her fears about his safety suddenly faded to nothing. They were unreasonable anyway. He was asking her to marry him. Overwhelmed by the infatuation of the moment, she replied, shaking her head with regret at having forgotten her vow and putting others ahead of him.

"William, I didn't mean to…"

He put his finger gently on her lips and shook his head. He held up the ring to her again, waiting for her answer. She smiled and nodded happily. *What else can I do?* Every part of me wants *this. Nothing else matters, and nothing would make me happier.*

"Yes! Of course yes! You are my true love and have always been!"

William smiled triumphantly, took her hand, and placed the ring on it with great love. Their foreheads now touched as they gazed upon it and the future it symbolized with them together soon, forever. They hugged each other happily.

All the loneliness and disconnectedness from family seemed to vanish now that they were together, and it seemed fitting and right to them both. They looked now into each other's eyes, and Jadwiga was overcome with a passionate love she didn't know she had. They kissed their first kiss with the light of the candles glowing a soft romantic glow. They now stood together, gazing steadily into each other's eyes, holding hands, realizing that the love that was planned so long ago was true for them. Not an obligation, not the fulfillment of someone else's plan, but something they both wanted—and left them alone in a universe of situations, single-minded in purpose and intention.

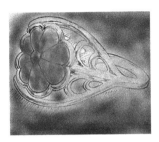

The very next day, Constance and Jadwiga, with some body-guards, left very early in the morning, as they sometimes did, for a forest ride on horseback. They came to a spot at which during the summer, they would sometimes stop to bathe in a stream that was on king's land.

"Guard, we are bathing here. We will bathe and call you if you are needed." The guards nodded. The two women began down the path through the trees. They walked beyond a deep pool to the shallow part of the stream, beyond where they should be. They waded through to a nearby clearing and waited for a moment expectantly. Ladislau emerged cautiously from the woods, motioning for William now that he knew it was clear of outsiders. The young couple, oblivious to the world, embraced and kissed and began to talk happily.

Ladislau and Constance, realizing their need for privacy, withdrew into the woods nearby and sat on a log.

"Ladislau, you have known me for some time now."

"Seven years."

"Aren't you worried about this sneaking around? You know Jadwiga made the decision for Jagiello mainly because she was concerned for William's safety and well-being? Aren't you worried about how the council will react to us taking matters in our own hands? How will everyone react if we see this marriage through in secret?"

"Who is the closest living relative in Poland to Casimir now that Louis is gone? It is *me*. They all seem to have forgotten that! I am

Casimir's great-nephew, I am the one who should have the greatest say, but because I've been gone for so long, so many of them think they have a greater position than me, but I'm the one who should be making the decisions here. And it's up to Jadwiga, and I will see to it that she is not forced either way. It should be her choice, not the nobles or the archbishop. I just want what's best for her, and I want her to be happy. I know how much she loves William, and I just wanted to give her the opportunity to not have regrets…to make sure she's making the right choice. She can't marry from compulsion as that would not be a true marriage. I just want her happy. And everyone *else* will have to deal with it!"

"I know you do, Uncle, so do I, so do I…" Constance sighed and hugged him, knowing they both loved her so dearly.

The next day, the meeting took place in the country, at the home of a great-uncle of Ladislau. Again, bodyguards waited respectfully outside, unaware that any meeting was happening. Ladislau and Constance had decided that it would be in the best interest of the young couple to speak and get to know each other better to make sure they both wanted to make this decision so hastily.

They went out from the back of the cottage to a nearby barn and rode the uncle's horses through the meadows until they reached a private spot in the far field near a stream. Ladislau and one of his men rode out nearby, but not so close that they would disrupt the privacy of the young couple. The two were now together sharing a picnic lunch.

"There is a Polish story that comes to mind looking at you now, young prince," Jadwiga said as she chewed on clover flower stems. "Tell it to me, Your Majesty." William smiled respectfully. Jadwiga stood to better dramatize her story. "Once there was a terrible fire-breathing dragon who would torment the poor peasants of the countryside of Krakow. He would eat the livestock and sometimes kill whole families with his fiery breath, leave nothing but ashes. The king did not know what to do and so offered a reward—the hand of his daughter in marriage for the man who could slay the dragon. But all the strong knights who dared try were burned by the dragon's fiery breath before even coming near! One day Krak, the shoemaker's son, who loved the princess from his youth—"

William pointed to himself, as if to say, "So now you're talking about me?" Jadwiga nodded quickly, not wanting to disrupt the flow of her legend, but blushing, lost her train of thought, so William assisted, "The shoemaker's son, who loved the princess from his youth…"

"Oh yes…he took a ram, cut and gutted it. He stuffed it with sulfur, sewed up the ram, and put it in the dragon's den. When the dragon awoke, seeing the ram, he gobbled it whole. Soon, Krak came out of hiding, jumped in front of the dragon, sword in hand as if to fight him! The dragon, thinking him any knight, tried to blow his fiery breath, but instead of killing Krak, he blew up from inside. The people were free at last, and the prince, he married the princess… Krakow is built on the dragon's hill."

"And what of the couple?" William asked.

"He became the best ruler Krakow has ever known," she finished triumphantly. "I love it out here, it's so peaceful… What if we were just normal people, simple peasants, and this was our home and we could have many children, and milk cows and collect eggs, and make cheese…"

"And have sheep and a garden, and you could spin wool…" William added. "It's beautiful, but difficult, you know… We weren't born for that life, I guess…" Grandmama came to her mind. She remembered her telling her this same thing. William's mood became sober and serious. "You're really at home here in Krakow. It feels like home to you now?" She nodded. "Would you leave it and come to Austria?" She shrugged. That question was far too complex to answer. He looked at her in a way she never saw him look at her before. It was with desire, and something about it made her timid.

"Jadwiga, we don't have to wait, you know…" he said as he pulled her close to him and took her face in his hands. "We can end this now, this waiting and hiding. Are we going to wait two more days? Why? I'm ready now. We have the church's blessing and God's. We are already married really." With this last comment, he kissed her.

Jadwiga, feeling timid, pulled away from him gently. "We can wait two more days." She needed to wait until the official time, even that was rushing things.

William, wanting only to please her and do what would make her happiest, answered resigned as he kissed her hand, "Yes, my lady, my queen."

～✦～

The still-bright waning moon shone again over the Franciscan orchard, where only the song of crickets could now be heard. There was a warm breeze and the smell of fresh earth and grass.

It was the next evening, and like metal to magnets, the two young lovers felt the need to see each other beyond anything else, even for a few moments. Jadwiga snuck out a servant's entrance into the beautiful walled garden she cherished so much. Jadwiga stayed along the wall so to not be observed until she came to the orchard, where the trees almost touched the wall and provided a screen from any observing guards from the castle. She gave a little dove whistle to hear where William was hiding, which was quickly replied. He was only twenty paces from her. *Good, he got the note from Clara.* He came out from under a tree, and they could barely make each other's faces out in the pale moonlight.

"Czesc!" Jadwiga could see how happy William was, as they gave each other a hug. "We don't have much time."

An unusual sound pierced the silent night and the cricket's melody. Suddenly, Jadwiga froze in her tracks, as did William. If Dobeslaus or the guards caught them now, there was no telling what would happen. Jadwiga stood frozen, cocked her head to listen carefully. She heard what seemed to be the sound of a young baby crying. It was getting louder and was more definitely the sound of a baby crying. A centuries' old gnarly grapevine climbed the wall of the garden. Jadwiga, impulsive and responsive to anyone in need, quickly climbed its height to see what was wrong.

"Jadwiga! It's just a cat…" He motioned with his arm for her to come to him quickly rather than carry on her intentions. "You'll get hurt. The guards may catch you. We don't know who's out there. It's not our problem, get *down!*" He whispered as loudly as he could. She motioned to wait, holding up a finger to her lips. The cry drew her up higher to the limb of a tree. William looked up, shaking his head as he cautioned, "Jadwiga, get down! You'll hurt yourself."

"But, I hear a cry...a baby...for sure, a baby!" she replied concerned.

"Jadwiga! Call the guard after..." Jadwiga, ignoring his counsel, jumped down over the wall and disappeared out of William's sight. He sighed and climbed the vine to observe and try to protect her from the danger she was now putting herself in.

Jadwiga landed on the other side of the wall with a thud, falling and getting a little dirty, but no one seemed to be around as she surveyed her surroundings in the dim moonlight. The cry was more distinct now as Jadwiga listened and moved toward the river. William, now at the top of the wall, decided to lie flat and observe her for a moment in case he needed to help her get back into the walled garden.

"Jadwiga, get back here..." William now risked more loudly.

Suddenly, the shadow of a woman ran from under a low tree, where the noise was coming from. Jadwiga stood frozen, but realizing it seemed to be a young woman only, she cried softly, "Wait, do you need help? Who is there?" But the young girl glanced quickly over her shoulder and ran away as quickly as she could. The girl had left the baby under the tree, in some bushes, and continued to run toward the bridge. Jadwiga's eyes adjusted to the dark. She came to the tree. "Who's there?" she repeated softly. No one answered, except the cry of the baby. She found where the baby was left in a woven basket, covered with some shards of wool cloth. She moved the cloth off the baby's face. With love and devotion of a mother, Jadwiga picked up the orphan and hugged and kissed it, the river gently running its course nearby and the crickets making a soothing song.

The baby lunged hungrily at Jadwiga to suckle on her face. She smiled and laughed, totally engrossed in the beauty of the baby and its angelic scent. Jadwiga gently rocked the baby. "Now, baby, it's all fine, all is well, shh...shh... I will take care of you, don't cry." She walked back to William, who observed it all silently from the wall, and stood decisively with the baby sheltered in her arms.

"William, tell the friars to open the front gate immediately." William hesitated, concerned about her safety. Jadwiga replied, "Go! I will meet them at the gate. It is only twenty paces from me. This mother has left the child, as an orphan…" William took another glance and, feeling there was no harm, disappeared to do her bidding.

As the friars were waiting for William's return, they quickly opened the front gate at his beckoning, and Jadwiga came in with the baby. The friars were used to receiving anonymous babies from mothers who did not feel capable of nurturing their own. They knew immediately what to do and began warming milk and cuddling the baby and checking its health near candlelight. Jadwiga, knowing the child was in good hands, said, "We'll bring her to the sisters tomorrow. I will come back early and take care of her until the sisters can take her. I think we should call her Serena, because I found her in the moonlight. I have to get back." She left the monastery hastily, now concerned that she might be noticed. William motioned to the friar with a finger that he would be back.

They walked together along the wall under large apple trees, which almost touched the garden walls, providing a shelter from any eyes of guards. William was quiet and seemed put off by her actions. They walked just beyond the point where they had met, each in their own thoughts.

"You never know who you save when you save a baby. They may be the most important person in your kingdom—a scholar, a priest, or a mason. God has some great purpose for them to fulfill," Jadwiga explicated. William shrugged. Jadwiga felt concerned and uneasy suddenly that they might be caught and felt like she needed to get back. She knew enough to trust her inner voice; it was usually right.

"Wait, don't hurry off yet, Jadwiga…" She paused, and they stood looking at each other. Somehow, the situation of the baby in need and the mother had put a degree of concern for others ahead of William for the moment and brought her back to real-life concerns. She couldn't seem to bring herself back to the romance of their secret meeting.

"I have to go, William…what if they catch you?"

William replied seriously, "Yes, Jadwiga, what *if* something does go wrong? What if I do get caught now? Let's not wait—you are the queen, you rule this kingdom. If we do it now, if we fulfill our marriage vows, no one will ever be able to stop us. You are the king of Poland! Be my wife starting right now." And he pulled her to him and kissed her.

Jadwiga, still in a pensive, serious disposition softened to the gentle and passionate kiss, but pulled away sadly. "William, look at us. Look at how we have to be… Did you stop to think at all about how we're supposed to live our lives? What are we to do, marry in secret today and then just expect all of Poland to comply with our wishes? Are we supposed to sneak around for years and years? What if someone tries to kill you? Don't you worry about this?"

"I don't know, and I don't care, Jadwiga. Did you ever think that if we have to, you could just leave Poland and we can live in Austria? Forget all this! All I know is that I want you. You're mine. Just fulfill the marriage now and then everyone will have to accept it. Don't wait, let's just do it now so no one can stop us."

"Soon, William, soon," Jadwiga insisted. She just had to wait, but another part of her didn't want to. Maybe he was right. No, she had to wait.

"Do you just expect me to walk away from my destiny?" asked William, suddenly worried and trying to make his case. "Jadwiga, a lot could happen between now and then. I have a bad feeling. Maybe it should be now. I don't ever want to leave you again, I can't live without you…"

Suddenly, a door slamming interrupted their conversation, and candles were lit in the looming Krakow Castle. Jadwiga, nervous and concerned, held his hand as she started to leave him. They both looked nervously in the direction of the castle.

"I can't live without you either. Tomorrow. Feast of the Assumption, with Mary's blessing." She turned to go, but he pulled her back to him, not having let go of her. He kissed her passionately, and she did also and then whispered, "I have to go…" She pulled away, looking back with love and concern then turned to quickly return home, hoping to not be noticed, as William looked on with love and concern as well.

✦

In another part of the city, Ladislau was residing with a wealthy elder nobleman and his family, an old friend of Louis of Anjou, Gniewosz of Dalewice. In the darkness, the residents of this peaceful abode were suddenly awakened and alarmed by a loud pounding on the door. Ladislau, a houseguest, was even more awakened when Dobeslaus burst into his room accompanied by castle guards with weapons fully drawn. Dobeslaus pulled a defenseless Ladislau from his bed and threw him harshly to the floor, his sword pointed to his throat—a rude awakening.

"Where is the Austrian rat?" shouted Dobeslaus. Ladislau did not answer, indignant and irreverent to his position. *"Answer me!"* he shouted loudly, holding his sword so close to his throat that Ladislau believed he would kill him.

"I already told you! Upon being turned away by you, he decided to return to Austria to gain his father's assistance. And that is a concern you might want to consider, that Poland may soon be at war with Austria due to your insolence," Ladislau feigned.

He barely finished speaking that Dobeslaus shouted once again, *"Liar!"* He then threw down a document next to his head, which Ladislau turned to observe so close to his face.

Gniewosz, the owner of the house, came in the door now with some men of his own. "Dobeslaus! How dare you enter my house like this at this hour, disturbing my guest? Have you lost your mind?" the frail older gentleman of court demanded.

"No!" he answered sharply. "But are we to lose a queen?"

Gniewosz looked at him questioningly and, even though he sided with William and Jadwiga, hid his position.

Dobeslaus barked in explanation, "This document, inscribed and hidden in town records, states clearly that there is to be a release of the prisoners of Krakow prison on the Feast of Our Lady of Assumption, in honor of the marriage celebration of Queen Jadwiga to *William of Austria*. A public and *legal* document!" The men did not respond but pretended to be as puzzled and concerned as Dobeslaus. They were surprised that such a document would exist.

"And what is that to do with my houseguest? You are not in authority over him! Leave the premises! We have no concern with William of Austria, who has returned to gain the help of his father, Leopold. Perhaps that is the matter you should be concerned about. Now leave before this becomes a matter for the courts!"

Dobeslaus seemed to waver. He didn't have real authority over either of these men. He abruptly, without saying another word, turned and left the household as quickly as he had come. After all, if Jadwiga was in his sight, under guard, there was no way for William to get to her.

As soon as they could be heard leaving the front door, Ladislau summoned the Gniewosz's teenage grandson, David, who had just come in, to lift him from the floor. As he lifted him, Ladislau began, "David, you must go to William. Tell him to exercise every caution and that they are aware of his intentions. Tell him I cannot be witness, as it is too dangerous. He must act alone and immediately. *Go!*" David nodded and, understanding the situation, immediately left the room in haste.

They all shook their heads in a somber, concerned state of mind as the sun could just be seen dawning on the feast of the Assumption of Mary. Just what would this day bring? They all breathed a collective sigh of concern and a prayer for the destiny of the young monarchs.

The Assumption of the Virgin, Bartolome Esteban Murillo, 1670

CHAPTER 19

Day of Decision:
The Feast of the Assumption

There was an evident increase in the number of guards patrolling the Krakow market this August morning. The summer sun warmed and wakened the town to its normal trading activity, the midsummer harvest now on display for sale in gracious abundance. David made his way to an elderly lady selling apples, standing by her crippled and apparently deformed son, his head covered to avert stares. David came to this "son" of hers and exchanged a quick word, as he took his arm, guiding him through the bustling town. David looked for a quiet, private place and escorted the poor cripple into the cathedral.

They came to a secluded spot within the mostly empty structure, except for some elderly widows praying. Finally, the two could speak privately.

"Ladislau says he cannot be witness, it's too dangerous. You must act immediately. They are aware of your intentions." He smiled a large smile of encouragement to William as if to say, "Way to go," fully aware and secure in the fact that he really beheld before him a prince who could always return a favor at a later time. "Remember me when you're king!" He continued encouraging.

"I will," William replied. He was frustrated and tired of the sneaking and worrying. He laid his head against the wall behind him, not sure what to do now.

David smiled mischievously. "I know a way into the castle. It is the worst possible way, but no one will think of it." William looked at him, wondering if he could trust his loyalty to him. He was feeling like he was beginning to miss home, and in this strange land, he felt outnumbered and unwanted, but he knew in his heart that Jadwiga loved him too, and that was all that mattered. Ladislau would not have sent him if he didn't trust him. For the moment, this young, skinny teenager was his only hope.

He nodded. "Fine, show me. Let's go."

The two young men exchanged their disguises for a worse disguise, the lowest possible imaginable sewage cleaners. David, knowing most of the young men in town, had swapped their trade on this day for a golden coin. The regular sewage cleaners gladly traded their chore without question or hesitation.

They came with a simple wheelbarrow and shovels. Their job was to remove sewage from the castle wall toilet. They walked by a guard, who disgustedly waved them by for their weekly ritual. They came to the opening and were repulsed and nauseated by the smell.

William hesitated. "Uhhh, is there no other way?"

"Not without getting caught," David replied. "They're on high alert. You have to climb up one level. Use the cracks to insert daggers, use these to climb. The hole is tight, but you can make it. Stay on the outer walls, they have very little filth on them," he advised. William paused. *Are you crazy?* But remembering the task at hand, he began to determinedly wrap clothes around his hands. "She better be worth it," David shook his head. "Send a trusted maid down in your place, dressed as you. Quick!"

William entered the stench-filled opening and turned to David one last time. "She's worth any torment this world can bring," and continued the otherwise impossible task of ascending the interior of the toilet facility, both hoping that no one would dare use it during these moments. *What would Paco think about this? What would father think? It doesn't matter. She's worth it.*

William scaled the interior pit wall as carefully as possible, using daggers as footholds when needed. What seemed an impossible task was labored but finally accomplished in reasonable time while David loaded the cart with a week's worth of excrement.

In the first-floor castle outhouse room, a teenaged maid cleaned the interior enclosure and spread flowers on the wooden bench, which served as a toilet seat. She had a soapy bucket of water nearby and opened a small shutter to let the air into the small enclosure. Suddenly, she saw a head from the opening of the hole, and although she had heard voices from below and was aware that the young men were cleaning the pit, she had never seen them come out this way.

William held one finger, still covered in rags—and now in excrement and urine—close to his lips. "Shhhhhh… William of Austria," he whispered, introducing himself, counting on the loyalty of the young maiden and his charm. "My good maid, in the name of Queen Jadwiga, I order you to silence. Lift the bench."

The wide-eyed, entranced young maiden, nodded, her lips tight and speechless. She guessed from the castle gossip what might be happening, as she found herself front and center of the romance story of the century, which every household and town's girl was well aware.

"Bring me clean soapy water at once," he ordered. "And you must return down there from this rope in my place, understood?" The girl looked doubtfully down the hole as William took a thick rope from his pack, tied it to the door handle and dropped the rope down the hole. "Oh, and this is what you get for your pains," and he handed the girl a bag of gold coins, which she grasped and shook her head in even greater disbelief at this great good fortune, changing from an attitude of disgust to a "can do" attitude.

She whistled softly for a young girl and waved her to the toilet room. "Fetch another bucket of clean soapy water."

The girl ran obediently, returning with the bucket, soap, and a cloth. As the older girl disappeared down the toilet hole, William received the clean water from the girl, who now fanned her nose with her hand and made a sour face.

"In a few minutes, when I'm clean, bring me to Constance. Shhhhhh." She nodded and sat outside of the toilet room until William summoned for one more bucket and then was semi clean and redressed. "Now child, take me to Constance," he whispered and smiled, giving her a golden coin. "And don't tell anyone but give this to your grandmother." She nodded and led the mostly clean William up the back stairway for servants toward Constance's quarters.

Constance received William at the door of her quarters. She sprang into action, pushing the child out the door, commanding her to silence and at the same time telling her to get her mother to bring hot water for a bath. The girl nodded willingly and scurried off. Constance turned to William in disbelief, shaking her head, trying to hide her doubt and concern.

"Constance, is she expecting me?" William asked.

"Well yes, but not like this. You are going in the bath!"

"Is she ready for me then, for us to be married?" he pressed.

Constance scurried him behind a screen as she pulled out clean clothes, which had been brought by one in Ladislau's company earlier. She hesitated and shook her head. An overwhelming feeling of melancholy and doubt was gripping her heart. All this hiding and fear didn't seem right. How would the Polish advisors react to this type of secret marriage on the part of Jadwiga? There was too much uncertainty, too much difficulty; this was not a good way to begin a marriage in fear and hiding and running scared, and she was afraid it could only bring bad things for the future.

"Constance?" William asked. "Is she ready? What's wrong?"

"There's nothing wrong. She will be waiting for you, so be quick, but at least one hour in the bath." Three maids came in and filled the bath with hot soapy water and left together with Constance.

～⁀～

The summer night was long and glorious as Jadwiga stepped out onto her balcony. It was her favorite time of day, twilight, and Krakow's lights were beginning to be kindled, and she smiled as she could hear loud and joyous singing in the square. She observed a high number of guards and was slightly concerned. Where was William? Was he going to make it safely to her tonight? She was feeling anxious, but the peaceful evening and celebration of the Assumption had left her with an underlying peace. She had placed her and William's life in God's hands at mass. She went inside, lit a candle near her bedside and knelt down facing a crucifix to pray her night prayers silently.

Shortly, Jadwiga felt a gentle touch on her shoulder. She turned and, realizing it was him, smiled lovingly, shaking her head.

"William! I can't believe you're here. You made it. You're here." He was handsome, well groomed, and clean. He knelt down beside her and hugged her tightly, and she took great comfort in his embrace. They looked at each other and then looked down as if to try to pray together, but they couldn't really. "Is this a dream?" Jadwiga said in the last pale glow of the sunset and with the candles' soft light, William kneeling by her side.

"No, it's not a dream, I'm here, and I'm not leaving…ever." He stood up, held out his hand, and pulled her up and toward him then kissed her.

"Jadwiga, of the house of Louis of Anjou, now that you have come of age, will you marry me, will you be my wife?" Jadwiga suddenly felt a rush of emotion. She thought about the past with her family, vaguely recalled her marriage, the priest making a tent over them, Mama and Grandmama's beautiful smiles, Papa's hug. Everything had brought her to this moment, and before her stood the most handsome young man she had ever laid eyes on, and she couldn't believe he would be her husband. How blessed she felt.

"Yes, William, yes, I will be your wife." They looked at each other for a brief moment with pure love and anticipation of their life together.

"Now, we will be married, and what is done cannot be undone, by anyone, ever. It is our bond which will always bind us as God has willed it."

As their hearts beat with the importance of this moment, there was suddenly some loud arguing from outside the room, down the hallway, which could only mean one thing as their loving exchanges suddenly changed to concern.

A group of men barged in, with Dobeslaus in the lead followed by four guards and Constance in the rear, pleading for them to stop. "*William of Austria, you are* hereby expelled perpetually from Poland!" Two guards grabbed hold of William, holding his hands behind his back. Dobeslaus came face-to-face with William. He was spitting mad, holding his sword to William's throat.

Jadwiga yelled a heartfelt cry, "Dobeslaus, *no!*" Trying to compose herself, remembering her authority over him as the Queen of Poland, she persisted with decisiveness and confidence she never knew she possessed. "*Release him*! If you bring harm to him, the same will be done to you and your entire family. I swear it!" This was so uncharacteristic of her and surprising to Dobeslaus that it changed his attitude slightly.

"If any harm comes to me, my father will invade Poland, with Sigismund of Hungary! And hunt you down and skin you like a fattened pig!" added William.

Dobeslaus removed the sword but repeated somewhat undaunted, "William of Austria, you are expelled from Krakow, from Poland, and your safety will not be guaranteed." Roughly, he shoved him toward the door.

"She is the *queen*, she commands *you*, fool," William shouted. "You'll pay for this, fool!" Dobeslaus and the guards held on to him, resolved to remove him from the castle. William turned to Jadwiga again, filled with passion. "Jadwiga, I love you, I'll be back, I promise!"

Jadwiga shouted, distressed and powerless, "I love you William, I will go to you!" Dobeslaus gave her one last warning look, as if, "Oh no, you won't, don't even think about it," looking at her as with disdain. They shoved William rudely out of the room as Jadwiga and Constance looked on with disbelief at the obstinate behavior of Dobeslaus.

Jadwiga began pacing her room with Constance looking on helplessly. She was in a frenzy of emotions: of love and anger at the same time and confusion. She paced like a caged animal. She was crying and angrily wiped away her tears, pacing three, four steps at a turn, pounding her fist in her hand, feeling frustrated and helpless at Dobeslaus's insolence. Constance observed from nearby, fretting, giving Jadwiga her space but not knowing what to do next.

Jadwiga lunged toward the window, which felt small and narrow, like a prison window. She fumbled for a glass lantern and set it on the windowsill, trying to light it *as a beacon of hope for William.*

She looked out into the distance. Constance helped her light it and looked back to Jadwiga, who was feeling out of her mind. She never saw Jadwiga so upset and distressed in her life.

Dobeslaus and the group of guards brought William roughly down the castle stairs, out of the castle to the outside and into the castle stables. Dobeslaus shoved him to the ground, onto hay. Still enraged and not sure what to do next, he paced for a moment, trying to work out his next move, staring at William, disturbed at the situation he found himself in.

William lay staring undaunted and remaining dignified, leaning up on one elbow. His intelligence stopped him from getting into a power struggle with an individual who had no real power over him, yet he was still full of youthful intent. He didn't believe Dobeslaus was stupid enough to hurt him, but he also knew he wasn't likely going to get back to Jadwiga easily.

Suddenly, from the darkness of the stables, Paco and William's bodyguard emerged, swords drawn to Dobeslau's back and to the backs of the guards. Paco spoke with his typical manly, cowboyish confidence. "So now, that's no way to treat a prince of Austria, tsk, tsk, tsk. Just wait until his father finds out. One move and I'll have all our swords pierce all your hearts." He motioned for William to get up. "Get a horse, William." He nodded toward the horses. William hesitated at this command but did not speak and obediently got a horse. He climbed gracefully onto the saddle.

Paco continued, "Go and get on down the back road south. We'll meet up down a way."

William paused, now looking down on the situation. "I will meet you again, Dobeslaus, but next, time it won't be this way. You'll be the one leaving," he swore. He turned his horse and ran off with some of the bodyguards with him.

The other bodyguards tied up Dobeslaus's men with reigns and leads that were hanging from the stalls. Paco tied Dobeslaus and now had him sitting on the ground. He nicked his chin with his blade, just enough just to give him a reminder of his words.

"We're on our way, don't you worry. Don't you follow us now or send your guard after us, 'cause then, we just might have to kill some

Polish. Leopold will be happy enough to have his son safe. It's all good now, no use causing war over young romance," Paco warned in his easy drawl. The rest of the group mounted their horses and rode off in the same direction as William. They left Dobeslaus scowling with anger, shouting curses as they rode off.

At the edge of the meadows beyond Krakow, near the darkened forest edge, William had galloped with his guard and now turned his horse back toward Krakow in the far distance. He could barely make out a light in what may have been Jadwiga's room. Was her heart breaking as his was? She was so upset; he had never seen her that way. Darkness and the sound of their horses breathing hard was all that surrounded them.

Paco and the other bodyguards now approached at a fast pace. "It's us."

William dismounted and fell to his knees as he looked on at Krakow castle in the distance.

Paco dismounted, "Get up, William, you are a prince, for God's sake." William just knelt and stared, his emotions getting the best of him. His worst fears were coming true, and he felt torn from his destiny after so close to it and torn away from his long-awaited marriage to Jadwiga, who he knew he loved. Paco pulled at his arm to lift him. They had to leave.

"I understand and am sorry, William, I pity you both and your suffering, but your life is in danger, especially if they follow, and it is my job to make sure nothing happens to you." It was late and the road ahead dark and uncertain. He had no choice.

"William, they might try to kill you, stop this! It's time to go, we have to hurry." William finally mounted his horse. Paco mounted his. The horses and men were restless. One guard lit a lantern and began down the dark forest path. William was the last to follow, urged on by Paco, but giving one last glance to the barely visible light in the window to now what seemed a fierce dungeon, which held his only love captive. He made a silent vow to himself that he would return and return with force.

Jadwiga finally went for solace to Constance, who hugged her as a loving mother would. She pounded her fists lightly on her shoulders. Constance gently took her hands in hers and held tight, speaking solemnly and honestly to her. "Jadwiga, we knew there would be problems. We knew this might happen. We know this could continue past your marriage. Maybe it isn't the right time now. Maybe we need more time to sort out a solution. And to be honest, it doesn't feel right to do this in hiding and haste and darkness. A marriage must be celebrated in light." Jadwiga sobbed now into her hands. She knew this all along deep inside.

"But we've been apart so long, and there are always so many miles and people and politics between us. Maybe I'd leave for Austria with him!" Jadwiga replied through a stream of tears. "If I let him go now, I may never see him again, do you understand Constance?" She didn't want to throw a tantrum, but she couldn't help stamping her feet and pounding the whitewashed, cold stonewalls that wouldn't budge anyway, just bruised her hands.

"No, it doesn't have to be…give it time child…," Constance tried to counsel.

"Don't call me child, *I'm not a child*," Jadwiga replied defiantly. And with that, she pulled away from Constance and headed for the door. *No way! They won't win.*

Jadwiga descended the spiral staircase as quickly as she could. Constance followed with difficulty. N*o, no, I'm the king! I am the highest authority!* I will command them. *They will do as I say!* She rushed through the kitchen, a late-night scullery maid stared, shocked, and then down another staircase into a wood storage room with a servant's exit, only to find it locked and barred.

She pounded on the castle door angrily with her fist because it had been barred. She spotted an ax sitting on a nearby woodpile and picked it up, brutishly smashing at the locked door. She was going after William. *It's my kingdom, my life. I'll decide.* She was trapped, and Constance just stood stunned, staying out of her way. Woodchips began to fly violently as she began to make progress on the wooden bar.

Suddenly, a very elderly Demytr, trusted advisor to the family from the time of Jadwiga's father, entered, looking upset and filled with pity for the circumstances Ladislau had updated him about.

He looked at Jadwiga and Constance, paused, and then went to Jadwiga, who by now had made some progress on the door. He waited and then grabbed the ax as she raised it to tear apart the wooden bar lock.

Jadwiga turned crazily to see who dared get in her way. *Who dared hold the ax?* When she saw her trusted and beloved grandfatherly advisor, whom she knew was holy and loved her sincerely, she softened, and her state of frenzied anxiety immediately stopped. He held the ax tightly and she lowered it and began to cry.

"My queen, forebear! Is anything worth this craze? You are the queen of Poland, a daughter of the church. What thing has driven you to this?" he gently and lovingly counseled.

She now turned to him as her helper, "Oh, Demytr, Demytr, they have expelled William. We were to be married! Tonight!" He understood and saw everything.

Just then, a young maid came and whispered in Constance's ear. Constance conveyed the message to an already-frustrated queen. "Jadwiga, the palace guards are outside the door!" Jadwiga shook her head in frustration and discouragement, unable to respond, feeling so discouraged and alone. *I am a prisoner, nothing more.*

Demytr reasoned with her with all due respect and simplicity, "Ah, good queen, my daughter. Come to Demytr, though not as appealing as a young lover. William has escaped with his guardian and bodyguard." *Escaped? At least he's safe.* But he was gone.

She came to him as a most precious and loving grandfather, whose love for her was selfless. Still holding the ax, she came to him and sobbed on his chest as he gently patted her back and her head. After a moment, he pulled back, took her face into his hands, looking her in the eyes. She looked up at him, sniffling, losing heart. The tears would not stop.

"You are still the king of this castle and all of Poland. No one is above you, not even the castellan. Is this what is best for you? Best for Poland and the church of Christ? Best for William…hmm?" He paused here, and she looked at him pensively.

Not the king of Poland, nothing but a prisoner! Wiping away tears, she now leaned on a nearby wall, emotionally exhausted.

"Now hear me out. The life of a king is difficult beyond imagining. He must give himself day after day to his kingdom, subjects, enemies, and last of all, his beloved family. The heart of a king is unselfish and giving. He gives over and over his will to the interests of his kingdom and politics. He wakes up each morning, unsure if someone will kill him or if he will be killed in this battle or that. He worries if this strategy is best or how to handle this unruly noble or peasant or mob. He seems to be the one who commands but is, in fact, commanded by every circumstance in his land. His family misses him as he is so often away solving disputes, and battles! Battle after battle, peace in our day is beyond him, and all he can do is dream of a better day. For all his wealth, he can only dream of a kingdom where there is no strife and greed and land claims and on and on…and most days, all the treasures of the kingdom do not seem enough to compensate him or his family, who must also sacrifice him. Why do you think the Poles have not yet found a king? Are there not enough men in Poland? The truth, which men will never admit or say, is that to be a king brings a life of strife. And though nobility demands obligations, it does not tear one from his family and a peaceful life. Nobility is preferred to kingship in Poland, and a heart large with courage, self-sacrifice, and good selfless intention is difficult and rare to find. You see the beauty in William and love him for it, but God sees the heart. Dearest Jadwiga, remember…that in all things, there is a *good* way…" He motioned with his one hand toward the door, which she had tried to tear down. "But in all things, there is a *more excellent* way."

He gently pulled at the long chain that hung around her neck, revealing the crucifix Jagiello had given her. And as he pried her hands from the ax handle, he put the crucifix in her hand and closed her hand around it. She shook her head solemnly then nodded and tried again to compose herself further. Demytr finished, "It is the Feast of the Assumption, let us put our trust in Divine Providence and the intercession of Mary most holy."

She leaned back against the cold stone, sliding down the wall with exhaustion. She sat on the dirt floor with her knees to her face and buried her head in her hands crying. She felt the truth in Demytr's words, her intellect now taking over again. She fought to put her feelings away to that little place deep inside, where she always had to tuck them. A flurry of mixed emotions fought inside of her. She felt almost sick thinking of losing William, as she felt sacrifice pierce through her heart and severing her from the person she cherished the most, as she resigned herself to letting him ride away, possibly forever from her and her kingdom. *He is leaving, as I sit here. He will be gone, if I sit here.* Something kept her in her lowly spot, and it wasn't lack of courage or zeal. The tears of frustration now turned to tears of sacrifice, burning her eyes and heart, burning away all self-interest and desire, until she would be resigned to the more excellent way.

Dymitr of Goraj, Jan Matejko

CHAPTER 20

Resignation

The morning dawned beautiful and bright as the roosters crowed and thousands of songbirds filled the air with their melodies. A cool fresh breeze made its way freely through her quarters. Jadwiga sat on her bed, introspective, and had not slept that night. She wondered where William was or if there were to be any more secret meetings. She wondered what this new day would bring. She knew that William must have left, and she realized that for his safety, it would be best. But a small part of her hoped that somehow she would see him in a secret meeting again. What if she had left in the night? Where would she be now? With him? Should she have eloped and left Poland for itself? They had her cousins who could have married Jagiello instead. No, they were not right for Poland. Papa had tailor-made her for this; no one else was meant to be here.

Her only place of consolation and comfort when she felt deeply upset, and she had never felt this deeply upset, was the great Krakow cathedral adjoining the castle. Here, she often took refuge in times of loneliness or discouragement, hoping that the grace of the Holy Spirit would supply for her many weaknesses. So this quiet morning, she made her way silently to the cathedral, followed only by her personal bodyguard, Henre. He waited inside nearby but gave her space as she entered the cathedral, now lit by the light of the sun bursting into the stained glass windows.

A choir of consecrated brothers sang morning Matins as she walked up to the front, normally a great comfort and fascination. She was oblivious to their praises. The smell of incense and beeswax candles comforted her. She came to a large black crucifix, knelt down, and tried to pray, making the sign of the cross to start. As she stared at the crucifix, still filled with mixed emotion and desires, she could not find the words to pray, so she just stared and tried to clear her head. *You gave up everything.* Tears began to stream down her cheeks. Had she been selfish? Would it have been wrong of her to leave with William? Was it wrong to love him and want him so much, to be with him and have a family? It had felt right, then how could it have been wrong? She felt so alone. *What do you want of me? What should I do?* was all that came to mind. No answer seemed to come to her, just the universal silence that most often accompanied her prayers, "Lord, help me, please!"

~~~

Days of travel had passed, and William and his entourage were now close to the Austrian border. They were headed home to Vienna. They stopped for food and lodging at dusk one night. The Mad Rose Inn was filled with a bustling community of travelers, merchants, and locals who were detached from the goings-on of Krakow.

William was sullen and melancholic as he sat in the inn, partaking in very little food and too much drink. Other travelers and peasants sang and laughed merrily in a corner, the effects of the gathering becoming cheerful and celebratory. The fire burned in the back where supper and stew had been cooked. The delegation had been given the best spot in the house because of their obvious importance, although they did not announce that William was indeed "William of Austria," to maintain safety and anonymity.

After a couple of hours, even William's men in his entourage began to feel happy and ignored the current situation from which they were escaping, and to which maybe they were now heading. They were lighthearted and ignoring their serious companion for the moment. They laughed and joked because they now were a day's journey home. William felt abandoned by their joy and merriment.

As the evening went on, William grew more sullen and moody. Every step away from Krakow and Jadwiga pulled at his heart and made him feel more and more that either a war or his death would be the end of this situation, and neither one was to his liking. He would rally Father. He knew that Father would back him if he insisted. If Jadwiga wanted him, she could apply pressure from her end. Or he could always just kidnap her, smuggle her out of Poland, and she could abdicate. Sigismund could help him. He knew he could count on Sigismund. He kept thinking of how much he loved Jadwiga and convinced himself that he could endure either death or war for her sake, if she wanted him to. No longer suppressed and no longer sympathetic, he began to resent the obnoxious Poles and Dobeslaus. *He would pay for sure*. And bitterness set in.

Paco seemed to be the only one who remained empathetic, and the voice of reason. "William, we enter Austria tomorrow. How shall you face the public of Vienna? With misery and despair over a woman? You are a man, you must play the man. You are a prince, you must play the prince. If you lose Jadwiga and Poland, you have to be accepted well at home. You cannot lose their confidence in your strength, strength of character. Though your heart is broken, pull yourself together now for this is no manner for you to enter your homeland as one whose soul has been torn from his bones and sinew."

William—now intoxicated, was feeling angry, bitter, and in tears from Paco's directives—scowled, trying to keep quiet. "Is it that simple? My soul is lost, my heart is weighed so heavily that it pains me… My purpose, my every dream is lost, my every hope and joy, my only love, my kingdom—all lost…" and he could not hold his head up. Trying to hide his tears, he put his head down on his arm.

A villager nearby noticed the wealthy group as well as the tension and tears. Not aware of whom he was addressing, he mocked, "Oh, poor spoiled little prince, what troubles and woes he must bear, pity him…" He called out loudly to draw negative attention to William and Paco, which they were trying to avoid. He tilted his mug to take a drink. William sprang into action immediately, jumped up, and grabbed his throat as if to strangle him, who was as tall but much huskier and older than William.

"I will show myself a prince and a man!"

Instantly, the Poles and the Austrians drew their swords and knives. The mood quickly changed with everyone's focus on the sudden brawl—everyone tense, uneasy, foggy in judgment. An Austrian guard slashed the Polish peasant's face.

Paco sprang into action, unarmed, diplomatically yelling out, "Forebear! Forebear! Prudence all!" Grabbing hold of William's shoulder, repeated to William specifically, "Prudence! Mercy, Your Grace…"

William released his grip, shoving the older man. Paco loosened his grip on William, directing William to the exit door. William hesitantly turned to leave while the bodyguard overlooked with their swords drawn. All eyes were on him. The man, choking from the hold William had on his neck, sputtered and shouted, "Austrian pig!" William spun around and punched him, knocking him to the ground. Enraged, William stomped outside with Paco close behind, leaving the guards to deal with the crowd.

William stumbled out of the inn to where other obviously poorer, very ragged elderly persons were seated around a fire, trying to warm themselves. He was overtaken by rage at not winning. He had failed Jadwiga. He grabbed an ax and began slashing at the fences and makeshift benches from tree logs and everything in his way, sending the innocent observers falling and scurrying for safety. They witnessed from the ground the ramblings of an enraged young man out of his mind. They just stared and blinked. He lost all reserve. "No love, no kingdom, no pride, no life, no wife, no man, no prince am I but just a restless gypsy with nothing…" And he fell to the ground yelling, "I will have my revenge! I will have her."

Paco grabbed William, pulled him up, shaking him hard, expecting him to stand; but when he let go, he fell again, as if he had no backbone. Paco picked him halfway up this time, grabbed the back of his hair roughly, and shoved him so that he was face-to-face with an elderly, sweet-looking bystander who had taken cover behind the log seat and was observing everything with meek concern. Paco had William's arm tight behind his back and shoved him roughly to the peasant. He was scolding now, in a temper himself.

"See him? See this man? He attests to one truth—that the dreams of youth are nothing! Look at him!" He lifted William's head, still gripping him by the back of his hair so William had no choice but to stare the old man straight in his face. "He had dreams, he once loved, had hope, and it all fades away! Such is the fate of mankind—that some dreams come true and they are Providence's gift, but you... young ass! Most of our dreams dissipate... He knows this best! Look at him!" He commanded the young handsome prince gruffly, "In his eyes, you see lost dreams, lost love, strife, difficulty, suffering, disappointments, struggle. Look at him! He knows the truth about life!"

He threw the prince down on his back. By now, many men had come out of the inn and were observing quietly the spectacle, their desire for revenge playing out in front of them. "A man knows that dreams are illusion, and all we have is reality and whatever we make of it, here and now! Not what could have been or should have been! Reality forces us to see that some things are beyond us..." He gestured toward William. "Some things are beyond you, be thou a prince of Austria or be thou a mortal man, most things are beyond even you..."

Paco looked around, noticing the silent audience around the fire and those who had crowded out of the inn and the bodyguard who all were silently observing the spectacle and Paco's speech like a well-rehearsed play. They began to nod in agreement, and some began to clap as the others shook their heads and returned to their merriment, now ready to forget about the earlier drama. They returned into the inn. Paco gave them a shake of the head and returned his attention to William, feeling bad that he might have been too harsh.

He held out his hand to help William up and continued, now quietly and heartfelt, with a sympathy which was not characteristic of him. As he held out his hand, William covered his face in self-defense, mistaking his intention to smack him hard. He helped William to a private quarters' entrance with beds of hay and roughly settled him in bed.

William lay down and looked up at Paco. He was exhausted and almost passing out, "You, Paco, you will go home to your wife, your young children, to your life… I, I have nothing. No love, no life…" He began to fade off to sleep.

Paco, playing the father, smiled down at him. "Leave boyhood, this night in Poland! Enter Austria a man."

Jadwiga had settled into a melancholy state, which was unusual for her, over the weeks following William's forced departure. She had, little by little, given up hope of William secretly surprising her somewhere on her path, and the thought that he wouldn't saddened her. Ladislau confirmed to her that they had left the region. A part of her heart hoped he maybe had made his way back to her, and if he had, she would have left with him.

The delegates returned from Krewo and confirmed the marriage arrangements to Jagiello. They looked sympathetically at Jadwiga after hearing the events that had occurred while they were gone. She saw they realized more and more the sacrifice they were asking of her but still expected her to carry out what they all thought was in the best interest of Poland. She tried not to resent them. They couldn't all be wrong about what was best for Poland, no doubt, but could they be wrong about what was best for her? Jadwiga took comfort mostly in the cathedral, feeling more and more her Krakow home a prison to her, confined and restricted by the ideas of everyone around her. The reality of duty was now a cross she felt put on her shoulders.

One day as Jadwiga knelt close to the altar and the crucified Christ, her head resting on her arms, she heard scraping. A worker was cementing an area of the cathedral floor. She noticed a young woman, who must have been his wife, come in with a number of young ragged-looking children. The eldest was carrying a baby. The mother seemed to be asking for something, maybe money, Jadwiga guessed, and the man shook his head. He had nothing to give them. The mother replied with frustrated but respectful gestures. He shook his head and continued to work. There was nothing to give. They left quietly, and one child noticed Jadwiga and stared at her. He was thin and pale with bare feet but smiled at her. Jadwiga smiled a little and waved. They left, and Jadwiga returned her gaze on the beautiful crucifix.

She focused all her strength on Jesus. *I love you, Lord, but what you are asking is difficult.* She tried to love God above all things with her whole heart, mind, and strength. *What is it you want of me?* Enraptured in this intense moment, her pain knotted up inside of her. She offered it all up to God. The intensity of her burden and her love of God gripped her heart. It was in this intense moment she received an awesome consolation, and a word from the great God she loved and wanted to serve so well: "Seek first my kingdom, and everything else will be given to you. Join your sacrifice to mine for the love of all mankind. You are my beloved daughter." The words were clear and seemed to come straight from the mouth of the crucified Christ, the Son of God. *Jesus! You spoke to me! Thank you, Lord, thank you, Lord!* A waterfall of peace and confidence, joy and love filled her heart and calmed all her inner turmoil. Tears of joy accompanied this moment of consolation. God was asking her to do this, but He would be her strength. She could trust in Him. She had to kneel still in this beautiful moment for what seemed like hours. Finally, Jadwiga pulled herself up and walked to a confessional.

It had been a month since her confession, before William had come. The priest listened attentively as she began, "For thinking only of myself, for giving way to despair, for pitying myself and neglect of my duty…for these and all my sins, even those of which I am not aware, I am truly sorry." She sighed deeply. *Help me not to be selfish.* She was ready to move on and didn't want to continue living like this. She wanted to get back to a peaceful, happy life.

The priest, always a source of great comfort and wisdom, which she took to come from God himself, paused for a moment and then in a consoling tone answered, "You are most beloved of all God's children. Remember, Christ said, whoever leaves mother, father, brother or sister for love of Christ, their reward will be great in heaven. My little one, seek first the kingdom of God and all good things will be granted to you. Whoever puts his hand to the plow and looks back is not fit for the kingdom of God… You have so much to give and to do for others…" Jadwiga nodded now with certainty and confidence as his words reflected and echoed that which she was hearing in her heart. *Lord, help me to be a strong ruler for Poland and bring peace to the land I inherited.* She nodded and was at peace again as the priest finished, "Now, for your act of contrition…" He granted her absolution. Her tears now turned to tears of sorrow for her selfishness as the face of the thin, pale child came back to her mind.

Jadwiga left the confessional. As she returned to kneel at her usual spot and pray prayers of penance, the scraping of the man who was still continuing his work in the cathedral brought her to reality. She looked over at him, taking pity on him, realizing he was poor. He and his family were thin, and he wore ragged, tattered clothes. She walked toward him. He bowed to her but continued his work. As she walked, she toyed with the ring on her finger that William had given her. She took it off as she walked toward him.

She came to him and said a word to him about the quality of his work. He smiled and nodded. Jadwiga didn't think he knew who exactly she was. She offered the ring to him, but he seemed startled and puzzled. She asked, "May I?" gesturing toward the wet cement. The peasant worker was too shy to reply and gestured as if to say, "Whatever you wish."

Jadwiga removed her shoe and put her footstep in the wet cement. Now she smiled at the worker, wiped her foot on a cloth and put her shoe back on. She surveyed the footprint then held out the ring to the worker. "My man, take it in payment for ruining your work... You must..." She took his hand and placed it in his palm, closing his hand on it. "If anyone questions you, tell them to speak to me. Put it to a great purpose." She walked out of the church, and the worker stared at her and the ring in disbelief as she left the great cathedral.

From that point, Jadwiga tried to carry on with her duties and obligations in a renewed way. She returned to the orphanage, which she had not visited in weeks, and to the sisters. The babies, as always, were a great source of joy and consolation for her. Here she cuddled and helped with her favorites, the little babies and baby Serena. She loved them dearly. She also returned to the castle and other political concerns, and if she was sad or upset, no one knew of it.

She did not allow herself to talk or think of William in these terms any longer, except when late October arrived, she decided to let William know that they both must set their course to different destinies. She sat down to scribe a letter to him herself, which she entrusted to Henre its safe delivery:

RESIGNATION

Dearest William,

It is strange how what seemed essential in the heat of summer and its passions has all been buried by the reality of autumn and winter. All that was alive and bore fruit is now dormant for the long winter ahead. And William, it is with a heavy heart, and both tears of love and endless devotion that I write to you to tell you that my love and respect for you will live on forever. In a different place and time, our true love may have been right, but what I fear worst in life is a life void of peace, a life lived in fear of losing that which I love most. You would have never been safe in Poland, William. There will be those who would have tried to kill you our whole life, and I love you too much to live with the fear every day of losing you. Losing you once is more that any heart could ever bear. Then there is the matter of the conversion of Lithuania. With me, offer our great suffering as a sacrifice of love for mankind that all may be one and so that Eastern Europe may achieve peace. I've prayed, William, and it is what God wants. Enter with me into this sacrifice together for the good of the world and His church.

Yours unto eternity, love, peace, and joy,
Jadwiga.

Seal of Jadwiga of Poland

William received the letter confidentially delivered to him in Vienna by Henre. He had been strategizing with his father as to what needed to be done and a proper course of action under the circumstances. Leopold was not interested in war with Poland, even at the urging of the Teutonic Knights and William. He was delaying a response by fighting smaller battles he had told William he had to resolve first.

When William received Jadwiga's letter, he was greatly disturbed by its contents. He had expected Jadwiga to fight for their relationship and wield her power and authority in their favor. He could not imagine that she had simply given up on them. But this was her handwriting, and he knew she was too young and good to fight the forces and pressures around her.

He crumpled up the letter angrily and threw it into the fire. He wiped away tears, disappointed and frustrated as he stared at the burning letter, shaking his head. He felt betrayed by circumstances and those closest to him, even Father. The love in his heart was overtaken by disdain and stubborn pride. Every day had brought them farther and farther apart. He wanted to go still and kidnap her, but he knew this was now a matter of the kingdom's security; the circumstances where overwhelmingly against them, and Jadwiga had resigned herself to it.

It was only a matter of weeks before another sword pierced William's heart. Leopold was killed in Switzerland in the Battle of Sempach Lake by a group of peasants, and both his spirit and intentions to resolve this matter were crushed by Leopold's death. Without Leopold as his help, William's powers were more limited than ever. The time to act was running out. Sigismund refused to return to Poland. His only allies now were the Teutonic Knights, more specifically their leader, Conrad Von Rottenstein.

CHAPTER 21

The King from the East

It was a cold, frozen, snowy December when no visitors would have been expected that Rottenstein opened the doors of Marienburg castle to see William and his men, covered in frozen rain, had arrived at his threshold.

"I am William, of Austria... My Father, Leopold...is dead...," William stammered, standing at the door, half frozen from the treacherous conditions they had just experienced.

"Leopold? I am so sorry, boy, my condolences. Come in, come in, and be warmed... This weather is not fit for the devil!" He welcomed the party in hospitably. "Welcome, William."

The party was sheltered, changed and clothed, and now were being fed at the supper table, with warm tea; and a large group of seventy men in the dining hall—knights, workers, and even servants— ate a hearty meal in a comfortable dining room with two extralarge fireplaces at either end. Servants continued to bring servings of ale, as the special visitors were well accommodated.

Rottenstein's mood became more somber as the dinner went on, and he could see that William was not happy and tight-lipped. He spoke confidently to his guest. "What's on your mind, William?"

"I came for your help. I want to stop Jadwiga's marriage to the Lithuanian. We were married at Hainburg as children, and I was to fulfill the marriage last summer, but they threw me out. I had to leave."

Rottenstein nodded. The last thing he wanted was a Lithuanian on the throne of Poland. "I simply cannot provide an army large enough to fight all of Poland on your behalf, William," he continued, disgusted. "There are other ways though..." He paused as he schemed different solutions to the problem at hand.

"Help me get to her, help me speak to her—that's really what we need! They are forcing this marriage on her. I know she loves me, she told me... The longer I wait, the less chance I have to get her back!" William continued.

Rottenstein held his hand up to William's ranting, annoyed with his personal teenage dilemma and narrow view. "This is intolerable! A Lithuanian on the throne of Poland? Lying and deceitful...mmf..." Rottenstein added to the chorus, his anger rising into his throat.

"She is convinced it is a good thing...a holy thing," William continued.

"The Poles have gone mad! Those Lithuanians are filled with pride to ever think..." Rottenstein grumbled.

"Get me to her..." William insisted. "Get me to her, and I will take care of this once and for all. She is my wife after all, and we consummated the marriage, and she is my wife, whether they like it or not..."

"You consummated the marriage? Why didn't you say so? So it is true! How can she even marry Jagiello if your marriage has been consummated?" Maybe the prissy little king was not so good as everyone had been enchanted to believe! The Pope will never approve. "We will contact the Pope on this point, speedily, so he can intervene from the southwest to put this insanity to its proper end! I will get you to her, and Jagiello will have difficulty as well. I will see to it!" William nodded.

A few days after William's arrival, Rottenstein received a personal summons to the baptism of Jagiello from Ladislau. Once Ladislau had realized the inevitable, he now sided with the Polish nobles for Jagiello's ascendance to the throne. He had requested the infamous head to be the godfather of Jagiello. None other than the idealistic king herself instigated this act. She honestly desired all involved to be at peace and share a common vision of brotherhood as neighbors.

"Leopold is dead, and now this…?" Enraged, he threw down the invitation. "Godfather? Godfather to Jagiello of Lithuania? Or shall I say godfather to Jagiello, king of Poland! Ugh… I am sick, sick!"

In light of Jagiello keeping his vow to become Catholic, nothing should have pleased him more, but hate is often rooted deeply and cannot be taken out without causing pain, and change was inevitable.

Looking at William, he realized he scarcely had an ally in this unseasoned warrior who had come with no troops and held interests vastly different than his own. He was a useless tool. He didn't care for this young man, but for now, he was his only ally.

"You there, you there!" Rottenstein now yelled enraged, making William jump. Everyone in his presence was customarily on edge and on high alert. "Scribe! You tell that pagan bastard devil that I am sick and the weather is far too treacherous and that I thank him for his thoughtful gesture, but it is impossible for me to attend his baptism and wedding, and far more impossible for be—to ever be—his godfather," he replied, throwing his stein at the messenger, who taking this as his dismissal bowed and left hastily watching his back.

What would be his best move now? Maybe William had turned up in time to be the solution. He had to be conniving to win this battle of wills. There had to be a way to undo them all. He rubbed his chin and beard, as was his habit when thinking through intense battle plans.

William smiled and shook his head, beginning to appreciate the severity of his new patron.

<hr>

Winter came quickly after the November letter, and Jadwiga waited patiently for negotiations to be finalized; but as she did, so her own anxieties began to surface. She was marrying this man almost three times her age who she had never met. She knew fear had a tendency to accompany the unknown, but what if he was just unbearable? How could a marriage work with him after she was so sure William was her soul mate?

She recalled how cordial Jagiello's brother Skiergiello had been to her and how he was quite normal in appearance, but he was his younger brother, and images of a marriage to an old, deformed man, as much as she tried to stop them, kept creeping into her thoughts.

She often worried that the Polish nobles were mistaken about his sincerity of heart. What if all this was just a ruse to fool all of Poland and this man-husband she was now to accept as a joint ruler was a fraud? What if her sacrifices turned out to be for nothing, or worse yet, what if for a deceitful purpose? Despite her prayers and initial resignation, she could not suppress these fears and doubts. What if this was the case? If the marriage didn't happen with Jagiello, is there any way William would take her back? She already knew their mind-set was fixed as they urged her to this great responsibility, but was their personal interest in using Jagiello and Lithuania as a shield ultimately going to be a good decision for all of Poland and Poland's future? What would this new life bring for her? Would Jagiello be good, kind, and honest, or would her life now be filled with even more pain and loneliness? She was the one who would have to live with the day-to-day ramifications of their decision, and she refused, even at such a young age, to blindly come into a marriage that could spell disaster for her plans of forging a dynastic family in Poland. He had to be right in her judgment. Everyone knew a forced marriage, not entered freely and willingly, was not a marriage at all.

So she enlisted Constance to help her set up her own secret delegation apart from the noblemen of Poland. Constance arranged a private meeting with Peter Szawichost, a steward of Krakow, to ensure that Jadwiga's wishes on the matter were cleared. "Well, you might understand her anxiety. She is to be wed within months, and these stories plague her mind. It is not too much for a queen to ask. She must enter the marriage freely, out of her own accord, not forced by the nobility."

Szawichost nodded in agreement sympathetically realizing that ultimately, this young girl standing before him was indeed the ruler over everyone in Poland. "Yes, you are correct to say so, but all the plans are set. This should have been dealt with much earlier. It is far too late to be dealing with such things!" he answered, facing Jadwiga now. "I have seen him myself, and I assure you, he is a normal man in every sense. These are maids' tales you are hearing. On my life, he is no part animal!"

Constance persisted, "All we need is sworn testimony that he is, in all parts, a normal man. Not like a horse or any other beast. She cannot find out after the marriage that he is not what we think!"

Szawichost, trying to hide his annoyance and remember his place, replied, "Fine, I will observe him myself to see if such tales be true or false. You women must be in need of greater occupation, so much time given to talk—you talk yourselves into frenzies."

Appalled by his disrespect, Constance, turning red in the face, scolded, "Peter! How dare you address Her Majesty as such! And furthermore, you are commanded to silence about this mission, and any breech will meet with stiff penalties."

"My apologies, my Queen Jadwiga, I am truly at your service." He bowed sincerely. Jadwiga nodded her consent as he left the room quickly to avoid the ladies noticing any more cynicism on his face.

∽∽∽

Peter's mission brought him to the Lublin castle of Spytek to "pay homage" to Jagiello, who was slowly making his way to Krakow for his February baptism. Upon his arrival, it was found that Jagiello and his brothers, Skiergiello, Kiergiello and Boris, were all guests. Jagiello still had his long braided hair and beard but, by all other accounts, was the picture of a fit and healthy thirty-six-year-old man. Peter simply wanted to accomplish this mission quickly without interference or delay and had only briefed his friend Spytek who trusted him completely of his purpose knowing his position was close to the queen.

"Spytek, there can be no hint that it is the queen's concern," he said as they walked down the castle steps to the lower level.

"Your timing could not be better. Just follow me. Trust me and look surprised!" The two men entered a medieval sauna room. They were fully dressed, and so much steam came from the fire and rocks that Spytek waved his arms frantically, immediately beginning to sweat in his full winter attire while acting like a tour guide for Peter. He stated loudly, "And here Peter, we have the sauna. Because it is so cold this winter, we make good use of it…"

Jagiello emerged, squinting from the steam, his entire abdominals visible, quickly surrounded by his brothers and cousins, all strong handsome men, sweating. The brothers were quite a sight to behold in their sauna as all the years of physical endurance had left them all brawn and well muscled.

Spytek and Peter just stared for a moment then shook their heads. Peter squinted and waved steam away to get the best look possible. "Ohhh, well, good men, excuse us, pardon, I was just showing old Peter here the pipe, uh, the piping hot sauna—whew, we are too old for this, Peter, how can you young men just stand there, uhhh, stand it? God bless you. Uh, see you at dinner." The group of handsome men just looked at them inquisitively, looking exceptionally good, while Spytek directed Peter toward the door. The two exited, slamming the door quickly and leaned on the door to make sure they had privacy, looking relieved, catching their breath.

Spytek exclaimed triumphantly, "Well, that was easy enough!"

Peter replied in his fatigued, annoyed manner, "And now how am I to reply to the queen? 'My fairest young maiden, you will be more than pleased?' or 'My dearest queen, he is quite satisfactory?' or how about, 'He is sure to please'?"

Spytek replied, tongue in cheek, "Definitely low risk to personal or national security. Maybe we should leave it to her to see he's as big as a mouse."

Peter, rolling his eyeballs, reluctantly answered, "Some days I loathe my duty. I'm glad this part of the mission is over with! Make sure they are shaven clean—at least."

Soon after Peter had been sent, Jadwiga received word from the archbishop, who summoned her to question her about her marriage to William. With the baptism, marriage, and coronation of Jagiello only months away now, the bishop had new concerns of his own.

"My lady, I must speak to you in private. Your maid may stay." Jadwiga asked all but Constance to leave the room. "I hope you are in good health. With the wedding plans coming upon us in such great haste, I wanted to speak to you in regard to your upcoming marriage. Firstly, I need to know that you are not being forced into this marriage and that you are deciding to marry Jagiello because *you* have decided so. You realize a forced marriage is not a true marriage?"

"Yes, my lord, I do realize and I have given my consent. The nobility has chosen to acknowledge Jagiello's request as valid. My mother has given me permission to choose, and I do so willingly." At least with her mind, she did willingly; her heart was not fully convinced just yet.

"I want you to know that the church is filled with gratitude at your willingness, as so much good and unity is needed at this time. Everywhere in Europe, there is bickering, strife, factions, squabbles, murder, plots, land claims. The sun rises and sets on restless, selfish pursuits and duplicity. We are eternally grateful for your cooperation."

An awkward silence followed between the three as the bishop reflected briefly how best to approach his next controversial question without offending the purity of the queen before him who, by all appearances, was the picture of meek beauty and reason.

"There is another difficult issue we must address." Again, he paused. Jadwiga could read the concern and pain in his face. Did he actually understand the pain in her heart? "It is the matter of your marriage of sponsalia to William."

"Yes, this I will renounce on my twelfth birthday. I have contacted him by letter to tell him I will not marry him," she replied definitely, but as she said these words, something in her heart tightened like a knot.

The bishop shifted in his seat uncomfortably. Jadwiga looked at him questioningly. "William is claiming that the marriage, your marriage, was consummated and that you slept together for weeks... and that you are being forced to marry Jagiello against your will."

At this, Jadwiga gasped, and her face turned red and redder as she just shook her head and stared in disbelief at what the bishop was implying now and at the implications that she would lie and that William was now "bearing false witness" against her. She couldn't speak. She felt something she never felt before well up from the depths of her. Normally meek and calm, she now found herself working hard to gain her composure and humility. "Oh, but this is false, these are false accusations!" Jadwiga exclaimed. "He is bearing false witness..." Constance simply could do or say nothing but gasp and shake her head open-mouthed.

"I have to ask you both, do you understand the meaning of *consummation*? Do you know what it is?"

Constance felt embarrassed in the presence of the bishop discussing these matters, but blurted out, "Well yes, I know what it is, and I instructed my lady when it was thought to be that she would marry William in August."

"It is the holy act of matrimony that God has made to bind two people for life," Jadwiga stated simply and thoughtfully. She had not bound herself to anyone for life.

The bishop nodded. "I am aware of what occurred in August and that Jadwiga was to marry him, and if this union was begun, then that is fine, you were perfectly able to give consent to it as you had been married already as children. You must understand that you would have done no wrong in fulfilling your marriage vows, and such a marriage would have to be respected. I am not here to accuse you of wrong, just to clear the facts of the matter to clear the way for your marriage to Jagiello or William. So did you consummate your marriage to William?"

"No, I did not," Jadwiga replied firmly. "The truth, I will tell you, is that we were going to the very moments that he was caught. That was our wedding night for us. That was our plan, but it never happened. Because of the castellan, it didn't, which I eventually took as God's will even though initially, I was alarmed and distressed at losing him. I loved him, but I have come to see that it was an intervention from God."

He then turned again to Constance. "Can you confirm this?"

"I can only confirm what I know, that it seemed to me the couple did not have time to do so, and until that time, she was always with me—well, mostly always with me."

"So there were times when they were alone?"

Constance stared thinking. "Well, not always," she answered embarrassed, as though she had neglected her duty. "Yes, there were times when they were alone," she admitted, and her head and shoulders dropped momentarily. "But I have known Jadwiga her whole life, since age four, and I have never known her to lie once, so her word is as good as gold. That's all I need to know."

Jadwiga listened silently as disappointment took hold of and sadness came into her heart. Constance was the only one who knew her the best. Not even William really understood her.

The bishop answered, seeming satisfied that he found the truth in Jadwiga's testimony. "I believe your word is solid, and I will attest that the marriage to William was not consummated." He advanced toward Jadwiga to hug her and Constance, assuring them that all was fine, happy that these necessary formalities were over. He left them to themselves.

The William she knew and loved was not who she thought he was if what the bishop said was true. In this medieval world of broken messages, she refused to believe that William would do such a thing to destroy her honor and reputation. She could only guess that this was his desperate attempt to have her back, and suddenly, her heart was filled with understanding.

The events of the day ran through Jadwiga's mind again and again. She began to think of the problems that this claim would cause in Poland, Lithuania, and for Jagiello, through all of Europe, and the church. She guessed that if William had really made these claims, he could not have possibly thought through the ramifications, and she was disappointed that he had not listened or respected the decision she had made and wrote to him about. Not even William listened to her. Did anyone respect her or her authority? It certainly didn't feel like it. She stayed in the meeting room all day as she thought and pondered all these things, barely able to eat despite Constance's urging. She wouldn't leave the study, and Constance was growing concerned. It was in the evening that she discovered what she would do.

Albrect, her beloved mentor from her youth, William's uncle, must have become the Duke of Austria now. It had been years since she had seen him at Papa's funeral. A sudden love rushed into her heart as she thought of the kindred spirit who had been such a source of love and understanding for her, her truest friend. She realized she must appeal to his good will to control William and set the record straight for her, to clarify the truth. She knew she could count on him to fix this dilemma.

So she sat down to write a second letter to Austria. Constance was relieved that she found a solution.

Dearest Albrect,

> *I hope all is well in Austria, my dearest uncle. Here in Krakow, as you have no doubt heard, my circumstances have changed. I regret that we will no longer be relatives as had been anticipated by both my father and your dear brother, Leopold. I was so sorry to hear of his untimely death. If he and Father had both lived, my circumstances and William's would be so different now. I often think of you and my time in Austria with great fondness and hope that our relations will continue peaceably.*

> *Without doubt, you have heard and know of the new circumstances in which William and I find ourselves. Even Mama and Maria are experiencing their own troubles in Hungary as I write. Ladislau will update you and clarify things.*

> *As you well may know, I have decided, for the sake of Christendom and in accordance with the will of my countrymen, to discontinue the marriage, which you yourself were witness to.*

I am disturbed by recent rumors as I undertake this sacrificial choice of marriage to Jagiello, grand duke of Lithuania, whose character, faith, culture, and heritage is mostly unknown to me. Disturbing rumors that my marriage to William was consummated. Please be assured that no such act was fulfilled. Please, Albrect, as an uncle and friend, I beg you speak to William to be prudent and understanding about this sacrifice, which we undertake for the sake of the church and Christendom. I have prayed and discerned it to be God's will, and for me a sacrifice, which will remain so for my life.

Please speak to him to help him see the good in it. As you taught me, this life is filled with strife, and above all, in all things, we should undertake those things that bring about goodness and peace.

I leave this matter to you to impart to William proper action and honesty in this case, and to correct any ill will so that he may live in peace and contribute to the peace of European society, which I undertake to develop in giving myself to the cause by love rather than war. You taught me to love peace. Please counsel William, and I will pray for both of you. God bless you, and you are welcome always to Krakow to visit.

Lovingly, your best of friends,
Jadwiga

She would send it by Uncle Ladislau, who was now residing in Krakow, watching everything closely, and request that he personally take this letter to Albrect and return with a reply.

She sealed the letter with her wax signet, pausing and sighing deeply as she gazed into the fireplace. She had not council of a father, a mother, or sister, but only Constance who, even though she tried to control her anxiety about the situation for Jadwiga's sake, was not very good at hiding her own feelings.

Her advisors and governors were older men who concerned themselves very little about the sensitivities or feelings of a young woman. They seemed to care little for what she was really thinking, but she was quick to always put on a good face when working with them. She knew the difference between duty and feelings. In her case, work was to be her home life, and the two could not be separated.

She sighed. One by one, all the people she had known and loved in her life seemed to be drifting farther and farther from her. Her heart ached as she thought of Maria and Mama, who she had just recently heard had lost the Hungarian throne to Charles of Durazzo from Naples, and that Maria's future marriage to Sigismund was now in question. She was so far away she didn't even know how to help them. Everything seemed to be falling apart, and everything and everyone she cherished seemed to be fading away. A tear escaped to betray the pain and loneliness that now pierced her heart, dropping on to the letter sealed now with wax and her tears of sacrifice, tears of duty.

CHAPTER 22

Deception

One day in late December, a messenger arrived specifically for Jadwiga. Since most business was conducted through her advisors, it was unusual that the messenger insisted on hand-delivering the letter to her in person. Was it news from Mama or Maria? She met with him briefly to receive the letter.

The young messenger bowed kindly to her. "My master, the bishop, would like to meet you at Oswiecim. He asks that you open the letter and reply directly to me." Jadwiga accepted the letter and gave an understanding nod to him. She was in a receiving room only with Constance and a fire burning brightly, to where she waved the messenger to sit by and warm himself. She read the brief letter, which was a summons from the bishop to Oswiecim, fifty kilometers from Krakow.

"Constance, the bishop is requesting that I visit his parish at Oswiecim without delay. He says it is regarding a confidential matter. He cannot come to Krakow, and I must come without alarming the castellan and the governors."

This was the first time she had ever received a personal invitation that had not passed under the watchful eyes of her advisors. The bishop's invitation and appeal to come to him and his parish seemed at first strange, but Jadwiga thought again that the matter was worthy of her honoring his request. What personal matter could be so important at this time? She felt that there were some matters the council possibly hid from her. She wanted everyone in her kingdom to have just treatment and a fair hearing. She felt somewhat concerned about making such a decision on her own but then quickly decided. For once, she would make a decision on her own and live with the consequences. This had slipped under their notice, and she would exercise her own judgment. She had been bound indoors for weeks and suddenly felt the need to get out. She turned to the young man, "I will come early tomorrow morning, but will have to return by early afternoon."

Constance was puzzled and somewhat alarmed. "My lady, the winter conditions!" The winter months were no time to risk travel in such cold, and with the upcoming events, Jadwiga and Constance were even less inclined to travel.

The young messenger waited for the final decision, and Jadwiga repeated, "I will see you at Oswiecim tomorrow morning. I will make arrangements at once."

He bowed, smiling happily. "My master will be greatly pleased."

Early the next morning, a small band of select guards and Henre prepared to leave at Jadwiga's command. "My lady…" Henre stopped her as she boarded the coach inside the carriage area, the light of morning just breaking, "Are you sure about this? The advisors are not aware of this. What if there is trouble? How can we know that messenger was true? They think we're only going for a brief tour," he said, nodding toward the castle gatekeepers.

"The fact that no one knows of these plans makes it less likely that someone can ambush our small entourage. Let us make haste and return unknown to all. The seal of the bishop was on the letter." They were leaving on this cold cloudy morning during the sleepy week of Christmas, where the late-night festivities would serve them well. The messenger and letter had been obscure as to why the bishop wanted to meet so quickly, but Jadwiga was concerned about her future and was ready to take charge of her destiny. She also worried that her subjects were being treated well. Maybe this was an issue of need. So she set out this morning, worried about what concern the bishop had and how she could be of service to him or the town.

Upon their arrival, Jadwiga entered to the church to pray. Jesus was present here. The bishop met her in her pew and embraced her.

She remembered him well from her coronation and meetings on various occasions. They were well received and escorted to the bishop's dining quarters, where a beautiful breakfast and warm fire was well prepared. Constance, Henre, and the few guards joined them.

"Thank you, Queen Jadwiga, for answering my request for a visit, and I thank you for your trust and confidentiality."

"Is there any matter that is pressing and urgent, my lord?"

"Well, I speak for most of my village and surrounding area, but we treasure your presence here in Poland and feel very blessed to have you as our divinely appointed queen, in fact, our king. This meeting, I implore you to understand, was not established for selfish reasons but to help you examine with certainty the destiny, which is about to unfold in your life and for the kingdom of Poland." Jadwiga now sat silently, feeling that something more was not being disclosed to her. "I set this meeting not on my behalf but on behalf of these two advocates…" He motioned to some servants who opened a nearby door. In what seemed like an eternity of anticipation and curiosity emerged William followed by Rottenstein.

Jadwiga gasped. She could not believe her eyes. In her young innocence, she took on a decision all her own, and she stood up to meet this unlikely pairing, feeling it difficult to breathe, for she had cast herself back into a dilemma that she thought she had resolved and moved on from. In her mind, she had detached herself from him. Now, she had to deal with the moment. William came to her and reached out to embrace her, but she held out her hand, meaning for him to keep his distance. Something about his pairing with Rottenstein made her concerned and uneasy about this meeting.

William stopped at seeing her expression. It was less than loving, less than welcoming, less than what he had known and felt only the summer before.

He stopped cold, shaking his head, like asking, "What?" He stood arrogant and in disbelief about her reception.

Rottenstein also looked at her judgingly and with uncertainty only steps behind William, but now moving beside him, he put his hand on his shoulder.

The bishop, quickly sensing the tension, interrupted the awkward silence. "I will leave you to discuss these matters." Jadwiga nodded as he left the room and closed the doors tightly behind him. She knew he thought he'd acted in her best interest. The bodyguard left also, leaving her with Constance and Henre.

Rottenstein, who arrogantly and mistakenly spoke first, while custom demanded that the king be the first to speak, broke the silence. "You are to marry a Lithuanian?" He did not attempt to hide his disdain and disrespect.

She could not chastise them; as she had made the decision to undertake this journey today, it was her responsibility to deal with the consequences that had brought her to this place. She also realized they had no alternative. They could not have come to Krakow, so she decided to hear them out and answer their questions, hoping that they would not undertake any foul play or wrongdoing. She was alone again, except for the butterflies in her stomach.

"Yes, I am to marry Jagiello of Lithuania. You both should have been informed."

William was now incredulous, "You're serious? Why are you treating me like you don't even know me?" He could see everything had changed. "Jadwiga…" was all he could manage softly. It pulled at her heart, which she closed.

"I have been told that you have been saying that our marriage was consummated. You know this is not true." Suddenly, his noble intentions appeared less than noble and appeared as a straight lie to her. She couldn't muster sympathy for him at this moment. Again, he found it difficult to speak, so she continued, "I feel that you have done so in order to preserve our marriage of sponsalia, and if I am right, you had a good intention on one level."

Rottenstein sat on the table, silently observing, waiting to conduct his business as the young couple was absorbed fully in their discussion. She was happy to see him back off.

William looked ashamed, and he looked down. What was he hiding? Perhaps he had boasted these things to the wrong people at the wrong times to bolster his ego rather than to preserve the marriage. Jadwiga thought maybe it had served a double purpose for him. He had a hard time looking into her eyes. Guilty? She wondered.

"Yes, what is so wrong? I would have done or said anything to have you!" Finally having found his voice and his love for her, he answered; seeing her, he became hopeful that he could reclaim her now.

"I wrote my letter explaining my decision, did you not receive it?" she answered firmly.

"Yes, but how could you expect me to accept it? It's not about riches or kingdoms or even power, Jadwiga. None of those things mean anything to me now…now that I've lost my greatest treasure…"

Jadwiga shook her head and again held out her hand. *Do not come near me:* a sign of her interior struggle to keep him at a safe distance so she could carry on with her new resolve. She stepped back from them. "Because I did not tell you in person but wrote in my letter, you did not take me to my word? I am resolved, William, to carry this out. I believe it is God's will."

"Did God not will you to marry me? We were married, do you forget? Because I remember that day! I remember our parents and our families… Does God change his mind?" It was one of Jadwiga's best memories of love and family she would always cherish.

She noticed Rottenstein raise his eyebrows and shake his head, seeming to bite his tongue to not join the onslaught to lower her resolve.

"He does not change his mind, but he changes our minds, changes our hearts and puts us in a place where we can love the most. He gave himself and asks us to give ourselves in ways that we would not, for love's sake, for mercy's sake."

"But you're the king of Poland, you can do whatever you want and no one can command you," William argued. "Why don't you just do what you want?" She was the "king" of a country, and it just wasn't that easy. She had everyone to consider first, besides what she wanted. God, her subjects, and then her, she was third. *I am third.*

Jadwiga prayed quickly and silently for William to see things her way too. She looked down, waiting for inspiration then looked back at him, "Christ is the king of Poland, and he commands me to do this."

Now William began to shake his head and become angry but didn't know what to say.

Rottenstein decided to join in. "So you will marry the Lithuanian?" he asked as he stepped forward, his question seemed menacing and threatening, his tone implying it was a stupid idea.

"Ladislau was to ask you to be godfather, did he not ask you?" Jadwiga now turned her attention to Rottenstein.

"Yes, but I could scarcely believe it to be true, knowing your marriage was to be to William and knowing the evils of the Lithuanian race firsthand, knowing how your father fought them also! But he did not live to warn you of these things. What possible reason could your nobles have to allow such madness?" Slowly, any control Rottenstein had been exercising was beginning to wear away. He walked toward her and spoke quietly to her, grabbing her arm firmly. "What is to stop us from taking you now with us?" She looked at Henre, who took a step toward them and shook her head. *I'll deal with him.*

"And then what?" Jadwiga replied confidently, unafraid. "All of Poland will be after you and William, and you would face trial and embarrassment or, worse, imprisonment? The mind of my advisors and my mind is made with them. Jagiello will be king!" She wrestled her arm free of Rottenstein's firm, uncomfortable grip and stood back firmly.

William now became the silent observer. She could see him realizing with every passing moment that he had lost her to her ideals and this new country.

Jadwiga, not intimidated, replied, "Great King Casimir began relations with the Lithuanians to establish peace and security. You must not act as though I am the first to will it. Why are you so shocked at moves toward peace? We must each do our part to ensure that the love of God and his peace and mercy are ever present, do we not?" Jadwiga left this last question open knowing that Rottenstein had not ever been known for these Christian virtues even while carrying the flag of a Christian.

Rottenstein continued, now fueled by his and William's desires. "You would marry a man three times your age, of pagan influence, a liar, and now accuse a noble organization of the church, which served by blood and life to allow peace and security to all of Europe for generation upon generation, which so many have enjoyed because of our sacrifice? Do not act as though I know nothing of these things!"

Jadwiga apologetically and humbly admitted her error. "Yes, Conrad, and with all my heart, I apologize for my presumptions, but I know you from *my* generation and reports of your order continually stealing and robbing from these people, all their possessions, and any progress they make toward civilization and Christianity itself. What then can this double life lead to but evil? We are to be singular in mind, will, belief, and action. We must remember that this is covetous behavior. You wage war against both the Lithuanians and Northern Poland because of greed and covetousness! Again, I will implore your order of Teutonic Knights begin to act like Christians and give and be merciful rather than take!" She had said all she wanted to say to him and decided to address him no further, for she would not speak to deaf ears.

She turned instead to William, deciding to keep it as brief as possible and say once and for all what was on her heart. "I understand that you may have acted out of love to save our marriage, but you must understand the serious nature of lying and slander. Consider that you have said convincingly something about us, which simply is not true. Consider how this is a lie, how this presents you and I, and me and my new husband for all of Europe and Christendom! It illegitimatizes our future marriages. You must stop this talk and undo what you have now done."

She could see William was having a hard time accepting it all. She walked to him finally and held out her hand to touch his face. He moved away from her, angrily and upset, with now his hands upward, stepping back. "I never wanted harm to come to you and would never play a part in bringing harm to you. We have now both serious responsibilities and duties to be fulfilled down different paths." She had grown tall since the summer, she noticed, almost the same height as him, almost eye to eye; she was in fact a different person now.

Now Rottenstein needed to get one more attempt. "So you know this man Jagiello to be honest and a man of his word?" She was happy she had sent Peter. He would tell her the truth. She was putting a lot of trust in her advisors.

"I have sent my best to meet him in Lublin. Barring any wrong they see in his person, our marriage is set for February. Let us live in peace, brothers."

At the mention of Lublin, Rottenstein was appeased as he now had intelligence that would assist him if he so desired to use to a secret advantage. For William, he heard her words, "barring any wrong they see in his person." And both were satisfied to now leave, knowing that they were not going to change this young determined king's mind unless some severe misfortune befell their enemy Jagiello.

The men bowed and left, and when they were out of hearing distance, Jadwiga motioned for Henre. "Do not allow them to leave until we have arrived back to Krakow." He nodded and left.

Jadwiga motioned for Constance. She held her hand tightly as they made their way to exit to return quickly to Krakow; only now could she let her guard down. "Constance, I hope Jagiello is the man we are expecting him to be."

CHAPTER 23

Regicide on the Eastern Front

She waited patiently for the answer from Peter Szawichost. He had spent weeks with the future king and his entourage including his brothers to judge the character and disposition of these men, but most importantly, the sincerity of the grand duke himself.

From the beginning, most of the nobles of Poland had all agreed to this arrangement. There was something in the character of Jagiello that endeared him to them all, and they trusted him for the purpose he would fulfill. Szawichost was going to be the careful judge on Jadwiga's personal behalf and was chosen because of his ability to be sensitive to the concerns of Jadwiga.

He returned to the castle and met with Jadwiga, trying to answer all of her and Constance's questions.

"Is he of good countenance?" Constance was the first to ask. They had been told that his looks were of good quality, but they wanted to hear from their own trusted advisor. He had always been faithful to her father and a great friend to Ladislau, like an uncle to her.

"Yes, all you have heard, I confirm is true, he is of a good height, build, and looks. He has the appearance of mercy, contentedness, and concern, but strength as well. He is a hunter of the best stature. He loves and is most comfortable with the outdoors and nature. He is sincere and appears by all means to be honest and not of ill will or deceitful but a man true to his word. He has intended to convert to Catholicism his whole life and always wanted to reach toward the west of Europe for liaisons. He has been anxious for your hand in marriage because of his love and respect for your father and his Uncle Casimir, whom he remembers well and held in greatest esteem his whole life. As you recall, his very own Aunt Ana was married to Casimir." Jadwiga nodded fondly, eager to hear every impression. "In my mind, he will make an excellent king and husband for you," he finished with love and concern.

"You should be most pleased and find him to be a good man to love and begin a family with. We look forward to the castle of Krakow being filled with the cries of young Christian princes and princesses and a family which will go down in Polish history as the most important reigning family in recent European history."

Jadwiga and Constance simply had nothing left to question or ask. They looked at each other and smiled. Jadwiga, for the first time in a long time, breathed easily and contentedly, knowing that Peter would never approve something that was wrong for her. The anxiety and uncertainty that plagued her all autumn and into the winter season now gave way to trust and happiness, and peace.

It was days before the Feast of Epiphany in Lublin, where Jagiello had taken shelter in the company of Zawisza Olesnica the vaivode of Krakow. Here he had been accepted as the future king. Jagiello busied himself with hunting as he waited weeks for his upcoming baptism and coronation at Krakow. He was anxious and would rather not have waited so long, but he knew he had to wait for her to come of age. He hunted for his wedding feast and for the castle pantry to be filled with meat for the months he would be too busy to do so.

Jagiello was on the hunt with his kinsmen. He had become separated from the group and was hunting along a river with a special friend of his from his youth, a Chinese man of his age named Guangming. He had traveled far simply to attend the upcoming great wedding of his cherished friend in Poland. He was also on a diplomatic mission from his dynasty, and his wife and children had travelled to attend the great wedding, all enjoying the hospitality of

Zawisza Olesnica. The two separated, and Jagiello continued along the river.

Jagiello dismounted to drink and find a spot to hunt quietly, as he often enjoyed complete isolation. Suddenly, he heard a voice from behind as he drank, "So, cousin, at last we meet again." It was Witold, Jagiello's cousin who had a serious falling-out with him over Jagiello's taking over of Lithuania after the death of his father.

Witold's father, Kiejstut, who had co-ruled with Olgierd, Jagiello's father, on the death of Olgierd, wanted to take over rule of Lithuania for himself and Witold and leave Jagiello and his brothers out of rule. He so much desired power for himself that he went blind with rage and wanted to wipe out and kill his nephews to take over rule for his family only. Kiejstut looked at his nephews as weak and a liability for Lithuania because of their diplomatic beliefs and tendency to Christianity.

Jagiello was frozen and shook his head. He did not expect this unguarded meeting. "Witold." He grabbed his heart as in his mind flashed the image of his uncle begging for mercy as Jagiello turned his back and left him in the dark castle dungeon.

"Jagiello!" had been his uncle's last desperate cry, echoing through the halls and ringing in his ears into the future to this moment, demanding, condescending, bullying, and threatening. Jagiello had paused briefly, thinking he would like to turn and offer mercy, but instead refused to turn to his uncle, who was a murderer and had tried to wipe out Jagiello and all his brothers.

Jagiello's brothers and officials of state were at a loss as to how to proceed. They wanted to offer mercy, but Uncle Kiejstut was blind by rage, greed, and jealousy, his heart void of love. One thing was certain: if they had set him free, he would have killed them all in an unrepentant, merciless bloodbath. Jagiello, the very next day, had been called to the dungeon, only to find his uncle murdered. He did not know how or who was behind the murder and could feel little remorse or pity, only a tinge of sorrow for the lost past of his childhood and for the lost soul of a relative drowning in his own hate.

Witold approached Jagiello, who defenselessly still knelt by the brook he had come to drink from, and held the knife at his throat.

"You left me, imprisoned me, and if I had not escaped with my wife as her handmaiden, I would be still imprisoned today."

"I'm sure you were safe in the hands of the Teutonic Knights," Jagiello answered.

Witold struck his face with a strong blow. "You murdered my father and left me no choice but to take shelter in the hands of our blood enemy!" He kicked Jagiello again in the stomach. Jagiello bent over in pain.

Suddenly, Rottenstein and William approached on horseback. Jagiello glanced up, not recognizing them, but he knew they must be with Witold. "I didn't kill your father, my uncle! I did not ever mean to kill you, but only have you realize that our rule in Lithuania was to continue as a diarchy, which I wanted you to be a part of with me! I just wanted you to see that in time, and my hope was that you would. Your father was beyond reason and not himself. He intended to murder my brothers and I. I need you now more than ever, Witold. Among my brothers, you are the best of them to rule, but you have to put aside your hate and you have to understand your father wanted to slaughter us. You aren't like him, Witold, and Lithuania needs you now."

As Rottenstein and William came toward them, Jagiello recognized Rottenstein. "So it's your new family." Jagiello spat after he noticed it was none other than their own enemy who constantly assailed Lithuania and burned and pillaged any progress the Lithuanians managed to make.

Now Rottenstein kicked him in the stomach as well. "So you think that you can just come along and marry the queen of Poland? You Lithuanian scum, you never know your place. You belong with those counted as useless in the eyes of God. You are nothing, and you never know your place!" His hate and prejudice raged through his words. Witold flinched, as though he had ripped open older wounds.

"My place?" Jagiello asked humbly, his humility being his strongest quality. William stood by, quietly taking it in and judging his competition. William was surprised by the quality of his character and peaceful nature and saw that he was a good man, someone he could entrust Jadwiga to, but then jealousy began to take hold of his heart. He would not allow his childish kindness to get in the way of his "manly" side.

"I am William of Austria."

Jagiello seemed astonished. "You're William? What are you doing here? You know Jadwiga has made her choice, was it not made clear to you?" Now William kicked him in the stomach.

"You don't look much like a king now, do you?"

Jagiello stood up slowly and wiped his lip. "So what is it you want with me then, do you mean to kill me?"

The three men now seemed like wolves circling him for the kill, and he felt as though the only thing sparing his death was the hand of God itself, because by now, they should have killed him and moved on before the arrival of his kin. He turned and repeated again to Witold, always the diplomat and negotiator, "I didn't kill your father. I cherish you as a brother. You should have waited. Why would you bring your household and side with the Teutonic Knights for the destruction of your people? Is that better than working for our people? You would throw away everything you worked for, that our parents built for us?" Witold, a man of simple words, was visibly being moved by Jagiello's words, which he knew always had a reputation for honesty. He lowered his dagger and replaced it into his sheath.

Rottenstein looked at him, disappointed because he hoped to pit the two against each other and use Witold to kill his own cousin. He couldn't personally take responsibility for the death of Jagiello and damage his reputation.

William now stepped forward; they were almost eye to eye, but Jagiello, the mature adult, and William, still very much the young man. Jagiello, in combat, could easily surpass him; and William, no longer sure of the motives of his comrades, fearing that now, Witold may turn on him for Jagiello's sake, could only utter threats. "Do you really think you are the best for Jadwiga? She is *my* wife! We were married! You don't speak her language. You don't know her. You don't know what it means to be part of the European family. You're an outsider. I have known her and her family her whole life, and her father wanted us married. It was his will, as it is her will. If you care at all for her, you will leave her free to do what her father and my father willed. You're just using her for your advantage, to gain power and position—you don't care for her, you don't love her! You are and always will be using her for your selfish gain, and you've bewitched the Poles to agree to this madness!" Jagiello stood speechless and sympathetic. "I should kill you now. But I am not a murderer," William finished, sounding defeated.

"Only a slanderer, from what I understand," answered Jagiello.

William replied with a swift strong punch to the stomach. Rottenstein jumped to hold Jagiello's arms behind his back, and Witold stood, still indecisively observing. William was now in his face. "Leave her, turn back, and change your mind and be happy in your kingdom."

"The Poles have agreed to this. It's under contract and not to be changed. They don't want you as ruler, and they have made that clear. Jadwiga knows this, and she has made her choice, not by what I look like or who I am, but by the duty she understands she is sworn to fulfill and her love of the church."

Rottenstein let go of his hold, throwing Jagiello to the ground. "And that is another lie! That you would convert all of Lithuania to Catholicism, you lying snake!"

Jagiello stood once again. "Is it really so hard to believe that we are converting to Christianity? Witold here has converted, has he not? You had him baptized on his arrival. My mother was Christian. What makes it so hard for you to believe our motives are true? Why won't you just see this for what it is, all of you? I am sincere, I love the church and the civilizations it produces, I am in love with it and have pledged my life to it. I don't even know Jadwiga, and I hope and pray I will be a good husband to her, but in my heart, I feel as though this is right, the right thing to do at the right time. Why are your own hearts so hardened? Think of what this means for Europe. We are no longer questionable enemies but brothers fighting for the kingdom of Christ. What is the harm, and where is the evil in this?" Jagiello's diplomatic stature and grace shone through his countenance and his every expression. It was easy for all of them to see in that moment why the Poles had agreed to his elevation to the throne, and for the moment. he disarmed all three by his meekness, humility, but strong dignity and certainty as well.

Guangming had meanwhile made his way silently back to Jagiello and the predatory triad. His training in the martial arts in his nation had left him a force to be reckoned with even among well-trained European knights and a warrior like Witold. He was not quite sure who these men were as his understanding of the European languages was minimal, so he did not unleash his full force but snuck toward the antagonistic group from behind. He stepped on a twig, which echoed with a snap that in the silence of the forest resounded and sprung the three to action and automatically assume a position of defense as they drew their swords.

They were startled as they faced an uncertain individual of Mongolian or other culture. Rottenstein and Witold sprung instantly to action with unquestioned zeal, assuming him to be their worst enemy. They presumed that his power was measured in his countenance rather than his training and acquired skills in the martial arts. They were no challenge for him whatsoever.

William had stood hesitantly by observing with his sword drawn, but when Guangming had disarmed them both and had a sword at Rottenstein's throat and his foot on Witold's neck as they both lay on their backs, William simply threw down his sword toward him and held his hands upward.

Jagiello wiped his bloody lip and eye with his coat sleeve and quipped to Guangming, "So you wait 'til I am beaten to save me?" Guangming, also a man of few words, shrugged and gestured, "I did my best."

Jagiello introduced the men to Guanming now, "Meet my best friend, Guanming. He is Chinese from Beiping, not Mongolian as you may have assumed."

Guanming bowed to the three in friendly greeting, replying, "I am the enemy of his enemy and therefor *his friend*!" He had often heard Jagiello introduce him this way to countless others.

Jagiello smiled and responded simply to him, "Thank you, my friend! You may let them up but disarmed."

Suddenly, from the underbrush came charging two large hunting hounds, fierce and ferocious toward the group, and from the woods could be heard the shouts of men and the running of horses in pursuit. Jagiello's brothers were not far behind and outnumbered the small triad that had assailed Jagiello. The hounds came between Jagiello and the men, baring their teeth threateningly. Knowing they were now the ones in danger, Rottenstein had his last word, "You have not seen or heard the last of me, you lying snake."

They quickly mounted their horses. Jagiello, ignoring Rottenstein and William, called out, "Witold! *Stay*, Witold! Stay with your kin. Come back to us, to your real family." Witold didn't answer but gave what seemed to Jagiello a subtle nod as their eyes met quickly one last time. His wife and children were at Marienburg. He could not change alliances in this moment. Jagiello nodded back, hope enkindled in his heart. The three charged off in the opposite direction of the approaching band of hunters.

Jagiello now petted the head of his ferocious hounds, which stood barking threateningly at the parting group, "Thank you again, Guanming."

Jagiello called out to his brothers and host, "It is Rottenstein of the Teutonic Order, make sure he returns to his home out of Northern Poland. It would appear to be an issue for the kingdom's security." His host looked shocked at this news but motioned for the security to follow after them. Jagiello remounted his horse, feeling that good was going to come out of something that may have turned evil.

Clovis and Clotilde, Antoine-Jean Gros, 1811

CHAPTER 24

Baptisms, Wedding, and Coronation Days

Jadwiga was never informed of the dangerous proceedings in the woods at Lublin. At Jagiello's request, these were kept secret to not upset or worry Jadwiga at this time. Finally, the day came in early February 1386, when Jadwiga was to meet Jagiello. Jadwiga, Constance, and her ladies-in-waiting, some giggling excitedly, hastily found their places from which they would greet the Lithuanian delegation. Jadwiga, although nervous, appeared serious, mature and diplomatic. She knew the consequences of this decision, good or bad, weighed heavily on her shoulders. The excitement of the ladies lightened her mood.

The Lithuanian delegation of handsomely dressed men, now shaven clean to reflect the European style, walked down a corridor leading to two large doors. Jagiello was following Dobeslaus, who stopped at the door, bowed, and gestured for the party to enter. He stepped aside to enter behind the party. Jagiello paused at the closed door, hesitated, as if contemplating his destiny and the moment he had waited so long for; looking downward, he pushed the heavy doors open. He had been told about the overwhelming beauty and grace of his queen. He was anxious to finally set eyes on his future bride, but nothing prepared him for her warm and inviting smile and a love and hospitable nature, which was disarming to everyone she met.

The previously excited young ladies now appeared diplomatic and properly attentive, showing no signs of prior preparations. Jadwiga was seated on her throne surrounded by her ladies, body-guards, and nobles. Jagiello walked inside the doors, pausing, giving just enough time to admit his group before proceeding, his eyes fixed on the woman on the throne who was surprisingly taller than the other women around her.

Jadwiga shyly was now able to look up. His handsome and manly appearance was much more comforting to her than she had imagined. Now she understood what the Poles saw in him. He had a beautiful face, intelligent, meek, and sincere looking. Their gaze met, and her beauty astonished him. She stood to greet him. He knelt before her and looked up at her, also somewhat timid. There was a reserved quiet strangeness that often accompanies new meetings broken by Jagiello's words.

"My queen, I am Jagiello, grand duke of Lithuania. I… I am at a loss for words, that is the beauty, your beauty, it takes breath away…"

Jadwiga looked down for a brief moment, then in a diplomatic way, which she had become accustomed to replied, "I am Jadwiga. My good man, you have come so far. Welcome."

There was a great feeling between the two of them, and despite their ages, they seemed comfortable together. "Thank you. I met your father. He was a great man."

Jadwiga asked pointedly. "Is it true then that you as well as your kin are to be baptized Catholic in a few days' time?"

"Yes, well, all except Witold. He is remaining Orthodox Christian." Jadwiga stood and extended her hand to him. He took it and kissed it; the young ladies of the court tried to regain their composure.

Jadwiga was appreciative of this quick gesture of affection. "So, we shall see you at the baptism Sunday. Until then, I hope you and all your kin are received well and have the best of care. I have asked Ladislau, my dear uncle, to be your godfather. A Pole is likely more suited for the position than a German."

"Yes, this would be good. I have asked my favorite sister, Alexandra, if she would be interested in a meeting with Ziemowit of Mazovia at our wedding. If he is interested, she is available for marriage."

Jadwiga smiled and nodded in agreement, "Ziemowit has reconciled himself to me this past December." Making one a family member made it harder for them to be your enemy or plan treason.

"I will see you Sunday at the baptism. And, my good queen, I hope you understand, I undertake this as I feel called to by the Lord Jesus not to steal your kingdom away. It is time for peace, time for His reign in the hearts of Lithuania."

Jadwiga was impressed deeply by his sincere piety and was moved by it. In this sense, she felt they had a kindred spirit of faith. He kissed her hand again, bowed, and turned to exit followed by his men. Was there any way he could be an angel of deception? Both were so relieved to have finally met each other and soon be united in marriage.

As soon as the men left, Constance and the ladies rushed to Jadwiga's side, each trying to express their impressions and hug her, excitedly talking about how handsome and normal Jagiello and his brothers were.

⁓

Thus the day came that the Lithuanian ruling family was baptized into the church.

Jagiello took the Christian name Ladislau, like his new godfather Laudislau of Opole. His three younger brothers Korygiello (now
Casimir), Wigunt, and Swidrygiello (Boleslaw) all received baptism
with humble devotion and piety on February 14.

Many observers were moved to tears and then a distinct joy as
they were washed with the water and spiritual water for their soul.
Cardinals and other priests were in attendance as well as a large number of Polish delegates and ladies of the court. Each baptism was
received with greater and greater joy and peace, until the feeling was
so warm and loving it was almost tangible.

Jadwiga breathed a sigh of relief and joy. The sacrifices she had
made for this moment had all been worth it. She knew that she
made the right choice as she witnessed its fulfillment and its fruit,
her prayers for peace being answered before her eyes. Each brother
and Jagiello was embraced and welcomed into the church by each
noble and priest. The joy and love was real, as where God is, love
is. In the background could be heard a hymn that grew louder until
everyone, including their Lithuanian brothers, joined in the chant,
"Ubi Caritas" (God Is Love). A spirit of joy and of gladness filled the
church and spilled on to the streets of Krakow, and the celebration
in the castle following.

After this great event, everyone in Krakow was growing excited,
relieved, and peaceful. What seemed like an incredibly unlikely plan
was slowly coming to fruition, and despite what anyone thought in
the past, the welcoming and loving spirit at the baptisms was talked
about and spread throughout the land.

The Poles now would have a Catholic king, someone who
could come to their defense, assist and protect them if needed. The
Lithuanians also now had a joint Polish ruler. No longer were they to
be enemies living in fear of each other. The excitement in the kingdoms could be felt throughout Europe and reached the great halls
of Marienburg, where stone hearts accompanied great stone walls of
the castle.

Rottenstein, filled with vile prejudice, only got angrier and angrier that his enemy was inevitably to be the ruler of the kingdom to the south. His seething anger and hardened heart could only think of one option to satisfy his festering energy.

"Zolner, if the Lithuanians are thus occupied, deceiving the Poles and bewitching them all in a fantasy rule, then who is left defending Vilno and Lithuania? It would seem like the perfect time to launch an attack upon these savages whose shepherds have come to drink and ravage the goods of their neighbor. Let us prepare for an attack. Someone has to stay alert and awake to reality. They will return to find that some of us have stayed on guard and not fallen into their deceptive traps. You will lead us again, Witold."

Witold nodded, listened silently to his scheming host. He had returned to Marienburg after the assault on Jagiello and was finished with this dictating enemy. Jagiello's last words in the forest rang true, and more and more, he loathed this "host" who had taken him in when he had run from Jagiello but now, he could see clearly, was using him for his own personal gain. Witold had nothing more to benefit from being with him. Nothing more to gain from staying and being used, but since he was concerned about what this could mean for his or his family's safety, he meant to leave without telling Rottenstein. He would leave by the cover of this night.

He had learned a lot from the Teutonic Knights in his couple years here, and as Christianity began to take hold of his heart, he could sense a change come over his person. He had learned from the industry and crafts of the Marienburg industries how to run success-ful operations and business, and he felt that God had used this time to teach him how to apply the industrious nature of the Knights to his own kingdom. He had gained tremendous insight and wisdom on how to make use of goods to promote the well-being of his own people. He now saw that he was like Joseph of the Old Testament, who had been sent away, far from his home for a greater purpose. His time was finished here, but he would not divulge this to the great leader.

William, still in Marienburg, spoke his mind. "I didn't come here to fight against Lithuania. I want to thank you for your services and hospitality to me, but I need to leave now. I will go to Krakow, and if Jadwiga will marry him, I will leave and return home. I need to see with my own eyes that she is married before I am satisfied. Until then, I still won't believe that she will abandon me."

"Young fools and young love," answered Rottenstein, "A bad combination. Go your way, and now that I've gotten to know you better, it's probably better for all of Europe that you don't rule Poland. You are faint of heart like a woman and seek only pleasure. You will never amount to anything!" William was visibly insulted. These comments touched on his interior struggle. Rottenstein had voiced the words that were echoing through his being, albeit a false voice.

"I wish you both well, as I may very well never see you again." Under his breath as he turned to leave, muttered, "God willing."

The next morning, Witold, his family, and some servants left under the cover of darkness. They were a small entourage on horseback, with some packing horses for the few goods they took with them. They left quietly and quickly travelling toward Krakow for two reasons: firstly, to be reconciled to Jagiello, and also to let them know that Lithuania was now going to be attacked by the Teutonic forces while the wedding ceremonies should be going on peacefully.

They travelled as the first light of dawn appeared over the eastern horizon, taking the main road to Krakow. It was later in the afternoon of this cold mid-February that the group was arriving to a village by the forest. As they travelled, Witold sensed a strong foreboding in his heart. As they approached the village, they passed a young lady of almost twenty. She watched them as they went by, and she searched the face of Witold and recognized it.

She recognized it as the face emerging from the woods from her childhood, destroying her peace and entering her memory and heart as the face of evil and destruction. She screamed and dropped her load of wood and ran toward the small village to warn them all of the villain approaching and to rally defenses.

The small party had stopped now, and Witold's wife Anna called out to him, "What is it?" Witold did not answer but, suddenly, as they continued around a bend in the road, realized the place was familiar to him. They came to a newly constructed church building, from within could hear Gregorian chants of the afternoon prayers ("Pange Lingua Gloriosi"). It was as if they had been drawn there by the song itself. Rain began to fall, cold and merciless from the gray sky.

As Witold approached the church made of logs, a sorrow grasped his heart, and the cold rain and wind was not enough to make him feel redeemed. It was the church where he had murdered the priests twelve years before. It had been rebuilt by these simple, poor peasants; and as the village men began to run and make their way back toward the church to defend it, Witold dismounted from his horse and knelt in the slushy icy mud. Grasping his heart, he suddenly could not breathe well, and he began to weep for the sins of his past. Perhaps it was the grace earned by the prayers of the very men who had offered their deaths for his conversion, but he knelt, gasping for breath and a pain in his heart made him feel suddenly like he might die in front of this church, which from within came the pious and holy songs of the monks.

He bent his forehead to the very ground on which he himself had spilled the martyrs' blood. The village men now reached him and his family with axes, knives, and any tools that could be used to inflict harm and defend the church. They saw only a small family, whom they encircled in front of the church, in the cold rain, and a man in tears, weeping, now looking up to heaven, striking his breast, crying out loudly, "Mea culpa, mea maxima culpa! Mea maxima culpa!" The scene moved the villagers to standstill and to tears of anger mixed with mercy, forgiveness, and gratitude for the conversion of this man who had been responsible for so much suffering and death among their own loved ones and neighbors.

His sorrow and repentance disarmed them all as they stood in the cold rain; it became like a confessional, washing away their sins of hatred, resentment, and prejudice. The largest of the men was the first to move from his spot. He dropped his ax and knelt down next to Witold, whose pain and sorrow was even penetrating his own heart. He embraced him, and Witold grasped the face of the man as a long-lost brother and embraced him. It was a miraculous event. Witold knew that he could no longer live a duplicitous life, like Rottenstein. It had to be whole to be true, and just as he left Marienburg behind him, he left the duplicity as well. He suddenly realized he did not know Christianity well because he only knew the example of hypocritical men who followed ritual on the outside but practiced hatred on the inside. He did not want to be that man ever again, thus he embraced the mercy of Christ and became a truer Christian years after his baptism. These men were his brothers, and God was their father.

"I am Witold, cousin to your king."

Everyone knew the baptisms, wedding, and coronation were taking place. They all felt that there was a strong wind of change blowing in the land and in the hearts of citizens. They were no longer enemies but brothers to care for each other. The men helped Witold to his feet and embraced him. They brought him and his family to their homes to provide food and shelter to this man who now knew the life of a refugee.

The success of the great union taking place was not to be based on written contracts, "but on the spirit of "fraternal love," which had to animate those involved for the triumph of a great idea."[1]

~⚬~

February 18, 1386

The marriage day of Jagiello and Jadwiga finally arrived, a day they had both anticipated, prayed, and dreamed about their whole lives. It was a frozen February day, anticipating the coming spring. But the sky was blue, and the sun was shining brightly through the cathedral windows despite the cool air inside. The black crucifix where she had prayed so many prayers watched her now be wed. Something in her past and upbringing had urged Jadwiga to this moment, and now, the thought came to her that it had been planned by God and revealed to her slowly.

---

[1] Oscar Halecki, *Jadwiga of Anjou and the Rise of East Central Europe* (New Jersey: Columbia University Press, 1991), 153.

By a firm trust in Divine Providence, they had longed for something and didn't know what, but today, as Jadwiga walked up the aisle of Krakow Cathedral, escorted by her beloved Demytr, surrounded by hundreds of beloved citizens and nobles, it was not such a sacrifice that it had seemed. For before her was a man of his word, a man of God, smiling and looking to her as the fulfillment of that same promise that would bind them together for God's purpose.

Demytr, looking small next to the tall princess of five feet and nine inches, even thought to himself as he patted her hand confidently and happily that she was Jagiello's equal physically. Both were named king of Poland, ruling as a diarchy, and their equality was etched in their equal stature. So she arrived at the altar of God, equal in all things to her husband, in intellect, wisdom, and love of God. She no longer saw him as a threat, a pagan, or someone to be questioned, but someone she was given to love.

Only when mass was over was Jagiello allowed to lift her veil and kiss her as a sign of their married love. This was her first true kiss—the one intended to be, which fulfilled her destiny and longing. It bore such beauty and weight for both of them who were so touched by the moment that they both had tears of joy. Jagiello presented a beautiful wedding ring with crosses embedded and jewels. The priest blessed their rings for their life together as a sign of unity and fidelity. It was the most beautiful ring she ever saw.

Jadwiga no longer had to feel alone anymore. Didn't have to wonder who or where or when or feel so isolated from all she had known and loved; for now before her eyes was her present reality and her new family here in Poland. Her heart flooded with joy and emotion as the reality of all her doubt, fears, confusion, and loneliness melted away as she held the hand of her husband and king. His strength fulfilled a part of her that was missing, and even their difference in age meant nothing to her now as all their differences melted away. How glorious was the fulfillment of the more excellent way, God's plan A; and in the moment, she felt its power and glory. For now, there were no enemies to the east, only true brothers and sisters. The songs and sounds of the hundreds inside and outside the cathedral echoed to the Carpathians and seemed to ring through the whole countryside, songs of joy, triumph, and best of all, peace.

Hidden in the confessional of the beautiful cathedral observed William, who had taken shelter in the house of the Morsztyns and now dressed himself as a religious to avoid notice or capture. He noticed in the crowds of nobility his elderly Uncle Albrect. He moved himself to a position next to him and prayed the prayers of the mass without drawing attention to himself. Finally, he gently touched his elbow to Albrect's on the pew beside him. Albrect, who seemed to have fallen asleep or be in deep prayer, finally looked into the hooded monk's face to recognize William! It had been months since he had left Vienna, and they were all extremely worried about his well-being. Albrect's gentle and loving countenance now looked with pity and love on his nephew, an outcast, almost considered a criminal because of his circumstances and passion.

He had done nothing wrong really but had been caught up in the negative outcome of his dreams. His mother, Viridia, had turned to Italy to arrange a marriage for him with an Italian princess, Joanna, daughter to the king of Sicily. Albrect patted William's back as a welcome and sign of love and shook his head in sympathy and pity. They both had such love and respect for Jadwiga, and it pained them both that they would lose her as a family member, but Albrect could see the good and divine in things as they transpired before their eyes. William would be all right, as Sicily was a beautiful country, well established and well provided for. Still, he looked with pity and concern as this beautiful young lady, who had loved William, was given in the sacrifice of the mass to this new man and felt they had to unite their sacrifice of her for the greater good.

As the wedding ended and the priests and bishops processed down the aisle, the happy new married couple processed finally to claps and words of joy and congratulations from everyone. Jadwiga's eyes fell on the face of Albrect, and she immediately recognized the beautiful, tall grandfatherly figure who had nurtured her as a child and treated her with such love and respect, her kindred spirit. "Albrect!" she exclaimed, drawing Jagiello's attention to the very elderly thin Austrian prince.

She brought Jagiello to Albrect and introduced him, "Jagiello, Albrect of Austria. He was like a father to me." Jagiello nodded and smiled, Jadwiga holding his arm and he having his hand on hers.

"Take best of care of her, Ladislau, she is indeed the fairest maiden in all of Europe and the wisest." He smiled, feeling the pain and isolation of William who stood beside him still, not revealing himself and not noticed by the couple.

"Please, you will join us tonight for the wedding banquet, and will you stay for the coronation ceremony as well?"

"Yes and yes, if it pleases thee, most beautiful Jadwiga, as the weather is harsh for an old man travelling."

"Good," answered Jadwiga. "It's settled then! Are you well accommodated?"

"Yes, of course, with Ladislau of Opole, all is *well*," he said.

Jadwiga hugged him and happily exclaimed, "See you tonight, please come talk to me."

Albrect bowed his head as the couple continued away from him and William. "You see, now you no longer have a destiny to fulfill here, and you must leave at once, or they may have you imprisoned if you are caught. Your mother has found a new bride for you in Sicily and both women await you eagerly. That is your new destiny, my son. So go and Godspeed." William knew he didn't have time for details, and seeing his destiny must now take another path, he nodded, hugged his uncle, and glanced at Jadwiga and Jagiello shaking hands with eager citizens. Would this be the last time he would set eyes on her? He turned reluctantly and, with a heavy, heavy heart, left for Austria and his future destiny in Italy.

After greeting many hundreds of guests, the cold, excited onlookers on the outside of the cathedral, and touring briefly by carriage through the crowds, Jagiello and Jadwiga now returned to the castle for festivities. It was a great wedding celebration with medieval music, dancing, and feasting. Jadwiga was seated on her throne, taking in all the festivities. Jagiello sat beside her, watching her speak to various nobles who congratulated them.

Ladislau of Opole introduced his beautiful daughter (another Jadwiga) to the couple, and she caught the eye of Jagiello's brother Wigunt, who was popular among the Poles. She would eventually become his wife. Jadwiga looked over to Jagiello and smiled, catching his loving gaze, his admiration and love for her growing with each moment of this magical day.

"If it were summer, I would have this room filled with roses and every sort of flower, and yet none would match your rare and exquisite beauty." He kissed her hand, and she laughed gently, shyly, and looked away, thinking that he was quite beautiful as well.

Now the time finally came for the two newlywed kings to be alone for the first time in the home castle chambers. As the night grew to a close, both were exhausted from the festivities that did not seem to want to end right into early morning. They were now alone in their room with a large warm fire burning in the open fireplace and candles lit at the bedside. The noise and fun jostling of the night had given way to peaceful quiet. They held hands, and Jadwiga knelt down by the bed, not too tired to say her night prayers. Jagiello observed her, trying to figure out what she was doing, with love and contentment on his face, taking delight in her determined piety. He saw her make the sign of the cross and knelt beside her, following her lead. Her gaze was on the crucifix, and he also stared at it; she prayed in her native Hungarian and then, looking at Jagiello, also, began the "Our Father" in Latin. "Pater noster qui es in coelis, sanctificetur nomen tuum; adveniat regnum tuum," the very prayers he would translate to Lithuanian for his people. After the sign of the cross, they stood, Jadwiga becoming timid having never had slept in the company of a man. Now the weight of the new union was real, from being so far apart, now to becoming one family. She went behind a screen to change from her gown to her nightdress. Behind the screen, she made the sign of the cross again, her own private prayer for strength.

After some time, Jagiello, who was quickly falling asleep because of the exhaustion of the day questioned, "Jadwiga, is everything okay?"

"No, I mean yes," she replied, too nervous to now come outside of the barrier, wringing her hands together hesitant. Finally, she took a deep breath and walked quickly to the bed and under the covers, looking straight up at the ceiling, making no eye contact with him.

Jagiello was humored by her modesty and shyness. Turning toward her, putting his head on his hand, propped up by his elbow, he just smiled at her, but she would not look at him. He laughed gently and touched her cheek. "My young wife, you can look at me." So she turned toward him, his strong muscles showing his strength, and she touched his muscle and smiled, feeling so protected now.

"It's just so strange, I am used to sleeping alone…"

"Yes, we are like strangers you and I, but no more. I will always be here for you at your side always, to keep you warm to watch over you and our kingdoms, and together, we will see to the conversion of Lithuania. Thank you, Jadwiga, for having me. We will be at each other's command." She nodded silently.

He kissed her forehead then leaned over to blow out the candles.

PART 2

Jadwiga's Legacy

March 4, 1386

Two weeks after the baptism and wedding feasts, Jagiello was crowned in Krakow Cathedral to complete the third major event in the capital city within less than a month. He was crowned with a new crown of gold and jewels, the crown previously used having been removed to Hungary by Louis. The happiness of all was felt in this momentous event as Jagiello took each step to the highest position in the kingdom. Jadwiga looked on with peace and resignation, feeling sure that he was the rightful king. She wanted to be by his side as much as possible. She smiled and prayed for her husband as he received his crown, happy to share the rule and placed great trust in him for all the affairs of state. He deeply respected her and included her in all thinking, planning, and ideas for the kingdoms. Jadwiga no longer felt like the little child being left out of things, and they were equally consulted and had the final word on all decisions. After the mass of coronation, church bells rang out loudly and repeatedly for quite some time to announce the new king. There was held a private gathering of nobles and important citizens to celebrate the coronation.

During the celebration, Dobeslaus came to speak to Jagiello. He summoned him to private quarters. "There has been a messenger and scouts who believe that your cousin Witold is travelling toward Krakow, possibly arriving today. He wishes admittance to the castle. The word is that he has returned to pledge allegiance to you."

"Be sure to admit him and his family. I believe he is returning to us and let me know the moment he arrives. Thank you." Jagiello returned to his coronation dinner and could not wait to tell Jadwiga the news of the return of his cousin. He knew their meeting in the forest had proven fruitful. Later in the evening, Witold and his family did arrive and received a welcome and introduction to Jadwiga.

They were clothed, fed, and given a room to rest, when Witold returned to speak to Jagiello. "Rottenstein is going to attack Lithuania. He also means to have an alliance with Andrew to take over Lithuania."

"They try everything to create division! Already, just crowned and I must address enemies. It didn't take long," Jagiello replied. "We will deal with this immediately after the public festivities of the coronation. Let the people enjoy a few more days of celebration before we continue with state affairs. But it will be a swift response, or they will mistake us for weak fools."

The next day, Jagiello sat upon a throne in Krakow Square, surrounded by his bodyguards near to the city center to receive the homage of the mayor, the city fathers, and the whole city. This was followed by several days of celebration, including jousting with lances and swords and dancing. But underlying the celebrations, Jagiello could not help but become somber and sober about the news of his home kingdom. He felt he could not leave Jadwiga alone so soon after their wedding. It would not be fair, and they had waited so long to be married. Everyone understood his situation, and the planning in the palace meeting rooms was beginning about how to respond, for a swift response was necessary. It was decided that Witold would return with Jagiello's brother Skirgiello, leaving his family in Krakow. They were given a battalion of Polish knights to deal with the invaders. The sobering reality of medieval rule allowed for very brief moments of peace and security.

CHAPTER 25

Tears

As dignitaries and nobles from all over Poland left Krakow after the final coronation ceremony, Jagiello was requested by the prelates and nobles of Wielkopolska to come and assist them in local land and ruling disputes as quickly as possible to avoid civil war. Jagiello agreed that he would go and attempt diplomatic solutions.

He was preparing to depart within a week of the coronation. Jadwiga was watching him get ready for his trip the night before his departure. They had only been married less than a month. "Can I go with you?" she asked him as he got ready. She didn't want to tell him, but despite the assurances of the nobles from Greater Poland, she was concerned for his safety. She felt her presence would offer protection for him. "I have been in this palace and town since last summer [she did not mention her excursion to Osveczym], and I know the state of affairs here very well, but I do not know the kingdom. I would like to see it and meet its people. Do you not think that a people who know that their kings love them and come to assist them would be best?" She wanted to assess the well-being and livelihood of the people of her kingdom, to know whether they were prosperous or oppressed by local tyrants. She wanted her kingdom to be just for them.

"What might the nobles think of you leaving? You know they have not wanted you to leave in the past," Jagiello questioned gently.

"They were afraid for my safety, but now, I have you to protect me," she urged. "They will have to get used to it because I want to be with you."

Jagiello shrugged and took her face into his hands and kissed her. "They don't want a vacant throne. They fear if something happened to us after all this, then there would be no one to rule from Krakow, or worse, Ziemowit or Ladislau!" he joked.

"We command them and let us not forget it. Take me with you *please*," Jadwiga pleaded.

She had grown used to traveling and enjoyed the outdoors and excursions. She had planned to travel the kingdom but knew she could not do this without his support. Finally, he gave in, knowing that he had agreed to a diarchy. He would take her requests seriously and based on how well they had been received as a couple in Krakow, he knew that it was not just him who was winning the hearts of the Polish people but her astonishing beauty, presence, and heart of kindness and faith. All these things endeared her to his people, and he knew her presence would bring the same effect in places where strife was the order of the day.

"Fine, you come with me to Wielkopolska, but I can't promise anything after that," Jagiello conceded. Jadwiga replied by hugging him tightly, nodded and bowed to him.

"Thank you, Jagiello, I will prepare immediately." Both were happy with the natural solution despite what any of the governors might think.

<hr>

The newly married couple traveled touring towns, villages, and hamlets. Kings coming to visit was something that the people of Poland had not known for a generation. Jadwiga meant to repair for them the image of the absent king and prove her father right in investing his own child to the throne. Her grandmother, father, and her great-uncle had ruled, but her presence was a sign to her people that her plan was to be different, and she was a queen for them who had willingly given everything for them.

They arrived in Gniezno where, as everywhere, it was important for the monarch to receive homage to form unity. The reports that had brought the kings here were of unjust rulers who were oppressing the people. When the Krakow party arrived at Gniezno, they expected quarters and provisions. This indicated allegiance and support for the monarch as well as hospitality and a natural reciprocation for the services and protection being offered by the kingship. Jagiello had been warned of his hypocrisy as his loyalty had been called into question.

The governor appeared at face value to welcome them warmly. Rather than provide from his own wealth though, the governor turned to the people to provide provisions. Rather than give to the kings a share in the wealth accumulated from the region, the greedy governor was like the Pharaoh of Egypt, heightening the labors of the poor Israelites in Egypt, making them grow and collect the grass for the bricks, demanding the surrounding villages provide all provisions. He was harsh on the people under his jurisdiction and now became even more demanding with the intention of having them despise the rule of the kings.

Spring was a difficult time as supplies began to run low as the new season began for farming. Families stretched the remaining vegetables and grains to the last month—spring and summer about to change the food supply to plentiful. Families struggled to feed their own. So when the wealthy nobles of Gniezno and governors sent forces from home to home, insisting on provisions and meat from households to feed the entourage from Krakow, the peasants grew even more miserable and hopeless.

Jagiello and Jadwiga, unaware of the severe pressures exercised by the local ruling class, were happy and seemed well received. They were feasted and ate at great banquets. Jadwiga could see that the reception from the townspeople and villages was less than friendly, although she tried to reach out to the common people.

A week later, one afternoon Jadwiga noticed a very large number of protesting villagers with their wives and children gathered in the town square. Jadwiga sent Henre to find out why they had gathered. Henre returned to inform her that they were there to protest mistreatment and abuses.

"They believe you might assist them," Henre finished.

Jadwiga decided to go to the parish priest to get advice or see what could be done or if he was aware of any problems. As she entered to meet him, she noticed an archdeacon exiting. She entered to speak to the priest. He stood looking ashamed, shaking his head and distressed. "Father, what is it?" Jadwiga asked.

"Here, the church is controlled by the governors. We are not free. We have been forced to put an interdict on our people." He could barely continue the discussion as a tear betrayed his frustration.

"Not here, Father, not in Poland."

"Just go see. Follow him and see," he said waving toward the archdeacon who had just left. Jadwiga stepped out on the church steps in time to catch the archdeacon addressing the crowd. They thought perhaps the new kings would be their advocates and hear their cries for justice but instead were met by hostility from their church.

The archdeacon, moved by the insistence of the governor, placed an interdict on them. Jadwiga watched in shock from the church steps as he was forced to read a proclamation declaring, "Anyone who is seen to usurp the God-given right of governors and kings to rule over them has usurped the authority of God Himself who has set these rulers over them...and are herewith banished from the sacraments if they continue to protest against their divinely appointed rulers." The archdeacon, feeling ashamed and guilty about the duplicity of this proclamation, quickly left Gniezno, too ashamed to face the saintly queen or the peasant families he served but did not feel able to defend.

As the spring rain began to fall on the crowd and the archdeacon rode away, Jadwiga was astonished as now a spiritual punishment was heaped upon the sufferings the people were visibly already enduring. Jadwiga felt certain it was wrong as she observed the crowd who had come out of a desire for justice. If even the church would not listen to them, who was left to come to their defense? Jadwiga could see clearly how the situation was playing out, highly perceptive in regard to the mind and true intentions of the heart of people, and she was not going to side with the oppressor. She summoned an aid to come to her. "I will speak to them. I will hear their complaints."

The twelve-year-old princess, whose height and stature made her seem a lady of near twenty, watched as a guard went to the head of the group and spoke to the leader, urging him to come forward and give his complaints directly to the queen. The farmer with his wife came humbly and cautiously to Jadwiga, the farmer with his hat in his hand, afraid to speak, suddenly thought of his home, farm, and possessions and feared speaking lest these and his family would put in harm's way. Local guards looked on, visibly taking note of him and close enough to hear what he would say. He glanced at them and quickly lost heart. The wife urged him, "Speak," but he could not; so finally, out of frustration, the middle-aged farm wife with a sleeping child in her arms stepped forward.

"My queen, without offense to you and the king, we are happy you have come to us! The nobles have taken the king's allowance, but so much, they have not been fair… It will take us years to recover. They have taken our best breeding animals… It was our under-standing that your mission here was to make peace… And yet, not a household has been left in peace and without tremendous hardship… There was drought last year in this region, and our provisions are minimal." Her nervousness and frustration made her begin to cry as she glanced toward the palace guards standing too close by. "And, my queen…" She finally decided she would risk everything, as Jadwiga intently and sympathetically listened to her request. "Normally, I mean during my lifetime… We live in fear…" She whispered this last sentence as the guards looked threateningly on, everyone know-ing that there would be payment for betrayal.

Jadwiga followed her gaze to the spies looking on and came closer to her, "Pardon, what is your name?"

"It is Anna," she replied softly and nervously. Jadwiga came near, the spring rain still pouring down on the large group; she put her arms on her shoulders. "I did not hear you, what is it you have to say?" And she leaned in so Anna could whisper her claim.

"We live in fear and *tyranny*," was the simple reply.

Jadwiga hugged her and turned to Henre. "*Guard! Call the king*," she stated loudly and clearly. Her guards led her back to the canopy, which sheltered her somewhat from the rain, but she already had been soaked as the peasants.

Jagiello finally came out. "My lady?" She bowed with her head downward to not seem to surpass his authority, as did all present.

"Speak," he continued toward her and lifted her upward.

Motioning to the soaked group of peasants, who now were a display of misery to be pitied, she said loudly for all to hear. "The governor's men have taken too much from the villagers. Our mission here is peace, and yet each and every villager in the surrounding region has been pressed far beyond their means."

Jagiello surveyed the crowd, sincerely hearing his wife's plea and, seeing the suffering of the people personally, realized the error. At the same time, he could see now that what they had enjoyed had unjustly caused the suffering of these people and had not been provided by the means of the wealthy through fair trade. He saw the problem.

"Tell them most property will be will be returned and the king's allowance will no longer be allowed to be collected except through fair trade." He bowed to Jadwiga, took her hand, and kissed it.

As he began to walk away, back to other concerns he had been resolving connected to the very visible issue at hand, Jadwiga called out loudly for all to hear, respectfully and with love with passion in her heart, "Much gratitude, my lord... We have returned the peasants' cattle..."

Jagiello stopped, partially turned back to her as if to return, her comment could be heard by all, *But who will give them back their tears?"*

Jagiello stopped in his tracks reflecting. *Who will give them back their tears?* The damage had been done. They had unintentionally brought suffering and oppression themselves upon these people instead of peace. Jagiello raised his eyebrows in understanding, giving a last sympathetic look to the group of peasants. He stopped and turned to them and loudly declared again, "You will be compensated for your sufferings." He bowed to Jadwiga and returned to negotiations with a better understanding of the hypocrisy and meanness of his hosts. Jadwiga felt the power in their united strength. They were a team.

Jagiello annulled sentences that had been unjustly passed by the justice of Poznan, locally called the Red Devil, putting him in prison where he resided for many years as a sign that unjust rule would not be tolerated in this revived kingdom.

⁓

The new kings returned to Krakow in summer after dealing with issues and tyrannical rulers. Jagiello was getting ready for his biggest endeavor yet, his return to Lithuania to fulfill the promise he had made: the conversion of his countrymen to Christianity and the destruction of paganism. He would model the state religion of his people, which he knew would bring progress to them.

Living with Jadwiga taught him the life of a devout and pious Christian who, daily by her example, challenged him to kindness, grace, mercy, benevolence, and peace. She fasted regularly, which made him careful about his own greed, and loved prayers, sacraments, and mass. He followed her lead in these things. His own mother had been devout and holy, and now his wife, who may have seemed extreme to many others around her in this regard; for him, he saw it as the very source for all the goodness and love in her. More importantly, he witnessed the secret life that gave spirit to her public graces, the tip of the iceberg most people only saw.

Jadwiga commissioned all churches in Poland to request of all women to offer as a tithe, a white woolen baptism cloak that would be given as a gift to the Lithuanians from their Polish family as a welcome gift. This great commission had gone throughout the kingdom, and the churches gathered the garments that would now clothe their people and united the women of the kingdom to a joyful generous giving through their talents and personal participation in the unity which would usher in a new age for Eastern Europe.

Jagiello had spoken often of his beloved people to her, and he suffered at their struggles and their need to catch up to the progress that seemed to be welling through the lands of Europe. He yearned for the progress that would bring them a better livelihood and peace and looked forward to its fulfillment, which both agreed would be achieved by education and spiritual development. They both could not wait for the fulfillment of this all important endeavor, and feeling like they had accomplished peace in Greater Poland, Jagiello was ready to head east to Lithuania.

Christianization of Lithuania, Jan Matejko, 1387

CHAPTER 26

Tears of Change and Long-Suffering

Jagiello travelled to Lithuania the year 1387 AD to fulfill the promises he had made. A sacred fire had been burning his whole life at Vilno, a powerful symbol of his family's heritage from his youth. It didn't matter. The ties that bound him to the past were to be quenched now and forever. He had seen that the fruit of his people's ways had not brought peace or prosperity, and although he loved his people, he wanted the best for them: a deeper, more true spiritual life that would bring his culture a much-needed revival. The day came when the high priest of his pagan people—old, knowing, and ready to accept change yet fearing it more—tried to convince Jagiello to just leave this last monument to their pagan beliefs.

"King Jagiello, how can you betray all we know? How can you make us all deny it?" He sounded strong despite elderly appearance, but genuinely terrified about the results of this dreaded act, his whole life purpose about to be taken from him in front of his eyes.

Something in the old man's demeanor reminded him of his father, Olgierd.

"We leave behind what is false and turn to truth," Jagiello answered him lovingly and confidently.

"But this is our truth!" he insisted desperately. Crowds gathered and mirrored the views of their religious leader, appearing very concerned and confused. "Aren't the Christians our blood enemies? The ones who had inflicted violence on us from the West? Why are we betraying our gods?"

"These gods are not true, nor are they real. Christ is God who became a man! Are we to neglect his coming?" This he shouted out so his voice reverberated loudly.

"Extinguish the eternal fire that has burned from antiquity, and the true gods will smite you and us all together!" replied the elder equally loud, sending fear rippling through hearts of the people.

"Then I shall see my error!" Jagiello pointed to the guards who had barrels of water to extinguish the flames. The high priest raised his arms, hoping to deflect the possible wrath of the gods, about to befall them.

Nothing happened, except Jagiello motioned for another group of men to erect a large wooden cross in its place. He stepped on to the platform and addressed the crowd.

"The light which you have seen extinguished is to now burn in the hearts of the people of Lithuania. The light of God's Holy Spirit, which desires to love here, within us, to better us and our homeland, to be our very aid and inspiration." In their poverty, suffering, and ignorance they had no choice, but to subject their understanding to this magnanimous king and put their trust in him.

The promise for the hope of a better future was a powerful thing for them, and they were ready for change. "Here, we will build a great cathedral. My brothers and sisters, I lead you to truth, and these good men"—he motioned to the groups of missionary priests he had brought with him—"will teach you about the one true God!" He grasped the hand of the old priest and lifted it to heaven and proceeded to shout the words of the "Our Father" loudly to the gathered crowd in their native language of Lithuanian. The pagan elder, overwhelmed by these words of prayer and the emotion of the day, began to cry mixed tears, along with many present.

"We have a God of love, who has come to his people of Lithuania, who embraces them and will now make himself known to them." A brotherly embrace followed this heartfelt prayer.

Now the elder pagan set the example and embraced the priests, kneeling before them to receive baptism. "I wish to accept Jesus as the Way, the Truth, and the Life."

"I baptize you in the name of the Father, the Son, and the Holy Spirit." Water poured over the elder man as he received baptism. His hands raised to heaven; he laughed, a spiritual joy overtaking him suddenly, and was dressed in a white wool cloak as a sign of his rebirth.

That day, most present received baptism because so many were being baptized simultaneously, coming as families. Many had already been taught the basic tenets of Christianity, and though many did not fully understand it, accepted baptism by the masses.

Jagiello was the joyful host who oversaw the building of the churches throughout, near all major villages, the installment of priests there, the evangelization and conversion of the multitudes who accepted new Christian names—"Mary," "Joseph," or "Paul"—given a white cloak from their Polish family, and the kingdom was rekindled with the light of faith and the fuel of hope and charity.

Jagiello selected a large group of willing young men to come to Krakow to receive education and become scholars and priests for their people, and many responded. He smiled knowing in his heart how happy Jadwiga would be to see the fulfillment of her prayers and sacrifice, which he himself was both instrument and witness.

As Jagiello took some time to achieve this great endeavor, Jadwiga was left in Krakow for almost a year, praying for the success of the mission in Lithuania, knowing she had a true partner in accomplishing her dreams for her kingdoms.

Constance, one morning in late summer, came to her. "Jadwiga, I have something to discuss with you, that I've been meaning to speak to you about for quite some time now." Jadwiga was very concerned suddenly about the seriousness of her tone and demeanor.

"What is it, Constance?"

"You know how I love you and am devoted to you?" Constance began.

Jadwiga began to sense that she was going to tell her she had to leave, "Yes, of course."

"There is a lot you do not know about me, about my life in Austria before I met you." Jadwiga listened silently and curiously, now wondering what the one person who had been everything to her and the constant in her life since then (for nine years her counselor, guardian, mother, aunt, sister, protector) could have to say that was so shocking. Constance failed at words. What secret had she had held in her heart and soul for all these years, dutifully living day after day and working?

She pulled from her underclothes a golden Star of David she wore on a leather necklace. "It was given to me by my father." Jadwiga knew at once that this meant that her father must have been Jewish.

"I am a Jew, an Israelite." Jadwiga was extremely surprised as Constance always had accompanied her to mass on Sundays.

She shook her head. "But why did you never tell me?" Constance looked with such love at Jadwiga as tears burned her eyes of both her past and now her present dilemma.

"I was concerned about the way I would be received in Buda, then in Poland, but every large community, I find my people and well-established communities. My employers knew, that is Albrect and Leopold knew, and your parents knew, but you were young and a child, so it didn't matter. My father was very close to the royal family, which is why from a young age, I was sent to work for them. Our family was well honored and trusted. So I gained employment there, and when you came, I loved you so and pitied you because you were so young, only four years, and beautiful—you became like my own, and I never wanted to leave you. It didn't seem fair that such a young, sweet, innocent child should be deprived of her parents then torn from her new family, and then when you were sent from Buda, I couldn't leave you either. I always felt that I should watch over you and stay with you because you needed someone, and your parents wanted it also." Jadwiga now was the one in tears as she had always been the subject of Constance's attention and love and had never even thought to ask her about her past or realize the sacrifices she had made on her behalf.

"Oh, that is why you would tell me the stories of the Old Testament by heart, that is why you loved them so and the psalms…" Jadwiga reflected. "You're the reason I know them so well." Constance nodded, smiling at her with love and admiration. Jadwiga hugged her. "I love you so much, Constance, and I want to thank you for everything you have done. Have you spoken to the Jewish community here in Krakow? Have you prayed with them?" The community was large, and an important part of the success, prosperity, and industry of Krakow.

Constance looked downwards, nodding, "I have. I do, every Sabbath."

Jadwiga reflected and then realized, "Oh that is where you go on your afternoon off all these years?"

"Yes, yes, but Jadwiga it's more than just that…"

"Tell me, please!"

"I have met someone. A beautiful man, who loves me and has asked my hand in marriage," she finally admitted, visibly in love and prepared to accept. Constance, being only ten years older than Jadwiga, was still very young and very beautiful at twenty-four years old. Jadwiga noticed for the first time.

Jadwiga, realizing what this meant for Constance, could not help but feel happy for her. "You're getting married?" she asked excitedly and hugged Constance tight.

Constance nodded. "Only if it pleases you, and you will permit it."

"It pleases me, and I permit it!" she answered quickly. "But I know this will take you away from me."

"Jadwiga, I will live here in Krakow and will work for you until I have children, and maybe after on occasion, but we will always be close, and I will come whenever you call me here."

"Yes, of course you can stay in daytime employment and have the Sabbath and Sunday for yourself for now. I will miss you, but I am so happy about this."

Constance smiled. "Thank you! Thank you, and we are family, you and I, after all." As Jadwiga hugged her tightly, suddenly, she began to sob, because the reality of losing her constant companion, realizing that Jagiello was to be away so often, and her family was so far away in Buda—even with Constance here, she suddenly felt the pain of isolation and loneliness, which had often been filled by the company of her beloved guardian. They hugged and laughed and cried together knowing a new chapter was about to unfold for both of them. Jadwiga was no longer a child but a young lady who had reached womanhood early, as most in her day, and was now losing any reminder and comfort she still held on to about her past life.

Weeks later, Constance married in the nearby synagogue, and Jadwiga privately attended the ceremony. She was so happy for Constance that her own sadness was overshadowed by the joy of this event.

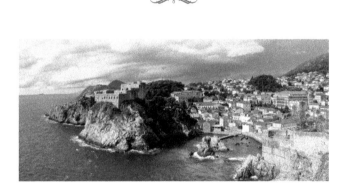

Weeks passed by with Jagiello still far from home when an important message came by way of Bosnia, Croatia. Maria, her only surviving sister, had been crowned the king of Hungary. Jadwiga's mother had tried to change the marriage arrangements to a French prince. On account of Sigismund's lax morals when it came to other young women, he had fallen out of favor with Elizabieta. Elizabieta and Maria had fled to Croatia in the uncertainty of what would ensue after Charles D'Urrazo, a nephew of Louis, had come to Hungary and claimed the crown of Hungary for himself. When Charles came, he forced himself to be crowned, intending to force a marriage to Maria, who already had been crowned regent. Most Hungarians did not want him in their kingdom, and he was murdered in the capital shortly after his takeover.

Elizabieta and Maria were blamed for his murder—the easy scapegoats for the angry Italian family who would seek blood revenge. Swiftly, the family came to where Elizabieta was staying with her family, stormed the castle, and imprisoned her and Maria as well. They were now prisoners and hostages. When Sigismund heard of all that was happening, he rushed to Bosnia to save his future bride. He and a Hungarian contingent arrived to fight and save the queen and her mother. Sigismund finally battled his way to her, but to save bloodshed, a truce was requested by the enemy. "We will give you the young one, Maria, but since it is her mother who likely ordered the death of our brother, we will not stop until a life is taken for a life." Sigismund was permitted to speak to the women in captivity as part of the truce.

When Elizabieta and Maria saw him, they were relieved and grateful. "Sigismund, you've come! Sigismund can you help us, can you save Maria?" Sigismund, unsure of his ability to even forgive his mother-in-law, but also feeling his own culpability in the situation by his promiscuous behaviour and infidelity, suddenly realized they were all paying now for whatever misjudgments they had made. Whatever differences they had had were over, for now the two were pitiable, and Sigismund knew the danger. It suddenly dawned on him that if things hadn't played out the way they had, he himself on the throne might have been challenged or killed by Charles D'Urrazzo.

"Mother, I can negotiate with them for Maria at this time, and then I will come with a larger army to get you."

Elizabieta, terrified and tearful, could only be grateful to save her daughter. "Yes, please, Sigismund, take her from here to safety…" She grasped his clothes, a desperate condemned woman who intuited her coming death. "And swear to me that you will never hurt her or cheat on her with other women! If you are to rule Hungary, then think of the example set by your father-in-law. You knew Louis, you knew he loved you and chose you and took you in like a son. He loved you. Please, I beg the God of heaven, think about him and be a man of God, for Maria, for your wife, for your kingdom. The way for you to be successful is through the way of holiness..." She begged this of him through tears, knowing and feeling in her heart this would be the last time they see her.

Maria clung to her mother, sobbing; the foreboding was as real as the words they were hearing. "Listen. Yes, you are correct, Elizabieta..." For the first time ever, both women saw this young man who had always been so stoic and serious have tears in his eyes, tears of sorrow, regret, and fear, as he felt the precarious situation weighing so heavily upon him, as he had risked his own life and safety to come to them.

"I swear to you these things you ask. I am coming back, as the Hungarians are to send reinforcement troops quickly, and they should be here within the week," he whispered the last words to Elizabieta. "We are coming to get you. I have asked for Maria, and they have agreed, but we are coming back." He turned to see the guard and now spoke more loudly, "We will negotiate a price for your release immediately."

"They will be punished," he swore, whispering again.

"Sigismund, *be careful*," a tearful Elizabieta warned. "These men are vengeful and not to be trusted. Leave with Maria at once and do not stop till you get to Buda, send the troops. Do not come personally. I trust in you to fulfill your oath to me. We only have each other now. We are family." She took Maria's hand and put it into Sigismund's and embraced them both. She then kissed Maria and held her tight, "Marry each other and trust and forgive." Both women cried as Sigismund now held Maria's hand and led her out of the dungeon, Maria looking back at her mother with fear that she would never see her again.

Jadwiga received this report in shock and silence in Krakow Castle. *Maria! Maria!* Her heart ached for her and her mother. She had been different than Jadwiga, more shy and reserved, less interior strength and uncertain, not overly concerned about her education and studies as Jadwiga had been. She had the personality of her mother, meaning well, but timid and unsure. Jadwiga's heart physically ached while she listened to the story play out for her from the reporter. Her eyes filled with tears. They were so far away, and she felt so helpless. The messenger stood silently, waiting to be dismissed. "You may go," Jadwiga said softly, barely able to speak, shaking her head in disbelief.

Demytr and the dear bishop of Krakow had accompanied the envoy into the room, and they all stood soberly staring at her, unable to move. Demytr came forward and sat beside her to hold her tight. "Jadwiga, there is more, terrible, terrible news…" Jadwiga looked at the group expectantly as if to say, "What could possibly be worse?"

"Your mother was killed before Sigismund could return with the ransom, Jadwiga, your mother is dead."

CHAPTER 27

Alone

With Jagiello away, Constance moving on, and now this terrible and tragic news of the death of her mother and already having lost her sister Catherine and father, Jadwiga, little by little, was feeling more and more alone. She wore black most often now. She spent much time praying to ease her loneliness, and the kindness of the nobility was good for the daytime and on the surface; but in her heart, she bore the sting of death, separation, and loneliness.

Despite the heavy obscurity of this dark night within the deep recesses of her soul, Jadwiga nurtured an inner stamina of faith, which spurred her to bring comfort to prisoners and needy subjects. She took comfort in visiting prisoners and feeding them bread and fruit and giving them consolation. The impact she had on them was truly saintly, as here directly from the hand of the great queen of Poland—tall, beautiful, holy, and majestic—they received their daily bread. They blessed her as she came and went, and she spoke to them of their problems and gave them hope and promise for the future when they would no longer be in prison. She encouraged them to pray. She loved them and empathized with their loneliness and isolation, for sometimes, she herself felt imprisoned in this life.

She often visited orphanages and sat and played with the infants and children, whom she could relate to their loneliness and sense of abandonment and gave them the love of a mother. She was really no longer a child but a woman now. She began to think of how nice it would be to begin her own family when Jagiello returned. She was ready for something new, and to start the family she always dreamed of.

Jagiello had been away for almost a year. Sometimes, she worried, with death always so close by if someday she would receive a messenger who would announce his death to her. The world of the Middle Ages was highly uncertain, but to kill a king would mean certain death for the traitor and would bring the wrath of a kingdom upon one's self, so most kept any evil inclinations in check; but still, Jadwiga worried about his safe return.

～⚹～

Before Jagiello had left for Lithuania, it had been decided that Jadwiga would travel to the lands of Ruthenia, which had been taken by her father from the Poles and resettled by the Hungarians. The nobles wanted now to use the queen's power to reclaim these lands for Poland. They claimed that they had been unjustly taken away in her father's reign. Jadwiga listened to their pleas to have the land returned to its rightful owners who had been drifters since that time. She had decided with Jagiello that they would reclaim these lands. The nobles and administrators had asked them to do this right away.

Jadwiga wanted to go personally without Jagiello, whose presence may have been too provocative to achieve these goals peacefully, as if to personally undo now the choice her father had made when he was king. She knew also that Sigismund would not oppose her now. So she personally accompanied a large troop of soldiers to Ruthenia with the intention of peacefully giving this land back to its rightful owners.

She achieved this mission, happy to see her country reunited and to ensure the rights of its people. In doing so, she displaced families from their homes, and as she watched the peasants walk away with their possessions and families to unknown destinations across the Hungarian border, she realized that sadly, war and politics was much more complex and had much greater personal individual impact than she had first realized.

When she returned to Krakow, Jagiello still had not returned, but it had been expected that he would be back in a couple of months' time. Happy to have been of service and having seen a new and beautiful part of her kingdom dear to her father, after months of travel, Jadwiga was anxious to arrive back to Krakow Castle and cathedral, the beautiful Vistula River running nearby, and the meadows and farms surrounding it. More and more with every excursion, it felt like home when she would return. With so many of Poland's knights accompanying Jadwiga and Jagiello in their campaigns, the normal defenses were somewhat depleted in Krakow. No one would have guessed what transpired in their absence.

When Jadwiga arrived, she found that there had been an attempt by Ladislau to overtake Krakow Castle. He was also a relative of the late Casimir, but everyone thought that he had been appeased and satisfied with the arrangements as they were. He had opposed the overtaking of the Ruthenian lands because he was to lose great amounts of land, and so when Jadwiga left Krakow with Jagiello away, in his advancing age, something deep within came to the surface, a hidden desire for power to overtake control of the Polish kingdom.

The castellan, Dobeslaus, sided with him. Jadwiga and all her men were astonished that he also had been convinced that they could simply on a whim take the kingdom. So when Jadwiga returned, the reality of the absurdity seemed to dawn upon them immediately.

"What is happening here, Dobeslaus? Ladislau?" she questioned as she entered the castle and found them both inside. "I have been told that you are here to stay, that you intend to take the kingdom for yourself. Do I understand this correctly? Dobeslaus, please leave." She knew that Ladislau was the one behind the takeover.

"Jadwiga, I only meant—"

"Only meant to overthrow Jagiello as king and myself as queen?"

"No, it was only, I thought—"

"Do you realize you could be thrown into prison and tried for treason?" She couldn't believe it, but Ladislau immediately saw the absurdity in his ideas. "After all, we have achieved, and Jagiello is achieving for the church, yet explain to me how you remain dissatisfied?" Jadwiga was angry, and Ladislau could see that no longer was she a child to be pushed or shoved but a queen with the heart of a king in her own right. And as she stood before him strong and sure, he realized her divinely appointed authority.

"I admit that I overreached my ambition. I meant no harm to you but to assist you to bring William back to the throne."

"Ladislau! I have known you from my childhood. Why must you bring William up again as I have forsaken all for my husband, King Jagiello! This is God's will, which Jagiello works to fulfill more than even you or I as we speak idly here."

"But, Jadwiga, your case of the invalid marriage is still in front of the pope in Rome! The pope may also declare your marriage invalid, and you could still have William—think of it! I know you love him."

"Have you gone mad, Ladislau? Have you completely lost your senses? Do you not know that I annulled my marriage of sponsalia to William on my wedding day? You were witness to it, were you not? And I am now married to Jagiello! Oh, please tell me you are not plotting to kill Jagiello?" She suddenly feared for Jagiello and looked carefully to read Ladislau's face for signs of scheming. "You would do no such thing, his own brother is to be your son-in-law!"

Ladislau shook his head regretfully and now wanting just to go home. "No. I would do no such thing. I wanted to help, as William claims still that you were married to him…" He now shook his head. After siding with William, in Jadwiga's presence, he realized she had been wrongly accused. Her honesty and purity was clear to him, as well as the certainty of her love and devotion to the king.

"What do you need from your kings, Ladislau? We have given you all we could, and I couldn't give you the Ruthenian lands without causing strife there." He shook his head and seemed resolved within himself to forget any former scheming or intentions. "I need your word that you will no longer assail us with these schemes and disloyalty. After all we've been through. We are family after all. You are my uncle! We can never act as enemies. Mother is dead, and you are all I have here in Poland. Please, Ladislau, can we not live in peace?" Seeing her pain and loneliness, he came and hugged her as a true and loving uncle.

He really didn't want to rule, and he only wanted her to be happy, whatever that would mean for her. "We will live in peace, and if you can take me at my word, and you have my word. I will never try to usurp you both as long as I live."

Jadwiga now let her guard down and began to cry, taking him at his word. She had taken on so much and lost so much, she did not want to lose him. "I forgive you, Uncle, but you must never do this again. I have forgiven you once, and the nobility might let me be lenient, but next time, I cannot promise that with Jagiello that there would be such clemency."

"I understand, daughter, my queen, my king… I am old and sometimes confused, but you have my word—we are resolved, and all will be well. We shall live in peace as relatives."

Situation by situation, Jadwiga showed herself to be merciful and forgiving and finding in every struggle the best way to achieve peace, even when disputes found themselves at her doorstep. Time passed and Jagiello returned home, heavily loaded with carcasses from the winter hunt and was well received in Krakow again, returning home after the baptism of a whole nation as well as seeing the establishment and building of churches throughout Lithuania. He returned a hero.

Jadwiga was especially happy to see him again after almost a year. He was her hero as well because he had worked so hard to achieve the church's and her dreams of unity. Her frequent prayers for the conversion of the Lithuanians had empowered his mission. Now, the sacrifice in the decision of her marriage to him seemed only a blessing to her. The time away had been good because it gave Jadwiga time to mature. Jagiello noticed she had changed. She appeared to possess a greater desire to bond with her spouse and to want to welcome children after the time of his absence. She was so happy to have him back and treasured their time together as they planned and talked about the children they would soon have.

Soon again, Jagiello departed from Krakow, as became his typical schedule, quarterly visits home and long extended periods away. Jadwiga knew about this from her childhood when her father would be gone for so long, as travelling was by horsepower and always slow, as well as all the dealings, hearings, meetings, and even possible battles that were endured by kings. Whether it was the time away, added to possible fertility problems, the coming of a new baby was not happening. Jadwiga began to fear and wonder if she could not have children.

～◦～

Year led on to year with Jadwiga continuing her charitable works within the castle. It came to pass that one time, when Jagiello had been gone for quite some time, she began to feel isolated within the castle from the servants and maids. It began slowly, but something had changed within the castle. Being highly perceptive, almost to the point of being able to read people's hearts and motives so well, being a great judge of character and subtle behavior, Jadwiga felt a change overtaking the workers within the palace. They were short with her and less open to talk. They were not mean, but not friendly either, and Jadwiga became distanced from them because of this change. She sensed this even in Krakow, in the center town, and even at church. It was a strange sense that people lost trust and the original love they had for her. She did not understand the source of this displeasure, only that it seemed real to her. It was so extreme that she began to go out in public less and less.

There had indeed been whisperings throughout the palace, completely rooted in a lie. A rumor that Jagiello, being gone for such extended periods and often on hunting excursions, and being a handsome man and being so often in Lithuania, must have a mistress or mistresses somewhere. Out of a desire for novelty and excitement, these stories and speculations were spread and retold, though not founded on truth. Jadwiga had not been aware of such stories until this cold spirit began to be felt in the relationships of the palace workers, but even then, she did not know about the cause of it. She prayed and left the matter in God's hands but prayed for a resolution.

One morning, as she came to the meeting room, Dobeslaus, the castellan (whom she had already forgiven for his scheming with Ladislau and for initially sending William away, who had often usurped her authority), noticed her and came to take the opportunity to talk to her in private. He came in immediately behind her and closed the doors quickly, motioning for the guards to stay out. His behavior was unusual and alarmed Jadwiga somewhat. He was not her favorite on account of the disrespect he so often gave them. She could not persuade the council to hire another individual on account that his family had held the position for so many generations.

"Dobeslaus…what is the matter?" she asked him, concerned, even for her own safety. She did not trust him at all.

"My beloved queen. Something… I don't want to be the messenger of bad tidings, or to make any insinuations, but it is the king…" Now, she was greatly concerned, as she always was for Jagiello's safety as she prayed for this each day. "He is away so often. And how could a man be away so much for so long from his wife? It's just something…a feeling that there is no way a man like him could stay so long without a woman. There is a chance that he has another woman or women." Jadwiga's reason for concern took a new and sudden turn.

"Well, what proof do you have of such accusations?" she could only think to answer. She had never actually thought of the possibility that Jagiello would not be faithful. He seemed to love her so much and to say so often to her how much he loved and treasured her. It never even occurred to her that this would be possible by what seemed like undying devotion he had for her; and after all he did, which he told her, he did both in God's name and her name.

"There is no proof, my queen, but the concern for the state of Poland is that if the king has a child by another woman—let us say, a

Lithuanian, and let us say that that child is his firstborn, a son—well, that would leave Poland completely without a Polish heir…"

Jadwiga never even imagined such treacherous thoughts. After they had waited so patiently for their marriage to be validated, could Jagiello now completely disregard the marriage bond and commit adultery? Suddenly, she began to have trouble breathing. She looked at Dobeslaus and considered the source for a brief moment. Dobeslaus had never done anything kind for her and had always been a source of trouble. Why should she trust him now? Yet something now made her concerned. He had planted a seed of discord.

"Dobeslaus! How could you think such a thing? The king is purehearted!" she finally managed to scold him.

"My queen, the king is a man." Jadwiga knew enough to know that Dobeslaus meant that men were different than women, less inclined to restraint, more needy. She turned her back on him completely. She did not want to give him anything, nothing of what she truly feared now that he had planted seeds of doubt, and not the power over her to see her in a moment of difficulty, which he so often seem to like to cause her.

"If that is all, leave now." Dobeslaus, not wanting to go too far and perjure himself, satisfied, bowed to her back and left the room.

Henre, not always trusting of Dobeslaus, looked in briefly to make sure there had been no foul play, simply observed Jadwiga pensive and disturbed, but well left her to herself. Now, she sensed she knew what was happening in the palace. The negativity and coldness grew out of the rumors that the king must have mistresses and that she was unsatisfactory as a wife, not being able to produce children. She finally turned on herself. Had she done all she could to be a good wife? Were there things about her that made her less than adequate? Suddenly, she was filled with self-doubt about the quality of her relationship with Jagiello. Worse, she began to think that if Dobeslaus was right, if Jagiello had another love somewhere or in Lithuania, a bastard child might be born. His Uncle Casimir had divorced wives after all. What was to stop him? Especially when he returned time and time again with no sign of a child. Her mind began to race as the talk of the castle had, with doubt, speculation, concern, and fear that the king may indeed have a Lithuanian child if she did not produce an heir soon.

Jadwiga's heart was heavy now, and even if she prayed every day, she could not seem to feel the light and peace of a beautiful cloudless day. As if the concerns already in her heart weren't enough, she soon received news that pressed her down as far as she felt she would ever be. Jadwiga had met with Sigismund and Maria with Jagiello six months before in a joyful and tearful reunion to discuss Ruthenian lands and how they rightly belonged to Poland, ensuring that they would have peaceful support from Sigismund. They were happy to be allies and family.

The royal couples rarely saw each other, even though the distance was not too far, both families were extremely busy with governance and could spare little time. The truth was also that Jadwiga and Maria had grown apart over the years because of the distance between them. Their love for each other was so strong, as after the untimely death of their mother, they shared in the quiet suffering that they only had each other of their family left, and that thought was comforting and precious to them despite the distance between them. This last visit was cordial, but business, and Maria and Jadwiga shared precious moments, discussing their lives and their attempts to have a child. Both were delighted and treasured every moment together, but Jadwiga had sensed sadness or loneliness in Maria's heart, as if she wanted to say more but couldn't. So they left on very good terms with Maria's secrets worrying Jadwiga on many levels, but one secret Maria had confided to her was that she had newly found out she was going to have a child. This sparked a flame of hope and joy in both their hearts, and Jadwiga swore she would come and stay with Maria when the baby was born. They had hugged and cried, not knowing when and in what condition they would find each other next.

Sigismund had sent a messenger speedily to Krakow, who rode straight without stopping to Krakow and the castle. He bore the black flag of bad tidings on his horse, and when the castellan received him, he knew someone had died. Dobeslaus stopped him, concern and fear on his face, not knowing what political ramifications a death might have on the castle and all of Poland. "It is the sister of the queen."

Dobeslaus, for the first time, shook his head in disbelief. "How much more can this young queen take? I can protect her from many things, but how to protect her from death? I cannot." And his heart grew sad and filled with love and pity for his queen. "If I let you in, you may break her heart, yet she must know." So he waved the messenger through, telling him, "You must be gentle and kind. The queen is so burdened by so many things, we don't want this news to devastate her." The messenger nodded with understanding and meekness, sighing deeply as he rode on to the front and was assisted to disembark.

Dobeslaus could not bear to accompany him to the queen. Watching him go, shaking his head, his heart filled with regret and pity that he had ever laid a care upon the queen's mind and heart.

Jadwiga was in council with the nobles when the door burst open and the messenger appeared with his black flag. Everyone in the room froze. Was it Jagiello? Was it one of his brothers? Who now? They stared silently, wanting to know out of curiosity, yet not wanting their world to change. Jadwiga, somehow in her heart knew that this message was going to be very influential and close to her heart, possibly had been given a premonition, walked backward towards her throne and slowly sat down, her heart wrenching within her chest. She had to take this news sitting. She bent her head and crossed her hands over her chest, waiting.

Ladislau was the first to greet the messenger, who stood paralyzed at the entrance of the room. "Well, come forward and tell us what news," he urged. At that, the messenger approached the council, "I am sent by Sigismund, king of Hungary, to inform the council and Her Majesty, Queen Jadwiga, that her sister is now resting with the Lord. Four days past, she fell from her horse, and the injury sustained to her head sadly and with deepest regret was fatal. The baby she carried also died. Sigismund sends his sorrow and regrets and all his love. He invites you to come to Buda if you desire. That is all."

All the men in the council were speechless. The last remaining of the queen's family was now gone. Poor Jadwiga. They had grown to love and respect her, revere her so that they silently wondered how much one young woman could take. She was the last of her father's house. They could barely look at her and simply looked down, murmuring silent prayers. Ladislau slowly made his way to Jadwiga, who now began to weep. He had known her since she was a baby and wanted to support her now more than ever. They didn't need to talk. She took comfort in his hug because it was all she had. Her Polish family and Jagiello was now her all. Even though almost constantly surrounded by people both inside and outside, she couldn't help but feel the weight of the reality that as far as her beloved and cherished family, they all had vanished from her grasp and her life one by one, until she was now undoubtedly, inexplicably, alone.

CHAPTER 28

Reunited

Finally, Jagiello returned from his long journey, which he cut short after hearing about Maria's tragedy. Jadwiga could never live in peace without resolving things, and she knew she would have to resolve the issue that Dobeslaus had raised. She could not keep this dilemma hidden or quiet, but she did not know how to question the king without making it seem like she was accusing him, so it took some time to bring herself to discuss it with him. Weeks passed since Jagiello had returned, and the festering question about what he did or did not do, or would or wouldn't do, was growing in her mind. She was also still in deep mourning from Maria's tragedy. These two things weighed heavily on her.

As was customary, Jadwiga ate dinners with her maids, and sometimes when Jagiello was home, they would eat quiet dinners together; but most often, they enjoyed and welcomed the company of the court at dinner. This was especially when Jagiello was home or when there were matters to discuss. The dinners were usually modest, but well supplied and always joyful occasions bringing the castle members and friends together, women with Jadwiga, and men with Jagiello. These happened more often after a long absence of the King, or when he would be parting again, or if nobles from different regions were in Krakow. It was customary to eat in the palace after visits or days of negotiations. Jadwiga always kept meticulous records of foods and stores needed for the castle and always personally oversaw that the food supply was accurate, plentiful, and prepared or purchased what was needed.

This particular night, after many weeks of dining and entertaining and what seemed to her like so few private moments where she had his undivided attention, she looked over to the men at the other end of the table and lost all interest in insignificant conversation, and began to listen to the men's conversations, but quickly lost interest in what seemed meaningless in comparison to the matter that really weighed her heart.

Something seemed different between them. She looked at Jagiello now, wondering if he indeed was capable of those things Dobeslaus had mentioned, and as he laughed and spoke with the men, she saw him not as the good Christian king or her good faithful husband but like any other man, like a man with needs. The idea that he would or could commit adultery and put his soul in a state of mortal sin was extremely concerning for her. She looked at him and thought, *What if he has done this already? What if he is in a state of adultery?* And her thinking made her blush and begin to feel panic. She wanted to speak but was suddenly overcome with such heart-pacing shyness and nervousness, speechless.

Jagiello caught her in this conflicted moment of wanting to talk and yet being unable and when his eye caught hers, he noticed her strange look of anxiety and concern. He looked at her as if to say, "What is it?" She smiled the best she could and finally spoke something trivial to him.

"What game graces the table from your hunting, my lord?" Jagiello smiled, happy that she would take such interest in his hunting, which was his favorite pastime after his work.

"My lady, I hate to disappoint, but only the pheasant and one deer to be cured. Much of it was left to Skirgiello and Alexandra and Ziemowit as gifts for hospitality." Jadwiga smiled and nodded replying questioningly, "Six weeks hunting and two fresh kill. Maybe the king will need find a new pastime, one that is more lucrative for the kingdom and closer to home."

Everyone at the table grew uncomfortably silent. It was completely uncharacteristic of her to direct the king in this manner. Jagiello was slightly irritated and disturbed by her unusual behavior. "Well then, I shall consider shortening my hunting stays." Jadwiga looked down, trying hard not to be overcome with tears. The men laughed and joked among themselves about "typical wives" and "women." The women were quieter as they saw Jadwiga struggle to contain her frustrations. They knew the depth of her mourning was taking a toll on her.

Jagiello looked again at her from across the table, this time with his own pensive frustration and skepticism. He had been told that William had returned in secret while he had been away and that Jadwiga had been possibly having a secret affair. Now, both were looking at each other with suspicion, unaware of the other's concerns.

~

Days passed and the coldness that had seasoned the palace now settled between Jadwiga and Jagiello. They barely spoke to each other and, although slept together, never spoke except to pray a night prayer together, both sad and upset, but neither knowing how to approach their concerns without accusing the other. The difficulties in their hearts transpired into their relationship and reverberated throughout the palace so that the suspicions, which started as gossip, now seemed to be more and more a possible reality. Neither one knew how to start a conversation that might help resolve the situation. Jadwiga, as always, turned to God for help in resolving this silent conflict that arose in their hearts. She felt anxiety because this was frustrating her goals to begin a family. The times that Jagiello was home were so short, and even though he was right here, they were a thousand miles apart, too far to start a family.

One June Sunday afternoon, Jadwiga joined the Corpus Christi procession around town and briefly along the shoreline of the Vistula. The tensions within the palace were high, but above all, she counted as most important the veneration of Christ's presence among her people in the Eucharist. She and some ladies-in-waiting and bodyguards joined the procession, following the altar servers bearing incense, and the priest carrying the monstrance housing the true presence. Four men held up a golden canopy over them. By the river, some families enjoyed the peace of the early summer breezes after the long winter and spring; they followed and sang hymns. Families and children came and joined in, intrigued by the presence of both God and their queen in complete adoration of him. The entourage headed back to the castle, happy to have shared their faith and the warmth of the summer sun. Jadwiga made a personal decision to trust in God and speak her mind to Jagiello tonight. She could no longer live this way. She decided to resolve this matter now before he left on his next venture. They were wasting precious time, and she could not let him leave this way, possibly in a state of sin. She left the matter in God's hands.

As they were returning toward the city gates along the river, she noticed a crowd along the shore near the bridge of the Vistula. They were absorbed in some issue, and loud weeping and mourning could be heard from the roadway. The priest and procession continued toward the cathedral, but Jadwiga stopped and left the procession to see what the problem was and if she could assist. A guard quickly obeyed and went immediately to see what the commotion was ahead of her. He returned and said excitedly, "My queen, a young boy, the coppersmith's son, has drowned in the river! It just happened! A fisherman in the boat got him out, but it was too late. He fell from the bridge into the river, but he was drowned. They have just brought him to the shore!" Jadwiga, shocked and horrified, her heart wrenched with the pain of a mother for this young innocent subject of Krakow, rushed to go to the group who had been too absorbed in the tragic drama to notice the royal entourage approaching from behind them.

Jadwiga broke gently through the crowd to where the boy lay. His parents were nowhere to be seen as he had accompanied some older children to the river. A man had tried to remove the water from his lungs and was breathing in his mouth with little benefit, as he was cold and his skin a pale shade of beige blue and his skin pruned from the water, his body limp—the look of death on his face. Jadwiga gasped, "Jesus, Jesus, be with us here," and she knelt down and picked up the child in her arms as though he was her own. Jadwiga hugged him rocking him back and forth. From her heart came a desperate plea to the Almighty, her automatic response when everything was nothing, when the universe seemed to give way from her feet, and she felt alone in the presence of God, "Almighty Father, do not abandon your servants! Holy Spirit, I beg you, return this son to his mother and father. Give him back to us to fulfill his life's purpose. Holy Spirit, give us back our son!" Her cries were desperate and from the depths of her heart and soul. Nothing else mattered in the world as she cried tears for the loss of this precious child. She secretly offered her life in exchange for his own, secretly in her heart she bargained with God, "Give him his life back, oh, Almighty and Holy God, who holds all power in your hands. In the name of Jesus, your Son, who raised the dead to life, I beg—your servant begs— give him back his life, oh, Lord, of creation, his life for mine if you wish, but give him his life, my Lord. Thy will be done." The others observed their queen kneeling, servant of the child, crying out to heaven repeating, "Jesus, we need you, Jesus, be with us! Do not leave us! Thy will be done." And they joined in with her heartfelt prayer.

This was the prayer of her heart to the Lord of the universe, and it did not fall on deaf ears. After moments of the group all in tears, praying along with their queen led by her example, saw her kiss the boy's forehead, and lay him on the soft grassy shore. She removed her cloak to cover his body, covered his body and knelt by him still in enraptured prayer that few had the privilege of witnessing was a part of her daily routines. She knelt now, as many people knelt with her and prayed for what seemed to be hours but was only minutes.

An extraordinary event occurred. The boy gasped and moved. Jadwiga and the crowd were startled as the guard quickly removed Jadwiga's purple cloak from his body. They witnessed the boy's eyes open as he gasped for breath, coughing and sputtering. Jadwiga, as amazed and fascinated as the group of witnesses surrounding her, cupped her hands to her face and shook her head in disbelief of what she was witnessing. She had relentless faith in the power of God, but she herself a witness to it was struck to her core with fear and awe at what she was seeing. The boy was blinking confused, crying suddenly, looking for his mother or comfort. Jadwiga once again embraced him in her arms, rocking him back and forth, "Oh, thank you, Jesus, thank you, Jesus." Crying now tears of rejoicing, the group could not help but cry with her as they exchanged tears of sorrow for tears of joy and disbelief that they had been the receptors of a great miracle, the greatest of miracles, resurrection from death!

From behind the crowd, a mother shouted, "David, David, my son," having been summoned by some frantic teenagers about the state of her child from the Krakow center. "My son, my son!" she shouted as she approached the shore. She found her son upset, crying, but alive, and Jadwiga gave him to his mother, who now took her place hugging and kissing him, happy that he was alive, not realizing the great miracle that had just occurred. Jadwiga began to laugh a beautiful laugh of joy at the awesomeness and joy of the miraculous event, as did now everyone exchange tears into laughter of extreme joy. The mother did still not understand the reason for the elation of those around her. Now realizing that it was the Queen Jadwiga who had personally seen to her son's well-being, she was at a complete loss for words.

"He was dead my lady," the man who had tried to revive him insisted to her. "He died, but he came back!" The mother now understood and was shocked. "The queen put her cloak on him, and he came back to life!" The peasants and entourage including guards, maids, and fisherman all nodded sincerely.

"Thank you, thank you, Queen Jadwiga! God bless you! You are his servant, God bless you... I am a widow, and he is my only son" was all she could say. She also became overwhelmed and began crying with her son. Jadwiga bent and kissed and hugged them both, tears still streaming. They were all overwhelmed because of being the witness to the event, as Jadwiga, now at the urging of the guard, turned to return to the palace.

The crowd was beginning to enlarge, every one of them watching her and following her gaze as she looked out back on the spot where God heard them and made His power known, and where his light shone so brightly that all darkness was touched by light and joy. In a world so filled with suffering of the mind and heart, God's holy hand touched and healed, overcoming darkness and sadness. Here was a queen whom God himself had come to the assistance of. Whoever could doubt her if even God was willing to help her?

⁓⁓⁓

News of the miracle traveled throughout the castle like fire and throughout Poland and Europe slowly and steadily. That very afternoon, many were speaking in hushed voices but with a new and excited feeling, like spring rushing through, ready to bring new life. Jadwiga, along with everyone, could not help but be fascinated by the afternoon's events. It was a sign of God's blessing upon the queen, Poland, and its people. Still, there was one place where the event and grace still did not shine upon it: the one spot of suspicion in both kings' hearts.

Constance had come to the castle to be with Jadwiga upon hearing the fascinating news. Jadwiga had asked her what she should do now, and Constance recommended that Jadwiga simply question her husband with patience and honesty in a nonaccusatory manner. Jadwiga knew that she was right, and with hope and peace filling her heart this afternoon, she resolved to speak with love to her husband. She gazed into the evening fire, anticipating his return so they could speak. Constance, helping her to get ready for bed, pointed out, "Sweet Jadwiga, don't look so solemn. The return of the king is a matter for the queen's rejoicing and another opportunity to work on an heir for Poland!"

The difficulties of her heart surfaced in tears of uncertainty and nervousness despite the wondrous events of the day. "Constance... how can I be with him now? Have I not given up enough, not uttered enough "Our Fathers"? And now, do I have to bear infidelity and intercede for the salvation of his soul? It's like sorrow upon sorrow. Would William have done the same?"

Suddenly, Jagiello walked into the room, wanting to discuss the day's events in detail with Jadwiga, at first excited, but at hearing the last sentence and particularly "William," his mood quickly changed. Constance hugged Jadwiga good night. "I'll see you tomorrow," she said, leaving, while Jadwiga wiped away her tears and turned toward the fire.

Jagiello began undressing, removing his outer clothing to a nearby chair, and he couldn't hold it in any longer. "William of Austria? You know, I've been hearing strange reports in my travels, probably all from the Teutonic Knights... But no, also from the courts of Austria...and from different local sources..." He paused to see if she knew what he was getting at.

"News of William?" she asked.

Jagiello, watching her to see if she might be innocent or guilty, replied, "Yes, strangely, he stated that your marriage to him was consummated, that you are his spouse, the Poles have taken you captive, your mother has prostituted you to me, and married you to a barbarian pagan... And there is news that he has been here and that you have been seeing each other."

Jadwiga, who had been preparing an offensive discussion, suddenly and surprisingly found herself in defense, and all the glorious events of the day were now quickly overshadowed by distrust and suspicion. Incredulously, Jadwiga protested, "Jagiello, you have to believe me. The marriage was never consummated! You know that was a lie! And I have not seen him since months before our marriage!"

"Only months before, I didn't know this!"

"Does that matter? They wanted to speak to me."

Jagiello, confused, "They?"

"Rottenstein and William, they wanted to stop the marriage, but you knew that..." She went to Jagiello, grasped his arm lovingly.

"You know it is not true, I have not seen or been with William, don't you believe me?"

Jagiello looked beyond her, apparently hurt. "A source close to the palace has informed me of this. And why were you speaking his name as I walked in, with tears? You love him still!"

"No! No!" Jadwiga protested and now remembering the possibility of his own adultery, replied, "No, I sacrificed everything—my desires, I gave it up for you… And now…" She looked at him, shaking her head, seemingly angry and disappointed, and he not understanding why she should suddenly be angry with him.

"Now what?"

"I should have known that you couldn't change!" she answered back to him.

"Change? I gave up everything! My heritage, my kingdom, my language, my religion…my freedom," he answered accusingly.

"Freedom?" Jadwiga asked. "And what if your firstborn child is a Lithuanian?"

"My firstborn? He will be Lithuanian!"

Jadwiga gasped and knelt down as if her energy had left her, "I knew it!" Jagiello looked at her with uncertainty about what she was saying but continued, "And Polish and Hungarian, and French."

Jadwiga gasped again. "Oh!" And began to cry. It was worse than she thought; he was admitting there was more than one woman.

Jagiello was becoming confused by the moment. "Did you consummate the marriage with William?"

"No."

"Have you seen or been with William since that fall or had any correspondence with him?"

"No."

Only having the word of this saintly young woman, he believed her and felt bad for his harshness and accusations. "I believe you."

"Have you committed adultery, Jagiello, are there other women? I am not your confessor, but I am your wife!"

"No." Now, it was his turn to answer, and she wiped her tears to try to see clearly. "No? Truthfully? No? What of the Lithuanian heir, the Polish, the French?"

Jagiello suddenly was humored by the situation. "Not an heir from each, an heir from your bloodline and mine, which contains all these..." Jadwiga calmed down at once, seeing his sincerity, love, and devotion, "Oh, my lord, then you have not been with any women?"

"No! How, why could I do such a thing, when every night whether encamped or in a stone castle, I think of you night and day...? I have no desire for anyone but you, all others are forsaken!"

Jadwiga finally spoke the truth of the heart of the whole matter, the underlying insecurity about herself. "And I have given you no heir..." And again, she began to weep about her barrenness and the fact that she had no child yet.

Jagiello's heart now softened with sympathy and understanding, and he came to her, embracing her passionately and lifted up her face to him. "You should try harder for that...it is true... But understand me, there is no other, only you, who I love and cherish from near and far. Only you... Why have you thought such things? Who has given cause for you to think that way?"

Jadwiga reflected for a moment, now in Jagiello's warm, fatherly, and husbandly embrace. "Well, Dobeslaus actually."

Jagiello now understood the cause of all the strife that was between them. "Dobeslaus! He is the same one who has accused you of infidelity with William to me!"

CHAPTER 29

Justice

Any wise king could not let such disrespect and deception go unpunished. Dobeslaus would now have to pay for his imprudence and disrespect. His slander was a poison to the kings and the palace family
and, ultimately, to the kingdom. So it was determined that his act,
no matter his prestigious position, could not go unpunished, and a
trial was set to seek justice. After swearing on oath, the court reached
a verdict in his case, and the highest judge in the land pronounced
it for all to hear: "Because of your meddling interference, spreading
none truths, and encouraging malicious distrust between the king of
Poland and his gracious wife…and due to the compassionate mercy
of the queen, who has asked for clemency in this case, the nobles of
the kingdom sentence Dobeslaus, long-trusted castellan of Krakow
castle, to reinstate his good name and show sorrow and regret for his
actions. For the malicious spread of rumors and lies, to crawl under
the king's chair like a dog and bark loudly so all here present may
hear and all to whom this poison has spread will thus be remedied…"

Dobeslaus's wife and family sighed with relief, and his wife
cried, humiliated, and blew into a handkerchief. Jagiello stood, followed by all the nobles, servants, and guards present to get a better
look with satisfied smirks. Jadwiga was seated, observing the verdict
with surprise. Everyone in the room clapped in agreement. Even
Constance was amused. Dobeslaus stood acceptingly, ready to make
restitution, realizing that if the queen had been of a different character, he may have been killed or imprisoned. The servants removed

the king's chair to the center of the courtroom. Dobeslaus, noticing the amusement of those around him, grimaced with embarrassment and resignation, shrugged, nodded, and crawled to the chair, under the chair, he barked like a dog. "Louder!" called the judge. "Louder!" chimed in the nobles.

Dobeslaus grimaced but barked louder. Then getting into the spirit of things, his humor taking over, he barked even louder, echoing throughout the room. The assembly now began to laugh and clap, pleased and appeased. Getting more into the spirit of the punishment, he looked at his embarrassed wife and howled then howled as loud as he could. The whole room lightened up laughing, reinstating a spirit of camaraderie and the proper humility needed to continue his role forgiven and knowing his proper place. Jadwiga looked on relieved and happy that now she would likely never have to worry about him again.

⌒⌒⌒

The next Easter brought joyful news from the Pope. After holding a hearing on the insistence of Austrian bishops, having received word of Jagiello's oath being fulfilled to Jadwiga and Poland, and his great accomplishments for the church in Eastern Europe, Pope Boniface IX declared Jadwiga and Jagiello's marriage valid.

Although summoned, William did not come to Rome to testify in person that their marriage had in fact been validly consummated, so his lack of testimony was interpreted as unfactual. The church officially declared that William was now free to marry, as though trying to compensate for his loss of Jadwiga. Austria, now under the directive of Albrect, thanked the Pope and, as a sign of fidelity, stated its new loyalty to the Pope of Rome over Avignon. An olive branch signal for Jadwiga from her long-devoted friend, Albrect, who knew the truth lie with her rather than in William's brooding over his loss with too many enemies.

Jagiello took her at her word and never doubted her. It was a relief for them both as well as the court and the kingdom of Poland to finally, after years of marriage, have the official declaration and approval to be recognized as husband and wife throughout Europe. For years, they had lived under the shadow of the scandalous lies of the Teutonic Knight leader and William. Jadwiga was relieved to finally have this resolved. Now that the accusations were resolved, she was hopeful peace would prosper. But evil never rests.

⌘

Things began to go extremely well between Jadwiga and Jagiello, and there was a time of peace and security after the trial and miraculous event, which continued for many years in Krakow throughout most of the realm. Most except for the realms of Northern Poland and Lithuania, which after Jagiello's and many other's great efforts to fulfill his oath there in regard to establishing churches and schools for education, had been met with constant embattlement from the Knights.

All their efforts for years had been met with opposition from the Teutonic Knights. Whenever they made progress, it would be destroyed and set back with their attacks. Their greed and prejudice never died but were continuing despite the signs that God blessed the kingdom of Poland and despite the Pope's urging for peace and harmony. Now that internal matters were settled, the council and kings turned their attention to the problem of the Knights in the northern kingdom and Lithuania.

Their relentless onslaughts brought constant complaints to Krakow and the kings. To ignore them would be to not be responsible. "Our tolerance of these people has reached its limits. We must go to war for the north and on behalf of our brothers and sisters in Lithuania, because that which was supposed to be a blessing has now become a curse on us. We have to plan for war," the counsel pressed.

Jadwiga, who hated war and never wanted to resolve anything by war but by peaceful diplomacy, stood up and spoke. "I will go to Rottenstein myself and speak to him. Surely, he will listen to reason, being an institution of the church and subject to the Pope. There is no way they will not be reasoned with for sake of peace." She persuaded the council to allow her a diplomatic mission to Prussia. "I will travel without King Jagiello, or an army, to speak to him that he may be persuaded to stop his persecutions on our people and our labors in Lithuania." The council and Jagiello agreed, realizing that she was their only hope to bring peace now, and the last chance before they waged war.

"You may go," Jagiello agreed with the council. "But you make it clear that it was only your pleading which has stopped the army of Poland from marching on them."

Jadwiga travelled north, north toward hope and trusting in God's intervention to bring peace. She travelled only with the amount of people she needed to and arrived to Marienburg feeling like she could convince Rottenstein to stop his senseless destruction in her lands. She decided as she travelled there that she would be kind and as understanding as possible. She could not understand what would lead a Christian man to such madness and felt in a way that she must be dealing with a madman. She decided she would treat him with love and respect regardless.

They arrived at the castle only just having sent a messenger to announce their arrival.

"Uh, you cannot be serious, why is that young vixen here? What business does she have coming here now?" He pouted. "She will not receive the welcome she may expect!" He knew he could bring no harm to her, as all of Europe and the Pope would bring him to trial. He had heard rumors of her virtue and so-called miracle, but he really despised her for her betrayal of Western Europe and for joining herself to the people he hated most.

He had interpreted his mission as being to despise and fight them rather than embrace them as brothers and sisters. But some have trouble reading the signs of the winds of change and the hope of a better world, and Rottenstein didn't see that his soul was in a pit of greed, resentment, fear, and bitterness. A pit with no ladder, only shadow and darkness that he had grown so used to. He feared that the light of the real world now would hurt him, and he could not live in the brightness of a new day dawning because he could not see life's purpose for him or recreate it. Most souls hope and wait for the dawn of a new day, but not him. His heart had grown so used to the darkness, it had become his god and the creed by which he lived and would die. Without an enemy, he would have no purpose, and all he ever had given his life to would be lost and in vain. So at the root of his life and behavior were the vice of pride, and the ignorance of the vastness of the possible ways he could live out his life. Oh, if only he could have dreamed a better way to live his life. So much suffering would have been saved for others and their tragic lives and deaths. But his pride and hate blinded him, and not even a saint could convince him of the truth.

When Jadwiga arrived, although she intended only to come and leave immediately, the coldness was evident as Rottenstein tried his best to be hypocritical. He had very little love in his heart and could no longer pretend to be kind.

Jadwiga was having a difficult time, concerned about how he would receive her. It had been ten years since she had seen him before her marriage, and he was really the last major obstacle in her kingdom of peace. As she walked toward him in his meeting room, she prayed for a way to get through to his heart so God could change his mind-set and at last have peace for Poland and Lithuania. It was the very thing she had given her life for, which he seemed now to give his life to make sure would never happen. She tried to love him regardless of his record, of his wrongdoing, for to do less would mean she herself was not being an instrument of peace. "Lord, make me an instrument of your peace, were there is hatred let me bring your love, where there is darkness only light, and let me not seek to be understood, but to understand," was her heartfelt prayer as she walked toward him.

She bowed with respect. "Conrad Von Rottenstein, I am pleased to see you again."

"To what does our order owe this visit from the king of Poland?" he asked directly.

"Why do you think I have come? You reject my invitations to Krakow, so I come to you. Why *have* I come?" Rottenstein stared beyond her.

"I knew your father. He understood me...he fought with me," was all he could manage, "I have arranged for dinner. You and your entourage must be hungry, so let us eat and discuss at the table your visit, and will you stay? We have prepared rooms."

"If it pleases thee, Grandmaster, no, but we will eat with you if that is your pleasure." So they moved to the dining room and sat down to dinner.

Jadwiga sat directly across from Rottenstein. As if in a private war, the Teutonic Knights sat on one side of the table, and Jadwiga and her people on the other. "We brought honey from Poland as a gift for the order," she began hopefully, Rottenstein shrugging, looking disinterested.

"I have another guest here, you should know," mused Rottenstein with intrigue, and Jadwiga froze, wondering if he would dare have William back to Marienburg.

"He is joining us for dinner... Oh, here he is now." And shockingly in came Witold. Jadwiga was confused. The last person she expected to see here was Witold.

"Witold?" she exclaimed. What possible purpose would he have to be here, now? Witold, why are you here?" she asked, concerned as she observed him come to the table, and instead of sitting on her side of the table, near to her as one might expect, he sat next to Rottenstein. Jadwiga looked at him questioningly. She knew that Witold was upset now with Jagiello and Skiergiello in Vilno and that he felt like he had not been given as much power there as he would have liked, but she never guessed that he would align himself with the Knights for assistance again. He did not answer her. She decided to focus on Rottenstein and let Jagiello deal with his wayward cousin.

The situation was uncomfortable with the bodyguards concerned and watching carefully the dinner for any attempt on the queen's life with poison, but Rottenstein really had too much to lose by such a treacherous act. Jadwiga had calculated even such acts were beyond him, although he may have done so if it had been Jagiello.

"You have come here for what reason then?" Rottenstein continued, knowing she would not leave until she had spoken her mind.

"You must know, sir, why I have come, can you not think of a possible reason?" He just shook his head as though he had absolutely no idea, and the thought of being told what to do by a young lady of twenty-something was revolting to him and showed in his demeanor. Jadwiga, for her part, although hungry could not eat because her stomach felt as though it was in knots, and everything she had come to say was trapped tightly in her throat as she could not help but wonder how this very food they would eat was acquired or if it had been stolen from other innocent victims. The table was laid with roasted meats and baked vegetables, onions, which filled the dining room with tantalizing aroma of a well-cooked rich meal.

She asked pointedly, "Why do you continue to assail Lithuania now that King Jagiello has made good on his vow and worked so hard to establish the churches there with so many good men and religious orders? How is it the mission of the Knights to work for the destruction of the church when your order's mandate was from the Pope? Is not the heart of your order and mission the *protection* of Christians?"

Rottenstein grew more and more disgusted that this prissy young queen would now dare sit at his table and question him thus, his pride welling and being pricked by her questioning. He did not have to answer to her.

Jadwiga stared at him and Witold, expectantly waiting for a reply, but did not receive one. He had grown obstinate and his heart callous and cold. She waited further, determined that he answer.

Finally, he spoke, "Do you really think that people can change? Do you really think these ignorant, heathen swine can just overnight change and care about education and Christianity, just overnight? Your childish whims are magically fulfilled by the wave of your scepter? Hmmm? You have not lived to see everything I have seen, and who are you to question me? The only way they will convert is by the sword!"

"I have been told to relay to you that King Jagiello and the Polish council are growing impatient, and that it was only my intervention that holds the hand of justice from striking against God's own servants, the Teutonic Knights, as I will not allow them to strike an institution of the church. It is your military strikes both against Lithuania and our kingdom in the North of Poland, which concern us. Can you not promise that you will cease your strikes against our nations? Perhaps you need to reexamine where your services are needed now that Lithuania is no longer a threat." Jadwiga innocently spoke the last sentence, intending no insult.

He stood threateningly, pounding the table and pointing angrily, shouting at the queen. "Who do you think you are? Are you above the Pope? You now command the Knights? You arrogant little…little…" He now composed himself just enough to not call her a name. Everyone sat staring at him in disbelief, waiting in anticipation for the insult, which did not come. He came to his senses and looked around at the company who stared at him with Jadwiga. "Ugh!" he sat down again. Jadwiga was not shaken or disturbed, but from deep within came a sigh as she pitied him for not being able to see his own fault. What had she come here to say? She lost her train of thought. Had she said it all, had she finished what she came for?

"I need you to not enter Lithuanian lands or Northern Poland without written consent from me of your intentions and purpose in these lands. No longer are you welcome in these lands, and you must abide by these regulations to avoid war with Poland and Lithuania."

"Avoid war?" he protested. "I do not intend to avoid war! I seek it, it is my life, it is how I fulfill God's will!" he shouted as he struck his breast. Jadwiga could not help but answer him now. They were engaged now and locked in, each for their purpose.

"God's will?" Jadwiga asked. "And what is that? Bloodshed? Violence? Armies that destroy and burn? Hate? Prejudice? *Wars start in men's hearts,* Conrad, *wars start in men's hearts.* Hearts where love does not reign and *God is love,* Conrad!" Now tears came to her eyes, but not of fear. She shook her head. Instead, they were tears of sadness, frustration, and sorrow for the terror and ignorance that made his mind like a rock that could not be penetrated. She could see that he had no intention to respect her request. Yet she refused to hate him. She refused to live his life, and she tried very hard to love him despite everything.

"Your father was my ally..." he mused. "We fought them together, he and I..." He was trying to bring the attention and blame back to her and her father.

Jadwiga rebutted, "My father fought for Poland, as I do now... and things have changed and are changing, can't you see that? It is my father who wanted peace, who taught me to cherish it and work for it." She could see that nothing she would say would change his mind. "Will you respect our request to ask permission before you cross our borders?"

"Huh!" he replied with disdain.

Jadwiga pressed for a clear commitment, "So you will not respect our regulations?" Rottenstein turned his head away from her eating his food, refusing an answer, visibly intending to do very much whatever he wished.

"I must tell you then that while I live, you will not be harmed, but upon my death, no more will you be sheltered from the justice of God himself. I wait and pray for you, but if you do not change, in your lifetime, you will pay for the blood and deaths on your hands for your crimes of hate, killing, oppression, and stealing. God will have justice, He is a God of mercy *and justice!*" she stressed loudly.

She now stood, and her entourage did also. She took off the ring that her father had given her, which she had learned came from this very place two decades before. "I return the ring, which was given my father, as it would only mean a betrayal to my people if I wear it. No longer will I wait for you to do the will of God, for you are bent on your own, but I will continue to pray for you, that your heart will belong to God and not the evil one." She removed her ring and set it before him on the table. "I cannot eat at the table of Judas. You are always welcome to Krakow, and I pray and wait for your conversion."

He now was acting as though he was ignoring her completely, like as if to say, "Just leave." His obstinacy began to test her patience and emboldened her to speak her heart.

"You and your order are not above the commandments of God, do not kill and do not steal! How dare you put yourself above the laws of the God you claim to serve! How dare you abuse innocent citizens!" Rottenstein turned his head away again.

"We must leave. I am sorry to have imposed, and may God bless you and let his light shine upon you." He refused to even look at her, just waving his hand toward her as if dismissing a common servant. She considered her mission here complete and bowed graciously.

"Thank you for hearing my request." And to Witold, "Return to your family" was all she could say. Then she and her group exited the great hall, back toward Krakow with always a glimmer of hope that the wisdom and light of God would break through and enlighten their hearts and change their destiny.

CHAPTER 30

Perpetual Praises

Jadwiga had done everything in her power to ensure peace in her kingdom. She decided she would live with peace in her heart by forgiving and praying for Rottenstein and focusing on the things she could do rather than what she was powerless to change. Her return journey in the north was spent collecting evidence and testimony from the people there about the crimes of the Teutonic leader. They were real and intolerable. These she did bring to bear witness to the truth about the order's actions to both the court of nobles in Poland and to the Holy Father in Rome.

For many years, she had dreamed of an idea to have an order of priests in Krakow who would constantly offer praise to God in perpetual adoration. When she returned to Krakow, she worked to achieve this dream. She also worked to establish and revive the university at Krakow began by her great-uncle Casimir, which without proper funding had not flourished or grown. In time, the town of

Krakow was always under the gracious spell of the groups of friars and priests who, at certain times of day and certain feast days, could be heard throughout the town singing praises to God. The numbers of scholars from around Poland and other European countries also grew within the town. Their presence and boisterous intelligent conversations could be heard throughout markets and inns and school.

Jadwiga gave to all who asked until the council questioned Jagiello, frustrated about the tax money being diminished greatly by her giving.

"My King Jagiello, the taxes have been diminished by the queen's giving of food and goods to the poor, who we have in great supply."

"Have you approved this spending?" Jagiello asked. Although he was in power, he always allowed the council a say in decisions.

The council looked at each other and, not wanting to convict Jadwiga, their beloved king, just shook their heads, just enough to make their point and no more, never wanting to diminish her saintly behavior in the eyes of the king. "My king, she does this out of her own accord."

Jagiello decided to address the issue of lack of treasury funds, and how to balance all of Jadwiga's and his dreams for Lithuania with the limits of money. He shook his head and, in a rare display of decisive frustration, left the council immediately to find Jadwiga.

He found her in her beloved orchard garden, with many children around her as always from the local orphanage. When they all saw the king himself coming to them, her ladies-in-waiting knelt silently, and the children suddenly became very quiet, imitating the ladies. Jadwiga saw Jagiello coming to her and happily walked to meet him with a small girl in her arms. Something about the gentle late October warmth and sunshine and the smell of the autumn air made Jagiello feel like he walked into heaven, a place of shelter, a place with no tears, love, a place of glory. She greeted Jagiello as a beloved husband, and he kissed her hand.

"Can we speak?" he asked kindly. Jadwiga asked the ladies to stand and take the children inside the monastery for lunch. The ladies did as they were told, leaving the two kings together alone in the late fall sun.

"What is it?" Jadwiga could read the concern on his face. He often had a hard time expressing his difference of opinion, so highly did he love and respect her, even in her youth. Her beauty also often made him swallow his words, most especially on this beautiful day, when her cheeks were tanned from the sun, which also brought out the gold in her hair. He felt like he was in the presence of an angel.

"You know I love you…" This was how he often would begin addressing her when he had some point he felt they might disagree on which was dear to her.

"The council informs me that the treasury is depleted commonly now by your giving to the poor and to those in need, and to prisoners who are leaving the jail. Is this true?"

"Yes?"

He looked at her thoughtfully, and whatever chastisement he had intended melted away in front of her idealistic and saintly purity. However, the truth was that her expectations for both kingdoms, her expectations of Jagiello to fulfill their ideas about a good kingdom, were costly, and he had to make her realize they couldn't achieve it all.

"You have asked me to build churches, schools, and villages, and we have done all this, and we must always support the schools and armies to fight for defense. All this costs money, you do realize, large amounts of money?"

Jadwiga nodded knowingly. She felt like she knew what he was going to say next, and she remembered all the times she tried to reason with herself about the limits of the country's treasuries; and yet her heart could not stop giving to those in need, and she felt like she was doing God's will but at the same time stretching things beyond what was possible. "I know I've pushed things to the limits, but, Jagiello, have you thought maybe that when we give and give people an opportunity, people can profit themselves as well as the kingdom? When we give to our people and invest in them, they in turn can invest and begin to profit all of Poland and become contributors? It seems to me that giving freely is the great secret to the success of a kingdom or town. When we invest in a person, we invest in a destiny, and each destiny we enhance, we enhance our country."

"Yes, I believe you are correct. I see this in Lithuania as well. The people have hope and work hard for their future, now they can see they have one. Our investments are the seeds of a fruitful harvest in the future."

He smiled at her now, but still concerned. "The treasury is running low, I have been advised. We will need to put off any giving or plans for a time to rebuild it, and the army and security needs to be paid as well. Will you lessen giving to the poor for a time?" Jadwiga now became serious, as serious as the cases her heart never let her turn her back on, and she realized she could not say no.

"Jadwiga?" he waited.

"How can I say no? How can I let anyone starve or go hungry? How can I eat comfortably knowing that people in my kingdom are suffering? I cannot. If you forbid me, I will not be able to meet with people or see people, for I cannot refuse anyone in need. We always seem to be fine, even with the giving." He knew she spoke the truth. "Perhaps we should look to the rich to support those who are needy, and perhaps the rich should see their duty to improve the lives of the poor around them by teaching them how to be successful?" Jagiello sighed and looked doubtful. The last thing the rich would agree to was to give more for the others around them or show them the way to prosperity for fear of losing something themselves.

"We will have to put aside a certain amount of money for different purposes then. You are right to say that when we give freely, it only helps everyone, and sharing is the key to prosperity and a happy people."

"It is God's way to share and give freely, so it has to be the right way," Jadwiga agreed.

"We will do our best then to continue in the direction we have been taking, but we also cannot deplete all our resources. We have to save for unforeseen problems. There will have to be some limits on giving." Jadwiga knew the realities, and she knew he was right.

"There is also the issue of the Teutonic Knights, Jadwiga. You know the reports are consistent that they continue to raid the Polish and Lithuanian villages, you heard firsthand the reports and their merciless killing is worse than before. Diplomacy has not worked. I have always respected your policy—*our* policy—which prohibits us from unnecessary war, but, Jadwiga, when does this policy become a hindrance for peace? We enjoy peace here in Krakow, but our subjects in the north have never enjoyed peace during our reign. Can we really continue to deceive ourselves with the idea of peace if it does not exist for others?"

Jadwiga was silent as she pondered his words; maybe he was right. She looked around at the walled garden, her little peaceful world. "I live in this little world of Krakow, and I've created for myself the illusion of peace, but your words are so wise, Jagiello. I…I…guess you are right to say it. I am lulling myself into a false sense of peace, but what is the answer then?" She suddenly felt lost and saddened by the realities of her world. "Father wanted me to work towards a world of peace…"

"And we have done that, Jadwiga, but when others are suffering, are we to stagnate in inaction? Your father took action only when it was needed for the greater good, no other reason. It has been over ten years, and we have waited for change, *patiently and diplomatically*, and yet nothing changes. Peace is a great idea, but in this world, evil must be stopped, shouldn't it?" He stopped here as he noted Jadwiga becoming upset.

"I cannot order the death of soldiers or my enemy…nor bring a child into a world of war…"

Suddenly, Jadwiga could hold her secret that she had been trying to keep no longer. She stopped him and smiled and looked suddenly so happy and happy to change the subject. He didn't know what could possibly be going on in her mind—maybe another plan of hers. He smiled back. She was irresistible to him and he always caved in to her dreams and plans. He just couldn't resist her beauty and intelligent spirit; even though she was so much younger, he often let her take the lead. He kissed her and decided whatever she wanted, she could probably have.

"So, what is it now?" he asked. She kept smiling the largest happiest smile he ever saw, until tears came to her eyes. She looked down and put her hand on her stomach.

"Oh, oh no, it can't be?!" he exclaimed. All she could do was nod and smile and laugh.

He picked her up and spun her around in the cooling noonday sun; as they were hugging, tears came to his eyes also. He couldn't believe it. It had been eleven years of marriage, and the two had begun to wonder if they would be barren—the subject buried deep within their hearts and too painful to even speak of.

"The Lord has heard our prayers and blessed us," Jadwiga finally said.

"He has blessed us!" Jagiello repeated. The moment was so great they silently made their way back to the castle holding hands. It was almost too good to be true. Finally, their union and the union of their countries were to be blessed in a new person and a new family, a new creation forged from two great cultures and individuals.

The Pope received the great news in Rome, blessed the couple, asking that the child be given his name Boniface, agreeing at Jagiello's invitation to be the godfather.

CHAPTER 31

Glory

The next months were a glorious and joyful time of expectation for Jadwiga and Jagiello. Finally, God had heard her prayer that she had asked constantly of him to grant a baby of her own. Jagiello stayed nearby, now after eleven years of marriage, and work in the kingdom. He wanted to spend time enjoying the family life and relative peace that had been established. It was a happy time of waiting. Jadwiga experienced sickness that was often typical of some women. Constance, now a mother of three children herself, came more often to be with Jadwiga at this special time and to be a comfort to her.

Sometime after Christmas, in a very cold and long January, Jadwiga confided to Constance one day something that weighed on her heart. "Constance, I have not told the king or anyone, but I have a feeling, something strange deep in my heart, I cannot explain—I think that I will die soon. I have felt this way for some time, even before the pregnancy."

Constance, who had suffered the fear and anxiety that came with childbirth in their day, comforted Jadwiga as any concerned woman would. "It is natural, honey, for you to feel that way. We all feel that way. Childbirth is frightening and delightful, even blissful at the same time. It is strange that Yahweh would put such great suffering and sacrifice with such a glorious event as the birth of a new person, mysterious and wondrous..." Constance tapered off, becoming lost in her thoughts and memories of the duplicitous nature of childbirth, such pain and agony and such delight.

Jadwiga set down her embroidery. "I know what you speak of, and I have these anxieties, and every time I worry, I lift it up to God and ask for a safe and happy delivery of my child. But, Constance, that's not it. It's more, as I said, even before the baby. Sometimes, I feel weak, most of the time all right, but these times of weakness, I feel in my bones, happens more frequently now. I never used to feel this way, and when I pray, I sometimes feel that God is calling me home soon and that I must prepare for heaven." Constance smiled, concerned, as Jadwiga was never one to draw attention to herself.

"What if something happens to me? Will you care for the baby for me, Constance, even be a wet nurse for the baby?"

"Jadwiga, you must put aside such concerns, you must think that God will look kindly upon such a faithful servant and bless you both."

"I do not pretend to understand the majesty of his divine plan, Constance."

Constance looked seriously now at Jadwiga. She had noticed that she had grown pale and tired more easily and more often, and she had just guessed it was part of her pregnancy. But Jadwiga spoke sincerely from the depths of her heart, and something in her sincerity made Constance believe her words were prophetic. From that moment on, both silently felt underlying the happy moments of the coming spring was a deep concern if her prophetic words were real or imagined anxiety.

Spring came, and with it a usual renewed force and energy that comes to the earth after a long winter. The servants gardened and harvested the early lettuces, spinach, and onions to grace the castle kitchens. Jadwiga frequently walked in the gardens. All around seemed oblivious to the weakness which both Jadwiga and Constance only seemed aware. They all excused her as being pregnant and nothing more. Jadwiga frequently prayed in the Cathedral as usual and was often accompanied by Jagiello at adoration and mass, praying for the country, for peace, and for the safe delivery of their child.

Jagiello was so happy to finally have a family, as now, he was forty-six and more than ready to settle and be a father, miles and far from what his father was, so different and transformed by a new culture and reality. He looked forward to the possibility of a son and heir or a daughter as beautiful as his wife. His happiness was tangible, as was the happiness of all in the castle and Krakow and all of Poland.

He did not see what Jadwiga and Constance saw, and Jadwiga could not bring herself to weigh him down with premonitions. She let everyone including the King Jagiello feel that her weakness was the pregnancy. After all, maybe she was wrong, maybe it was just the nervousness of childbirth coming.

One night almost June, she had a dream. It was her father. She never dreamed of him. He appeared to her and was happy in an aura of peace and security, almost glory. Suddenly, in the dream, came her mother. They were with her sister Catherine in a sunny golden field. They did not talk, only smiled and waved with love to her. Maria also joined them, holding a beautiful baby in her arms. They were all surrounded by an unearthly radiance and glow that could only be heaven. She went to join them, but could not reach them, and they disappeared farther and farther until they were out of sight, and she woke up crying but comforted by the peace and security she had felt in their presence. How much she missed them in her life was always pressed out of her mind to fulfill her duties and obligations with maturity and unselfish devotion. Jagiello awoke and noticed she was crying; he embraced her and comforted her. "It was a dream, I saw Papa, Mama and my sisters."

Jagiello kissed her head and stroked her hair. "Are you well?"

"Yes, fine," she replied assuredly.

She told this dream to Constance later in the day. Something in both their hearts was giving way to the idea that Jadwiga's premonitions may in fact become a reality, yet there was nothing they could do but hug and pray and wait.

Finally, the long-awaited day came when Jadwiga began to experience labor pains. It was a month earlier than expected, and everyone was somewhat concerned as her time had come, but too soon. Everyone in the castle waited anxiously and prayed. The labor was long. It lasted a full twelve hours. Jadwiga's weakened state and pale complexion, along with her too thin large frame, which should have appeared plumper with the weight gain of childbirth, did begin to concern her nursemaids and the best midwives in southern Poland, who had been called to duty in the castle.

Jagiello, for his part, prayed with the nobles, bishops and priests also for a healthy and safe delivery.

At last, Jadwiga delivered a beautiful daughter. Jagiello came in shortly after the delivery. He would not wait as advised by the midwives but pushed through regardless to her side. He knelt down at her bedside, eager to see his firstborn child. Jadwiga was so weak; she could barely hold the child. He made up for her lack of strength, and he kissed her forehead, took the baby from her arms, and cried tears of joy at the sight of his child swaddled in his arms. Jadwiga smiled at the delight of her husband then leaned back, exhausted, closing her eyes.

"She has a fever, Lord Jagiello, both mother and child," the midwife warned him. Jagiello hugged the baby close to him, sat beside Jadwiga on the bed, and could barely speak, overtaken by tears and the beauty and hope of the moment.

With the baby in one arm and his other hand caressing her, he kissed her head, saying, "Well done, my love, well done."

Everyone present was happy and relieved. "What will you call her?" asked Constance as she wiped Jadwiga's head with a cool cloth. She was really concerned that Jadwiga was conscious and awake, and recovering from a difficult first labor.

"Elizabeth Bonifacia, after mother and the Holy Father," Jadwiga managed weakly.

"You must nurse the baby soon, Jadwiga," Constance advised.

Jagiello hugged and kissed both again and asked the midwives if everything seemed to be all right. They nodded and continued their work. "God willing, all will be well in a few days' time and a full recovery made. The baby came early, so she will have to be watched closely."

"We must baptize her soon, tomorrow…" Jadwiga struggled to say.

"We will, and I will make arrangements," Jagiello replied. "You have done it, my angel! Good work! We have our daughter."

He left the women to work, as Constance and the midwives looked and worked with great concern that they hid from the king. Jadwiga, so weak she could barely hold the baby, was not a normal reaction for a young woman to have shortly after childbirth. A healthy mother quickly gained strength to hold and nurse the baby, and the long labor along with the fever weakened her so that she barely had strength. The little premature baby was not as full as she should be and did not have a strong cry. Both of these worried them as they did everything in their power to bring both mother and child to full health. Constance, filled with concern for what her and Jadwiga had so often discussed and consoled each other, worried most of all if this in fact was going to be the fulfillment of the premonitions Jadwiga had been expressing. She fell on her knees beside the bed and, over-whelmed with all sorts of emotions, prayed that God would preserve the life of her beautiful friend and her little innocent child.

Elizabeth Bonifacia was baptized in the great Wawel Cathedral the very next day as requested by Jadwiga to ensure her baptism because of her frail premature birth. Jadwiga was not in attendance, as a proper celebration would be held at a later time when both were in better condition.

Jagiello went to see Jadwiga, bringing the baby back to her himself after the baptism. "She's now a child of God." He smiled. Jadwiga could barely respond. He now began to realize that Jadwiga was somewhat ill more than normal. She did not have the healthy glow and excitement of a new mother with a new baby but seemed weaker and sicker than the day before. Little did he realize that something worse than he imagined would transpire.

Every day for the next three weeks, Jagiello came to visit. He took note of the midwives, who strangely were still in attendance after weeks, and Constance, who were all solemn and serious and still working as diligently as the days before, trying to encourage Jadwiga to eat broth at least. They also tried to get Jadwiga to nurse the baby, but she was so weak that they began to discuss whether they should call for a wet nurse. They all knew it was critical for both the mother and baby to nurse, and to start a wet nurse might even work against the healing and recovery of both.

Jagiello became more and more concerned as the weeks passed. "Constance," he summoned her. "Is she going to be all right?" he inquired, whispering. Constance looked up to the face of the king. In all the years she had been with Jadwiga, this was the first time the king had directly addressed her. She had a difficult time looking at him, but also out of fear that he would read her expression. With all her heart, she could think of nothing but that this was the end for her beloved charge, and the pain in her own heart at losing her great friend, relative, and queen was so strong and so bitter she could not face him with this reality. "Constance, will you not answer me?" he pressed.

She summoned up the little courage in her heart and spoke painfully, "I fear… I fear she is not well at all good, Jagiello…" Here she stopped and could not even speak because of a lump that welled in her throat like a knot.

Jagiello, seeing the pain and agony in her face questioned, "What do you mean?"

Constance sat down and cried after many exhausting sleepless nights of caring for Jadwiga with very little change or progress. The baby seemed to weaken as well. All the prayers of the kingdom seemed to be falling on deaf ears. She did not want to be hopeless, but all of Jadwiga's warning began to take on a reality. She shook her head back and forth, looking down. Tears began to stream down her cheeks as she sat on a nearby chair and collapsed from exhaustion began to sob.

Jagiello stared helplessly and turned to a midwife, "What is it?"

The midwives, also tired and fearful, also just shook their heads and began to cry as the king's expression began to turn from serious to the realization that they did not give much hope to the situation at hand. They did not have to speak. Jagiello suddenly realized that he had naively trusted that all was well and that the wonder of his life with Jadwiga, his most beloved wife, friend, advisor, guide, saint, and spouse was perhaps close to its end.

"No!" he whispered. "No!" But no woman in the room could give him assurance of anything. They were all so weak in the face of life. Jagiello knelt at the side of Jadwiga's bed, trying to speak to her. Their God would not let this happen to them. How could he?

As if she read his thoughts, Jadwiga felt his hand and squeezed it weakly, "He is all good and has given me a blessed life... He has given me a good husband, a good father, and all that is good..." Now that she spoke this way, Jagiello began to cry. How could he live without her? How could the kingdom of Poland live without her? Her life was so much a part of his now, and he loved her with all his heart. How could this good God not hear their prayers and preserve her? "I am going soon, Jagiello... If I die, my cousin Anna of Cilli...marry her..." Jagiello could not believe his ears. She was speaking of death. Something in all this made him feel like it was inevitable. "When I go, leave all my possessions for the university here in Krakow..."

"Jadwiga, stop it, I command you do not speak like this. You will recover, and the baby will do well..." Jagiello answered her strongly but with love and gentleness. Tears now streamed down her cheeks, but oddly, her expression remained serene and calm and happy.

She touched his face and said, "Thank you, Jagiello, for you have been a great husband to me..." Now her hands touched his tears.

"You will recover Jadwiga... God will heal you..."

She shook her head. "He has told me in my heart my blessed and happy life is over...so many suffer so much, and I have been blessed with so much..." She smiled. "Just take care of Elizabeth, have a wet nurse, and raise her up..." Jagiello bent his head down with her hand still in hers. Everyone in the room was in tears. Although they all had great faith, they could see God's will taking a course always most difficult, the course of a life well lived at its end.

Each one knew what a loss this glorious soul would be for the kingdom and for her spouse, and they each wept as they had stopped their comings and goings and listened attentively to each of her words, which appeared strong considering her weakened state. "Tell the nobles and servants I thank them..." Jagiello now stood.

He realized he had to let the nobles know her state, for until this afternoon, no one had understood what was really transpiring as far as Jadwiga's health. "I will my love, shh, shh, rest now" was all Jagiello could say as he kissed her hand. "I will return this evening… and stay with you."

She nodded in reply and smiled slightly. The nurses tried to give her the baby to feed, and she tried to take her and put her to the breast. "Wet nurse… Constance…" was all she could say. As she gave her child to another's care, tears again streamed down her exhausted, weak countenance.

That night, Jagiello woke to the hustle and bustle of midwives and Constance crying. At first, he thought it was Jadwiga, that she had died, and it felt like a sword had torn his heart in two. Instead, Constance came toward him carrying his newborn infant, silent and still. As she walked toward him holding the child out toward him, he saw her grief was not for Jadwiga but for baby Elizabeth, the daughter he barely had come to know. A look of confusion and upset came over him as he shook his head as she walked toward him. The child, his only child, was gone?

"No, no it can't be, the baby is gone?" Constance only nodded, weeping over the small, thin three-week-old infant, who for whatever reason Providence did not supply, had died. Constance held her toward her father to hold her one last time. Jagiello grasped the bundle swaddled in cloth and pressed his lips to her head. She was cold, beautiful and tiny, her life not to be lived out here below. He took her and knelt to the floor, holding her to his chest and crying, rocking her back and forth, "Oh, my daughter, my baby, you are gone?" He was a sight to be pitied, and there is no heart in the world that would not have been moved to tears to see him mourn his first child. But maybe, God would relent now that he had his child and spare his wife!

He cried on his knees, holding the little delicate corpse tenderly, crying so much; he never knew he could cry like that. Finally, sighing deeply, he asked, "Has Jadwiga had been told?" Constance shook her head. They could not bring themselves to tell her. He went to Jadwiga but sat on the chair beside her bed and held the baby in his arms until morning, deciding not to wake her up in case her sleep would somehow revive her and bring her strength to overcome this illness that seemed to take the life from her so quickly. He turned inward to the life of prayer Jadwiga had taught him, "Holy God, I believe in you, help my disbelief, take my child into your arms and spare my wife. Take this child's soul into your heavenly kingdom, until we can see her again," and he continued his prayer until morning to put this sorrowful turn of events into the hands of the Almighty Father and King, who was above all things, above even two great kings of Europe.

In the first light of morning, Jadwiga awoke to see Jagiello holding the baby. The look on his face told her that it was not good. The child was weak as Jadwiga, and she feared the baby might not live. Something told her in her heart that she was gone. "Oh good, Jagiello, she is gone to heaven?" she questioned him in a labored voice and reached out to grasp the cold little hand of her baby. She did not appear stronger or better than the day before. He nodded yes and could not bring himself to say it. He looked at her in her weakened state and felt so helpless. "I will go to take care of her there," she continued.

"No! God will take care of her, just stay here with me, with us. We need you here for Poland, for your people. Stay! You must think this way to become strong and grow well, and there will be other children!" She smiled lovingly and sadly at Jagiello, and he leaned to kiss her now.

"We will have to make funeral arrangements," was all he could say as both their eyes filled with tears.

Suddenly, Ladislau came in the room and rushed to the bed as he had just received news of the baby's death. He was in tears and so sad for the couple that he had grown to love. He stretched his arms over Jagiello and Jadwiga both and kissed them both. "My hearts, what is the good God doing to us? Is it true the baby is gone?"

"Yes, Uncle, and I am to follow her soon, God is calling me also," Jadwiga managed weakly. She knew he as well as the others had not known the serious state of mother and child. He knelt by her bed, cherishing her as one of his own daughters, picked up her hand

and kissed it, admonishing with loving concern. "No. You will stay and have a family of other children and heirs to the crown." Jadwiga closed her eyes peacefully, tears were streaming down as she managed to smile and shake her head gently no.

Ladislau looked at Constance and the nurses tending her bedside, who could not reassure him, and then at Jagiello, suddenly realizing the truth about the situation. He knelt by the bedside and said a prayer for a miracle of healing. After all, she was only twenty-four, but the way of the Middle Ages was that one had to always be ready to face eternity as there were no guarantees—no hospitals or medical procedures to prolong her existence. Rich or poor were subject to the methods of their day, which left them all at the mercy of nature. Ladislau took the child from Jagiello, who kissed her one last time, offered her to Jadwiga to kiss one last time, which she managed to do. As she kissed her, she sighed in her soul. *Oh, why must we all die, such pain, why must everyone I love die? It must be like this in life, but eternal life we will live and never have to die again.* That inner voice consoled her. Thus she said good-bye to her long-awaited daughter and gave her up to God, too weak to attend her funeral.

Baby Elizabeth had her funeral mass the next day, and her death filled Krakow with such sadness and mourning that one would think an adult of full stature and life had died, as they considered her their own. Empty now sat the silver cradle Witold had sent, forged by the new industry of Lithuania. The gifts for the new mother and her child, worth two hundred and twenty-five florins, sat untouched—a beautiful token of the love and devotion so many had for her and her child. It would be granted to the Krakow University as requested by the dying young mother. Suddenly, the sadness was doubled because the news of Elizabeth's death also brought with it whisperings of Jadwiga's state of health. Everyone prayed and hoped for her recovery as news spread.

But God said, "No."

The next three days saw Jadwiga's condition deteriorate, and as she had not eaten, she grew pale and thin. And in her weakness, she tried to take in some broth each day, but even the warmth and allure of the summer sun through her window could not heal the ailment that had taken over her body.

Jagiello stayed close by as the Krakow doctor only could shake his head sadly and offer no solution; they all knew Jadwiga's time had come.

It was the middle of the night, that dreaded dark hour, that Jagiello was awakened again by attending workers. He slept in a separate bed in their bedchamber. There was a hushed silence with a warm summer breeze blowing in the window and candles lit enough to light the room.

Constance motioned sadly for him to come. "It is time," she wept softly. Jadwiga was only partially conscious and seemed to be struggling for breath. The caretakers knew the signs as her breath became labored. She opened her eyes and managed to whisper, "Thank you," with such a look of love and a heart filled with love for these special people around her, and mostly to Jagiello, for being her hero, her family, and her strength and guide as she his.

Her face was now filled with peace and had such a sublime expression that Jagiello had to ask, "What is it you see, Jadwiga, tell us! What do you see?"

Her eyes opened and closed and as she labored to answer, "Joy… Love… Peace…" was all she could answer.

Ladislau quickly entered the room, having also been awakened by the doctor. Jagiello turned to Ladislau, "Oh, I can't take this, I can't take this," and he turned away from the bed and knelt with his back to the heart-wrenching scene.

Ladislau grasped Jadwiga's hand. He had witnessed enough deaths to know this was the bitter end. He loved her like a daughter and wanted to be there for her, but he could not help but sob, broken and helpless. "Thank you, Jadwiga, for showing us the way…," he said as he kissed her forehead. "Jagiello, come," he urged.

Jagiello came to the bed again and gave Jadwiga her final kiss. She breathed a final sigh and was gone. They each wept deeply, yet her peaceful and beautiful expression showed that she had indeed seen something beautiful and sublime and had entered that realm. Only this gave them comfort in their agony, yet they stood frozen in the moment and prayed at her bedside quietly. The servants blew out candles until only the faint glow of one or two was left as well as the bright moonlight streaming in the window and the gentle warm fresh breeze from the pasture she had loved so much as if all of Krakow was bidding her farewell. Jagiello knelt at her bedside with his head on the bed and her hand in his, her body growing cold and lifeless by the minute until the first light of sun crept into the room, and that giant construct of time and eternity continued its cycle, and a glorious era for Poland was severed by the death of their beloved Piast and Angevin queen on July 16, 1399.

The death knell tolled loudly in Wawel Cathedral that morning, and ever so quickly did the news spread throughout the realms that the beloved Queen Jadwiga had died. Children cried, mostly orphans who had personally known her, and people of all ages who had been prisoners. Still fresh in the mind of prisoners was her kindness and generosity as in families and the poor whose lives had been made better by her graciousness. Every heart was broken, and so many tears shed; so deeply had she affected and cared for her people. As all of Europe heard the news, the well-regarded queen who seemed so young to die, and too soon, was mourned and revered, leaving every-one solemn. So was chronicled in the *Calendrium* of the Krakow chapter a brief obituary notice: "Today at noon died Her Glorious Majesty Jadwiga, Queen of Poland and heiress of Hungary, indefati-gable promoter of the glory of God, defender of the Church, servant of justice, model of all the virtues, humble and gracious mother of orphans, the like of whom has never been seen on this earth."[2]

The funeral was held three days later on July 19 with all of Krakow, Poland, and Lithuania mourning the loss of their beloved "king" and the era of peace that was felt to the outer edges of her realms. Her sacrifices and love did not go unappreciated, and as the death knells rang from town to town, along with royal messengers,

---

[2] Fr. Boleslaw Przbybyszewski, *Saint Jadwiga Queen of Poland (1374–1399)*, Postulate for the Canonization of Blessed Queen Jadwiga, Rome, ed. Fr. Michal Jagosz, trans. Prof. Bruce MacQueen (London: Veritas Foundation Publication Centre,1996, English publication 1997), 81.

gratitude for her marriage to Jagiello brought unity, which was spoken of in both realms as "Jadwiga's Ring."

Nagrobek Jadwigi Andegaweńskiej w Królewskiej
Katedrze na Wawelu

CHAPTER 32

Valley of Tears

Ladislau and Jagiello greeted guest after guest the whole day of the funeral. Their love and condolences gave them some comfort, and their communion united them all in a common bond. Finally, at the end of the long, tiring day, the two were left alone and sitting silent in front of Jadwiga's coffin. It was late, nearing midnight, the church cleared and locked, now lit only by candles. It had been an exhausting month, with such sudden and dramatic turn of events. The two sat in the whirlwind of change and uncertainty in front of the coffin, as if only now resting. They were both exhausted and into their own thoughts, trying to offer up prayers for Jadwiga, but more for themselves.

Finally, Jagiello spoke, "Why did you allow me to be crowned king, Ladislau? Why me, of all the men in Europe? I was a stranger after all, almost your enemy. Why me?" He suddenly doubted himself for the first time since his proposals for Jadwiga's hand. Ladislau shrugged then answered what he could. "When tragedy hits, it's so easy to forget all the good reasons we did the things we did, those deeds which would not have been accomplished without the life of the lost one who is gone. We are in the valley of despair and cannot see the light in it. Part of our heart is gone and buried with them, and life as we know it will never ever be the same. We are left with a void that can never be filled. All we can do is honor the beloved by living the things they taught us, live the things Jadwiga taught us. That is our only way. We have in her holy intercession a tremendous recourse for aid when we need it. She is our ally in heaven now. But we will honor her life by living out her virtues of peace and charity and making these more real than ever in the realm." Jagiello nodded silently. "Don't forget," Ladislau continued, trying to encourage and uplift the sullen king. "You were her hero. You achieved what she dreamed of and what she sacrificed for: the conversion of Lithuania, peace, and justice in Poland. Together in your marriage, you achieved so much, Jagiello, you made her *happy*. You were chosen because everyone who meets you sees your kingly stature, sees you as divinely appointed. We see in you what you don't even see in yourself because you have humility and a heart of greatness. God gave you these desires to join to Western Europe and to marry Jadwiga for his purposes."

Jagiello didn't answer. He was exhausted, fatigued, and feeling the weight of his position to the point of doubt. He could think of only one thing. He was leaving Poland with Jadwiga. He was done. He had no desire to be here or to argue his case to stay or to face competing claims to the throne or to marry any other woman who had claims to the throne. He would return to Lithuania and let the Poles, his friends, and brothers deal with the kingdom.

All he wanted was to be alone, go back home, and disappear into obscurity. This sediment was sudden, but certain. "You have been as a father to Jadwiga and a great friend to me. I thank you for all you have done for both of us, and may God bless you abundantly." The two men embraced, Ladislau nodding and shaking hands, not taking this the way Jagiello was thinking—that he may never see his friend again. They walked back to the castle together, finally saying good night to each other. Jagiello watched his godfather walk down the hallway to his quarters while planning to pack his belongings immediately with a few trusted servants and make his way back home to Lithuania to find a new direction for his life.

It was over a week after the burial that Rottenstein, while fighting a campaign in the northern reaches of Prussia, received notice from a messenger of Jadwiga's death. He was shocked as he read the announcement. He was seated in a middle of a field of battle in which the Knights had had victory over some simple native people of the region, and strewn about him were the bodies of the dead, his men going about salvaging whatever they could from them. Fresh blood was spilled in pools near his feet. It was a scorching-hot, stifling summer day; and after reading the notice, he suddenly felt as though his armor was a coffin to him, and he called loudly and impatiently for assistance to remove it. He suddenly found it hard to breathe. His assistants ran hastily to help him. He threw off his helmet, his breastplate, and leg plates. He was sweating and red. He sat down on a log, with the blood of a nearby victim leaking out and touching his foot.

He was saddened somehow. He had toyed with this "little" queen, and their relationship had been filled with anything but due respect; and for a moment, he felt bad for the way he had treated her. He could not believe she had died. He felt her loss as he reflected on her goodness. He never imagined he would outlive her. He looked around him, and in light of her goodness and the images of her in his life, he suddenly felt unjustified for the bloodbath and destruction around him.

For the first time in his life, he wondered what he was doing. The pool of blood was now surrounding his feet, and he stared at it and put his finger in it, looking remorseful and confused at the same time. He thought for one moment of an admonition she had given to him when he last saw her which echoed in his mind, but most loudly at this moment, "While I live, you will not be harmed, but upon my death, no more will you be sheltered from the justice of God himself. If you do not change, in your lifetime, you will pay for the blood and deaths on your hands for your crimes of hate, killing, oppression, and stealing. God will have justice, He is a God of mercy *and justice*!"

He scowled at his own weakness of mind. He pulled his finger from the pool of blood, raising it to his eyes, and watched the drops of blood drip, drip, drip onto his foot. Ignoring any command other than his own will, a will so far gone and bound to hate and killing that he could scarcely imagine another way of life, he brought his finger to his face and drew lines on his cheekbones and forehead, solidifying himself for the life he was still determined to live. Nothing would change his course.

◦∽⌐∾◦

William received news of Jadwiga's passing almost a month later. Austria had sent notification to him in Naples, quite the opposite Mediterranean landscape to Rottenstein's rugged cool landscape in the north. He had refused to marry after Jadwiga's marriage. He had waited for some misfortune to befall Jagiello. He was clinging to a thread of hope that he could still have her. There was no one that was good enough for him. He spent much time between Austria and Naples. He was now engaged to the heiress of Naples, Jadwiga's niece, who still had not come of age.

He had grown accustomed to his new life in Naples. After all, he calculated, it had been twelve years since the disastrous events between him and Jadwiga. Parts of what happened had left him embittered in life. His very young fiancé came to serve him lemonade in the August sun. Almost twelve years to the day he was kicked out of Krakow. "What news, my lord?" She was so young, but he would indulge her.

"Nothing, just Jadwiga of Anjou has died after childbirth. Her child also died." Joan studied him carefully. He seemed surprised and very deeply saddened.

"Just an old friend from the old country, a childhood friend," he finished after noticing her examining him.

He had never disclosed to her family or anyone the details of the painful events of those years. His pride would have no one in his new life know of these events from him. He would deny any of it if asked. Joan nodded, satisfied, and went off inside. As he watched her go, he realized she was almost the same age Jadwiga was at her marriage when he lost her. She was really just a child. Now he was twenty-eight. He thought about how young they both were when they were so much in love, just kids really, but it hadn't felt that way at that time. As he reflected on the news, it occurred to him that if he had married Jadwiga, he would now be without a wife. He wondered if Jagiello had done anything to harm her, and for a moment he tensed up, hate welling in his heart. It wasn't his problem, he calmed himself. He shook his head at the brevity of life and the complexity of destiny. As he drank his fiancée's lemonade and lay back on his hammock near the Mediterranean, he said a quick prayer for her soul and savored the privileged life. He married a year and a half later in 1401 to Joan II of Naples but died five years later in 1406, childless.

～◦～

When the Polish nobility, including Ladislau, noticed the message left by Jagiello of his intention to abdicate the throne, they met quickly to debate the future of Poland without a king. For a month or so, they continued governing, trying to decide whom, if anyone, should replace the line of Piast kings. Each one in their heart agreed that they could see none but Jagiello as the king. No one wanted to replace him. Their sadness and displeasure over the loss of Jadwiga left everyone feeling she would never properly be replaced by anyone.

Constance, in meeting Ladislau in town one day, mentioned Jadwiga's request for Jagiello to marry her relative Anna, granddaughter of Casimir, who was residing in Cilli, Styria. Ladislau brought this proposal to the council. Ladislau himself was long over the desire to rule and, advanced in age, had planned to retire soon to a more peaceful life away from government affairs. Ziemowit had settled in the Ruthenian lands and was living a contented life as Jagiello's brother-in-law. No one had the heart to come to Krakow and claim the throne.

The governing council decided to travel to Jagiello and ask him to return to Poland as the crowned king in his own right, with the proposal that he marry Anna, Jadwiga's cousin. They found him hunting in the far reaches of Ruthenia.

As the delegation headed by Ladislau approached him, he guessed that possibly they were coming to ask for his return. He stood silently as they rode toward him and studied them.

"Hunter, good hunter, have you seen the king of Poland in these woods? We seem to have lost him. He is tall and handsome. He is Christian and trusts in God. You would not have by chance seen such a man as this? You see, his kingdom has lost him, and they are lost without him. They need his divinely appointed presence and wisdom to guide them. But if you have seen no such man, then we shall continue our search."

Jagiello smiled and chuckled slightly. "Ladislau! Nice to see you again." And Ladislau came off his horse to embrace him.

"We've studied all options, searched the kingdom, and you're it, you're the only one who can do the job."

Jagiello shook his head and smiled. It was good to see them all again. His wonderings had made him feel lost, and he could see no purpose or had no will to fight, had no will for anything but seeing his trusted friends and advisors. He suddenly felt like they were his family, his heart and destiny. What he knew was how to govern Poland. "Do I have to marry Anna? What does she look like?" he joked with them.

"Well, I guess you'll just have to wait and see…" Ladislau teased.

Jagiello walked off with them, the cold wintery air upon them as they all made their way to the home fires of Ziemowit and Alexandra's castle.

⌣⌒⌒⌒

Jagiello agreed to marry Anna of Cilli, although it was a marriage of necessity and paled in comparison to the marriage that had been forged with Jadwiga. It had been a marriage of minds and equality. Anna was a simple woman, called to service, simple in mind and desires with no interest in governing or the matters of state. Both found themselves in a marriage of convenience for Poland. Jagiello had not thought that he would ever find true love again and set himself to continue governing Poland. Within himself, he always treasured his first young wife and thought often of their conversations and the great things she had inspired him to achieve and the person he had become because of her. As Ladislau had advised, the only way he could bring justice to her death was by living out her ideas. The following year, he founded the University of Krakow and guaranteed its funding, bringing in doctors and masters from Prague.

He lived in peace for a decade within Poland despite the Teutonic Knights' continuous bullying presence in the north. He continued to apply diplomatic means of reaching out to Rottenstein, who still disdained him as the evil Lithuanian who had stolen Poland's throne and, in his mind, likely assassinated his own wife and child. Any diplomatic attempts were hypocritical on Rottenstein's part.

The Prussian master invited the king and councilors to Torun for a three-day tourney meant to embarrass the king and his council. The best knight though turned out to be a Polish knight Dobieslaw. Not wanting to leave not having embarrassed his enemy enough, the next morning, Rottenstein insisted on touring the town and surrounding area with the king. A cook "accidently" threw kitchen slop out the window, landing perfectly on Jagiello. Rottenstein called out the cook and sentenced her to drowning, but Jagiello calmly excused her, feeling with certainty he knew the true cause, his Polish entourage feeling equally insulted.

～⌇～

Witold, over the course of time, having been made the grand duke of Lithuania, had always been the one at the battle zones with the Knights in the north, always the one who dealt firsthand with their tactics and brutality. Not that he was perfect in his judgments, but he was closer to the unjust violations of diplomacy, which the leader of the order constantly excused himself from. Things grew worse and worse between Witold and the Knights, the real problem being that Witold, with the king of Poland, was a force to be reckoned with and did not let them get away with senseless decisions.

The same evening of the disturbing humiliation of the king in town, they sat down for one last meal before all would depart, Rottenstein acting innocent of everyone's suspicions. He suddenly began to rant to the king, after he had drunk his fill. "Shall we talk?" he asked as he motioned to walk the grounds in the summer night. Jagiello's bodyguards looked concerned as the two began to exit the festivities, but Jagiello gave them a nod. *Give us space but stay close by.*

Rottenstein put his arm around Jagiello, "Witold gives me no rest, constantly shifting loyalty. One minute he is our ally, one minute our enemy, and I have tried to bear it all patiently, as you know. But as of late, I have had enough of him. Surely you must understand our situation and frustrations?"

"Yes, my cousin does have the habit of changing loyalties so often that even I never know if he's with me or against me, but lately, I think in his older age, he is settling." *Settling with me*, thought Jagiello.

"I need to know if I attacked Witold…would you support me?" Rottenstein asked, finally getting to the purpose of all his grand elaborate designs. Jagiello furrowed his brow, amazed how alcohol could let a man's guard down, as he pushed Rottenstein's arm from his shoulder and left Rottenstein staggering for his balance.

"So that's what this is really about? You expect me to fight my own cousin, who *I* appointed?"

"Or let *us* take care of him for both of us," the sinister elder leader replied. "You know how much trouble he's been for you, well, what if he suddenly was *dead? Gone!*" The last two words were uttered strangely high pitch, like a whine.

"So this is what this whole thing was about, that's why you brought me here?" Jagiello repeated incredulous.

"I am a man of action as you should know by now," Rottenstein boasted.

Jagiello shook his head, "He's my *cousin*. Blood is thicker than water."

"He's an idiot!" shouted Rottenstein. "A *fool!"* Their walking had led them to a nearby tall cliff overlooking a deep ravine. The body-guards were following a reasonable distance behind, nervously keeping a steady eye on the situation.

Rottenstein came close to Jagiello again, face-to-face, so that the alcohol on his breath made Jagiello move his head back somewhat. "We are the same after all, you and I," Rottenstein hissed and then began to laugh a psychotic strange laugh in Jagiello's face. Jagiello stared at him with disgust, wondering what he could possibly have in common with this selfish, evil man. "You are my *brother*, Jagiello, I am your *brother*."

Jagiello paused. Did this crazy man mean in a *Christian* sense? It felt like the ramblings of a fool, so Jagiello waited for him to clarify. "Your *father* is *my* father!" He began a soft foolish laugh, which crescendoed, again concerning the bodyguards, echoing down the ravine as if nature was laughing foolishly with him. He took a few steps back toward the cliff, Jagiello not sure of his intentions or what he was saying, straining to make sense of his words. "Olgierd, *your* father is *my* father Olgierd," he mockingly clarified, speaking exaggeratedly slow. His sinister laugh continued again as he stared at Jagiello's strange expression. "He was a rapist who raped my mother in Eastern Germany. That's right, an innocent young Christian girl of eighteen, who gave birth to a bastard *son*." And he bowed graciously with his hands extended out, taking one step backward to the cliff, so Jagiello felt sure he meant to throw himself down.

Jagiello stood frozen, shocked at what he had just heard. Was he lying, or was this shell of a man actually his own brother? He didn't really care if he threw himself down. He went toward him, and suddenly pitying his pathetic state, he grabbed his wrist. "Don't," he stated firmly.

"What's to stop me from pulling you down?" Rottenstein also now had a firm grip on Jagiello's other wrist. His hysteria now turned to rage. "Choose a side! Choose me or *him*! You fight with me or against me!"

"Are you threatening war against Poland?" Jagiello asked, trying to draw him to reality.

"I've had it with your hypocrisy, you're either a true European *or not*," Rottenstein taunted.

Jagiello shoved him away from the cliff, breaking free of his grip, and sending him falling into some nearby rocks. "Say you'll fight with Europe," Rottenstein stammered.

"Poland and Lithuania *is* Europe," Jagiello clarified.

"We are to be at war then, you and I?" Rottenstein shouted as Jagiello began to back away, making his way back.

"If you go to war with Witold, you go to war with Poland," Jagiello confirmed.

"So be it then," Rottenstein shouted spitting in an insane pitch continued, "Prepare for war against all Europe, *fool.*"

"You mean the *Teutonic Knights*?" Jagiello turned, wanting to walk away but stopped briefly, concerned about Rottenstein's earlier comments. He wasn't sure if they were true, but why would this crazed leader say these things? He felt it could be true, or he could just be deluded; but if it was true, this man was really his brother. Jagiello managed to calm himself enough to reach deep inside himself, searching for truth and insight, realizing that one way or another, he was his brother.

"You know, we are all forged in the flames of human passion, Carl. It isn't really the circumstances of our birth that matters at all, just our rebirth really." He gazed at him with pity and charity despite all the circumstances surrounding them.

"Prepare for war, *fool*," repeated Rottenstein, not allowing or caring what bits of wisdom might have been being offered to him. Jagiello looked at him with pity one last time, turned, and walked away, Rottenstein yelling out from behind him, "Then it's war!"

That summer, Lithuania had experienced crop failures, causing famines, to which Jagiello responded by sending large sacks of grain by boat. The Teutonic leader illegally seized the grain, claiming it was arms being sent. Jagiello's councilors advised him that it would be better to "stomach" this wrong than to embark on war.[3] When he was asked by an envoy to return the grain, Rottenstein would not and began other destructive behaviors in retaliation.

For the next year, the Teutonic leader meaning to carry out his threat had Jagiello in a state of preparation for war. Jagiello, nor his people, could live in peace with the continued threat of the Teutonic Knights to the north. Since diplomatic means had failed, the Polish council, feeling harassed, and defending their king, agreed that their only recourse in the situation was war.

Witold was sent by Jagiello to Sigismund to ensure that their treaties would be upheld if they went to war and to ensure Sigismund's support, as Jagiello found himself now surrounded by uneasy alliances.

Witold met with Sigismund, only to have him propose to join him in defeating his own cousin and thereafter be made the king of Lithuania.

Witold immediately left to inform Jagiello of Sigismund's hypocrisy and intention to side with the Knights if they paid him

---

[3] Jan Dlugosz, *The Annals of Jan Dlugosz (Annales seu cronicae incliti regni Poloniae)*, trans. Maurice Michael (West Sussex, UK, IM Publications, 1997), 368.

enough money. Sigismund's greed voided him of any loyalty to anyone but himself. Jagiello found himself now surrounded by enemies.

~⁓~

Finally, Jagiello reluctantly began to travel northwards toward
Prussia. His loathing of war troubled him. He didn't know how he
could attain victory when his heart wasn't in it. As leader, he risked
losing everything if he did not show total true leadership. He felt he
did not have the heart of a king after all. He stopped for two days
in Slupia. On his first night there, he said a prayer before he slept in
which he asked for the intercession of Mother Mary and Jadwiga. He
fell asleep uttering the words, "Speak, Lord, your servant is listening."

He dreamt in the night of Jadwiga. He often thought about
her and prayed to God for guidance and direction. In the dream, he
saw her, and she came toward him carrying a glowing sword in front
of her, erect and ready for battle; but there was no mistaking it: her
hands were in a position of prayer over the sword's hilt. Jagiello was
deeply moved and suddenly concerned that he had disappointed her.
For nine years since her death, he had worked for peace, but things
had escalated to the point that all of Poland lived under the threat of
the Knights as did their king. And yet throughout the year of preparations, he had accused himself of being the evil one by preparing
for war. If he was to be a true Christian, did God not now own his
heart? How could he dare go against Christ, who he now felt he had
betrayed? His heart had been heavy for a year because he was acting
logically, but his will was not in it.

Jadwiga came toward him, not in battle armor, but in a beautiful golden gown; and as she came, he reached out to her, and his love
for her was still so real that tears of anguish at his love and betrayal
of her began to pour. His soul truly was in anguish over his dilemma
and frustration at failed diplomacy and the prejudice he knew so
many held in their hearts against him. He felt so alone. She reached
out to him and he to her, and Jadwiga crowned him with a wreath
of beautiful white flowers and handed him the sword, which turned
into a rosary as he grasped it. He was suddenly enlightened that he

now held in his hand a new type of weapon he had not thought of, prayer.

He looked to Jadwiga to advise him, and she said to him in a clear tone, "My son, pray. You are a faithful servant, pray that God may direct your path and for your enemy." Jadwiga suddenly turned into Mother Mary as she backed away from him, "Let it be, my son, you will be an instrument of God's justice." He awoke from the dream in tears at the potency and reality of its meaning. It was a dream that marked the rest of his life.

Jagiello awoke at dawn with a particularly heavy and reflective heart. He had been preparing diligently for war for nine months. Jagiello knew at the top of the mountain stood the monastery of the Holy Cross. He desired to speak to no one or to think of earthly concerns but to do as he had been commanded and pray. He climbed to the monastery and spent the day on his knees in prayer and began to feel the weight of his responsibility. He felt like Jesus in Gethsemane. "If this cup can pass over me, then please let it, Lord, but not my will but thine be done."

It was eleven years almost to the day of Jadwiga's passing, in a hot July that Jagiello, together with thousands of warriors, including many knights from all over Poland, Polish from Hungary, nobility, and hired men of Czech blood, knew the call to war in the north and responded. Jagiello was well planned and prepared for the task.

The king's army was large, strong, and united. Most especially the Polish knights of the north and Lithuanians who had withstood the Teutonic Knight's brutality for a generation.

Continuous last-minute negotiations between Hungarian envoys, Jagiello, and Rottenstein for a truce were unfruitful. The Teutonic Knights would make no amends whatsoever, or promises.

Sigismund's only real interest was payment from the knights of forty thousand florins, even to the point of hypocrisy and deceit:

> The Hungarian envoys, in a private audience, [told] the King how the Master would not listen to reason, so the Hungarians have achieved nothing…: "Since the King of Hungary… is Regent of the Roman Empire…is not at liberty to abandon the Order and its Master in their need, for they are part of his Empire, the Hungarian envoys have ordered me to hand to Your Majesty this letter, a declaration of war by the King of Hungary, who now breaks with Your Majesty and sides with the Master of the Order." Before he [left], the Hungarians' messenger whisper[ed] to the King that he must not take this breaking-off of relations too seriously, for that letter is to cost the Order 40,000 florins and will have little other effect. The King, he says, is not to worry, but to continue with his plans and not delay starting hostilities…[4]

It was on Tuesday, July 15, that Jagiello began his day hearing two masses, "during which he pray[ed] for divine assistance."[5] Jagiello cried tears at the prospect of war and the bloodshed and loss of lives that would transpire at his command. He could not recon-

---

[4] Maurice, *The Annals of Jan Dlugosz,* English abridgement, 384.
[5] Maurice, *The Annals of Jan Dlugosz,* 386.

cile himself with the great mechanism that had brought him to this moment of truth.

Jagiello was deep in prayer, begging that the God of mercy and love, whom he had come to know and serve, would intervene by the power of His Holy Spirit. He felt sick at heart at the bloodbath about to unfold at his command. "Lord and Master, God of love, God of peace, hear me now, and intercede. You have commanded me to love and pray for my enemy, and this I do! Please, hear your servant's cry, and through the intercession of your handmaid Mary, and her servant Jadwiga, I beg you, Lord, to grant us peace…"

Suddenly, Witold came running in the tent breathless, "Jagiello! Jagiello! In the name of all that is good, the Teutonic Knights are advancing on us now! There is no more procrastinating, cousin, for war is upon us! Get off your knees, cousin, to battle!" His voice reached a crescendo of urgency. Everyone was put on edge. Jagiello dressed in his suit of armor for the first time since long before Jadwiga's death.

Władysław Jagiełło z Witoldem modlący się przed
bitwą pod Grunwaldem, Jan Matejko, c.1855

The Teutonic Knights had advanced so near to the Polish army that they could see each other's faces now; the Poles determined to "conquer or die."[6] Jagiello urged the men after mounting his beautiful, large Chestnut gelding:

"Men of Poland and friends of Poland and Lithuania! Friends of Europe! We have met here on this day of sorrow, to meet not with our enemy but with our brothers. Our brothers who, through hatred and bitterness, will not accept us as such but refuse to embrace us and want to see us as their enemy. The Lord is saddened by this day! The Lord does not wish for brother to kill brother! Through every diplomatic means we have come to our brother and tried to reconcile our problems, and yet they despise us still, have disrespected and dishonored Polish and Lithuanian territories year upon year, and threaten Poland with war. This is the hour of vengeance. Vengeance is mine sayeth the Lord! Today, the Knights pay for their brutality, theft, greed, and disrespect of their neighbor who, for an entire generation, they have brutalized. Our God is the same! He does not divide us according to our nations! We serve one God, and this day, he allows us the heart of courage and fortitude to stop the affliction of evil that has scourged Poland and Lithuania for generations! To battle! This is the day the Lord has made, let us rejoice and be *glad* in it because we will be the ones to protect the innocent victims who, time and time, year upon year, they have preyed upon mercilessly. Fight for the dead, fight for the injustice, fight to put an end to it all. Fight for Poland!"

Suddenly, two heralds arrived from the enemy's camp: "Your Majesty! The grandmaster of the Prussian Knights…sends you and your brother these two swords, so that you may fight him and his army without further procrastination or hiding in the woods and thickets to deceive him, but to fight him *now*…"[7]

Jagiello accepted and examined the swords carefully and sadly. "I have no need of other people's swords, for I have plenty of my

---

6 Maurice, *The Annals of Jan Dlugosz,* 387.
7 Maurice, *The Annals of Jan Dlugosz*, 388.

own, but, in the name of God, I do accept these two sent to me by an enemy that desires my blood and the destruction of my army, so that these swords may further strengthen the help being given me by God, into whose hand I entrust everything.[8] Tell him, that this is his absolute last chance for peace."

The Polish and Lithuanian fighters joined in a loud resounding national anthem, "Bogurodzica." Jagiello, regardless of Rottenstein's taunting him personally to war, was then escorted by a group of Knights to a higher plain outside of the immediate fighting. Witold personally joined the fighting, leaving his destiny in God's hands.

Rottenstein received his heralds back. "Well, what did the pestilence answer?" The heralds shook their heads, forgetting the exact response. "Is he fighting? Is this the glorious day when I shall rid Europe of its hypocritical enemy?" They shook their heads and shrugged. "He isn't fighting? The idiotic coward! Some king! Made of pink blood! Then I shall go find him and cut his cowardly idiotic heart from his body to end the misery of Europe!"

The messenger, suddenly remembering Jagiello's last words, stammered, "He also said this was your absolute last chance for peace!"

"Chance not accepted!" He finished his last words in a rage of hatred, spitting and red, putting his helmet ready for battle his last commands. "Take me to him! To battle!"

So the long-anticipated moment came when both unleashed hate, resentment, and determination one against the other in the battle of the century. It was hard to know who had the advantage at first. As hour went on to hour, blood was shed, lives lost, and destinies reformed.

Halfway through the fighting, suddenly, a troop of German Knights noticed the king's group and began heading toward the king. From the group charged a German Knight from Lusatia, heading straight toward Jagiello. Jagiello readied himself for battle. As the

---

[8]   Maurice, *The Annals of Jan Dlugosz,* 388. For a full and detailed account of the Battle of Grunwald and events surrounding it see AD 1410, pp. 374–405

knight charged, suddenly, from the side came an unarmed secretary with the shaft of the broken lance and pushed the knight from his saddle, as he could not be seen from the side view. The man fell, unarmed at the feet of Jagiello, who held his lance at his forehead, but Jagiello's knights finished him off.

This began a final battle between the remaining Knights of both sides. It was not hours more of fighting that the Poles could see that their enemies were few and far between. Almost all the Teutonic Knights were killed or taken prisoner.

Witold finally rushed to Jagiello to announce the victory. "Jagiello, it is over. He is dead, and so are most of the marshals and all their knights and commanders!" Witold, having become a Christian and having lived with the Knights, made his bittersweet announcement, not feeling bragging or gloating over the slaughter of humans he had just endured. Witold, feeling sick himself now of the gruesome displays of the dead and those robbing them of their possessions in payment of their crimes, but feeling relieved, felt that this was the end of the road for him. He was done with this. With the death of this lifelong enemy, he swore silently to himself he would never fight again except in defense. He somehow felt he would never need to. "It's done, Jagiello."

Battle of Grunwald, Jan Matejko, 1878

Jagiello could not believe that after so much preparation and prayer, it was over. "Take me to him if it is true." They stopped at a section of the field where their enemies had fallen, their horses dead or dying around them, all slaughtered in a bloodbath. Witold led him to the area where Rottenstein lay dead in a pool of his blood, already pillaged by soldiers desperate and greedy for their pay. His position along with his major knights marked by one of Witold's marshals.

Nearby, thirsty living warriors had found and pillaged a cart of the Knights, which contained barrels of wine; and now, the majority were drinking wine pouring out of large oak casks, using helmets, boots, or anything. Jagiello, noticing them gorging themselves, so ordered his knights, "They will drink themselves stupid and be attacked at night by those that have run off. Spill what is left out!" he commanded.

Jagiello's knights went over and dispersed the hundreds of soldiers, splitting open the barrels with their axes. From the cart flooded out over the field of battle wine, which poured out, mingling with the blood upon the fields so that the wine and blood mixed in a strange adulteration. It began to rain and then rain harder. In the strange mixture of elements and a dizzying halt of adrenaline, Jagiello dismounted his horse.

He was led to Rottenstein, or the shell of the man, and two fatal wounds were pointed out by Witold, who now seemed sickened also and remorseful: one on the forehead and the other in the chest. "Only fourteen Polish Knights killed," Witold mused.

Suddenly, tears of sympathy for their fate streamed from Jagiello's eyes down his cheeks. As he stood by the body of his "brother," a strange mix of tears, wine, water, and blood streamed down around the bodies. He knelt down and closed Rottenstein's eyes, which seemed staring in desperation.

"*Those who live by the sword, die by the sword,*" he uttered Christ's words thoughtfully. Witold nodded, reflecting. Here, he thought for a moment of Jadwiga, who was fond of this quote of Jesus; and thinking of her now, he nodded as tears streamed down his face, thanking God for his assistance and Jadwiga's intercession for a quick victory.

"May God, in his mercy, grant you eternal rest, my brothers," he prayed sincerely. Tears continued to stream down his face. "Wrap them in clean clothes, place them in a wagon, and send their bodies to Malbork for burial..." he commanded and stood up.

"A new day will come," he said gravely and sadly. "A day of diplomacy and peace, but this was not that day." Jagiello wrapped his arm around Witold's shoulders as the dusk made everything seem surreal around them and the sun finally shone strongly through the clouds. "Come, cousin, we have sown the seeds of peace and diplomacy, fertilized by the blood of our brothers."

Valley of Tears

For a time we lose our way
Shed off unwanted skin
And live another day
And die and rise and
Die and rise again
Until year moves
Onto year and we
Are formed and reformed

We have lost our way
And live another day
And live another day

And put to rest
Those shameful deeds
By which we lived another day

For a time we lose our way
Deny our soul in brutal shame display
'Til metal upon metal falls
Or there is nothing pure

Those who live by the sword or greed
Will die by the same
To their shame, to their shame

They will beg "mercy" to make
Them right again.

Establishment of Krakow University, Jan Matejko

AFTERWORD

Jagiello married Anna of Cilli on January 29, 1402, three years after Jadwiga's death. Anna died in 1416, after fourteen years of marriage, leaving behind one daughter aptly named Jadwiga. This Jadwiga died three years before her father in 1431, without an heir.

Sigismund remarried to Barbara of Cilli (Anna's cousin). William did not marry until after Jadwiga's death and died childless in 1406, seven years after Jadwiga.

One year after Anna of Cilli's death, Jagiello married an elderly Polish widow of "three not too prominent husbands" (Halecki, p. 287). She died after three years of marriage. Jagiello's fourth and final wife, "a young Lithuanian princess, Sophia Halszanska, 'Queen Sonka,'" he married on February 7, 1422 (Halecki, ibid.). She bore him three sons, two survived infancy; the eldest was born October 31, 1424, named Ladislau (d. Nov. 10, 1444 being nineteen years of age, Battle of Varna, as regent of Hungary). In 1427, Casimir was born to the couple, whose six sons (of thirteen children) with Elizabeth of *Austria* were to form a strong dynasty in Eastern Europe in the spirit of Jadwiga and their grandfather, Jagiello. This dynasty now was accepted throughout Europe.

Oscar Halecki's thesis regarding Jadwiga's decision to marry Jagiello was that it impacted a turn of events in East European history felt for centuries for the good.

Constance is a fictional character, who likely would have existed as an aid in Jadwiga's journey. In chapter 22, the meeting of Jadwiga with Will and Rottenstein in Oswiecim is fictional (not documented), as is the meeting with Jagiello, Will, Rottenstein, the character Guangming being fictional as well in chapter 23.

The "brother" allusion of Rottenstein in "Valley of Tears" is fictional. There was a Conrad Von Rottenstein, one Teutonic leader, but there would have actually three different leaders over the course of this story. Although it is documented that Jagiello did stop to pray at Slupia on his way to battle, all dream sequences are created; Jadwiga's dream sequence of William returning to her was inspired by a dream of the author, who pondered the situation, and the dream clearly showed that their love was real for each other. The Battle of Grunwald, as well as Jagiello having two masses said just prior to battle, was well documented in detail by Jan Dlugosz, as if reported by court reporters.

Certainly, the death of Jadwiga at such a young age was tragic for the kingdom and everyone around her as she was so cherished as a leader and wife. Keeping in mind the average life expectancy before the 1900s was forty-three years old and medical care was so limited, it is possible that Jadwiga suffered from Rh blood issues, which could not have been corrected, and might be deduced from ill health of mother and child. If this was true, then not conceiving until age twenty-four was a great blessing. Jagiello always wore their wedding ring; despite three other marriages, he never took it off and said at his death that it was his most treasured possession. Jadwiga was held in high regard by all of Jagiello's successive wives and children.

Jadwiga is a great model for young people in discerning what is God's will in our relationships, and even though love feels right, is it the person God has planned for us? We need to pray and be discerning about those all-important life decisions. St. Jadwiga, pray for us! God bless.

BIBLIOGRAPHY/REFERENCES

Dlugosz, Jan. *The Annals of Jan Dlugosz*, c. 15th century. Translated from Latin by Julia Mrukowna. Translated to English by Maurice Michael. Chichester UK: IM Publications, 1997.

Halecki, Oscar, *Jadwiga of Anjou and the Rise of East Central Europe*. New York: Social Science Monographs, Columbia University Press, 1991.

Przybyszewski, Boleslaw. *Saint Jadwiga, Queen of Poland, 1374–1399*. Translated by Bruce MacQueen. London: Veritas, 1997.

PHOTO AND ILLUSTRATION ACKNOWLEDGMENTS

Teutonic Castle in Malbork (Marienburg) Pomerania (Poland)
Mike Mareen Shutterstock
Wawel Royal Castle Krakow, Poland
S-F Shutterstock
Fisherman's Bastion, Buda Castle, Budapest
Karel Gallas Shutterstock
Wawel Castle Day, Krakow Poland
TT Studio Shutterstock
Three Sisters at Farm
Sunkids Shutterstock
Little Girl with Flowers
Tatiana Bobkora Shutterstock
Pink flowers/orchard
Maria Uspenskaya Shutterstock
Wielpolska Salt Mine
Puchan Shutterstock
Tatra Mountains /Poland Koscielisko Village
Magmac83 Shutterstock
Castle in Dubrovnik, Croatia
Scott Biales Shutterstock
https://en.wikipedia.org/wiki/Pope_John_Paul_II#/media/
File:JohannesPaulusSimonis1985.2_(cropped).jpg
http://muzea.malopolska.pl/en/obiekty/-/a/11437349/11491905

https://en.wikipedia.org/wiki/Royal_Prussia#/media/File:
PRVSSIA1576Casparo_Henneberg.png
https://en.wikipedia.org/wiki/Jadwiga_of_Poland#/media/
File:Nagrobek_Jadwigi_Andegawe%C5%84skiej.jpg
Sketch drawings by Jaime LaBonte, Windsor, Ontario

Thanks to Jan Matejko for his superb contributions to historical artworks of Poland and for all the artists whose work falls in the public domain. Thanks to the authors of the above resources for their love and dedication to history for the rest of us. Thanks to *Wikimedia Commons* for photos.

ABOUT THE AUTHOR

Dawn Ibrahim achieved religious studies and education degrees at University of Windsor, Canada, with continued studies at Sacred Heart Seminary, Detroit. She is the mother of nine children and a high school teacher with a personal interest in history, philosophy, and theology. Historical biography is a favorite genre, and bringing important women and Christians who shaped their time and the future through Christian sacrifice a special interest.

Readers are encouraged to get in touch at jadwigasring.com or jadwigasring@gmail.com. We love to hear from our readers.

CPSIA information can be obtained
at www.ICGtesting.com
Printed in the USA
BVHW022327300622
641075BV00006B/47